THE
ROOTS OF
BETRAYAL

THE ROOTS OF BETRAYAL

Volume 2 of THE ARCIST CHRONICLES

DANIEL AUSEMA

GUARDBRIDGE BOOKS
ST ANDREWS, SCOTLAND

Published by Guardbridge Books,
St Andrews, Fife, United Kingdom.

http://guardbridgebooks.co.uk

Roots of Betrayal, The

Cover art © 2022 by Alex Storer

ISBN: Paperback: 978-1-911486-71-8
E-Books: 978-1-911486-72-5

*Dedicated to all those storytellers
who use their stories to create space for everyone
and topple the walls that divide us.*

N
W E
S
THE FROZEN SEA
Jarnur
Romnai
Volcanic Springs
Mine

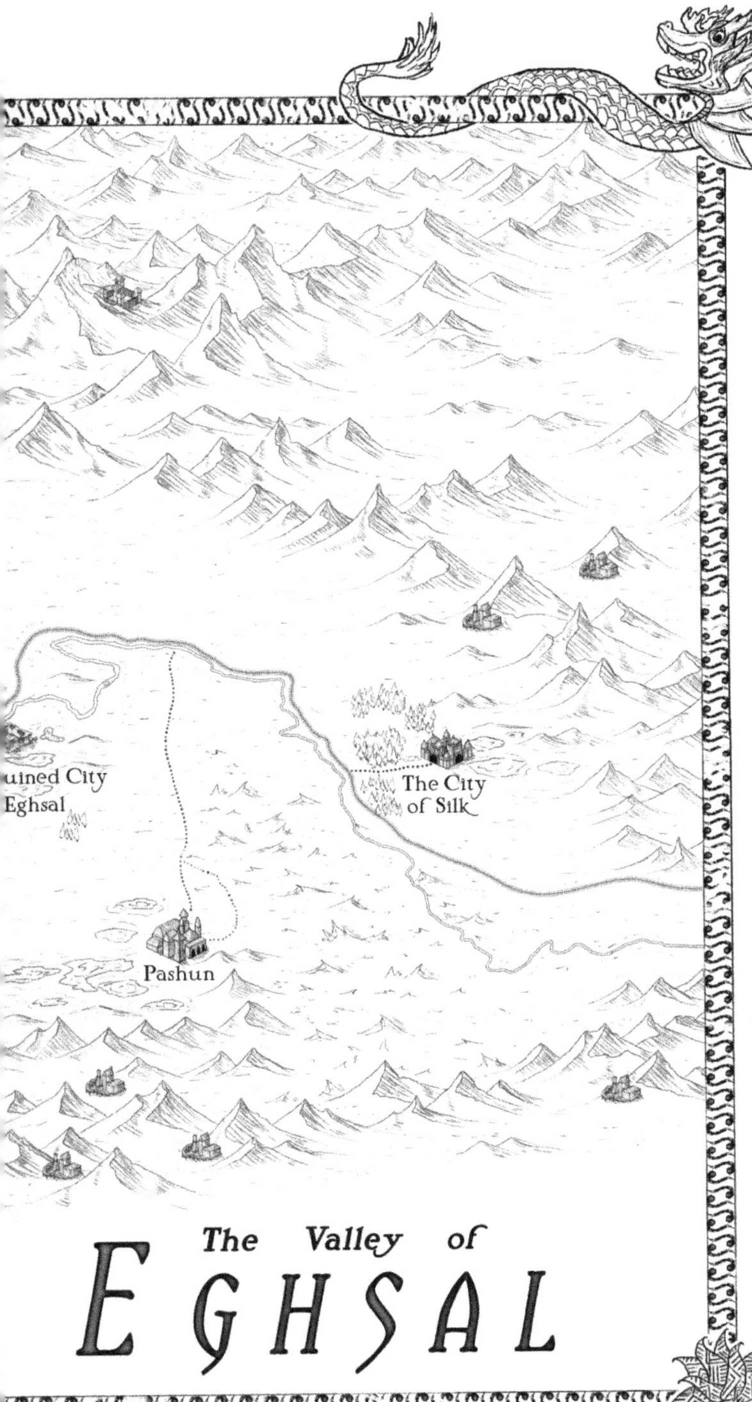

Ruined City
Eghsal
The City
of Silk
Pashun
The Valley of
EGHSAL
© Zach Bodenner 2017

Chapter 1

Pavresh approached the mumbler village as he'd been taught, hands open and empty and a bundle of dried willow branches carefully tied across his pack. With each step he shook snow from the criss-cross webbing of his oversized shoes. A chunk of snow, dislodged by the low-hanging sun, fell from the south-facing rock overhead onto the rough trail.

Here on the southern side of the vast Eghsal Valley there were few hot spots to warm the air, but the summer sun, visible for much of the day, kept the snow from being altogether permanent.

Pavresh stopped to wait at just the right distance from the village, the trader's pause. Then with magic he cast the idea of a trader over himself. Arcist magic played on patterns in people's minds in powerful but subtle ways, and even here among the mumblers it worked, giving him the appearance of someone who belonged. Even so, he did nothing—magic or otherwise—to make himself appear to be a mumbler. To disguise his face or skin would have been a crude insult, and he wanted welcome here, not to insult his mumbler hosts.

The mumblers kept him waiting a long time.

They'd seen him. Five years of visiting mumbler villages made him certain of that fact. No doubt they were discussing his presence, debating whether to trust him. A trader, seemingly, yet not. His bronze skin was too dark, his features, if they could be distinguished through the many furs, too fine to be a mumbler's. And yet knowledgeable he was about their ways, in a manner that few of his people were.

At last, a village leader marched out to meet him. He wore a mask over his light-skinned face, a plain oval with two holes cut for the eyes, its surface daubed in simple lines of paint.

Pavresh tensed. Masks like this were common among the villages to the west. They held it taboo to be seen bare-faced by outsiders. But a trader, by definition, wasn't an outsider in that sense. He pulled the bundle of willow branches closer, as if they were a shield.

The man's webbed shoes were sleek and his gait the rolling pattern Pavresh had yet to master, letting the man run on the top of the snow, if need be. His blade gleamed like silver—metal mined and forged by Pavresh's people, maybe even originally from his father's mine. Even years after he last saw his father or the mine, it struck him as strange to feel that reminder of home come crashing over him, like a current that's been released.

Pavresh spoke first, the trader's greeting. "I bring fresh goods." Not entirely accurate, unless the definition of *goods* were expanded to include the stories and news he brought, but true in their way. More important than their truth was the ritual meaning they leant to his presence. The protection they gave him. Or *should* give him.

The mumbler drew out his blade and answered in words Pavresh didn't understand. If he had known, back in Romnai, that the mumblers had not just a single language for him to learn but many dialects and languages, each distinct, he might have given up his plans then. Fortunately, a trader's pidgin gave him the chance to communicate, to understand their stories. To fit them into the patterns of the magic.

"I am a trader," he clarified, shaking the willow branches. The word meant both the person who traded and the act of speaking the pidgin. "I bring fresh goods," he repeated the ritual phrase.

"We do not trade with miners." The man's words were halting, and he emphasized them with his unsheathed knife.

For a moment Pavresh thought the man must know him, must know that he'd grown up on his father's mine. Did it show in his face? Could a person's history be so visible to a stranger? But then he remembered where he was. The nearest city of his own people was Pashun, a city that controlled dozens of vast mines in the nearby mountains. They were hated by the mumbler villages situated nearby and the wandering bands who lived in those parts of the mountain.

Should he leave then? If they thought him a miner from Pashun, there was little he could do about it. He gave himself the space of four breaths to consider the matter. Of all the villages he'd visited, the suspicious ones were the most important, their stories the most likely to be unknown outside their members.

Pavresh resisted the urge to take up his own long knife for protection and drew on his magic. Harmless, let that come through. An innocent wanderer. No, innocent wasn't right—that would make him seem weak. A rugged, experienced wanderer and exile who had nothing to do with the people of his birth.

Uncomfortably close to the truth.

Carefully, he said, "I am not a miner at all. I am a trader. I wish to trade with your village."

The man held himself still as a cold wind cut down the mountainside. He stared at Pavresh as if waiting for him to break. Maybe he'd made the wrong choice. Was it too late to grab his pack and run from there?

Not with how easily the man could run on his webbed shoes.

After what felt like a long time, the man slowly put his knife into its sheath—loosely—and gestured at the willow branches. "I will bring you to our trader." Or *our pidgin-speaker.*

Pavresh bowed in the mumbler style—hands behind his back—and followed the warrior into the village.

The houses were typical of mumbler homes—thick furs

overlapping rounded wooden frames. But these frames were more permanent than Pavresh was used to seeing, old trees wreathed in living needles instead of the more portable branches that other mumblers chose. It spoke to a sort of peace out here, so far from Pavresh's people. The land offered no promise of safety from the dangers of the frozen landscape or the bands of wolves, but those factors felt like a peaceful danger, if that were possible. A danger that didn't disrupt life in the same way that living nearer the cities of Pavresh's people did. Nothing like constant war with a more advanced society would.

Was there any way to carry that same sense of stability to other villages? And even back to his own people, a stability that did not fear its neighbors? If Pavresh could pull them into the magic, add their stories and ways of seeing the world until his own people accepted them, who could say what their villages might look like in a hundred years? The whole valley might be transformed, his own people and the mumbler villages both.

The pidgin-speaker was an old woman, seated close to the hearth inside a communal fire building. Her hair was white and her skin the color of ash wood. Because he'd been invited into the village, she didn't bother to wear a mask for him. She was sorting a variety of threads and bits of cloth. A brick enclosure around half of the roaring fire served as a mumbler version of an oven. It spoke, as the houses themselves had, of the permanence of that village. The room shimmered with heat. Pavresh bowed again and waited for her to speak.

She wasted no time on pleasantries. "What do you trade? We have little need for anything from beyond our village." Unlike the man who'd met Pavresh, her words were smooth and well-practiced, which argued strongly against her claim of needing little trade.

"Nothing, tisrah." Pavresh opened his empty arms in

apology but smiled as he said it. With magic he pulled over himself a subtle hint of a joker. "No goods, only words. And ears, my own." He touched his ears as he said it.

There had been times in these years of wandering when this answer was met with anger, times when the mumblers had turned on him and shoved him out of the village into the cold. They'd never done him serious harm, always stopping just short of that, but they'd made it clear that they would, if he tried to pull such a trick again.

In other villages, the traders laughed, welcoming his arrival, perhaps expecting more of a show than he ultimately put on, but still pleased to speak and share.

The woman in this village narrowed her eyes at his words. The impression he'd had of the village's permanence struck him. What if, in those other villages, he'd only been saved by fear of retaliation from Pavresh's people? And what if these mumblers lived so far from Pavresh's people that they had no such fear? Rather than letting the scene play out slowly, he rushed to add, "I seek stories. And I pay in the stories of your neighbors, give you word of the events in villages near and far."

The woman's eyes relaxed and she leaned back on her stool. "The tale teller? We have heard of your travels. Very well, offer me your own story, and I will determine what it is worth."

A story. Pavresh liked to lead off with a tale of a neighboring village. Something light to make his listener laugh, but with a hint of news about current crops, hunting patterns, or trading information to make it feel useful as well as entertaining.

"One story I heard as I came through the village of Reppdahl—"

"No." The woman swept her hand as if sweeping away the aborted story. "Of yourself. Who are you and how do you come to my village dressed as a trader?"

Himself, the story of who he was… He sometimes told that story eventually, but it didn't strike him as the best story to begin with. Pavresh held his hands in front of him as if to demur. "I am only a simple—"

"We're all simple in our own ways. Tell me your simplicity, if that is all there is to tell. We have heard strange rumblings of events in your cities from other tale tellers. I would place you within those stories."

Pavresh bowed, wondering what stories she had heard. It had been so long since he'd visited his own people. "Give me a moment to collect myself, and I will tell it as well as I can."

The woman narrowed her eyes again. "I have little time for a tale teller who cannot tell a tale the first time. I will allow you some time while I begin to sort these threads, but it is mindless work. If you cannot keep me awake, you will not be welcome in my village, pidgin-speaker."

Not welcome was a strong threat among the mumblers, one that removed any protection given traders. Pavresh nodded and drew his magic around him, more to compose himself than for her sake. A trader, a taleteller, a wanderer.

Reaching back to his first arrival in Romnai, to the naively overconfident youth he'd been, he tried to recapture the aura of a world-changing genius he'd thought he was back then. It was the biggest stretch for his magic. His years of traveling had taught him a lot, more than he could have imagined at the time, but what it taught most of all was how little he'd known, how little he still knew. And of how the world resisted change at all costs.

Taking a breath, he opened his hands to show he was ready to speak. The mumbler woman gestured for him to proceed.

The challenge was to tell the story in a way that would make sense within the mumblers' pidgin and way of seeing their world. "I was born among the mountains. When it came time to seek my path, I traveled to the big village, to Romnai."

That "Romnai" the word existed in the pidgin was one of the many things that would have shocked him five years ago. Or he would have chalked it up to it simply being an important city, even to the mumblers because it was their enemies' home. But the word was much older, because the city was far older than his people thought. It had been a city long before any of the people of Eghsal acknowledged, long before they'd traveled north to this valley. And the descendants of those original city founders now lived out here, in scattered villages, speaking many dialects and languages. One of which was a pidgin that preserved the word "Romnai."

These thoughts flashed through his mind without him pausing his tale.

"I came to learn an art, an art connected to stories, though not quite the same." Pavresh avoided the word *magic* since it meant something very different to the mumblers. He pictured Chaitan, old and ill, and the vibrant group of outcasts and dreamers who'd gathered in his house. "My teacher led me on the path, but other paths came together there. The chiefs of the village treated many of the villagers poorly. They fought among themselves over who would be in charge. Those villagers who'd been treated poorly were friends with my teacher. They wanted change. I helped them, but I also helped one chief who wasn't entirely on their side but still wished to treat the villagers well."

So many people, so many memories. People who had died in the struggle against the princes, and others who had gone into exile. Including him, in a way. Wasn't that what this journeying was, an exile self-imposed?

"Once I had to flee the city, and my path became more twisted. I visited the silk village, traveling by train." This word was the Eghsal word, but it had spread to the pidgin, and the woman gave no sign of not understanding, though the train never came down near this southern edge of the valley. "When I returned, many of those who wished to change things had been silenced. Imprisoned, killed, or driven off. I helped the rest of them as long as I could, but in the end I sided with the one chief who wished to help.

"There was a big fight in the village. Friends of mine died, maybe because I sided with that one chief. I cannot say I did right, but I did what I thought was best and wept for my friends.

"The chief who I helped succeeded. He cast down the other, worse chiefs because of my help. But I couldn't stay in Romnai any longer. My path became one among the villages of your people." There was no word in pidgin for mumbler, no clear distinction between the pale-faced mumblers and the darker-skinned people of Eghsal, and sometimes that made stories confusing, but he used his hands to encompass the mountains and hoped she understood. "I learned to speak pidgin." *To trade.* "And now I come to your village to hear your stories and share those of other villages and places."

The woman set down a spool of dark-streaked wool in one pile and met Pavresh's eyes. "Why?" She rolled her shoulders and stood to hand Pavresh a bowl of snow-melt water—a typical sign that he was accepted as a trader, though the question remained in how she held herself. "Why do you care about stories? What is this art, and what will it cost us to trade our stories with you?"

Pavresh stroked his chin while he shifted his magic. Less world-changer, more solitary monk. "Few ask that question. It costs you nothing, I hope, and may even gain you much, in how my people interact with yours."

He paused to sip from the ceramic bowl of water. A metallic taste lingered on his tongue after he swallowed. The woman waited for him to explain, cautious but not yet throwing him out of the building.

"The stories let me create…something. Like music, except you can't hear it. Or jewelry that each of us wears but no one can see. I listen to your stories and the stories of others, and I combine them in new ways. The better I understand a story, the easier it is to work that idea into a new song. And it changes the people who hear it. Or wear it."

"Song is cheap," the woman answered after he'd taken a second, longer drink. "But jewelry is expensive. Help me sort thread, and I will tell you a single story this evening. For every new story beyond that, I expect a day's work, for me or others in the village."

A day's labor for food and shelter as well as stories was certainly fair, as far as Pavresh was concerned. He often had to make do with less. And yet, if he could learn more… "Tisrah, you drive a hard bargain, but surely a single story will only loosen your tongue. Tell me two for each day's work, and we have a deal."

The woman rocked in her chair and held her hands to the fire. "One story for the work, one story for each story you tell."

Pavresh bowed and gathered a handful of cloth scraps to help the woman sort.

***

As often happened, the first stories the woman, Ezheeli, told were no more than events in the village's recent history. Or if not recent, exactly, within the trader's lifetime. Pavresh called them *happenings* rather than stories, and they seldom played into arcist patterns, except in the most general ways.

Even so, after each one he thanked her, and before the next he always rephrased the way he asked, to try to get the kinds of stories he wanted. The words "legend" and "folktale" did not exist in pidgin. When Ezheeli prepared to tell him her fifth story, he said, "What is a story from longer ago, but one all the children know? A story you heard as a child and pass on for them to tell when you are gone?"

"The past? We don't keep it walled off from the present. We welcome it in as something that's part of us today too." She tipped her head back and closed her eyes. "Ah, I will tell you the story of Dimmar, the fur mender. It is an old one, old to the oldest village, when we still lived in the warm valley."

She eyed Pavresh at those words, as if expecting him to challenge her or ask for something different. He leaned forward to show his eagerness to hear.

"Dimmar took the furs of wisents and wolves, the skin of deer, the fur of the musk ox from the mountain heights, the pelts of animals we no longer know. She made magnificent houses of those furs, houses that even Romnai today could not have rivaled for luxury or comfort.

"But the chief, ah the chief. He wanted ever finer houses. Each was never enough. He commanded her to build newer and greater houses for him, one for each village he visited. And Dimmar did as she was commanded, using every fur he sent to her.

"The great houses crowded the villages, taking up their land. None was to stay in his houses when he was gone. Only the villagers who cared for it could enter, costing the villages much time they might have used to hunt and gather and grow food.

"But still it wasn't enough. The chief sent his hunters for more furs. They hunted until those unknown animals were all killed, and to this day their bones lie along the streams but are otherwise forgotten. Dimmar mourned the last of those beasts, whose pelts had been highly prized, but the chieftain gave her no time for tears.

"The other animals grew scarce, too, and the last herd of wisents came to visit her, the last family of musk ox. Their mournful eyes begged her to put a stop to the chief. Even the wolves, down to a weary pack, begged her with mournful howls. The deer still numbered many, but they too fretted, and a great stag stood on the hill above Dimmar's home, outlined against the moon, and silently asked for help.

"But what could one fur-mender do? When she knew the chief would be coming to visit her, she began a new house, pulled from her own skin. At her house the chief found a palace, tiny but so perfect he knew he had to own it, too. While waiting for Dimmar to appear, he entered.

"The palace closed around him. And all the chief's houses were said to fly away from their villages and collapse into the palace prison, absorbed into the chieftain's final home. And Dimmar was never seen again."

Pavresh had to sit in silence to absorb the story before he could thank her. It was gruesome, in its way, and rough in the pidgin speech, yet there was much he could work into arcist themes. The cruel leader, the destruction of the land to sate him, the way people would fight back even at the cost of their lives—these were arcist themes that he could weave into the magic in intricate ways.

But what stood out, above all else, was that it was a story he knew. Not in this form and not with that exact ending, but one he'd known since he was a child. A story, he'd been told since he was old enough to listen to stories, that came from the Forgotten South.

Supposedly.

How had a story of the Forgotten South come here to this isolated village of mumblers?

Maybe it had simply spread from his people, as the word *train* had spread in the pidgin language. But he didn't think so. The story felt old—old in its very mumbler telling, not some recent story grafted into mumbler traditions.

"Thank you," he managed at last to say. "I would like to

hear more like that. Old stories, for as long as you will welcome me here."

Whatever the woman answered, Pavresh quickly forgot as the story commanded his full thoughts. The story was old in the same way the name of the city Romnai was old.

What that meant, he had no idea, only that there was far more to the history of his people and the mumblers than anyone's story had ever told. And the more he learned, the more he built his understanding of the arcist themes and patterns of these mumbler villages, the more uncertain he became about what he knew.

About anything.

***

It was only later that it occurred to Pavresh to circle back to Ezheeli's comment about stories of his own people and ask her about them.

"Ah, you wish me to pay you in your own people's stories?" She laughed deep in her belly as she said it.

Pavresh shrugged. "No, not really. I would rather earn your own stories of old times. But if there is news I should know, then I will exchange my stories for one of my own."

Ezheeli nodded. "Then this will be a gift for you."

One he would pay back with his own gift, though it wasn't required. To fail that would make him a lesser guest.

"The story is vague but recent. We had a tale teller come through only a few months before you arrived. She said there is war among your people. Or fighting, anyway."

Pavresh's hands went still over the basket of cloth scraps he'd been sorting.

"Some person in one of your cities is calling himself the Son of Ryo. I do not know if I am pronouncing that right, but one of your gods?"

Pavresh nodded, though it wasn't his own religion. "Yes,

Ryo is a god of my people. But the god of rules, not war." The god of proper behavior, of strict castes, of the old and established ways, no matter what the exact situation calls for. Certainly, the god whose ideals the people in Chaitan's circle had resisted, back in Romnai.

"Well, I don't know much more. Your gods are the same to us, your people all alike. But some fights in Romnai were by him. Or caused by him. A full battle in the streets. And other, smaller fights in other places. The miners rising up in Pashun." She struggled with the pronunciation, but he understood her. "The carters rebelling in the silk village. The only thing that our tale teller found important was that your soldiers would be busy away from our grounds. If we wish to reclaim land, now is the time."

Soldiers in the streets, riots and fighting. And who would bear the worst of the violence? His former friends.

"Thank you. For the story and for making it a gift. I will give you a gift before I leave, but that will have to come sooner than I had hoped."

A vigilante who wanted to restore old rules and laws could spell trouble for so many people Pavresh had once known. Not least for himself, if any people there had any recollection of who he'd been and what he'd done five years earlier.

The past was reaching out to him in two ways. One came with uncertainty, casting doubt on the things he thought were true. The other cut across the more recent past, snaring him to pull him back.

Neither one was something he dared ignore.

Nor anything he could trust.

CHAPTER 2

Jaritta ran along the western edge of the city ruins, trying to reach a better vantage point before the vandals were out of sight. Undignified for a woman her age to run so, but no one cared about dignity, least of all the dignity of a fire-scarred untouchable in the ruined city. She clipped her foot on a tumbled wall, stumbled but regained her footing. After a few more steps she stopped. No way she could reach the hilltop lookout in time. The strangers would already be heading around the curve of the river, lost to any curiosity or worry. Or vengeance.

As if an old untouchable like her, already within a few years of her fortieth birthday, were capable of vengeance against a band of armed men.

The buildings around her were all too broken down to afford much advantage, but a taller wall still stood a short way away. She ran to it. The rocks at the base were steady. She scrambled up to where the rocks became looser. No view yet. She climbed higher, placing each foot with care. The rocks were dark, volcanic stones from the surrounding area. No moss grew on such rock and little in the way of any vegetation, but a thin coating of something organic covered the edges, making them slippery.

When she'd lived in Romnai, Jaritta had climbed over roofs far more precarious and never slowed down. She made it to the top, and only once did her feet slip beneath her.

The strangers were just rounding the curve. Soldiers, no doubt about that. At least a dozen, possibly others who'd already passed out of sight or were hidden from view at this angle. Jaritta fumbled with a spyglass she'd salvaged from the river. The eyepiece had a small crack spider-webbing its way along the bottom, but she could still squint and see some details of the people marching away.

Wolf jati soldiers. As she'd suspected. The wolf jati were the ones who protected the valley from outside threats, the only ones likely to be found beyond the cities. They were the wild ones, the legendary warriors of the people of Eghsal.

What did it mean that they were stooping to vandalism? Why bother the untouchables of Old Eghsal City this way? Surely it was beneath the honor of such a proud jati of soldiers.

Unless there was someone commanding them to act thus. The wolf jati soldiers spent most of their time far from the cities, but their base was in Romnai. Someone back there must want to disrupt life out here among the untouchables.

Were they all soldiers? Maybe she could pick up a clue if there was someone from another jati commanding them. If only there were some chance she might recognize one of them or catch a hint of their future plans in their outfits. But she'd lived out here for five years without any contact with the people of Romnai. Before that she'd been an untouchable on the streets of Romnai for years, far from most circles of influence and power. And even earlier? A fifteen-year-old girl—even from the princely jati—didn't pay attention to lower caste things like soldiers and minor jatis. If there was any other clue to find in these people heading calmly away, she wouldn't be the one to recognize it.

Jaritta let the spyglass dangle from her hand once the soldiers had all rounded the curve. Nothing else to see and no new answers. She spat muttered curses at them. *May the Fire burn their backsides before they arrive back to their homes.*

Even so, learning what she had might prove important. The wolf jati served at the command of princes and priests, the groups in charge of the valley of Eghsal. They had always kept a wary eye on the untouchables and mumblers out here in the abandoned city, but that used to mean a patrol passing by once every month or two. This made five patrols spotted just in the last twelve-day. Plus, how many more were they not even aware of?

And now vandalism. Soldiers had marched right into Eghsal City and pulled down a building. There were few enough stable structures amidst the ruins as it was.

Why the increased interest? What was special now? Five years ago, the princes had nearly sent an invasion of soldiers into the ruins to clear them out. Or rather, they'd planted the idea that it might be necessary in order to hide what they really planned. But what if someone still harbored the idea that it would be wise to do? Even a false and foolish plan might linger in people's minds long after it had been shown to be worthless.

Or did someone back in Romnai have other plans tied to the city of untouchables?

Whatever it signified, Jaritta didn't like it. She and the rest of the people out here were already cast out from society. Couldn't society just leave them alone?

Jaritta stepped down from the tower's summit, and the earth shook. A violent rumble made everything around her ripple and shiver. She threw herself down to grab at the rocks. They fell away from her grasping hands, shaken loose, falling. And she fell too. The world flipped, or her eyes did. Nothing made sense except that she was falling. Striking a lower part of the tower that wasn't collapsing, she clutched at the rocks, stopping her own fall. The pieces of the tower's peak kept dropping around her.

When the dust settled over the ruins, Jaritta was at the top of a much shorter ruin, one with no view of the surroundings at all. Her leg was twisted awkwardly, and her shoulder throbbed where some rock had struck her on its way down. The spyglass was gone, no sign of even pieces of it remaining.

Other buildings had fallen as well, and people shouted to each other from across the rubble.

Jaritta slid down to the ground, afraid to put weight on her left leg. Once off the rubble, she tested it. She screamed at the pain.

A man she didn't recognize ran over from a nearby alleyway between the rubble to help her, which was a sign of either how spooked the people were by the soldiers' incursion and the earthquake or of how pained her scream must have sounded. The people of the ruins almost always left each other alone.

"What happened? Can you walk?"

If there was a law to the city, that was it. Each to their own, unless left with no choice but to become involved.

The stranger eschewed that tradition as he held her upright while she gingerly put her foot down again. She might hop, but she couldn't step.

And then she played into the same mindset when she answered, "I think I'll be able to. Thank you." As if she should just let him walk away. As if it was what she wanted him to do.

He hesitated. "Let me find you a stick of some kind for a crutch.

She tried to wave the offer away, but the movement made her wince. "Thank you. I should probably use one, if you can find it."

A short time later the man returned. The branch wasn't much—firewood was too precious here to be left lying around—but it would support her while she hopped. "Thank you. I'm Jaritta. Untouchable," she added, gesturing at the twenty-year-old fire scar that covered half of her face.

He was a short man, a decade or two her senior. "I know you. Vyovek. Same." Vyovek gave no indication of what had made him untouchable as he turned and walked off. The right pattern of old Eghsal restored, now that the shock of earthquakes and soldiers was fading.

Jaritta leaned on the branch and hopped and hobbled off deeper into the ruins.

***

The gathered few fancied themselves the leaders of the ruined city of Eghsal, though such a lawless place acknowledged no official leaders. Besides Jaritta herself, there were two other untouchables, one mumbler who'd learned the language of Eghsal, and a widow from the coast who had simply left city life behind by choice.

Jaritta hobbled into the circle of rough leather sling chairs, leaning on her stick-crutch. Her leg still throbbed. The mumbler took one look at her leg and then shouted something back behind him in the mumbler language. His pale features looked worried. Thamiba, her former lover who was one of the two other untouchables, smoothed out her chair so she wouldn't have any trouble sitting. He was his usual, unperturbable self, though she realized now how age was getting to him as well. Forty might not be especially old back in the real cities, but an untouchable life aged anyone quickly. She nodded her thanks.

The widow Driyya spoke even as Jaritta was getting comfortable. "There were words on the walls they pushed over. 'Sons of Ryo.' Anyone ever hear of that before?"

"Ryo is the god of rules," Jaritta said. "So he hates untouchables. But beyond that, I don't know."

"Hates untouchables and certainly doesn't approve of mumblers," Thamiba added. "At least not of us all living in one place together."

No one else knew anything to add.

"Hmm," Driyya cleared her throat. "The patrols increase. I don't like it. You don't like it. No one likes these soldiers sticking their blades in here. And they won't like it either, if they keep sticking deeper. Vandals and ruffians in a ruined city. Why would anyone do that? What's going on?"

Poorma hit her chair with an open palm. She was a death jati untouchable, one of those from the jati charged with handling corpses. Anywhere outside of this city of untouchables she would have been shunned as superstitiously bad luck. "Why do we wait until 'if they keep doing it'? Maybe we need to do something to them *now*. Show them these reactions they won't like, instead of waiting until they knock over a building with people inside, or worse." She was light-skinned for a member of the people of Eghsal Valley, her face like sand, as if she might have mumbler ancestry as well, many generations ago. But anger brought a bronze glow to her cheeks.

Thamiba's voice was calm—deceptively so, Jaritta suspected—when he answered, "You mean attack them outright?"

Awful idea. It would just make the princes send more soldiers. Jaritta opened her mouth to argue, but the mumbler Azheeran was already answering in his slow, careful voice.

"No, you do not attack, unless you must. I know this from my people." None of them needed a reminder of the many wars between the people of Eghsal and the mumblers. "We stay within the ruins. Hide, if we must."

"Hide where?" Poorma asked.

"There are buildings deeper inside. Ruins we don't make full use of. It may mean squeezing together, for a time."

Thamiba shook his head. "Many wouldn't like that. Telling people they have to share buildings, share a fireplace?" He chuckled. "*I* wouldn't like that. There must be something else we could do to at least figure out what's going on."

Crowded, sure, but more importantly, those buildings deeper in were often less stable, more prone to collapse than the ones in use. Unlike many who found themselves drawn to the ruins, Jaritta didn't dislike interacting with others, sharing meals, sharing space. Even as an untouchable in Romnai she'd found ways to join with others, at Chaitan's house and among the other untouchables when she couldn't do that. But the ruins further within the city weren't safe.

A mumbler woman interrupted them for a moment. She had the wider face of her people, her skin a color like undyed wool. Instead of speaking with Azheeran, she approached Jaritta and gestured at her leg. Jaritta had to think for a moment before she remembered that Azheeran had shouted for someone to help dress her wound. She gritted her teeth as she stretched her leg out. The woman unwrapped Jaritta's attempts at bandaging and set to cleaning the visible parts of the wound.

Driyya sucked in her cheeks and released them with a popping noise. "I agree. Hiding, sneaking, it'll only make the soldiers more suspicious. I say avoid them, as much as possible, but don't do anything to *look* like we're avoiding them. Continue on as if the soldiers are nothing. Soon they'll lose interest."

"Unless they don't," Jaritta said. Her own cousin had been the one who once pushed the princes to believe attacking the ruins was necessary. "Maybe these Sons of Ryo are fanatics. Maybe it will get worse instead of better. We can't just hide, and we can't just ignore them." She looked around at the mess of rock and rising plumes of steam from the dangerous ground all around. "But maybe we can run instead. Find a new home."

No one said anything for a moment. Jaritta held her breath, swallowing a cry as the mumbler healer woman rearranged her leg, sending pain shooting up her hip and back. Then at the same time widow Driyya said, "Where?" and Thamiba said, "And you'd be leading us, I suppose, like some hero from the Forgotten South?"

It was spoken without malice, with even a hint of humor, but it cut Jaritta just the same. She was from the princely jati by birth, and Thamiba had never forgotten that. Had never let her completely forget either.

As if to drive it in, he added, "Like a prince?"

Jaritta's scar flushed, and she reached for the extra loop of cloth she used to always wear. It wasn't there, but the old reflex to pull cloth over her scarred face remained.

Poorma broke the silence. "It's what we five are doing anyway, right? Trying to be this place's circle of princes, whether it wants us or not?"

The healer finished tightening the new bandages and bowed her way away from the group.

Thamiba held his hands open in the odd shrug that was as much a part of his personality as his way of talking. "I suppose so. But I'll argue a better path forward instead of fleeing the safety of these ruins. I'll head back to Romnai, spy out what I can learn about their interest in us. Figure out who or what these Sons of Ryo are, if it means anything. Then we *princes* of untouchables can make a better decision what our answer should be."

Back to Romnai… Just the words struck her a blow. What was happening there? With her brother, Prince Jasfer? As far as she heard, he was an important figure in the city, a close figure to the High Prince himself. What was happening with Chaitan back in his house—or dead? Surely he had had little time left to live, even five years ago, with how sickly he had been when she'd known him. And what about Rashul, released from house arrest…and what? Still inspiring the thinkers and malcontents, or hiding like she was, trying to forget the past?

She should be the one to go back. Someone was sending the soldiers out here to harass them, probably someone from

Romnai. She could see all those people she'd once known, learn things no one would tell Thamiba.

And be arrested on sight, tried, executed within days of her arrival, more likely than not. She should be the one, but she couldn't.

The faces of the others in the circle told Jaritta the discussion was already over. They kept debating each option—attack, hide, or flee—but Thamiba's plan to learn more first was clearly going to be their only choice. Beyond that, their only task would be to wait while soldiers and collapsing buildings picked them off one by one. Jaritta hung her head and listened to the discussion with only brief comments now and then.

No matter how convincing Thamiba sounded, she couldn't shake the idea that by the time he returned, they would have waited too long.

***

Jaritta climbed down from the hill she'd been trying to reach the other day. She still hobbled along on the crutch, though the mumbler woman's ministrations had helped ease the swelling considerably.

Thamiba was off. She'd watched him slip away along the river, heading downstream toward a world where she could never return.

No soldiers in sight to intercept him. She'd released the breath she'd been holding and wished the fire's protection on him as he traveled. Now at the bottom of the hill, breath coming hard, she wished the fire's protection for herself and her home. Let the gods or whatever cared for the things of the world keep them all safe while they waited.

Waited for something, some answer to what was happening in the world beyond their city.

A family of mumblers gathered brush for firewood along

the route back to where Jaritta was sleeping. Was one of them the woman who had tended her leg? She was ashamed to realize she didn't know. She, who'd been raised to keep track of every person she interacted with, to know their caste and jati and connection to others without delay, couldn't tell one mumbler from another. She dipped her head in greeting, and as she hobbled past, she vowed to do better to see them, each of the mumblers, as individuals.

Her home, such as it was, lay along the western edge of the ruins, so she didn't have to travel far, in among tumbled buildings. Out here the fumaroles and steam vents were fewer. She turned south, away from the river. A warm patch of ground forced her to detour out of what had once been a street. She slowed down to avoid tripping on the transition from old, nearly buried cobbles to hard-packed dirt.

Where the trail rejoined the original road, the remaining walls were well over her head, giving the area almost the feel of a true city. She wondered if she'd chosen the place, without realizing it, because it reminded her of Romnai. It was, at least, the closest thing those ruins had to offer to anything like the city.

Yet she didn't live within any of those standing walls. Instead, she lived in a lean-to structure against one wall. The roof was made of scavenged fabric held in place by sticks. The walls were carefully layered stacks of whatever she had managed to gather—mostly rubble and trash. Her pride was the section of wall made of old pottery, chipped urns and pots whose glaze at least gave the home some color.

As she pulled aside the cloth door to enter, a blast of heat made her pull back. The cloth tore off, as if she'd taken it with her, but she knew she'd let go. How could that happen? The heat made her squint. She held up an arm up to protect herself. Instead of falling onto her, the door rose into the air as Jaritta stumbled backward. Her crutch twisted and she tried to catch herself with her injured leg.

Her knee crumpled, and she cried out in pain as she fell over backward.

Something fell on her face, but she couldn't identify it at first. Dust? No. Sparks from a fire? No, but it was hot, hot enough to hurt. She brushed at her face, and her hand came away wet.

Before she could figure out what that fact meant, her house disappeared in a gush of steam and hot water. The geyser tore into the standing wall. She stared into the chaos of the jets of superheated water. Spurting danger, a death that reached out to grab her.

Fire take it. As if she hadn't paid her dues already, twenty years an outcast for the burn on her face?

Not taking the time to turn around, she scrambled backward, arms and healthy leg and even her injured leg pushing, scurrying. Desperation. The fire wouldn't burn her again.

The branch that had held her roof crashed down beside her. Twisting away from the remains of the roof got her facing away from the geyser. On hands and one knee, the other leg dragging behind, she crawled as fast as she could along the hard packed dirt path while the water continued its ferocious destruction through a swath of neighboring buildings.

When she'd retreated far enough to feel safe, she collapsed onto her belly. She sucked in dirt with each gasping breath. The sounds of the new geyser eased up, but there were other noises of rocks crashing and the earth opening.

A familiar part of life in Old Eghsal, she tried to tell herself. But no, it shouldn't have to be. They needed a new home. No matter what Thamiba found or anyone else learned, they couldn't simply wait.

It was time to leave, even if not everyone would follow.

Time to create a new, more stable home.
    Somewhere.

CHAPTER 3

Prince Jasfer rode in his carriage to the rail line along the river. Every few blocks gave him another view of soldiers conspicuously visible on the streets. It kept the city quiet, at least. The feeling of always being watched might not be the way he remembered Romnai when he was young, nor the way he wanted it to be necessarily. But it was a small price to play to keep the city at peace in the middle of insurrections and rumors of war.

Shopkeepers still ran their shops. Walas still made their deliveries. The people still visited the chapels to worship. Beggars still begged. The only change was they did all those things under a more watchful eye than before.

And in exchange, no one tried to overthrow the High Prince, no one cast the city into the chaos that had enveloped the city five years earlier.

"A small price," he said out loud this time.

His wife Datri sat beside him wearing an orange silk dress that brought out the cool brown of her skin. She likely knew exactly what he'd been thinking. She saw the same things, after all, and knew him well. And had the mind to put such things together easily. But she turned the statement into the earlier conversation they'd had as they were getting into the carriage. "The reception? Yes, it shouldn't cost us much."

She wasn't referring to money. Jasfer ran a hand over his face, a richer and deeper brown than his wife's, and considered the cost to his honor to be much greater than she implied. "Let him stay an outcast."

"He's your cousin. You already have a sister who's an outcast and a traitor. Best to cut back on the suspicious relatives somehow."

"I have no sister." He said the words out of reflex, without either the anger or sadness he might have felt at one time.

Datri took the response in stride. "Right, but soon you'll have a cousin who's grateful to you. And in sponsoring his return, you'll have clearly shown who has the power in this. To the other princes and to him."

The carriage climbed the slope of the Bridge of the Forgotten South, crossing the wide Eghsal River. River boats dotted the water below with sails, and one big steamboat floated beside the quay to be loaded. Ahead was the line of the tracks, under a haze of black smoke. "Right, a grateful cousin…who hates me. I'm not sure I end up ahead on that count."

Datri smiled, a look that most people probably would have seen as innocent pleasure. He knew it for what it was, though, the look of a devious plan. "As for that, leave him to me."

Jasfer answered her with his own sheepish grin. Datri had a gift for discovering a person's secrets and weak spots, turning them into reluctant allies. Or at least neutralizing them as enemies. He had to trust that she could pull that off with his cousin as well.

"We shall see." The carriage pulled up to a loading platform for the trains, one of many along this part of the city. Steam from the engine obscured everything on the platform beyond a few paces. Prince Jasfer held out his hand for his wife as the driver opened the side door. "And now for this task, shall we?"

Datri took his hand and climbed out with him.

They should be seeing trains unloading their piles of ore. Ore that belonged to Jasfer's household—the profits from it, anyway. Yet here, again, it appeared that no shipment had arrived.

A prince, especially a ruling prince, *especially* one of Jasfer's standing among the thirty rulers of Eghsal Valley, should summon the foreman or some other underling to the office in his manor. He would not be expected to meet the trains himself. Which was exactly why he and Datri did that. No time for the foreman to hide or come up with careful excuses.

The foreman must have seen them coming, as he was standing before the storeroom doors to greet them. Turang—Jasfer had checked the man's name and history before leaving his manor—was a solid man, no hint of blemish on his record.

Datri took a look at the other workers around the building and squeezed Jasfer's arm. She'd seen someone she could get information from. He nodded without looking at her, and she slipped away into the storeroom office. Yatim, his personal servant and bodyguard, would keep an eye on her, from a distance, while Jasfer and the foreman spoke.

Turang looked nervous, wiping his hands several times on his trousers. "Tisrah. How may I help you?"

Jasfer looked over the goods piled in various ways throughout the trainyard. "Where is the shipment from Pashun?."

"Yes, tisrah. We…it has been delayed."

"Is that all? It is more than two days late."

Turang swallowed. "No, tisrah. You should have received a report—"

The sound of a train approaching cut Turang off. Maybe the shipment was coming at last after all.

Jasfer opened his mouth to say as much when Turang grabbed his arm. "Something sounds wrong. Get back, tisrah!"

The pitch did seem off. Jasfer let himself be herded back from the building. The noise of the train sounded higher, wilder.

"Datri!" he called. "Someone get my—"

The train's roar turned into a shrieking cacophony of brakes and bending rails as an engine without any cars came crashing into the warehouses.

Jasfer screamed for his wife. The noise of the crash drowned out his voice. He shook himself free from Turang and ran toward the devastation.

There were voices calling, cries for water, for assistance. Jasfer ran ahead and found Yatim with his arm around Datri, leading her away from the wreckage. She gave him a weak wave. A spot of blood on the silk of her sleeve near her shoulder snapped his attention to her ashen face.

"Where are you hurt?" Before she could answer, he said to Yatim, "Why is she walking? Carry her."

Yatim bent to scoop her up, but Datri said, "No. I can walk. Just hit by a broken board."

"Come into the shade, then." He gestured to a canopy beside a warehouse office, a good distance from the wreckage. "Then Yatim can summon a doctor to make sure."

Datri's color returned to normal as she sat in the shade. Jasfer fussed over her arm until she told him to stop.

"That train was fleeing something," she said when he'd finally consented to sit calmly beside her.

"Fleeing? What do you mean? Nothing can keep up with a train."

"I don't know, but it was. I saw their faces. The driver, the coal shovelers. They were scared about something." After a moment she said, "I suppose they won't be able to tell anyone, will they?"

Jasfer had no answer for that. But what could possibly be a threat to a speeding train?

A train with no cars, though. "What happened to the rest of the train?" he asked out loud.

Datri nodded as if he'd finally voiced what she'd already been thinking. "The answer to that will probably answer both. Someone should go investigate."

Yatim returned with a doctor, and after a brief

consultation, Datri and her own servants returned by carriage to the manor. Jasfer, at Datri's urging, lingered to learn more.

Plenty of people had converged on the crash site while he'd been helping his wife. Going over now would only get in the way. He waited with Yatim until the cries grew less urgent.

As they made their way back, Turang plodded away from the debris toward his office. His face was smeared with soot.

Jasfer hailed him. "What happened? I would like to get word to the other princes, if this is more than a common accident."

Turang bowed tiredly. "No clue yet. No survivors, I can tell you that."

"Can you identify the train? Any idea what it would have been carrying?"

"Come inside." Turang held open the door and belatedly added, "Tisrah. I will check the books with you."

Turang paged through a ledger, shaking his head. "Nothing stands out to me. I was expecting a train from upriver later today. Carrying whatever goods needed to come this way. But mostly empty. With no ore coming from Pashun, we often have empty trains coming downriver."

A shipment of valuable silks from the Silk City might have tempted bandits, though he'd never heard of bandits taking an entire train behind the engine. Or they might have tried to pick up a shipment from Pashun, only to anger…someone. Mumblers? Outcasts? Could his sister's makeshift city of untouchables mount an attack on a train? It seemed unlikely, but who could say? "Send for a squad of soldiers to head upriver and investigate. Find the cars, and hopefully you learn something more."

"Yes, tisrah."

"And I'll make sure we get some more soldiers here as well, to protect you. No telling what danger might be heading your way."

By the time Jasfer and Yatim were back at the main road, a carriage came for them, sent by Datri. Jasfer urged them to hurry so he could be assured her injury was as minor as she insisted.

Datri refused any effort to nurse her. "It could have been bad, certainly. But it wasn't. So what did you learn?"

"Not a lot." Jasfer offered her the glass of water that was sitting on the desk in front of her. She glared at him until he set it down. "They'll send some soldiers up along the river to try to find the missing cars."

"And before that? Did the foreman say anything interesting?"

Their conversation had been interrupted, hadn't it? He thought back to what little they'd said. "Some kind of disruption at the mines. That was about all I got from Turang. I think he was being honest, as far as that goes. But we should have heard more from Pashun."

"Not if someone is trying to hide the problems from us," Datri said.

Jasfer leaned toward her. "Did you learn anything different?"

"Maybe." She cocked her head. "I don't understand it exactly, and I didn't have much time to look closer. But I suspect it's more than just a small disruption at the mines. More likely a full-scale rebellion of some kind."

A sound of soldiers marching past made Datri pause. There was a time when such street noises couldn't reach into the manor, but the squads grew ever larger, and their boots seemed to ring ever more piercingly through the city.

When their tramping had passed, she continued. "No one has been into the city. Even when deliveries were still coming through, the workers loaded their wagons outside the city and then came north to the train. It's been months since anyone went there."

Could miners take over a whole city? He thought of his sister's coup and the ideas that had led to it. Of their inspirational leader Rashul. He was still in Romnai and watched closely, but his ideas might have spread, might have inspired a dangerous revolution.

"We'll need to look into this more closely," he said after a moment's pause. "I'll speak with the Ruling Thirty and see what we should do."

Datri held up a finger to stop him. "Just speak with Baram first. The High Prince might know something already. Or might have an idea that doesn't involve the rest of the princes."

Jasfer opened his mouth to object then stopped. He didn't trust all of the other rulers of the valley and sometimes clashed with one or another. None seemed likely to stoop to the treacheries of the disgraced Dartak or Jasfer's own cousin Samatrit. But then *they* hadn't seemed likely to stoop that low, either, five years earlier. Yet they'd done their best to manipulate the anger of Rashul's movement to turn it to their own advantage.

"You're right. I will speak with him as soon as possible."

***

Jasfer stood between two of the High Prince's elite falcon jati guards and watched Baram. The High Prince cut an impressive figure, holding the reins of his snow chariot as he guided it around the frozen track. He was in his later fifties and had ruled as High Prince since before Jasfer was a prince, but he held himself like a younger man, proud and in command of his team.

The horses wore funny looking boots to give them traction. The track itself was in a hollow above the city, an hour's ride to the west. The sun rarely warmed it up, and the heat of the volcanic fields below seemed to pass right by, so that the track held its deep layers of ice.

Baram slowed his team and came alongside Jasfer. "Come up. We'll talk while we ride."

Jasfer had always admired good horses, but the horses he was familiar with worked in matched teams to pull carriages steadily through the streets of Romnai. These were a different type of horse, the chariot a very different vehicle.

A falcon jati warrior climbed in with Baram—he might be allowed to ride alone, but even a trusted prince wouldn't be permitted near him without at least one guard in attendance. Jasfer climbed in, surprised at how much room the chariot had for three people. He sat on a cushioned chair as Baram handed the reins to his guard. The horses started off smoothly with a quiet hiss of chariot blades on ice.

Baram spoke from the opposite cushion, his voice easily carrying over the noise.

"Such a relief to escape the city and come here. I don't make the journey as often as I should, but I need it to keep me ruling wisely."

"It is a lovely place. Cold, but the air..." Jasfer waved his hand around and breathed deep. Only a distant hint of sulfur marred it, much less than even the clearest day in the city.

"And impossible for anyone to overhear," Baram added as the chariot glided to a stop on the far side of the track.

Jasfer listened to the emptiness, the complete lack of anything human. After a moment he asked, "What have we found out, then?"

"The cars were found, not far east of the city. Empty and burned, so no clear indication of what the cars held. And pieces of the cars stripped away before they were burned, as far as the soldiers could guess."

A horse stamped its foot and snorted at the cold air. Jasfer watched the vapor of its breath freeze and rise, as if he could read something in the way it curled around itself.

"No real idea still, then?" Jasfer asked, when he'd taken a moment to think that much of the story through.

"Maybe. Our best guess is bandits boarded the train sometime. Maybe quite a ways back, up the river. When they tried to attack the engine, the driver panicked. Someone disconnected the cars from the engine—whether it was the bandits or the driver, we might never know."

How close did the railroad get to the ruins of Eghsal City? It stayed on the north side of the river, so never too close to those untouchables. To his sister who wasn't his sister anymore. But they had to at least consider those outcasts.

"Old Eghsal City?"

Baram shook his head. "Doubtful. We could look into it, but I don't think they'd have the resources to take over a train. This required weapons, tools…"

"Mining equipment?"

Baram glanced around the empty, icy hollow, as if someone might be even there, listening. "That's what we need to determine. What you said about the porters not entering the city—what your wife discovered, I should say—is concerning. There are many princely families there, and their letters indicate nothing wrong. The priests admit there has been some unrest, but claim it's nothing serious. But I no longer know whom to trust."

Jasfer leaned forward. "You can trust me." If he hadn't sided with Jaritta in her coup five years earlier, he wasn't going to betray the princes for some other rebel force.

"I know." Baram tapped Jasfer's shoulder in gratitude. "That's why I wish to give you this task. I need to know more, but I don't want any rumor spreading among the other princes."

He was not a spy, nor skilled in anything that seemed likely to help. But Datri would know how to proceed. "I may involve my wife?"

"Yes, please. I was counting on it. I also will introduce you to a cousin of mine. A distant cousin of my wife's, actually. Mahendri. He is originally from Pashun but has lived here in Romnai for a number of years. He can explain things about the city that you would have no reason to know, and I hope he can help you plan how to learn more."

Not a name Jasfer knew, but he would check with Datri. "Do other princes know he is your relative?"

Baram shook his head. "Doubtful. But as with everything you do on this matter, have excuses and alibis." He swept his hand at the empty hollow around them. "And meet in places where you can't be overheard."

***

"Mahendri," Datri said, running her finger over the coded notes she kept. "Approaching sixty years old and still very healthy. He has been here in Romnai for fifteen years, no scandals. Reports to a prince here when anyone from Pashun is visiting, and to the mayor back in Pashun when there's no one closer. Before that, he oversaw some of the soldier jatis, but nothing noteworthy there. A minor, bureaucratic role."

Jasfer nodded. "Any record of his involvement on any side during Jaritta's coup?"

"None. It was so quick, it would have been over before he even knew of it, unless he was directly involved. And well..." Datri chuckled. "I'll just say he doesn't strike me as someone to get caught up in that. His wife is here with him. No rumors of any liaisons, so either a very upright man or extraordinarily careful. Four children, the younger two born here."

"A family man, then. And if he's related to Baram's wife, he must be from the princely jati, right?"

Datri set the papers down. "Technically. But most of the families of Pashun princes have never ruled. Sometimes a daughter might marry into a family with a real chance to be among the Thirty, but he has no close relatives who have ever been anywhere near the thrones, apart from Baram's wife."

"Could be involved in a coup to get himself among the Ruling Thirty, though."

Datri shrugged. "Anything is possible. I always approach everyone that way. But no way he would try to set himself up as High Prince. He wouldn't get the support. If some other aspirant promised him support... Like I said, anything is technically possible."

She stood up, ready to go play the welcoming host that was expected of her.

Jasfer rose to help her with her papers and walk her to the office door. "Perfect, I will keep those details in mind. Will you listen in, or be interviewing the servants he brings along?"

"Oh, I don't think he has enough of a retinue to bring more than one. I have some correspondence to deal with, but I will still be in earshot."

Datri returned a moment later, escorting a short man into Jasfer's office. Jasfer rose to greet him and invited him to sit as Datri withdrew.

"Thank you, tisrah. You honor me." There would be no danger of anyone overhearing Mahendri's soft voice.

Officially they were discussing trade with Pashun, the mines, the missing ore, and they did spend some time on those subjects, reviewing things Jasfer already knew.

After this back and forth, Mahendri lowered his voice even further. "The real question is what to do about Pashun."

"Yes." Jasfer set his pen in its holder as a sign that they spoke in perfect confidence. "What do you think the real story is? And how will we learn more?"

"I think the situation is even worse than the High Prince imagines."

"How so?"

"Pashun is full of rivalries and divisions. Caste against caste, jati against jati, their distrust thin as silk in the best of times. If the miners are causing trouble, it won't take much for those rivalries to turn violent."

"Can't the princes control it?"

"Alone? No. They are weak and share too much power with the priests. The seminary there rivals the princes for power."

Jasfer drew in a deep breath. He belonged to the temple, to the hierarchical religion that dominated both Romnai and Pashun. But that didn't mean he trusted the priests. They'd cast out his sister. Not sister. A faction of their number had even sided with the princes who'd manipulated her coup and plotted against Baram.

"Then what should we do?"

"An informant, if we can." Mahendri looked up at the ceiling as if for inspiration. "Would the High Prince be willing to send one of his guards?"

Would a falcon jati warrior consent to going in disguise? Only by direct command. They were known for their elaborate, feathered headpieces and dangerous staffs as much as for their dance-like fighting ability.

"I will speak with him."

Mahendri leaned forward and added in a whisper, "But what they really need is a strong ruler. A high prince of their own." He leaned back but still spoke low. "Subordinate to our own High Prince, of course, and in service to the whole valley. But someone who can resist the priests' influence and bring all the factions to heel."

The words lingered in the silence that followed, a teasing invitation and urgent request.

CHAPTER 4

The mountains on the southern fringe of the Eghsal Valley gave way to lower foothills inhabited by scattered mumblers in their villages, each different from its neighbor in important ways. On his way out, Pavresh had stopped at many of them, as many as he could find welcome. Now on his return to the valley, he avoided them to pass through as quickly as he could.

Returning to chaos and violence, from what he'd heard, but here on the southern side of the valley, far from the cities of his people, all was peaceful and still, as if he alone saw that land.

The sun would set too early for him to stop, but as it bounced above him, along the mountain peaks of the southern horizon on its way toward setting, Pavresh paused to light a small fire.

Once the flames reached as high as his knees, he stood and removed the rope belt, the kusti, from around his waist. In the splinter Enshi religion, the knots on the end represented the cosmos—spark and fire, ash and smoke. He stood before his little fire touching each knot in turn. Then holding the rope out in the smoke, he performed the rituals of the fire. Balance, movement, the careful curves and twists of both rope and body. Even here in mumbler lands he'd kept up his observances as often as he'd had the opportunity, keeping the kusti movements light and smooth and keeping his mind united with the fire.

The rope curled around his wrists and twisted itself loose. He passed it behind his back, behind his neck. He moved through the stances in the prescribed order then repeated them in their own ways, each leading to the next without a preordained pattern, letting instinct and the fire determine what came after. He dipped his hands close to the flame and held them in the smoke. For a time the world disappeared.

The fire was the cosmos; the fire in each of its stages giving birth to the world around him, giving birth to himself. Flame was not greater than spark, and spark not greater than ash, but each equally a key part of reality.

When he came back to himself the sun was gone and the fire low. Pavresh lit the wick in his traveling lantern—mumbler style combined with Eghsal materials—and continued on the dark path down from the peaks. A slow journey now, but if he ever wanted to reach the valley proper and the cities of his people, he would need to spend some days walking both after the sun set and before it rose.

The path cut over ridges and through broken gaps of scattered stones, and Pavresh—a part of the fire, a part of the cosmos—carefully descended through the mountains.

***

Coming back down into the valley of Eghsal, Pavresh felt the familiar ambivalence of it, the sense of returning to a place, a home, he no longer knew. The descent from the mountains through the foothills was gradual. Boulders cluttered the downslopes, among scattered pines. Game trails leading through the snow became mumbler hunting trails before petering out to nothing.

Yet there was no question that he'd arrived in a different place. The air felt warmer. The slopes led ever lower, even if he sometimes had to climb between ridges to pass to the next slope. And sometimes the hunting trails hinted at something more, at paths used by the people of Pashun for trapping and scouting, at civilization.

Civilization—what did that mean within the arcist magic? Five years ago he'd have said progress, a positive push into a future of humans overcoming the world's challenges. Learning to tame the fire. But then, the fire was everything, sparks and flames and ashes forming the cosmos. By that, the tenet of his Enshi faith, was civilization not an evil sign of pride? Civilization led to princes fighting for authority. It led to a caste system that held the lower classes captive. It led to extremists like the Son of Ryo, whoever or whatever that was. And it led to betrayal, even by those with good intentions.

Pavresh climbed over a rise and saw a distant haze of the steam beds near Pashun. Dirty air but life-giving. Without that heat, there would be no people of Eghsal, no mighty cities. And no castes, no corrupt rulers, maybe even no betrayals.

When he'd begun his journey among the mumblers, he wanted to see civilization itself as a sickness. Better to be pure and untainted by such false fire, violence, betrayal. And so he would leave it behind, learn the mumblers' language, become one with the fire far from such a taint.

Except it hadn't worked.

The path came over a low rise, and Pavresh found himself face to face with a maned wolf, its long legs tensed to run. The animal stared at him. One leg was scarred with an old hunter's wound, long since healed over. Even out here there was no escape from civilization, whether in the wounds on the land or in the gifts of advanced tools and trade goods.

Pavresh did as the mumblers had taught him, standing still and tall, opening his arms so that his open furs would make him look bigger. Dangerous to attack was the image he wanted the animal to have, but no direct threat. The wolf matched his stillness.

Even the most perfectly remote, untouched villages of the mumblers weren't necessarily better than the civilization he'd tried to reject. That was the most difficult thing to wrap his mind around, to accept. Arcist magic rose up against any unfair, unjust actions, yet those injustices were everywhere, no matter how advanced or primitive, as he'd once seen those categories.

The wolf shook its mane, yipped its fox-like bark, and loped off away from the trail.

Pavresh headed on toward Pashun. It was his fourth time in five years returning to the valley, though he'd never stayed long. Something felt different this time. The previous returns had been with the idea of heading back to the mountains a certainty. He was returning to cross the valley to another region or simply to learn what stories had grown and spread since his last time. Now, he wasn't sure he would be going back.

He should feel accomplished. Learning the trade pidgin was a big step toward understanding the mumblers. He'd collected hundreds, thousands of stories over that time, finding the connections and the ways they varied from one village to the next. He was seeing patterns that should improve his understanding of the magic, make it more powerful and capable of intricate effects at the same time. Yet each new pattern seemed to undermine something else with the magic.

He'd set out sure yet curious. He returned uncertain and weary. He could only hope that the time back among his own people would at least restore his curiosity, if nothing else. And that the violence had not irrevocably destroyed the things he'd once loved.

Pavresh hadn't passed through this part of the foothills before. He expected to find some kind of path heading toward Pashun once he reached the valley proper. A route for hunters, if nothing else. An old route to the upper reaches of the river, where the cataracts made any further travel by water difficult. But he still had at least another line of ridges between him and the valley when he came across a surprisingly well-established path that headed between ridges toward the city.

A mumbler path or one by the city dwellers? In the trade pidgin, the people of Pashun were called miners. There was no sign of any mining speculation out here, but still it had the look of something done by his own people. He hesitated for a moment between following the trail and continuing on his original plan. But was he even sure there would be a route on the other side of the ridge? He turned and headed west between the ridges.

Pavresh followed the trail for the next several days. There was water to be melted, and he carried plenty of food to sustain him. He added pine nuts when he came across stands of the trees and chewed on pine sap. And there were a surprising number of patches of the winter berries that mumblers prized—surprising if they hadn't been cultivated specifically for those who used the trail. If not for the near constant wind blowing into his face, it would have been a thoroughly pleasant journey.

Eventually the trail veered up toward a gap in the ridge above. A smaller path continued forward within the narrow valley. Pavresh stopped to rest. He could try to press onward. No telling if it would lead anywhere or simply fade into ephemeral game trails. Better to stick with the wider path for now.

As he was about to tackle the climb up the ridge, the wind carried a noise to him. Voices. Not trade pidgin or unfamiliar mumbler words, but Eghsal words. The exact meaning didn't carry on the wind, but they were words with the rhythm of his own language. A sound he hadn't heard for so long.

Without even taking the time to wrap any glimmer of magic around himself, he rushed along the path, drawn toward those strange yet welcoming voices.

The path curved in toward a rocky enclosure that

resembled a mine entrance in miniature.

"Halt, mumbler."

Pavresh shielded his eyes and squinted into the darkness. The light from outside reflected off what looked like bare blades "I'm…" The words came rough from lack of practice. "I'm not a mumbler. I'm from the mines. Not the Pashun mines. From Romnai."

The blades pulled back but weren't put away. "A mumbler might have learned to speak real words. How do we know—"

"No mines anywhere near Romnai. Why should we believe you?"

Pavresh looked back and forth between where he thought the two voices came from. And a third? There appeared at least three figures within the darkness. "There is a mine near Romnai, across the river to the north, up in the foothills. My father owned that mine. I went to Romnai to work, to the city. Now I travel all over. Can you…could you light a torch or something?"

Were they miners? Maybe they were building a mine out here, getting things ready for an exciting future. He played with that image while his eyes adjusted to the low light. Wouldn't likely be the actual miners. The workers in the mines were low caste laborers and wouldn't be allowed to work out here on their own. A speculator, from a brenil or mid-caste jati, might choose to explore new locations. Or might be sent by a prince or other high-caste member.

It took a moment, but one of the figures lit a dim lantern at the back of the space. All it did was turn them into silhouettes.

"Why are you here? And how'd you find us?"

I belong. He wrapped that magic around himself. An official, but harmless. He tried to layer and smooth the magic to ease their tension, but the blades stayed out.

What if they weren't miners at all? Or miners who'd escaped and were hiding here where they might not be found?

The mumbler woman's words came back to him, of unrest and danger. "I didn't mean to bother you. I heard your voices as I was passing by."

Without warning, the figure nearest Pavresh lunged toward him. His kusti movements saved him. With the grace of his religious meditations, he danced away.

There were two others, at least. He stepped backward, away from the entrance, and his grace fled him. Loose stones slipped beneath his feet. He wobbled, fell to one knee.

All three were on him in a moment. More than three, it seemed—other figures pouring from the darkness to subdue him. Or was that simply an image that the stories led him to expect? He was sure of little, only that they stopped him, that they would never let him go.

They pulled him back into the darkness and bound his arms behind his back. Then they wrapped a blindfold around his eyes. Light filled the room, bleeding around the edges of his blindfold.

"Who are you really? Who sent you to look for us?"

"No one. A wanderer. I was sent by no one." Pavresh tried to see past the blindfold. The promise of light, the knowledge that it was there but inaccessible was worse than its absence had been.

"Look at him. He's some mumbler that's learned to talk, I tell you."

"No, I think he's a cheetah jati servant dressed to look like a mumbler."

"Did a prince send you, traveler? One of the false priests?"

False priests? That was an interesting thing to emphasize. "No one sent me. I was in the mountains and decided to return." Would confessing that he'd been visiting mumbler villages be wise? Probably best to keep that silent. But he did apply his magic, emphasizing the idea of a lone wanderer, of a rugged person who cared nothing about civilization. It was a figure common in many stories and easy to evoke.

"I doubt it. What do you know of the Sons of Ryo, traveler?"

Careful here. These outlaws or whatever they were might well be the Sons of Ryo the mumbler woman had heard of. Or they might be the enemies of the Son of Ryo, might have been driven out because of that person or group.

"Nothing. Is that you? Ryo I know, and the other gods, but I didn't know that Ryo had sons." An innocent, he said with his magic. No danger, no threat.

"Whom do you serve?"

Pavresh leaned even more into his magic and tried to extend its effects. "Nobody, since leaving Romnai." True words, and he let their truth infuse the magic. "I serve only myself."

That made it sound selfish. He wasn't selfish, was he? He served the valley as a whole, the peoples of the cities and villages. He served the ideals of arcist magic.

"Myself and the Cosmic Fire, as all of us must, humans or gods."

"He's no threat to us," one of them said. "Just an innocent wanderer."

The words reflected Pavresh's own thoughts so closely that he was taken aback for a moment. Then he redoubled his work on creating the magical effects.

"Maybe not." The voice sounded both more skeptical and more distant. "But now that we took him, what do we do? He can't just go free."

Pavresh reached farther with his magic, tried to make it cast its effect on the more distant speaker.

"Kill him, before—"

With a sharp hammer blow of arcist magic, Pavresh brought down all the images he'd been trying to create. Something felt different, a level of magical influence he'd never felt before. No one spoke. But as if they were under his control, one removed his blindfold and another released his bonds.

They parted wordlessly to let him pass out into the open.

Was he really doing that with his magic? He'd never tried to force such an image on others, to build the images up into something they were powerless to resist. Had never tried to control others.

He stumbled out, holding them in place while he hurried away from the hidden false mine. At the top of the ridge, he released the magic and collapsed beside the road, retching.

That was not what arcist magic was for, controlling people. It was more like the evil that the mumbler groups associated with their word for magic. Yet it had set him free, had maybe even saved his life. Was it wrong to use in that way? Was it even so different from the ways he'd used it to influence people, ever since he'd discovered arcist magic?

It felt different, though. Wrong at some level the magic itself rejected. He climbed to his feet and hurried on down the path. When he tried to reach out and sense the arcist images of his escaping, the magic felt soiled, no longer the pure thing he'd always sought. If his captors pursued him, he would use his magic to hide, to make himself seem like a worthless target, to escape.

But he wouldn't use it to control someone in that way—never again.

Chapter 5

The sea wind shook the paper in Harkala's hands so she could scarcely read it. But no matter, she knew it by heart, the old words, the oddly structured description that no one had been able to decipher. No one until she had.

Six hundred and fifty or so years ago, the first people of Eghsal had fled the Forgotten South. Had come to Eghsal. Even the name they'd given the valley was an old version of the word *exile*, if she was correct. They'd arrived in their boats here, not far from the mouth of the Eghsal River.

Was it a thousand people who'd come through those terrible waters to land here? Two thousand? Most scholars placed it somewhere between those numbers. Shouldn't it be even higher, though? By her calculations there must have been more than ten thousand, and even then those first settlers would have been extraordinarily fertile.

And that meant, what, fifty huge ships at least. But a smaller ship might have made it through the rough seas more easily, from what she knew of modern fishing boats, anyway. So probably hundreds of ships arriving.

Then where had so many ships ended up? They couldn't have all been buried in the silt of the river mouth or turned into the first buildings of Jarnur. That would only account for so many. Somewhere there must be remains of the ships.

The only clue was in a silk paper record from a century or more after the fact. No one had been able to figure out what it meant, though, not until she had the chance to study that scrap of ancient silk.

She scrambled up a rise, pausing halfway to the top to examine the soil. The servants waited below with all the gear she'd need for her fieldwork. She gestured to her student

Nakhil, a would-be scholar from a low-caste nefli family.

"See this?" The rock had a characteristic white line rippling along its surface. It extended for what the original settlers would have called a hundred *purusha*. "This was a riverbank once. The Eghsal River shifted from here to its current bed."

Nakhil bent down to see. "When, tisrah? Aren't these rocks far older?"

"Thousands of years, that's what the other scholars say." Harkala waved them away with her empty hand. "Is that what you were going to suggest? Well, what if it wasn't so long ago? The salty sea wind ages everything faster, buildings and boats but soil and rock as well. The river flowed through here far more recently than anyone realizes."

But six hundred years ago? Seeing the rocks, Harkala felt a voice of doubt. What if it wasn't the age of the rocks she should question but the time since the ancestors arrived? Add a thousand years to that, and the story required far fewer settlers, far fewer ships, much more time for the remains of those ships to disappear. No. She shook her head to clear the thought away. Now was not the time to stumble after some new errant idea, not when she was so close to proving herself as a true scholar.

Nakhil straightened and studied the line of where the river must have gone down toward the sea. No one born to scholarship would have submitted to being mentored by such an eccentric teacher, so she often drew students who were outside the normal. In the case of Nakhil, she'd lucked out. The young man was quick to listen and eager to follow her lead. Those were the key skills she required. He could think for himself, too, which was a pleasant bonus.

"And if the river mouth was along here instead of its current location, then this description makes far more sense." She waved the paper in her hand, her own copy of the scrap of silk. Knowing the ancient path of the river alone didn't explain everything in the paper. She'd also had to translate an archaic measurement the settlers had used, the *purusha*, which she'd deduced would have been roughly a typical person's height. And their compasses must have all been shifted slightly off true, perhaps by the iron of the mountains or some difference in how they constructed them.

She sighted her compass, making the adjustment for the ancient error, and set off along what had once been riverbank.

Farming had altered the land, even after the river's course changed. Rows of gourds and shell beans lined the ancient ridge, and grape vineyards stood closer to the current river, where the air was warmer.

The ancestors would have brought the ships up the river this far, the paper suggested. Perhaps they wanted to salvage some of the timber or perhaps they hoped to protect the ships from the storms of the shoreline. No doubt some of them harbored the hope to one day find a way back through that unforgiving sea and to the Forgotten South. Or the Not-Yet-Forgotten South, rather. Whatever the reason, the remains of the ships should be a short way in from where the banks had been.

At least, she hoped to prove as much. Then let the other scholars laugh.

To find that evidence of their earliest ancestors would be a truly great achievement, one that should make her famous in all the cities of Eghsal. And those cities needed something to celebrate these days. Give them a distraction from the tensions between castes, the violence between jatis. It could be a powerful reminder of what united all of them. Was it grandiose to think she might bring them all together, even if only for a brief time? Then let historians someday call her grandiose, because they would surely write about her.

"Right here," she told Nakhil, scanning the ground ahead.

The dirt was especially rich, so that a fair-sized bowl of a valley, shallow but clearly lower than the surrounding land, grew an abundance of crops. "There would have been an oxbow of some kind, or other stagnant offshoot of water. You can see the shape of it in the fields themselves."

"Did they sink the ships, then? Do we have to dig beneath the fields?"

Harkala shook her head. "Not if I read this scrap right. It seems to indicate that they pulled the ships out of the water and stored them in a protected…area of some kind. I can't make that out. What do you see nearby?"

Nakhil strode in among the mounds of carrots and cabbage and peered across the land. Harkala focused on a rougher patch of ground to the southeast of the fields. The remains of the ships could have stayed undiscovered there, as it looked like land that had never been excavated. It didn't exactly match her recreation of the silk paper, but perhaps she'd misunderstood part of it.

Nakhil pointed at a different location, a flat-topped ridge that marched down to the field. "If this looked like I imagine it did, wouldn't that be a better, more protected space?"

It did fit the description in the silk paper better. She looked down at her copy and back at the ridge. The location was a better fit, at least, but the ridge was much too small. "For the number of ships we're talking, it had to be a bigger area." Another glance between paper and ridge. "But we should check it out, at least. Let's take a look straight across here first, where the ground rises." The fertile soil gave way as soon as the ground sloped upward, with a rock-strewn terrain of tough grasses rising toward the mountains. "If we get stuck, we'll head over toward the ridge and see what lies there."

***

Stuck? Stuck was a mild word for the morass they found themselves in where Harkala had hoped to find her evidence. Figuratively, anyway—the water that had once been there had left with the river path, leaving it a dry land, but maybe not dry enough to preserve her ships.

An early plow blade had been the first evidence that it was less pristine than she had hoped. Some early settlers had planted terraces around the massive boulders that surely hadn't moved in thousands of years. Whether they'd managed to grow anything, Harkala doubted, unless the change in the river's course had swept most of the fertile soil away. What soil remained blew away with a simple brush of the tools the servants carried. Beneath was only solid rock.

No stray timber left behind by rotting ships. No indication at all that the ships had ever been anywhere near the area.

The laughter of her fellow scholars echoed hollowly in her mind. She could already see the covered smiles of those who'd never liked her and the embarrassed way her few one-time allies would turn away upon seeing her.

No, there were more sections to examine. She mustn't give in. But she needed a break from this field of rocks. "Come on, Nakhil, let's check out your ridge." They could always come back and search through the farther reaches of that rock-strewn area later.

The day was getting late. The servants, two aging retainers who'd been reluctantly lent to her for her studies, set up the supply tent below the ridge while she and Nakhil examined the area.

The lee of the ridge proved no more fruitful. Harkala dug a bit at the base, but the hard rock was far too ancient there to hide any ships. Nakhil wandered inland from the former wetland, peering into the hardscrabble trees. He paused for a moment beside one shrub to dig in the soil, but after a moment he shook his head and moved on.

Harkala went down to where the water would have been. Any scratches in the rock to indicate where ships had been pulled out? Any artifacts buried in what had been mud? The crops grown in the former wetlands over the centuries since that time would have surely destroyed all clues down there.

An old hand plow lay against the tip of the ridge, where it came closest to the fields. A mockery, a sign of all the farming that had destroyed any hope Harkala had of ever finding her ancient ships. She picked it up, surprised at how light it felt in her hands, and walked over to find Nakhil.

"Find something?" Nakhil was sweeping aside many years' worth of fallen needles and branches beneath a line of shrubs.

Harkala tossed the old plow on the ground. "More farming implements. Even here they must have disturbed the land more than I thought."

Nakhil picked up the plow. "Strange looking grain, though. I wonder what tree this wood is from."

Harkala snatched the plow back and took it into the sunlight. Too late in the day to see it closely. She strode over to the supply tent. The servants helped her train the lamps onto the plow.

"It is strange," she said over her shoulder to Nakhil. "Most of what's here today doesn't have this tight arrangement. And even old wood from further into the valley tends to be much lighter colored than this."

"Is it a tree that used to grow here and doesn't any more?"

Not that he actually believed that. Harkala could tell he was already leaping ahead—to the same place she was—but wanted to rule out other possibilities before he dared to state it out loud.

"I am not aware of any extinct trees here." Might as well just say what they were both thinking. "Say some early farmers used the timber from an old ship, though. A wood-poor place like this, they'd have wanted to make use of whatever they found."

"Is it… Can you tell?"

Is it wood from the Forgotten South? She remembered how she'd tossed it to the ground roughly. Now she hardly dared to handle the wood, as if just the possibility had turned it sacred.

She took out a lens to examine it more closely. There was nothing to compare it to, no other samples from the Forgotten South to know if she'd analysed it right.

She put the lens away. "I wish I could say."

She looked around at the fields of rich soil and the rocky land just outside the rim of greenery. "But I know this. We'll stay here tonight, and tomorrow we'll keep up our search, expand it outward. Those ships must be around her somewhere.

****

Shovels and dirt and a wintering sun, those would be Harkala's life now. For how long? However long it took, she decided. Long enough to find the evidence she needed, to write up her findings and submit them to the other scholars of the valley. To earn respect.

They dug into the side of the ridge, but the rock quickly grew too hard. Perhaps the seaward side had once been more protected. She and Nakhil made their way around to that area and found more evidence of centuries of farming. Terraces cut up the land into little plots of fields that looked like nothing the people of Eghsal used elsewhere. Most were unused today, since the better soil near the river's current course produced far more food.

"Maybe it was these farmers who made that plow," Harkala told Nakhil. "Let's see if we can find more scavenged wood among the terraces."

They tore apart one retaining wall and found only old

stones. The dirt held back by the terrace gave scraps of pottery and the metal from what might have been an old plow, but no more scavenged ship timbers.

It could take days, months to find their next evidence. She tried to temper her expectations. The one plow they found was proof that they were on the right path. Now it only took patience.

She hated being patient.

As the sun set one day, many days into their fruitless searching, Harkala decided to take a look at the terraces from above. With Nakhil's help she boosted herself up a ledge on the side of the ridge. She kicked at the soft rock as she got herself up over the lip and stood. Dirt tumbled down on Nakhil's head.

After brushing himself clean, he called up, "What do you see?"

The ledge was wider than it looked, and she could see an easy route higher, just scrambling over the rocks. But the view didn't show her anything new. "Not much. I'm going higher. There's a gap in the rocks I can climb up easily."

A small rock collapse, so long ago that no little, loose stones remained, gave her a safe route up the rocks. Even after she thought she'd have to stop, she found the slope gentle enough to keep climbing. Ancient rocks. This slope had loomed over those ancient farmers, the unknowable ancestors. And now, little changed, they loomed over her. Dark rocks and pale green lichen, more ancient than thought. She paused once to look back. Nothing special, and the sunlight was fading. She'd better hurry if she wanted to see anything.

Nakhil called up from below. "It'll be dark when you're trying to descend. Don't come down until I send for more light."

She had no intention to climb down yet. The top of the

ridge opened before her. She had to climb one tricky rock and get around another, then she leaned far forward to scramble up the last stretch to the summit.

The terraces were much more striking from above. Sinuous lines followed the curves of the landscape. The few larger patches that still grew crops were a noticeably darker shade of green than the fallow land.

Where might the ships have been stored in that land? And where would they find other remnants that had been used for other things?

There was an old barn up close to the higher slopes of the mountains, stone walls leading to a collapsed roof that must have been wood. Had a farmer used the ship timber to build that roof? That would be a place to look. The mountain slopes were too distant to have been the initial resting place of the ships. And in general, most of what she could see would be too distant from the old wetlands to have made sense. Only right here at the base would have fit what she'd deciphered from the ancient scrap of silk paper—or more likely at the other side, where they'd already found nothing.

Would that be it, then? She was so sure she would come out here and find some real proof right away. She wasn't naïve about the time real fieldwork could take, but she'd put in so much time just to get to this point. Months spent poring over ancient silk fragments, barely legible maps, copies of copies that were themselves crumbling to dust. Months avoiding the growing violence in the other cities as different factions vied for the favor of this god or that. Who had time for gods when the mysteries of the past were so much more compelling?

She *knew* where the river had gone, and hadn't that time proven fruitful? The evidence of the old riverbed was right where she'd expected to find it. Just like she knew where the scrap of paper pointed to, where it led her to look for the ships.

All for a single piece of wood, its origin no more than guesswork.

Her discovery might lead to finding some more remnants of the ships, long since repurposed and likely rotted. Buried ships would have lasted longer, especially in this cold, but maybe she would never find those.

Harkala turned around and picked her way across to the other face of the ridge. Was there something on that side she'd missed?

A stone rolled under her foot, and she fell, dislodging another rock. As she brushed off her hands and stood, she noticed the surface of the ridge itself. Flat. She'd seen that from below. And the soil was surprisingly thick for the winds that surely scoured its edge.

The place where the rock had been drew her attention. The soil was scraped away from a span the size of a flatbread.

Underneath was wood.

She had to swallow, make sure she wasn't just seeing what she wanted to see. She brushed away more dirt. The grains of the wood were clear, tight and narrow like the plow handle had been. Instead of a single, short length of a handle, this was a wide plank. She couldn't find the edges.

"Come," she called, her heart racing even as she forced her voice to stay calm. "Come up here. You have to come up. Bring some lights."

It took some convincing to get Nakhil to climb up in the mid-afternoon dusk. Finally, he and one of the servants, Darkoosh, scrambled up over the edge. The servant got four lanterns going and set them up around the ridge top.

Harkala could hardly contain herself, as she ran between the clear spot of soil and the lamps, adjusting their angle and brightness to see and memorize every detail. "It's all here," she told Nakhil excitedly. "A full ship so old no one even knows what ships looked like back then. We might be looking at a completely different style, a vessel unlike any we know today. Maybe we'll finally discover how they made it through the seas to land here in the first place."

Nakhil matched her excitement as he took measurements and sketched in a notebook.

Harkala paused to breathe and examined the ridge top. How much space did the ship take up? She paced off her best guess. It took her along much of the ridge. A sinking feeling tore through her. How many ships could they have towed up here? Four? Five? Out of the hundreds of ships that must have come through the sea, had so few remained?

Nakhil seemed to reach the same question as her just then. "Is it…do you think the ridge might be made entirely of ships?"

It would solve the problem. A hundred ships could create a ridge this high, even after years of settling. Too bad the explanation didn't fit. The ridge was rock. They'd seen it below, and she'd seen it as she climbed. It was too ancient, ageless, too clearly rock. Even her thoughts on the sea winds aging rock faster couldn't explain that fact away.

Harkala shook her head and led her shoulders droop. "No. But we'll excavate what's here. And hope it will lead us to the rest."

The rest of the mystery. Surely it wouldn't escape her searching now.

Chapter 6

Prince Jasfer stood before the assembled Thirty. He wore his finest silks, a brilliant orange color slashed with deep blue. His beard was oiled, and he knew he radiated power. No matter how little he liked what he had to do today, he would cut a memorable and striking figure before the other princes.

As the High Prince announced him, Jasfer read the crowd for influence. His cousin, shaven and wearing rags and kneeling before the assembly, held no influence. It all came toward himself, all the power of the room flowing through High Prince Baram's words and to Jasfer. It made him giddy. No matter what was happening in Pashun and along the routes between there and here, at this moment he had all the power he could ever want.

When Baram finished, Jasfer read his prepared statement.

"I am Jasfer Talai, ruling prince of the Valley of Eghsal, son of a ruling prince, and descendant of many who have ruled our land through history. Today I am sponsoring my cousin Samatrit's return to society. I do not absolve him of his crimes, which are serious."

He went on to enumerate exactly what Samatrit had done in the attempted coup and how he had worked to betray the High Prince. The words tasted of sulfur as he read them, of bitter spices and food that had gone bad. How could he sponsor his cousin's return when the dangers out of Pashun seemed to repeat the dangers Samatrit himself had represented? But he was changed by his shaming and exile, so everyone assured Jasfer. He kept the bile from his voice, speaking strongly into the room. Power gathered and spilled into him.

"At the High Prince Baram's own personal request,

Samatrit was approached. The falcon jati soldiers questioned him, and the priests as well. He is untouchable, and being untouchable does not itself purify him of his past. Yet the fire is at work in each of us, as Tiespetre wills it to be. They vouch for Samatrit's..." The paper said *worthiness*, but he couldn't spit that out. "They vouch for Samatrit's future, that it will be cleansed and made worthy despite his past. The High Prince's sentence remains, that Samatrit and his children shall never rule among the Thirty, no matter who sits as High Prince. This decree is burned into the law with a fire that none can change. But he is returned to his place with his family and declared once again a member of our caste and jati."

Samatrit lifted his head, tears on his cheeks, and for a brief moment Jasfer pitied him his five years of exile. Then he thought of his former sister's exile and the price Samatrit would have gladly forced her to pay for his own betrayal, and the pity drained away.

"As his cousin, I now lift him back into the graces of his birth. May the Fire consume him." No, that wasn't what he was supposed to say. He looked again at the words in his hands. "Consume his past and lead him forward, at our sides."

Jasfer stepped down from the dais and held his hand out to his cousin. Light glinted off the tears on Samatrit's cheeks as if he'd planned it. Samatrit took his hand, gripped it hard. Still strong, still defiant toward the cousin he'd never liked. Jasfer returned the grip without smile or grimace and focused on a point slightly above Samatrit's thinning hair.

The ruling princes and some of their families clapped. Samatrit's wife and children wept. Datri stood to one side, a calm smile on her face, as if this were all part of her control, something she had orchestrated. For once that wasn't entirely true, though once it became clear that Jasfer would have to sponsor Samatrit, she had made sure he did it correctly.

Samatrit spoke from the dais as well. The words were fine

and proper, but Jasfer let them drip away. The power in the room never wavered toward Samatrit.

When he'd finished, a few cheetah jati servants who worked in the Assembly escorted him away. No great honor afforded him, and a clear message that the work of the ruling princes would only continue after he was absent.

Jasfer bowed toward High Prince Baram. "I thank you for your clemency, tisrah. It shows your honor and strength. And I pray that the fire will continue to inspire us to justice and mercy, tempered by wisdom."

Baram took his words as his due and resumed his position of authority. The power in the room returned to their leader, but not all of it. Jasfer basked in the sense of his own position among the Thirty. All was not perfect—in the city, in the Eghsal Valley, even within the chamber—but all was right, arranged correctly to keep making Eghsal Valley a better place, under the High Prince's leadership.

***

Jasfer went to meet with High Prince Baram in his own chambers, rather than journeying again to the racing rink outside the city. Baram came from a decorated family with a long history. Instead of being built over the lava beds like many others, his home stood on a small hill north of the lava beds, commanding an impressive view of fumaroles and geysers.

Laborers trudging along the streets cast them sullen looks as they disembarked at the gate. A walla delivering meals among the workers called out something rude, but by the time Jasfer turned toward the men, the walla had ducked out of sight. Jasfer put his hand on Yatim's arm. "No need to pursue them. We'll be safe inside the manor."

Probably safer there than just about any part of the city, in fact. The violence wasn't confined to Pashun these days.

The lower castes were growing increasingly violent here. He hadn't heard of any attacks on princes, *yet*, but merchants had been attacked, and some people took to the streets complaining loudly about the princes. Some were describing it as a low-grade war, a fight without pitched battles or familiar strategies.

One faction calling itself the Children of Kwona, the horse goddess, complained about the princes' power. Another group, the Sons of Ryo, attacked untouchables in the name of their patron god. If either of them was involved in Pashun, hopefully their informant would uncover that piece of the puzzle. It was only a matter of time before the violence spread to Romnai if they couldn't do something soon to defuse things. The soldiers out in force only seemed to add to the danger and fear everywhere.

Gardens, an uncommon sight within the tightly packed city, led up to Baram's wide porch. The scents of the gardens chased away any lingering smells of sulfur and chemicals.

A dozen falcon jati soldiers, the personal guard of the High Prince whoever that prince may be, stood at attention along the porch. They were fierce women, each holding a long staff of fire-hardened wood. On duty they always wore a distinctive helmet with a falcon beak jutting out above the forehead and a multi-hued cloak made of overlapping fabrics and strips of leather that could turn many a blade. Pity the prince who thought to attack the High Prince in his own home. Pity the nefli laborer who thought to take out his anger even more.

A high-ranking servant in a fine white robe, a man with his own entourage of two lower-caste personal servants, bowed to Jasfer as he climbed the walk. "Tisrah, you are welcome. Please come this way."

The floor gleamed, so that the oil lamps along the walls reflected below—a hint of the fire's power and support for the

High Prince. The flowers decorating the hallway added to the flame coloring with reds and oranges. Their perfume gently filled the house.

Baram welcomed Jasfer to his study. He wore no crown or other ornament in his hair, which was graying at the temples but still dark, its dark waves oiled away from his face. His skin glowed in the light. Touched with the Fire itself, the priests might insist. If they were choosing to support him at that moment.

A fireplace in the corner burned some kind of treated wood that produced a rainbow of flames, so that greens or blues would dominate for a moment and then return to the usual yellows and reds. The High Prince sat behind his desk and gestured for Jasfer to sit in the comfortable chair opposite him.

"That was well done, Jasfer. A fine speech."

"Thank you, tisrah. I…I did not enjoy it."

"Please, inside my study it's Baram. And I know. That's why it had to be you. I couldn't ask anyone else to do it."

Jasfer studied the fireplace. A gout of blue flame burst out then faded back to yellow. "As you say. Certainly having some other prince sponsor him would have been far worse." Datri might have arranged an assassin if that had happened. But for Baram or for Samatrit or for whichever other prince it was? He would have argued with her against the High Prince but probably not the other two.

"And you earn greatly from this, you will see. Will Samatrit be grateful?"

Had his cousin ever been grateful, even as a child? Jasfer shook his head. "Only to his own cleverness, unless he's changed drastically in the past five years."

"Being untouchable has been known to do that."

Was Baram referencing Jasfer's former sister? Jaritta's life on the street had changed her immensely, but he wouldn't have said it completely erased the person she'd been underneath. Not until she sought to overthrow the Thirty Princes, anyway. Perhaps it was only an observation, though, nothing to do with Jaritta.

When he didn't answer, Baram went on, "Well, the other princes will look up to you more now. Your power grows in that way."

"Never a threat to you, tisrah."

Baram waved his objection away as not even a concern. "You came to speak of something else, though?"

"I did. Mahendri and I want an informant in Pashun. Someone loyal to you who could report back on the actual state of the city. I was hoping you might spare a falcon jati soldier."

"One of my guards?"

Jasfer nodded.

Baram ran a hand over his beard as he contemplated the request. "I do not like to diminish my own protection, now of all times. But I may have someone who could tackle a task of that sort. I will let you know. Would you expect someone who could blend in with the mines? That may be challenging. We would likely want to look for someone else, not one of my guards. Among the princes? The priests? The other city folk?"

Jasfer hadn't thought that part through, and Mahendri hadn't given him a thorough view of the city. "Not the mines, I think. The people in the city, I imagine. And I do wonder about the priests. They were a part of the coup, of course. And the ones involved were cast out. But did they include influential families down there?"

"They did, some." Baram rose and crossed to the bookshelf that filled one wall of his office. He reached high for a volume of official looking documents, bound in plain leather. He opened it on his desk to pages of his own handwritten records. "I have their family lines recorded here."

They were nonsense to Jasfer, but he read through the list dutifully. "Could you have one of your servants copy it down and run it over to me? Datri might know more about some of these people."

Baram nodded and passed the book to a servant who waited discreetly outside the door.

They moved on to other topics concerning the princes, the unrest in the streets, continued raids along the railroad tracks, the future, but none of them consequential. Jasfer found his mind wandering over that list of names, imagining a plot hiding behind each of them.

***

"We've reestablished contact with the princes of Pashun."

Jasfer leaned close to be sure he heard clearly. Mahendri spoke low despite the noise of the carriage. The curtains were drawn as they clattered along the streets.

"What are they saying?"

"It's bad there, worse than we thought. But they've carved out a safe part of the city. Up on the… Are you familiar with how Pashun is laid out?"

"Not at all."

"Well, it's like this." Mahendri held up one hand almost vertical. "The city is built into a steep hillside. Not that steep, I suppose." He angled his hand more. "But you get the idea. Down at the bottom are the steam-beds, keeping it warm. They stink."

"I have heard that." Even the people of the city had a reputation for smelling bad, carrying that stench with them.

Mahendri shrugged as if conceding the received image. "Our reputation precedes us. Anyway, the seminary is down there near the bottom. It's safe from the rioters, and maybe they have ways to communicate to the priests here, but if so, they aren't talking to us."

Fools in their temples. Jasfer gritted his teeth but said nothing.

"The princes, though, they live mostly up here, near the top of the slope. The smell is better, and the winds usually keep the air fresh, if colder than the lower parts of the city. So they closed themselves off when the strikes turned violent."

"They've been safe the whole time, then?"

Mahendri nodded. "But cut off. Trade doesn't come from the heights, and there aren't reliable roads that lead from there. Not without any messengers they might send being vulnerable as they left."

"So how did you hear?"

"It's dangerous. The rebels have been patrolling the roads. Even attacking the trains, as we saw. So they cut a new path. It meets up with the trade road, but farther north, avoids the worst of the rebel activity. To get through they have to send out a large contingent of their own soldiers, so they don't dare do so frequently."

Jasfer leaned back in his cushioned seat as the carriage slowed for something outside. "So, what do we do about that?"

"One thing to consider is that the old Eghsal City is a prime location for the rebels to hide, a base to strike from. We might try to clear the place out, force the outcasts to come back here to Romnai where we can keep a closer eye on them."

"That would require a lot more soldiers than you'd think. We've tried it before and never had success."

"Perhaps so." Mahendri tapped his lips. "It's something to keep in mind, though. Those untouchables may not be a direct threat now, but it's a vulnerability some enemy might exploit."

Was it only because Jaritta was there that he resisted the idea? No, Samitrit's false piety in urging them to attack the outcasts certainly played into as well. He gave a weak, "Let's keep that in mind, then." Then in a more sure voice he said,

"For now, should we send soldiers directly out to help the princes of Pashun?"

The carriage came to a full stop, and Jasfer pulled aside a curtain to see what the disturbance was. Mahendri stayed silent. Soldiers had blocked off the road and were checking every person and vehicle coming through. He opened the small window at the front to ask the driver what was happening.

"Apologies, tisrah. Came up suddenly, and now we're boxed in."

"Can you turn around?"

"Too tight, but I've signaled some of the soldiers. They'll open a path for us."

Good. Jasfer slid the window shut and waited for Mahendri to continue.

He sat silent, listening, and only after the carriage began moving again did he continue. "They would appreciate our assistance, I am sure. Would the High Prince approve of sending a soldier jati to Pashun to assist?"

Would he? Not his falcon warrior jati. They didn't have the numbers to send an entire troop, and it wouldn't be safe to deprive the High Prince of them, anyway. But there were other jatis. Jasfer could demand Baram place an entire jati under his own command, enough soldiers practically to conquer the city back himself. Jasfer had the influence to do so, but that didn't mean it was the best way forward. Better not to confuse matters.

"We might assign soldiers to help protect the routes, but I say we wait with anything more. I should hear back soon on the idea of sending an informant. I expect no difficulty there. Let's get a read on the situation from her first, and then make our plans from there."

Mahendri concurred. "We should send a message back the same way, without exposing our informant. What shall I say?"

"That we are aware of their situation and working to rescue them." Jasfer rubbed his cheek for a moment to think. Good to have it be explicitly from himself, to get them familiar with his name and influence. "Bring the letter to me before you send it. I will sign it so they know this is a matter the Ruling Thirty are aware of and working to solve."

***

Jasfer walked up to Samatrit's house with Datri on his arm. The party was a modest one, as befitted the family's status. No other ruling princes were there, only some of the lesser high caste families. He didn't know any names and left that to Datri, who whispered to him when he needed to know anything about them.

Samatrit's wife, Mashunri greeted them effusively. "Thank you, again. Oh, thank you for your sponsorship. You are truly an honor to your family."

Embarrassed, Jasfer dipped his head to acknowledge her thanks but wasn't sure what to say. Datri took charge. "You are family, dear. We take care of one another, no?"

Mashunri nodded and escorted them into the ballroom. A dancer performed along one side, wearing red silks and traditional face ornaments. Everyone else stood in clusters, talking and eating.

"Mashunri isn't priestly jati, is she?" Voice low and lips scarcely moving, a skill they'd both mastered long ago.

Datri shook her head slightly. "Princely. Good family with no big scandals. I think your mentor Apijet was her uncle?"

Apijet, killed by Samatrit's allies. And him already married to her at the time, right? So much for good family connections protecting you.

They made their way together across the floor. A servant handed them each a gourd of tisane, and they turned in opposite directions to see what there was to see. Datri would be looking for familiar faces, for those who hid a secret she already knew or who might know one she didn't yet. She let her fingers linger on his arm for a moment, then she glided off to join a group of women.

Jasfer observed the other guests' body language to judge the power in the room. Everyone deferred to him, even after his wife had left his side. That was to be expected, as a ruling prince and the one who'd sponsored his cousin. Under that deference hung a wariness, though, also directed at him. No other source of power or interest was clear in the body language.

Sipping his tisane as he walked, Jasfer approached the nearest group.

"Welcome, tisrah," an older man said. Jasfer acknowledged the man with a nod while he tried to place him. An uncle of Samatrit's, on the other side so not related to Jasfer. Kamlash. He owned some of the silk trade that Samatrit had been forced to relinquish when he was cast out.

"Those are fine robes, Kamlash. How is trade these days?"

"More stable than the mines, from rumors I've heard, prince. Some disruptions here and there, but no different than you might expect."

"Stability, yes. Pashun seems to have its share of unrest these days. Perhaps I should look into silks instead of mines. Let me know if you're selling."

Mindless chatter, yet Kamlash's reaction surprised Jasfer. He narrowed his eyes as if considering how much money to ask for his own shares. Of perhaps considering trading influence in Silk City for influence in Pashun. Now of all times? Either the man didn't know anything about the situation there or he knew more than Pavresh did.

The conversation moved on, but Jasfer steered it now and then back to the question of selling and buying silks and ore, and each time, Kamlash looked interested. Let it sit, simmer, see if he or some associate came to Jasfer in the coming days to inquire.

When he left that group, Datri gave him a subtle look, gesturing toward another group of men. Jasfer didn't recognize them, but he drifted over and joined them, letting them introduce themselves.

Names without meaning, they fled from his mind even as he tried to remember them. Silk weavers, though. That part he had no trouble noting.

Thinking of his discussions with Kamlash, Jasfer asked, "How are matters in the Silk City these days? I hear little from my wife's family." Datri's family corresponded frequently, in fact, but easier to play uninformed.

The men glanced at each other and one answered, "We are based here in Romnai. I am, anyway."

The other two nodded as if to say they were as well, though he noticed they didn't quite say as much. Perhaps one of them traveled between cities. Perhaps between Romnai and Pashun.

"My apologies."

"Not at all, tisrah. We should have made that clear. We often hear from the Silk City, so I can tell you that the work is good. New fabrics and old techniques."

"We shall never lose them," another of the men piped in. "The old ways. We have to keep them strong."

"No doubt." Jasfer nodded as if it were a wise and deep saying. "And peaceful, too? No mumblers attacking? None of this Kwona and Ryo unrest we face here in Romnai?"

The silk weaver gave a dismissive wave of his hand. "Mumblers. Not a problem out there. Our soldiers do well."

"But the soldiers…" Another chimed in, quieting when the other weavers looked at him.

"Oh?" Jasfer let all the power that accumulated on him rest on that one word.

The first weaver shrugged his shoulders. "Some sort of argument between our soldier jati and the wolf jati, I think. Or between our soldiers and one of the servant jatis. The reports weren't clear. Lots of the lower castes arguing with each other, but nothing that caused problems for us."

Jatis arguing in the Silk City. Perhaps some who claimed to follow Kwona and some who honored Ryo? Miners rebelling in Pashun. And the streets of Romnai were a fire laid out, awaiting a spark. Likely much the same in Jarnur. So much for the stability of investing in silks. Or anything.

As if sensing his thoughts, another weaver said, "It never interferes with our work, though. The servants argue for a bit and then make up and the work goes on."

Jasfer gave a light laugh that released the pull he'd been exerting on the room's power. "Hard to find good help. Doesn't matter where you go, I suppose." Banal and far from true, but the weavers quickly agreed with him, and their conversations moved on to discussing the silk trade itself and some new fabric they were testing.

Jasfer and Datri made their farewells early, as befit their greater prestige. A gust of wind blew some light snow from over the volcanic fields, each flake carrying the stink of sulfur. No sign of mobs or angry revolutionaries preparing to strike at the moment. An entire troop of soldiers guarded the party, from various positions along the street.

An unfamiliar carriage pulled up between them and their own carriage. Yatim, standing beside their carriage, startled and rushed around the strange carriage.

The guards who stepped out were anything but unfamiliar, though. Two women in the matching uniforms of the falcon jati, one intercepted Yatim and the other held a door open for Jasfer and Datri to enter the carriage.

Baram. He owned many carriages and kept each as indistinct as possible. Jasfer waved Yatim off and helped Datri inside. The interior of the carriage was fine without seeming ostentatious, smooth and well brushed fabric over cushions that wouldn't tempt anyone to sleep there.

The High Prince greeted them with only a nod and tapped on the carriage window. Once they were rolling through the streets, he spoke, his voice tight and low.

"Thank you for joining me here." As if they'd had any choice in the matter, but such feigned courtesy often kept the valley in order when chaos threatened. "I need you to share what you know of events in Pashun. Names, clues, any suspicions you have."

"Of course, tisrah." Jasfer caught Datri's eye, and she gave a hint of a shrug that no one but Jasfer could have read. What might have brought this demand on? "Anything you need."

Baram nodded and tapped again on the window. Without the carriage stopping, the door to the carriage swung open inward. Datri gasped and leaned away, pulling Jasfer with her. There was no wind, though, as if the door didn't lead outside. Jasfer craned his neck and caught a glimpse of a narrow compartment between the outside and the interior of the carriage.

A falcon jati warrior climbed inside and stood before the High Prince with her head lowered. Despite the fierce uniform of her jati, the warrior looked young, her cheekbones still soft. A blush spread up her face as she waited for Baram to speak.

"This is Valni. She will be your informant in Pashun. I am hearing of problems from other sources as well, so her journey there has become urgent. The rebellion there may well have support here as well."

Valni dropped her distinctive falcon jati cloak and wrapped a white cheetah jati robe around her shoulders. She didn't hold herself at all like a servant, even a high-ranking cheetah jati servant. Too bad he could no longer call on the arcist Pavresh instead. He could blend in wherever he was sent. They would have to work with her, try to train her before she headed out on the High Prince's mission.

That was, assuming he was asking them to get her on her way.

Only a breath later, Baram confirmed what Jasfer has suspected. "She will leave from your manor. With others or alone, openly or in secret, I leave that up to you. I need you to create a way for her to communicate back here, something that doesn't involve me or any of my household."

No doubt she would have a way to contact them as well, through her own jati. Jasfer knew enough to not ask about that.

"And we will take her back now, as if she were our attendant?"

Baram nodded. "I do not know who is behind any of this or who might be watching. Some of these factions may well have members in the households of the Thirty, and who can say where else? So I thank you for your discretion."

Another tap on the glass, a different pattern this time, and a moment later the carriage stopped. A falcon jati soldier in her own outfit opened the door for Jasfer and Datri and the disguised soldier.

A shout somewhere along the street cut off abruptly. A fight? Someone arrested by the soldiers? Or otherwise silenced? It was too far away to be any threat to them.

Yatim stood before the open door of their own carriage with two other armed servants standing beside the horses. Jasfer and Datri quickly got inside without any other word. The young falcon jati warrior in her servant's dress followed quietly, but her alert eyes and erect head had nothing of a demure servant's posture.

CHAPTER 7

Jaritta woke up shivering. Frost etched lines on the inside of her rough tent. She kept her furs around her as she made her way out into the bitter outside.

The refugees of Eghsal City camped as close as they dared to the volcanic fields. The land to the north glowed, and no doubt that glow kept the worst of the winter freeze away. But its heat seemed too distant to appreciate. The nights were cold out here, and their furs enough to survive but too little for comfort.

A fire blazed in the space before her. A dozen tents faced the fire ring, the people clinging to whatever warmth they could. That such a number would choose to pitch their tents close together was testament to how bitter the cold in the camp was. The untouchables and mumblers of the ruins did not take easily to having others nearby if they could avoid it.

No longer slowed by her injured leg, Jaritta strode to the edge of the circle of tents. Other circles and clusters spread out to the east and west. No geysers tearing them apart, no cracks opening in the ground. A rumble shook the area, followed by the distant sound of rocks falling.

She shivered and turned away. Before she could return to her communal fire, Azheeran came out from another cluster of tents to greet her. His grouping seemed to be set up differently, probably following some ancient mumbler wisdom that Jaritta couldn't define.

"There is ice on your people's tents."

"It was a cold night." Jaritta fell in beside him to head toward the fire.

"You spread out too much, don't build your tents like I told you."

What could she say? She agreed, but the other untouchables and outcasts were stubborn and hadn't listened.

"What we need is a new place. Simply start over. Not try to recreate the ruins out here within sight of them." It was that or end up back in the cities, begging for the scraps to survive. Unless Thamiba came back with better news, anyway.

"Then let's look for a new place," Azheeran said, "before it's too late."

***

An old mumbler camp sat in the lee of a low hill. Jaritta climbed over a fallen tree and half slid down the slope to reach the remains of the camp. Azheeran helped her to her feet at the bottom. A touch on her hand as she rose, pale skin against her burnished brown—even now, that brief connection could surprise her, after so many years an untouchable.

"Thank you." She brushed dirt from her hands and looked around. It was good to get away from the camp and the threat of geysers and earthquakes, to take her mind off Thamiba's trip to Romnai and wondering what was happening there. If she couldn't go to the capital city, at least she could look for a new place for the outcasts to live. "An old site, or recent?" It might well be a seasonal camp, empty now but occupied other times of the year. She didn't want to create new troubles by taking over an established route of one of the wandering tribes.

Azheeran stuck his hand into the mixture of ash and dirt where a fire would have been. "Used often, but not for a few years."

It was a potential place to move to. She scanned the area around the old camp. Dense growth, though mostly shrubs. They could clear an area, leave a wall of shrubs around them. This was a part of the valley where the railroad tracks left the river for a stretch, cutting off an isolated peninsula where they could at least still have access to the river.

No steambeds meant even the thicker vegetation was still a hardscrabble mixture of plants that could survive the cold. A layer of snow that probably only melted away for a month or two each year, if that, lay under the sharp branches. Could they build up a pocket of warmer air, trap it here somehow? She didn't know enough to guess, but the bitter cold of the refugee camp was absent as well. Or at least she told herself it was. Maybe the trees already trapped some heat that they might take advantage of.

Ilshu came through the undergrowth to join them. As with many untouchables, he had a lighter cast to his skin—his cheeks had a hint of pinecone in their color—still nothing as light as a mumbler. People often claimed the untouchables had mumblers in their ancestry. Jaritta wondered whether that was true or simply something they said to justify how they treated the untouchables. Like the others, he wore thick but rough robes to protect himself from the cold and the underbrush. The widow Driyya had sent the young man with Jaritta and Azheeran in her place.

"How far to the river here?" Jaritta asked.

Ilshu gestured back behind him. "A ways. But there's a little stream closer. Mostly frozen right now, but might give us cleaner ice to melt than the snow."

"A longer trip for fish, though." Too bad. Even from the refugee camp, many of the outcasts were still circling the dangerous ruins to fish the river, though, so it might not be impossible here. Jaritta picked up a large branch and tossed it aside, imagining moving the refugee tents to that place. Or better, more permanent structures of wood and furs to keep them warm, several linked together so they could even pass from one to another without heading out into the cold. "We might fit a dozen in here," she muttered out loud, as if her thoughts on tents and structures had been a conversation.

"A dozen people? That's not many, for all the people we're trying to resettle."

"People?" Jaritta frowned a moment then realized how Ilshu must have misunderstood her. "No, I meant a dozen families. A dozen…tents or something of the sort."

"That's still not necessarily many more than twelve people, with how we like things in Eghsal City. Maybe back in Romnai you squeeze more together, but are we going to demand that with the mumblers and untouchables?"

Leave Romnai out of it. She didn't want to be reminded. "Maybe we'll have to change. That's not impossible, is it?" But she didn't believe her own words. The evidence of the current camp proved him right. "Maybe not twelve, though. I'm only thinking out loud. Anyway, that was just this one circle. Then we could have another group over there, and there." She gestured broadly around the shrubland.

Ilshu paced a handful of steps from the old fire scar and stopped to peer out into the bushes. "Maybe. If we could get them to all move here."

Azheeran stood and brushed the ashy mud from his hands.

Jaritta helped steady him when his legs appeared to buckle. "What do you think, Azheeran. You mumblers have camped here. Is it a good place for a bigger group to live?"

"*We* mumblers? *I* never camped here." The words were automatic, as if he didn't expect an answer, so Jaritta waited for him to continue. "I want to see the stream Ilshu found first. And head toward the river."

They forced their way through the brush, and the stream surprised Jaritta, opening up at their feet. The needle-thick ground simply dropped abruptly down a hand's width to the water. A soaked branch bobbed against some rocks opposite them, the depth not enough to carry the branch farther downstream. The exposed portion of wood was covered in a shiny coat of ice.

"Not a lot of water," she said.

Azheeran nodded. "No, but it's flowing. Even in winter. That's good." He dipped his hand in and drank.

Jaritta did the same. The water had a tang of old rot but still tasted cleaner than the sulfur-tainted water they often drank in the abandoned city. So cold. She quickly dried her hand and wrapped it again in a fur.

"This flows north." Azheeran waved his hand downstream. "I want to see the route to the river south of here."

The Eghsal River to the south was very near to the ruins and their old makeshift homes. The land rose to a respectable ridge beside the river, so it took some time to make their way through the shrubs up toward that ridge. They left the trickle of a stream and made their way upward. Deer ran from them, a good sign that they might find game in the area, though there were also many tracks of the long-legged wolves that prowled that part of the valley. Competition. And a threat as well? Jaritta wasn't sure, had never lived in such a wild region where she had to worry about protection from wolves.

They camped halfway up the ridge, huddled close together in the mumbler way, with the fire close and a hastily built windbreak to funnel the heat toward them. From untouchable to such an intimate—and yet chaste—way of life. Hard to believe and hard to imagine the journey that had brought her here.

She fell asleep to a light snow drifting onto their tiny camp.

***

The morning was frigid, freezing their breath into clouds. Not as cold as the open camp where their people were living now, she reminded herself, or was that only her imagination, her wishing for it to be true? They warmed themselves by climbing the rest of the way to the top of the bluff.

The cliff wasn't high, but enough of a climb to take them to mid-morning, when the sun was well above the southern mountains. It shone on the river below and a wide expanse of land with the steambeds around the abandoned city plain to see.

"Much warmer here," Azheeran said.

Ilshu stretched. "Well, the exercise helps. I can feel my joints again. That's good."

"Not that." Azheeran shook his head. "The sun. It wasn't terrible yesterday during the day, but I bet it gets awfully cold overnight. Put a city in where that old camp is, we freeze. Probably flood in the summer, or live in mud at least. But it's winter that makes it a bad place to camp. Spend a few days in the fall, while hunting, sure. Or maybe spring to harvest young wood for making baskets and tools. But not year-round."

Jaritta turned around to look at where they'd been. It was still dark below them, the line of sunlight perhaps just now reaching the mumbler camp they'd found. Deeper in the winter, it wouldn't even see that brief sunlight. And to make room for enough people, they'd end up tucked in closer to the bluff, where the sun would be even less present. Her spirit sank.

"You're right," she said after she'd surveyed the land, her heart sinking as she saw yet another plan drift away into nothing. "It won't work. But then where?"

Ilshu shrugged and pointed down at the river. "The islands?"

Jaritta looked down at the tiny islands in the river. One was bigger than she'd realized, but even that couldn't have room for many outcasts. "We might as well visit them on our way back. Can we make a way down the bluff here?"

Azheeran led the way. A deer track cut down, steeper than

Jaritta might have liked, but they helped each other where the way grew too muddy. At the bottom of the bluff, they had to make their way upriver to view the islands.

The bank made travel beside the river difficult. They had no flat space to walk on, and trees grew out from the bank right to the water's edge. They traveled as close to the river as they could, moving up and down the bank as they had to so they could advance.

As they climbed over the angled trunks of a group of pine trees, there was a crashing in the underbrush ahead. Jaritta rushed forward just in time to see a herd of deer racing nimbly up the face of the bluff. That's what they needed, a deer's feet and grace.

They came down near the spot where the herd had been drinking. The bank leveled out there, and they took a moment to rest where they didn't need to brace themselves against a slope. The river was calm, dotted with shards of ice that broke up and re-formed as the current pulled them downriver.

There was something disappointed about the river. How was that possible, for water to be disappointed? As soon as she thought it, Jaritta couldn't put a finger on what she meant, but it was there. The arcists would probably say it was an arcist theme, something her mind reacted to as she paused beside it. Or maybe it was the sighing noise the water made, and the rest she simply imagined. No need to throw in magic.

Even so, as they left the watering hole to resume their trek, Jaritta was struck by that same sense of chagrin, and from the corner of her eye she thought she saw some vast shape moving away through the water. A predator that had hoped to dine on deer? To dine on humans? A more superstitious person might attribute it to the nagas of legend.

After that rest, every time she was able to take her attention away from the path ahead, she looked into the river, hoping to catch another glimpse of the creature.

The path beyond the waterhole followed an easier route, an animal path or even something human-created, though if so, by infrequent passage or very few people. They walked well into the afternoon, and Jaritta almost convinced herself that she'd only seen the shadows of the clouds in the river.

Still, she watched the water closely, if not for whatever shadow had caught her eye earlier perhaps for other animals that might live in this cold water. If other creatures could, it made it more likely she might find a way for the outcasts of Eghsal City.

A flash of movement, serpent-like. Jaritta gasped and paused beside the river. The idea that the nagas might be real, even here, seemed to bless that stretch of river. A moment later, though, a small head broke the surface of the water. Not serpentine. It had fur, slicked back by the water from a small otter face. The animal twisted and disappeared again beneath the water.

Before she'd had a chance to consider her disappointment, Azheeran hissed, "Down!" and pulled her to the ground.

Ilshu ducked in beside them. "What is it? You saw something?"

"The island." Azheeran pointed upriver. "There's a house already on it."

Jaritta stretched herself upward to see. They'd already reached the biggest of the river islands, and she had been too distracted by the possibility of animals in the water to notice. A house stood on the downriver side of the island. Or rather, *above* the downriver side. It stood on stilts that raised it a person's height from the ground. To protect it from floods? Or from animals? Perhaps both. It would be worth remembering, if they ended up trying to move to the islands or some other wetland.

But why was Azheeran afraid? It looked like a mumbler building style, above the stilts. Not only that, but there was a figure at the opening of the house. Jaritta leaned up further. Mumbler clothing, pale face.

"Come, why don't we at least approach? He's a mumbler, so you can lead the way, Azheeran."

"You still think we're all the same? We don't call ourselves *mumblers*, you know." Azheeran didn't wait for an answer, though Jaritta puzzled over the question as he continued. "To put it in your words, he may be outcast. Or may think I'm outcast. May belong to a different city or god or—" he said some word that Jaritta didn't recognize. "An enemy jati. Does that exist?"

"I suppose so, in a way. You think he'd just attack us, if we approached openly?"

"A trader can come, but we are not traders. A city dweller like you two, never."

Ilshu stood. "Maybe a group of three is more of a problem. But a lone traveler? He won't blindly attack me without worrying I might have friends back in the city. That threat has always protected the people of Eghsal from you mumblers."

Holding arms open, Ilshu headed on up the river closer to the island. Azheeran made as if to stop him then held back, keeping close to Jaritta in the shelter of the brush.

"Hello. I'm coming in peace," Ilshu called out as he walked calmly forward. "In peace. To trade, umm, assistance. Help for help."

Whether his voice was even enough to reach across the water to the island, Jaritta doubted. It was easy to overestimate how far a voice could carry.

"Can you understand me? Can I ask about your island?"

The mumbler made a movement with his arm. A dismissive movement, as if to tell Ilshu to go away. Or that was what Jaritta thought until Azheeran swore and Ilshu dropped down to the ground.

Azheeran shot from the brush and ran, bent over, toward

Ilshu. Jaritta followed, but dropped to the ground when she heard a whistling noise. The bare twigs above her head exploded, and a pebble struck the ground just beyond where she lay. A sling. Was Ilshu seriously injured? The thought made her stomach drop, both for him and for Driyya. The mumbler wouldn't have wasted a sling bullet on him, if a pebble would keep them from crossing the river toward his island. But even a pebble could kill.

Pressed to the ground, she wriggled forward, having become the naga she'd imagined, having become the otter she saw. Only without the grace and swiftness. No further pebbles slung at her, and no sign of Azheeran anywhere. Had he already reached Ilshu? She expected to find him bandaging Ilshu's wound or dragging him back farther from the island at any moment.

Instead, she reached Ilshu and found him propped up on an elbow, grimacing in pain. Before she could check on his wounds, he held up a hand to her for silence.

As if she would listen to him.

"Are you hurt badly? What happened to Azheeran? I thought he'd be helping you."

"Hush," he whispered back. "I'll be fine. Azheeran is sneaking on ahead. Wouldn't tell me why."

"So we just wait here? Let's get farther away from the island, at least." She paused. Where exactly was Ilshu wounded? And how badly? "If you can, anyway."

Ilshu nodded. "I can." He started toward her and pursed his lips. "If you don't go too fast, that is."

May the nagas guide us. Jaritta twisted around and headed back downriver. Ears alert for the buzz of a sling or the whistle of a slung pebble, but nothing sounded over the noises of the river's current and their own passage.

A wolf cry echoed off the water and over the woods. Odd to hear at this time of day.

"That's Azheeran. I hope we're far enough away," Ilshu said. Then he struggled to rise. Over his shoulder he said, "Keep pretty low, but pretend there's some bigger group of us coming down the bluff."

Jaritta looked back and forth for any clue whether or not she'd understood him right. Behind her, Ilshu waved his arms as if up the slope and called out, "Down here, but be careful." He jerked one hand toward the island.

Jaritta whipped around toward the island, saw the mumbler there looking their way, his hand moving at his side. A second mumbler was leaning out from inside the dwelling. They were much too close.

Jumping, she tackled Ilshu and lay on top of him as she imagined a pebble hitting both of them. Azheeran would return—from somewhere—only to find them both dead. Not that it was possible for the man on the island to hit them both from that angle. Still, she rolled away from Ilshu so at least one of them might survive.

But why did they need to draw the mumbler's attention? There must be a reason. She was lying near a good-sized branch, dry but nearly weightless with age. She grabbed it and tossed it as far as she could from her low position, up the slope. It didn't go far, but the sound of cracking branches carried through the woods. And hopefully out to the island.

"Come on, that should be enough," Ilshu said. "Let's get farther away now."

As they scrambled away, half crouched over, Jaritta asked over her shoulder, "What was that all about? Why did we do it?"

"No idea. Azheeran wouldn't say more, only asked me to do it. Safely."

Well, the safe part they'd only barely managed to do. As they got farther from the island, Jaritta straightened up and sped up, until Ilshu called for her to slow down for his sake.

A moment later, the path came right down to the river's edge, and there was Azheeran, sitting in a strange boat. His clothes and hair dripped, but he seemed to shed the water without shivering. He gave a whoop on seeing them. "I decided he owed us his boat, for injuring one of us. Good job with the distraction. I don't think he ever saw me."

"Will it hold us all?" Ilshu asked.

"If you don't rock too much."

Jaritta grabbed his shoulder before he could climb into the boat. "First let's dress your wound, Ilshu. Azheeran, looks like there's a blanket in the bottom of the boat. Wrap yourself up while I tend to him."

And then back to the refugee camp, alive and plus one small boat. But without any plan for where to go from there.

***

Thamiba returned a twelve-day later, with a few other outcasts from Romnai in tow. His journey left him less bedraggled than Jaritta had felt after crossing the river, but his news of Romnai was no better.

"There's no place for us there, that's certain." He shook his head to emphasize his words and looked from one of the city's self-proclaimed leaders to another. "I don't think most of them realize just how bad it is, either."

"What do you mean?" Jaritta pictured the old familiar streets. There was always room—as long as you weren't too worried about comfort and safety. "How bad is it?"

Thamiba shrugged, his arms wide open. "Not safe at all. It's a geyser about to blow." Before Jaritta could ask, he added, "Not literally, like here. Just... Brenil cheating nefli, nefli stealing from brenil, and everyone getting set to rise against the princes."

Which was why Rashul had been right about getting rid of the caste system entirely. "That's not so different..."

"It is, though. Beggars beaten and killed, that's what it'd be for us. The Sons of Ryo, that's what we saw on the building here, remember? They're ambushing beggars in the streets. The Children of Kwona is some other group that's stirring up people against the soldier jatis, attacking them when they have the numbers, telling people in the streets about terrible things the soldiers are doing. And then the two groups fight each other. I don't think the princes have any idea how bad it is, how little a spark might set the whole city burning."

Jaritta closed her eyes. Romnai burning, literally or not. Over five years she'd been here, but Romnai was still home in a real way. A strange emptiness seemed to open up inside her. A seed of something new was filling that emptiness, but she didn't know what it was, couldn't put it into words.

"What of Rashul? Chaitan? Did you manage to speak with them?"

"No." He avoided meeting her eye, and Jaritta felt a foreboding inside that emptiness, reaching out to crush the seed. "Rashul is watched. I didn't try to get close to him, but he seems to be a shadow of who he used to be. Quiet and submissive to the princes. And Chaitan—"

One of the people who had followed Thamiba came forward and put an arm around Jaritta. Jaritta started as she recognized the woman. Tanjali had been Chaitan's personal attendant as his sickness grew increasingly worse. As an untouchable, she'd been forced to leave Chaitan for a time, but as far as Jaritta had heard, Tanjali had been allowed to return to work for him later. "Tanjali! It's been so long. I'm glad to see you."

"I'm glad to see you too, Jaritta. But you need to know that Chaitan is dead. I'm sorry to be the one to tell you. He died last autumn."

Tanjali kept talking, telling about his illness, that it was expected, the natural progression of the disease and not any kind of underhanded act or… But what did it matter? The emptiness expanded. No Chaitan. Rashul finished as a leader was hard enough to imagine. He'd been their inspiration, the spark of charisma that got them making real plans for their dreams of a better city. But Chaitan dead, that seemed to end the ideas he'd encouraged, to end them entirely, to snuff out the dreams they'd created together in his house.

What did an extra boat matter in that? Or a river island too small to live on? Or a camp too cold when it wasn't too muddy? Let the castes be, and she could go off and live by herself. An island would be big enough for her and maybe a few others. No need to worry about the rest. That was the ethos of the Eghsal City ruins after all, each person taking care of their own.

Finally, Tanjali paused her talking to squeeze Jaritta's shoulder one more time then released her. "It's good to see you too, Jaritta," she repeated as if to draw Jaritta back from her thoughts. As if to emphasize the words she might have missed. "And I hear you're the one to carry on his work. I'll be here to help."

Jaritta looked at Tanjali's face. An untouchable, like herself. Beyond her were others who'd been cast out or otherwise found themselves outside the society of the cities. Maybe that was the seed growing in the emptiness, a new place for all those people.

Maybe, but for now the emptiness overpowered anything else.

CHAPTER 8

A bitter wind dogged the falcon warrior Valni along the trade road toward Pashun. The princes Jasfer and Datri had found a way to get her on a train disguised as a cheetah jati messenger. She wasn't even the only messenger. Whispers about the events in Pashun had spread among some of the princes, at least. Those with relatives or business in the southern city all wanted to know what was happening. No one thought it strange that she kept to herself—each of the servants guarded their own tasks jealously.

When the tracks reached the overland trade road south, they left the train and joined a caravan away from the river. A heavy presence of soldiers patrolled the route, some accompanying the caravan and some stationed at intervals along the road. Another train would have been better. The tracks along the river had existed before locomotives did, with cargo drawn up and down by boat. But surely the time was long past when some wealthy prince or other could fund new tracks here as well. Maybe it was already happening, for all she knew.

Once in Pashun, she would have freedom to decide where best to serve. Probably not among the princes where the other servants were headed. She needed to be able to see the whole city, not just the wealthy masters behind their barricades.

Masters and servants. She hated the way these non-soldiers spoke. Her jati *served* the High Prince, but she'd never seen herself as *servant*. It demeaned the work she was there to perform.

She stuck with the caravan for most of the way along the road heading south. It was a bare land of black and gray rocks and little else. Besides the wind.

The caravan master was a small man who spoke as if to make up for his size. Or as if he thought he were an imposing figure, laughable as that idea was. He was almost as anxious as she was to get to Pashun, now that there was an open path he could follow, people he might trade with. Yet all his shouting was ineffective at getting them going as fast as she wanted them to go, and he was frequently sidetracked into trying to jest with the messengers and ingratiate himself with anyone he thought might have power in the city.

A tedious bore, through and through. Much as she wanted to strike him with her staff, Valni forced herself into the role of a cheetah jati servant on an important but not quite urgent task for her master. The role sat awkwardly on her.

She gritted her teeth and pressed on. Her demeanor wouldn't have pleased those princes back in Romnai who'd tried to teach her. A servant didn't snarl at delays or glower at the slow pace of a caravan. She should bear the journey with grace and calm.

Well, failure number one. But all this was for the High Prince Baram, so she resolved to do better with what remained of the trip. And more importantly so when she reached the city. That was where the High Prince needed her most of all. She listened for talk of the Sons of Ryo and Children of Kwona, but if anyone had any secret connection to those groups, they kept their tasks as hidden as she kept hers.

When the caravan stopped early in the afternoon at an inn less than a day's ride from the city, she lost her patience. There was playing the role, but then there was getting the job done, and she didn't want to draw out this wind-wrecked journey any longer than she had to.

While the drivers and other hands rushed into the inn, Valni cornered the caravan master outside, pinning him against one of his wagons with a glare. "Why are we stopping now?"

"I'm as anxious to keep moving as anyone." He pressed himself against the plank sides of the wagon. "But the hands wouldn't hear of it. It's tradition to stop here before we reach that city of stinks. Drink and dance. Take a last few breaths of clean-smelling air." With a hint of a leer, he added, "You shouldn't miss our celebrations. They are legend."

Valni stared him down. If it were a group of soldiers, her own jati, maybe. But she had no wish to drink with this group of traders. "I have a job to do. What's the plan after we leave here, then?"

He squirmed away from her pointing finger and pointed at the road beyond the inn. "The new road comes in just over that rise. I don't know it well enough to say how long. That means we'll get up early, and Fire take the hangovers, because it might take all day to make our way up to the top of the city."

"We're close, then? If we weren't taking the new route?"

His eyes narrowed, calculating. "Why are you asking?" When she said nothing, he added, "I hope you can't mean to go on by yourself. Alone, in this cold? No, you shouldn't attempt that. It's too dangerous."

"I just want to know what the route used to be like, for my report." Not the most elegant of lies. Datri would be disappointed in her.

"If you insist. The route is simple, the road straight. But the stench…" The caravan master scratched his thin beard. "You're from Romnai? You're used to those steam beds, clean steam, a faint smell on some days of sulfur. Pashun is warmed by the steam, too, but it's more mud. Boiling mud close to the city. And that means a stink of a different kind. We were always glad of the wind, when it continued."

"So, you'd follow the road until you smell that?"

"Until? No. You'd smell it as soon as you crest the next rise. That's why we stop here. Have a few drinks while they still taste good. Nothing does once you smell the mud. But you have to keep on, even as it gets worse."

He took a deep drink of his mug, as if to ward off that smell already.

"What else should I know about that road?"

"It's not safe." He said the words slowly, as if she were dense. "That's why we take the new route, remember?"

Failing in her questioning. How did Datri's real spies do it? She did her best to keep any embarrassment from her face. "I still want to have an idea. How long did it used to take? You'd let your teams sleep off your hangovers and still get there before dark?"

"Dark? Before midday. It's just a straight road mostly. No more buildings between here and there. Sometimes a mumbler family might wander through, but little else. It gets boggy near the city, but that's mostly around to the west."

Oh, enough with the playing coy. He would know soon enough that she'd gone this way when he couldn't find her or her horse. "How long will it take me, then?" Might as well be blunt at this point.

"You? I thought you said you just wanted to send a report. It's dangerous, remember?" When she didn't answer, he said, "Well, if you don't push your horse too much, a few hours, certainly by midnight. You'll have the sun for a while this time of year, but—"

"Thank you."

As she made her way toward the door, the caravan master grabbed her elbow. "You shouldn't go alone. Let me send one of my junior traders with you."

Valni made a show of looking around the inn's common room at the traders growing rowdy with their drinks. "No." In case he was tempted to offer to go himself, she quickly added, "You either. I am well trained to go alone and intend to do so."

He opened his mouth to answer, but Valni shrugged his

hand off her elbow and left through the door.

The wind whipped her breath away. The sun dropping toward the southwest cast the road ahead in a bronze haze. She left her horse with the innkeeper, taking a fair payment that she hid within her traveling robes—it meant a longer journey, but caring for an animal within the city would only make her conspicuous. She set off to get as far as she could before the light was gone.

As soon as she'd left the inn behind, the road began down a slope. The caravan master's words proved true—the haze settled around her full of the smells of sulfur, stagnant water, and rot. Valni refused with a soldier's willpower to give even the least reaction. Focusing on the road and the barren land it passed through, she ignored anything else.

A few pine trees dotted the slope, scraggly and standing each alone, separated by wide swaths of leaf-less brush. None of it blocked her view except for brief moments. If she hurried, she might see the lights of Pashun by the time the sunlight was gone.

Where the slope flattened out shortly after, a break in the brush seemed to promise an even better view of the way ahead. The road swerved around the edge of the meadow. There was a different smell to the air, though, and Valni paused before heading across. Stepping onto a rock, she craned her neck to see. She could just make out a hint of water near the far side of the clearing. There was something almost wave-like even in the plant-covered portions of the meadow. The trees around the edges had the look of pines but their branches were bare, except for here and there a cluster of yellowish needles.

Best to stick to the road. There was something uncanny, dangerous about the meadow, and she hated the idea that it was a danger she wouldn't be able to fight.

She left the meadow behind, but the sunlight faded quickly

after that. She lit a small lantern and held it low so it only shone on the road itself. As long as she didn't stare long at the circle of light below the lantern, she could still see into the darkness.

No lights of the city. And the sunlight gone as well. A dim glow up ahead might be the city. Or might be the lava fields, if they were more than just the boiling mud the caravan master had described. The smell was unchanging. Too bad humans couldn't track smells like some animals.

How long in that darkness? She lost track, peering at the road ahead. Surely it was after midnight. The shadows promised rest, as if she could form them into comfortable bedding. She jerked her head upright. How could she call herself a soldier if she couldn't stay awake? What would the High Prince say of her, if he knew? She stiffened her spine, willed her eyes wide, and tried to make her pace one that would wake her up.

But still she slowed, and her eyelids flickered, free from her control.

Where was the city? She'd lost the road in the dark, surely. Was she on some mumbler path away from the city? It looked like more than just an animal track, from what she could see in the slight illumination of her lantern. Though as for that, a wild animal attack wasn't necessarily any less to be feared than a mumbler attack or an ambush by outcasts and outlaws.

Those thoughts at last managed to break through her sleepiness, trading it for a jumpiness that grew toward panic.

At last, she saw a light that wasn't her own lantern. Then a second, one off to either side of the road. The first glimmers of the city, and soon she would come around a bend or past some hidden obstacles and find the full lights of the city all around.

But no new lights appeared, and these flickered more like firelight than lanterns. Not only that, but the road was leading her past the lights. Much longer, and she'd be beyond them, again into a darkness only barely affected by the glow ahead. Valni stopped.

A falcon jati soldier was trained to fight without weapons. She carried a knife, just in case, as well as a staff that was much more deadly than it looked. But better to look innocent first, if she had to approach strangers in the nighttime. She stretched her arms and legs, both to wake herself up and to be ready to defend herself, if necessary. The cold air made her efforts to warm her limbs largely in vain.

She headed off into a darker patch of trees to wait for more light. This was where the caravan master's warnings were relevant, even if she chose to ignore the solution he offered. Better to wait for the day than to stumble into an armed insurrection.

The night passed slowly. Valni leaned against a tree without letting herself doze off. Slow as it felt, at least the sun rose early this time of year. She crouched low to approach for a better view.

It was a soldier camp. That was obvious as soon as she could see well enough. The straight lines of tents, the orderly arrangement of fire gear, the sentry. Two soldiers sat beside the fire as lookouts. All others were, presumably, asleep. If she felt herself in danger, she could take down the two awake soldiers without drawing a weapon, likely even without waking anyone else.

She longed to warm her hands by that fire.

The tents were pitched on top of cut cattails, which likely meant the frozen ground would quickly turn to mud with any heat. There were trees around the camp, though none especially large. Wetland trees? She couldn't tell in the dim light. The other firelight she'd seen opposite her path wasn't visible, but the land seemed to rise in that direction.

What could its purpose here be? It was a camp, an outpost,

and soldiers wouldn't be permanently stationed there. They were real soldiers, not some ragtag group of revolutionaries. Maybe they were getting ready to retake the city from the miners. Maybe they were planning to go into the mines themselves and teach the rebels a lesson.

Sending soldiers into the mines? The very idea was beneath her image of a soldier's job. That didn't really make sense with this location, though. The mines were all on the far side of the city, where the mountains rose up to impassable heights.

What it looked like, more than anything, was an outpost to intercept travelers on the trade route, which meant they weren't on the side of the princes at all. A jati of soldiers conscripted by revolutionaries. The thought sickened her.

It wasn't a short-term camp. The fire pit had a permanent look to it, built up with logs to hold the dirt in place and lift the fire out of the mud. The space around it was well trodden in a wide space.

Wide enough for dancing, even. The soldier jatis had a number of traditional dances, some unique to each jati but others that were shared among all soldiers. Valni traced the steps that she would have taken, tasted the fire liquor she and her jati would have sipped as they danced. There was even an empty earthenware jar lying on its side near the fire bed.

She felt a pang of longing for her own jati. Revelries with the traders hadn't tempted her in the least, but here… To spin, drink fire, join with a group of people like herself.

It was the sight of scavenged pieces of train cars that shook her from the image. A piece of metal beside the fire had surely once been the side of a freight car that roared along the tracks. A wheel had been repurposed into an anchor that held the guyline of the biggest tent of the camp.

She had to press on before she let herself be seen, but how to slip past? She might return to the road behind her, though as the sun lit up the woods, it looked open, vulnerable. Studying the land ahead through the haze of early dawn, she could see a portion of the city ahead. The road led over a hill where she would surely be seen and then out of sight. But at the base of the hill, there was a narrow trail.

What *might* be a narrow trail.

Valni made to circle the camp. After only a short way, a horse within the camp whinnied at her. Or maybe at nothing, but could she risk it? She peered close. No one stood guard on this side of the camp, at least no one she could see.

She crept around silently to the hint of a trail she'd seen on the far side.

The path wended among the trees, so that she quickly lost sight of the soldier camp. The smell grew stronger as the trees thinned, sulfur and soil and harsher chemical smells she couldn't identify. As if the steam beds had tried to mimic the various smells of human industry.

The trees opened. A gurgling sound, even louder than the wind, told her she'd reached the mud pots. She pulled a portion of her shirt up over her mouth. The ground glowed before her, a huge expanse of volcanic activity. And up to her left, the lights of the city rose, adding their own illumination to the dawn's light.

That path was narrow. The people of the city likely hesitated to use it, even by full daylight. Valni was a soldier, though, with the full grace of the falcon jati's training.

The mud bubbled and hissed as a light snow fell. Valni made sure each footstep was secure despite the snow, threading her way past the boiling mud. The flat rocks, carefully placed between the pools of mud, all seemed solid, with enough debris over top to give some traction. Where the trail swung near one of the mud pots, an expanse of mud covered the paving stone. Clearly the mud sometimes rose up over the rocks. Valni paused and studied the path. No reason to assume it would happen as she passed by. But no reason to assume it wouldn't. The area sometimes covered by mud extended some ways ahead and could well be more slippery.

It might be a regular, predictable eruption, like some of the geysers back near Romnai. She waited, her body tense. The steam field hissed and sputtered and mocked her for waiting, mocked her fear. She let the feeling pass her by. A soldier was above mockery or she wasn't worthy of the title.

The sounds of the city began to trickle down into the steam fields, morning sounds of carts creaking through the streets and markets beginning to open, though the sun would be some hours yet in rising. Perhaps she should forget her worry and press ahead. Certainly, she should have done so at the first. Plenty of time had passed for even a cautious passage.

But she continued to wait. The patience of a falcon, the patience granted by the gods. The noise of the mud changed, a spitting, growling kind of sound deep within whatever underground chamber lay below the mud. The world's fire pushing to the surface. With a pop that seemed much too quiet for its violence, a gob of hot mud shot into the air and spattered down onto the trail. Valni pulled back from the noise.

After her breath eased, she made the way onto the mud-spattered path, confident she had plenty of time before a second explosion. Her feet slipped briefly. After a few steps she figured out how to ease her foot into each step, deliberately squishing the new mud out of the way.

About halfway across the muddy section, the mud pot began to spit and splutter again. Damn. She had been sure the wait would have given them plenty of time, that it wouldn't explode again so soon. She sped up as much as she dared.

She was still in range when the mud pot erupted again.

A dancer might have stayed upright. An average person

wouldn't have stood a chance, would have flown into the middle of the mud pot opposite the eruption in surprise.

Valni lost her balance but kept her wits. As she was falling, she threw herself down to the edge of the path. Her elbow brushed the scalding mud, and she twisted away in pain. Gritting her teeth, she jumped back to her feet. Her leg twisted when she landed. But she was past the danger of the sputtering mud.

By the time she could clearly make out something resembling a sidewalk—the transition from steam beds to city was much less clear here than in Romnai—Valni was limping. She sat down out of sight to get her bearings.

From what she could see, Pashun by morning looked much as Romnai did. People going about their tasks. Wallas delivering goods. No cheetah jati servants—that set the place apart. Those with such high-ranking servants would be cut off up above. And there were soldiers, always visible.

Soldiers. She studied them more carefully.

They looked like real soldiers. Well disciplined, coordinating their actions. They should have noticed her tripping along the volcanic path, but that simply meant they didn't expect any threat from that way.

The barricades further along the walk showed where the threat was, to the south. The priests were that direction. What else was on the map she'd tried to memorize? Mostly just the massive seminary building, squatting over the corner of the steambeds. Peering up, she could make out barricades that way as well. That was the focus of the soldiers' attention, the streets directly above.

Those guarding the barricades did not have the look of well-trained soldiers. Miners who revolted? Or maybe some other group who'd taken advantage of the chaos to carve out their own space.

She'd have to do her best at figuring out those dynamics

and let that play into the story she would give when she made herself known.

And she needed a better story than she'd given the caravan master, one to make Datri proud.

She watched for much of the morning, paying special attention to the soldiers' movements through this narrow strip of the city that they controlled. Several hundred people likely lived here, in the space marked off by the barricades. Maybe as many as a thousand. A small part of such a large city, but big enough for her to learn some things, to find out the bigger story of the rest of the city, and to begin to fulfill her task.

Valni stood up, in full view of anyone looking, spread her arms wide as if embracing the neighborhood as her rescuer, and began to make her way out of the steambeds and up.

Upwards into the strange new city of Pashun, divided.

CHAPTER 9

On his hurried journey away from Pashun, Pavresh tried to scrub the way he'd used the magic from his mind. Arcist magic was a celebration of the patterns and stories of people everywhere, not some tool for controlling others. What he'd done was treachery, a betrayal of the magic's purpose. Treachery was something he knew well from stories. And from his own life as well. That familiarity didn't make it any easier when he turned around and committed it again, nor any less shocking.

The land below the foothills was an inhospitable place of jagged rock formations that hid shadowed pockets of snow that never melted. It was a good place to calm his thoughts and recover from the attempt on his life. The southern faces of the rocks were usually clear, so he made his way from one open stretch to another.

A bobcat paced beside him at dusk one afternoon but dashed off after some other prey when Pavresh didn't show any hint of fear. Even so, Pavresh didn't like the vulnerability of that land. There were animals far more deadly than bobcats that lived in the area, beasts that wouldn't be deterred by Pavresh's refusal to run. He wrapped himself in arcist magic, gave himself an aspect of belonging. But as far as he'd ever been able to observe, arcist magic had no real effect on animals. And why would it, if the magic drew on childhood stories?

There was a reason the valley's few trade roads and other paths avoided that land.

The howls of a pack of some kind of wolf sounded, impossible to track its direction among the rock formations. Each night he stopped sooner than he'd have preferred, forced to find shelter by the early sunset, though at least the days lengthened as his journey continued. He wrapped himself in his mumbler furs—deer and wisent stitched in alternating layers—and took what shelter he could find. A shallow cave, a jumble of fallen rocks, a scooped-out section of ice and snow if nothing else afforded itself.

One morning he awoke, his back sore from the rough rock, to find a comfortable mumbler shelter just a few steps away from where he'd slept. No sign of any mumblers—they must come this way rarely. He would have enjoyed much better rest inside its walls, but too late to dwell on now.

The land sloped down toward the trade road to the west, an incline littered with rocks and uneven gaps. Pavresh kept his distance, heading north among rock formations.

The snow grew deeper, but it was a hard snow, almost ice. His shoes, mumbler shoes, kept him comfortably on top. The north faces of the rocks were solid ice, but so pitted and uneven that he was in no danger of slipping. In the darkest part of the shadows of one towering rock formation, he could see nothing, not even his feet as he stepped. He could see the way again not too far ahead, so he kept on rather than swinging wider where the way would be lighted.

The sound of his footsteps changed.

Pavresh paused, peered closely at the ground. Nothing to see, but he turned and made his way closer to the rocks. The noise of his steps led him on, guided him back to the hidden path when he strayed.

At a gap in the rocks, Pavresh stopped. Something about the way the hidden path led into the rocks caught his attention, something about the layout of the rocks themselves, as if they'd been placed rather than merely fallen. The pattern suddenly made sense to him, the hint of a mumbler village in the way the path led into the shadows.

Could there be people within? And if so, would they

welcome him or try to kill him? His body shook with the memory, with a sudden indecision. Last time he'd stumbled across strangers and made himself known it hadn't ended well.

Mumblers had never attacked him in that way, though, he had to remind himself. Meeting strangers had been his life for the past five years and more. Arcist magic was a powerful protection, but so too was the way a guest was treated throughout the mumbler villagers and even among most of Pavresh's people. Welcoming a guest was a sacred duty, a command of Tiespetre as well as a key thread of most mumbler villages. That one group of miners had ignored that duty shouldn't stop him from learning who might be within this cave. Story after story from all over the valley and mountains combined with experience to reassure Pavresh.

He pulled the trader's bundle of willow branches from his pack, though there was no way anyone within would be able to see it. His hand only shook slightly. With his magic he made himself nonthreatening. A weary traveler, a simple trader. Then he called out in the trade language, "I bring fresh goods."

There was a scramble within the rocks. Then silence. After an awkward wait, a wavering candle flame appeared and made its way toward Pavresh.

"You speak," a man's voice said from behind the candle. Or perhaps, "You trade."

"I do speak/trade. I do not actually have fresh goods today, but I found your path. It would be rude to pass by."

"Not rude. But you are here. Share our fire." A movement beyond the candle seemed to be the man's hand gesturing for him to follow.

Pavresh had little choice, as the man's body blocked most of the candlelight and began to move away from him. The rocks closed around them and soon formed a broken roof.

A short way after the roof blocked out the clouded sky, the passageway turned sharply. There the walls opened wide without losing the coverage overhead and a cooking fire lit the cave.

It wasn't a large space, big enough for the single family that used it at the moment, but not much more. That space had a history, though. Firelight flickered over drawings and paintings that must have been added to over many years, generations. How long had the mumblers been coming here to spend the night in their travels?

And a short stop for traveling it was, no doubt. The land around was no place for even the most hardscrabble of mumbler families.

"We have a guest," the man said, speaking the trading language for Pavresh's sake.

An old woman by the fire—the man's mother perhaps, or his wife's mother—muttered something in what he guessed was their own native language. But then in a voice clearly intended for him, louder and painstakingly pronounced, she spoke in the trade pidgin. "And already you let him see us. How are there valley people learning to speak/trade? Better when no one—"

"Hush, mama," the younger woman said. Then she continued on in their own language that Pavresh didn't know. As she spoke, she handed Pavresh an earthen bowl with something warm inside. A savory smell rose from the food.

All three of the mumblers had dark hair, his with a hint of red in his beard, and skin the color of a fawn's soft hide, though darkened with dirt.

"Are there others?" Pavresh asked no one in particular. Then to the man, he repeated, "There are others of my people who have learned to speak/trade? Who are they? I would like to meet them."

The man shrugged and gestured for Pavresh to sit beside

the cooking fire. "Not *them*. One man, but we didn't meet him. Heard his rumor around Pashun. Visiting the villages south beyond there."

Probably echoes of his own travels, then, coming back after the years.

"Well, I thank you for your welcome," Pavresh said formally, taking a bite of the food. The heat was all that mattered, after so long eating mostly cold food. It was something thick, a meat porridge of some variety. "I would help you in return, if I can."

The man ate a bite of his food and nodded. "Perhaps you can. Tell me what you've seen."

It was the familiar trading Pavresh was used to from traveling to mumbler villages. He fell into the patter, paying attention to what bits of information drew the man's interest. He tensed whenever Pavresh spoke of the villages to the south, beyond Pashun. Had he fled them, for some reason? Been driven out? Even the mumblers had their outcasts at times. Perhaps he had stolen some goods or insulted his wife's father. Or was the mother's comment about seeing their faces some indication? He could see one traditional mask leaning against the packs at the edge of the cave. He tried to let the arcist possibilities roll around and fit themselves to the travelers' situation.

If they came from the south and were stopping here, then likely they were heading for the city of outcasts in abandoned Eghsal, just as he was. Or at least near there. He steered the conversation toward the city.

With a glimmer of magic, he made himself seem mysterious, wise, knowing—but he held back from making the magic controlling. Then as that arcist feeling settled onto the conversation, he asked, "And what do you hope to find in Eghsal City among the outcasts?"

The man's eyes narrowed. "How did you know..."

His wife laughed, and Pavresh heard something unexpected in that laugh. Among some mumblers, it was common for the men to be in charge—of the house, anyway; as they grew to the age of wisdom, the women elders often took leading roles in the village. But a young wife was often expected to stay silent, to serve food and care for the children. Perhaps it had not been so in their own village. Or perhaps it was why they had left. Either way, that laughter was not the demure sound of a woman relegated to the side.

Squatting beside the fire, she scooped up a bite from her own bowl. Once she'd finished chewing, she said in the trading pidgin, "He's been studying you, just like you've been studying him. He's probably learned a lot that you didn't mean to tell him."

Pavresh sketched her a bow. With his magic, he made himself a wise man, but an entertainer as well, nothing too mysterious. "Indeed. I guess you are…" What was the word to use in the trade pidgin? *Leery* wasn't a word he knew. "You are worried you will not like the city. You will not fit in. So you plan to see how it is, but then continue on to the north or some out of the way place near the city's steam beds. Probably. How is that?" The fact he guessed they were fleeing some event in the villages to the south wasn't something he was going to admit to.

The man frowned, but his wife again laughed. "You see? You are easy to read, Ellechandran. But he has misunderstood one thing." To Pavresh, she added, "If it were to his choice alone, we would continue on no matter what we see. Or at least that's what he'll claim he wants to do. Maybe try to stay here and not bother extending our journey. But no, we enjoy traveling, but he especially would grow weary of being alone, even if he doesn't admit it. I think we will try to find a way to live in the city."

Pavresh conceded with a gesture. "Well, then I can pay

you back in that way. I am going there myself, to meet some friends who are influential among the outcasts. Travel with me tomorrow, and I will introduce you to them."

The woman swung an arm from her husband toward the pot of soup. "Well, then, let's feed him some more. A favor like that is worth much more than one bowl."

They spoke well into the evening. The wife's name was Chhayasheela, and she sometimes shortened her husband's name to Chandrie, sometimes to Ell. The older woman was never given a name, was only referred to by a word Pavresh recognized as a variation of "mother" in what was likely their own language. She fell asleep long before the younger members had stopped talking together. Pavresh felt safe in sharing his real name.

The time spent over the food healed the terror he'd felt at the attempt on his life, terror he hadn't realized he was still carrying. He even let go of the more innocent magic he'd used to make himself seem safe and wise—and felt a sense of relief at releasing that as well. Even something that should be a natural part of arcist magic still left him feeling slightly unwell.

The space was a comfortable one, the walls cozy and well warmed by the fire in the center. It wasn't quite a cave, or at least Pavresh wouldn't have described it as one once he'd studied it. The roof of rock stopped short of meeting one wall, and no doubt much heat escaped that way. But they still managed to stay warm inside. The family had stretched a hide over a portion of that opening to trap some heat within.

The almost-cave easily could have housed them for many days, even as a permanent home, if not for the inhospitality of the land around. They had no extra water, after what they'd used to make their porridge. Nothing to wash with, nothing to drink without scraping up ice-like snow and melting it. Pavresh shared what was left of his own water bottle.

In the morning they packed up and left early. They were well along the Pashun trade road by the time the sun rose, late in the morning. They didn't stop until well after the sun had set, far along the road. Pavresh saw some of his own people in the distance along the road a few times and tensed, wondering how they would avoid unwelcome attention. Were they people like the ones he'd met outside Pashun? Were they soldiers? He didn't relish meeting either one. But the people ignored the four of them, even seemed to go out of their way to avoid meeting up with them over the next days. It took three days of hard travel, eventually crossing the trade road and heading toward the west, before they finally saw the ruins of Eghsal spread before them

A surprising amount of the city glowed with smoldering fire—or lava—beneath its uneven blanket of snow. Figures were visible, milling about the widespread clutter of rough tents that squatted between them and the ruins.

***

Pavresh brought the mumbler family to a grouping of tents along the eastern edge of the ruins, close to the river. They had to avoid a patrol of wolf jati soldiers, but the soldiers seemed more intent on the people within the ruins than anything happening beyond them.

One of the self-proclaimed leaders of the city met them once the soldiers were past, a mumbler man, middle aged with graying hair and beard. Pavresh had been introduced to him before he first headed out among the mumbler camps, but he had forgotten the man's name. The man had been too busy at the time to teach Pavresh their trade speech.

Now he invited them to squat around a fire set within a circle of makeshift tents. Pavresh's time among the mumbler tribes told him immediately that these tents wouldn't be warm enough to keep their sleepers comfortable. They shared a small meal of hard lava bread and cooked river weeds.

After they'd each eaten a few bites, he spoke in the trade pidgin. "I am Azheeran. If you are looking to move to the city here, you should know that you are likely too late. The fields are active. Buildings that were safe aren't so any longer. People are frightened, looking to leave."

Before Pavresh could say anything, Chhayasheela asked. "Is it even safe out here, then?"

"Nowhere is safe," he answered right away, as if it was a line he spoke often. "Not the river, nor the mountains. Not here."

Pavresh pulled back his hood so his Eghsal Valley features were clear and said, "Is Jaritta nearby? I would like to speak with her."

Azheeran frowned and ignored Pavresh, speaking instead to the others in a mumbler language Pavresh did not know.

Ellechandran shook his head and answered in the trade pidgin Pavresh knew. "Speak/trade. We understand that, as does our guide. Your words are—" He used some word Pavresh didn't know, but he could guess it meant something like "dialect."

There was a story in how Azheeran shrugged, turned toward Pavresh with an expression that seemed to mock him, and said in the perfectly clear accents of Pavresh's people, "And it makes you so mighty, does it not?" As if he'd come straight from the streets of Romnai. How many languages and dialects did the man speak?

He resumed speaking in the trade pidgin, directing his words to the other mumblers, but Pavresh tuned it out as he tried to identify the arcist theme to explain Azheeran's reaction. His...was it fair to call it antagonism?

There was pride in his bearing as well as offense. Pavresh had offended him, that much was clear, yet it was an old, familiar offense, more of a general reaction than a personal offense caused directly by Pavresh himself. Triggered by Pavresh's actions, certainly, but still a reminder of an older wound. How? Pavresh thought back through his own actions. Nothing stood out, no actions that he had learned to avoid when visiting the mumbler villages.

The draped furs and skins offered no clues.

Except, that ramshackle circle of tents was certainly no mumbler village. There he would be a guest, but here…was that the difference? He'd asserted himself, emphasized his non-mumbler appearance, tried to take over. No wonder Azheeran took offense.

With his magic, Pavresh made himself pull back—the old man in the corner, the hermit who seeks no fame. Physically, too, he relaxed downward then leaned forward again to listen.

"We have been searching for places," Azheeran said, and Pavresh tried to think back to make sense of the statement. He'd been talking about the dangers of the city. Searching for places that are especially dangerous, to avoid them? Or parts of the city that were safer? He couldn't follow the thread once dropped. "Do you know of any?"

Ellechandran and Chhayasheela caught each other's eyes. "The southern foothills…" Chhayasheela grimaced as she said it, and Ellechandran shook his head.

"Not there," he said after a moment. "Too many miners wandering about. More than enough people there already."

Their mother hummed tunelessly, eating her food and saying nothing, though Pavresh thought her alertness had become more focused at their words.

Clearly, they'd fled from there, as he'd already suspected. And now he began to see the shape of the conversation he must have missed. Worries about the volcanic beds here, wondering about the safety of living in other places. Were there any places he could think of that might be more stable than this? Places not already claimed by mumbler tribes or his own people?

Before he'd thought of any, Azheeran said to him, "You say you know Jaritta?"

Pavresh nodded. "An old friend from Romnai."

"She's recovering."

Pavresh shot to his feet. "She's injured? Let me help her."

Azheeran waved him away. "Injured a while ago by a fallen house. But this, I don't mean an injury. We have been up and down the river, looking for a site. She is resting from travels."

Shifting his magic to that of the rugged traveler, Pavresh asked, "What are you hoping to find, then? Have you looked at places far away from the river?"

When Azheeran didn't answer right away, Pavresh pressed on. "I am a trader. I have visited most of the valley and even into the mountains in every direction. I know the villages, the peoples who we call mumblers but are no more your own people than mine." He forced himself to keep the sense of humility he'd drawn about himself earlier so that pride didn't overwhelm his words. "I can help you find a suitable place."

Azheeran looked at Pavresh' pack, as if to see the proof of his words in the things he carried. Then he stood to leave. "When Jaritta is awake, we can discuss this more. You may tell us what you know."

Without another word, he left.

***

"So, you are back."

Pavresh pushed himself from his bedroll outside the tents where he had been taking a brief rest in the sunshine. "Jaritta." Pavresh's mumbler companions sat together with Azheeran beside the fire. They didn't look his way.

Pavresh dipped his head to Jaritta. It was not the first time they'd met since their time in Romnai, and they'd even had times of friendship since then, or if not exactly friendship at least something approaching it. But each time they met there was always their history between them. Her coup. His betrayal. Her escape, because of his help.

He might have been able to play his magic just right to make the awkwardness go away, but he resisted that impulse. Instead, he took her hand in his, and the cold distance they each maintained dissipated. The power of human touch. For someone who'd been declared untouchable, it was the one thing that could always break through, a reminder of how terrible the priests' punishment was and how it was—at last, blessedly— in the past. At least out here. She squeezed his hand in return, ever so briefly, as he said, "It is good to see you again."

Jaritta shrugged and pulled away, pulling her dress over the scars on her face by old habit. "Just in time to be cooked by the ground."

She walked away from the tents, and he fell in step with her. The sun had not set yet but she held a lantern against the ash-filled sky. The ground to the north glowed enough she might not have even needed that.

"Is it so dangerous? I heard you were thinking of leaving."

Jaritta led him up a rise before answering. A mist hung low to the ground here, a fog made of the volcanic steam. It stunk of sulfur, much more than the last time Pavresh had come this way, or at least much more than in his recollections. Jaritta gave no sign she noticed it as out of the ordinary.

"We have to." She swept her hand around the ruins of the city, black shapes above the glow of lava. "Already people are slipping away, but that's always happened, back and forth. Too many of us don't have another place to go, though."

"You could lose yourself in Romnai. No one would ever know."

Jaritta snorted. "You know, I get the feeling that's what the soldiers out there really want. Harass us enough so we leave and then herd us over there. But not if I can help it. You think the Thirty have forgotten my coup? Not a chance. I show up, Prince Baram knows within a twelve-day, and they don't risk me escaping again."

"If they're that worried, don't you think they'd hunt you down out here?"

"Who's to say they haven't?" Jaritta resumed walking, and Pavresh hurried to keep up with her long strides. He might be a great traveler, but she moved as if to cover as much distance as he had, only back and forth among the ruins.

"There may be no geysers in Romnai itself," Jaritta said after a moment, "but sounds like it's not much safer for people like us. You remember Thamiba?"

She'd spoken of him, even back at Chaitan's house years ago. Another untouchable who'd shown her the ways of the streets when she was first cast out, before coming out here to the Eghsal City ruins long before Jaritta's coup. He nodded and gestured for her to continue.

"He just returned from Romnai. We were having troubles with soldiers harassing us out here, even tearing down buildings, so I sent him to Romnai to see if he could find out what's happening." Her voice stumbled over the words for a moment, as if saying the name of her home city still stung.

"I saw some soldiers, when I was coming—"

"His report is pretty bleak," she rushed on, refusing to acknowledge any emotion she might feel. "Soldiers everywhere, people afraid. But that's not so different from...from before."

Before her coup, the fear had definitely reached a fever throughout the city. Pavresh remembered the feeling that any mis-timed action might push the whole city over the edge. An arcist image for sure.

"Chaitan's dead."

Pavresh went still. It wasn't unexpected, exactly. Chaitan

had been sick for so long. Pavresh had mourned his mentor when he fled Romnai five years ago, had known he would likely never see the old man again. It still opened an emptiness inside him. To mention his death while talking about the unrest in the city...

"The soldiers?"

Jaritta shook her head. "Nothing like that. Sickness and age. But still...dead."

Pavresh tipped his head back and closed his eyes. The inventor, or rather discoverer, of arcist magic, gone. Death had its place in the magic. He could trace how it formed a part of the stories he knew, how it formed a part of his own mind. The pain wasn't what he would have guessed, not as intense or immediate, but it was pain nonetheless.

The community they'd created in Chaitan's house had died five years earlier. Namrani's music. The dancing of Ekana and Indima and others. The arcist magic as performance. He mourned those again, as he'd mourned them for five years of wandering. Chaitan himself had been in such pain as long as Pavresh knew him. Stronger than the ache of knowing he'd died, Pavresh felt the resolve to carry on his mentor's work. To understand the magic. To use it to create a better valley.

After giving him a moment to accept that news, Jaritta continued. "And it might have nothing to do with everything else, but it feels like just one more sign that it's not Romnai anymore, not the place we knew." She released a deep breath. "There's something more. Factions are fighting each other. The soldiers—"

"The Son of Ryo." He hadn't meant to interrupt, but the words spilled out.

"Sons," she corrected. "You've heard of them, too? Who are they, what do you know?" Her words were urgent.

Nothing and less. He ran his hand through his hair. "A

story out in the mumbler villages, but I didn't know what it meant. You mean you don't know either?"

Jaritta frowned in disappointment and started walking back down the slope. "Only a name. It was painted on the rubble the soldiers left. We think they must be some faction of soldiers. A new jati, a new mystery religion, I don't know.'

She paused to avoid a block of stone that had once been part of a wall. Even out this far there were some ruins. For the first time in their walk, Pavresh noted a slight limp as she changed directions to go around it.

Jaritta didn't acknowledge any pain, so Pavresh said nothing. "But Thamiba said something strange is happening with the soldier jatis in Romnai. The soldiers aren't working *together* to make the city afraid. Not like it's some coordinated plan controlled by any one prince or priest. It seemed to him that they were competing instead. As if someone came in, divided the jati into smaller teams, and then promised power to whichever group terrorized the city the most. There's no hiding there for long. We'd just all go back to being beggars. And victims for the soldiers whenever they grew bored."

So that was where the Sons of Ryo fit in. One faction competing for…something. Maybe. He still couldn't figure out the big picture of who or why.

They were heading back toward where they'd started by this time. Azheeran and the two younger mumbler travelers walked to meet them.

"Besides, I know the princes," Jaritta continued. "Out here I'm forgotten as long as I'm no part of anyone's power plays. And maybe you're even right and I *could* disappear back into the streets of Romnai. But that's just me, one person. What about the rest? They can't all flood into the other cities without anyone panicking and…" She shrugged. "Who knows what they'll do."

The leader in exile. That was the theme he felt as Jaritta

spoke. And the conflicted ruler. He set aside the thoughts of Chaitan's death and mysterious factions of soldiers so he could focus on what she was saying. She was still longing to be the High Prince, only now it was to this hodge-podge of peoples out here in the wild. She wanted to be their benevolent ruler.

Another blast of sulfur swept over them. He'd smelled air as bad before, in an empty wasteland that he suddenly imagined filling with Jaritta's unruly followers. It was near the villages Chhayasheela and Ellechandran wanted to avoid, but separated from them by an upthrust of higher rock.

"I know where you should go, then."

She cocked her head and stopped walking just as the mumblers came up to meet them.

"Pashun. Or rather, not the city itself. I don't think it's much better than Romnai right now." He shied away from the memory of the people he'd compelled with his magic. Their words had hinted at the dangerous times in their own city. "But opposite Pashun. Near the steambeds, so you'll have heat. It's an empty swampland. You might have to drain it, but the soil must be worth growing something to replace the fish you won't be catching." Unless the soil was poisoned by volcanic chemicals. Worth exploring, anyway. "Or maybe even set your city up the mountain slope a little ways, if you can manage it."

"Why is no one else living there?"

Pavresh shrugged. "The swamp, I suppose. And the smell, but that's no worse than here."

He cocked an eyebrow at Azheeran to see if he had any answer, but the mumbler shook his head.

She studied Pavresh, and there was a wariness to her eyes, as if she thought he might betray her again.

"It is a good place," he insisted, "and no one living there. Not our people and not the…the mumblers."

Jaritta pursed her lips and gave a single, curt nod. "Thank

you. It sounds worth looking into. But only if you agree to go with me to see the lay of the land." So he didn't betray her while she was heading there. She didn't say the words, but she didn't have to. He'd revealed her plans to the princes once, and she wouldn't want him to have the chance to do so again.

Hearing about the conditions in Romnai made him want to go that way. To speak with Rashul, their charismatic inspiration back then? To visit the house where Chaitan had lived? No, but to somehow connect who he'd become with what had happened in Romnai last time. Maybe he could understand what had gone wrong when he'd used his magic to compel his attackers. Maybe he could find a way to make it feel whole and wholesome again.

There was something right about agreeing to Jaritta's demand as well, though. What was the arcist image here—the wanderer returning home or the knowledgeable guide setting out to share his knowledge? It was whichever one he chose it to be. Finding healing could be a part of that journey, no matter what the destination was.

Pavresh nodded. "I can do that, at least for the start of the journey. As long as I hear all the stories you have to tell, you and whoever else accompanies us, as we go." Ellechandran and Chhayasheela, would they be willing to return south so soon after fleeing...whatever terror or shame had driven them out? Theirs was a story he wanted to hear.

And they would know more of that land in the south as well. About mumbler ways of healing that were also true in their own ways. He would ask them, but not with Azheeran present.

To Azheeran he added, "And perhaps we can find some of your own people with the knowledge to get us the rest of the way. And a willingness to join with you in a new city."

CHAPTER 10

The tisane cooled as the princes talked. Prince Jasfer gestured for a servant to rewarm his, only to realize what he'd forgotten—the servants had gone home. Only the Thirty could be present for tonight's discussion.

Prince Baram finally summarized the long report he'd personally given them. "So, while there is much we don't know yet, and my agents work to uncover what they can, we know this. Pashun has fallen into the hands of rebels. Trade is disrupted. The rebels have even attacked trains quite near here, though for the moment we have pushed them back away from the river. Our relatives of the princely jati have secured the edges of their own neighborhood, but they need our assistance. The question is, how shall we proceed?"

Several voices shouted to be heard. No one that would matter. Jasfer read body language to find the lines of influence and see if he could guess how the discussion would go. The big players of the past were gone, some dead or retired and others cast out in the aftermath of Jaritta's coup. Those absences threw the lines of influence into confusion, a mess that hadn't yet settled after five years. When the influence didn't revolve around the High Prince or around Jasfer, then it could range and wander without fixing on any prince for long. But at the start, no one of consequence would speak up.

Jeevendra talked about the long-standing history of the connections between Romnai and Pashun. He was a scholarly prince, middle-aged but removed from the big events of the city as long as Jasfer had been among the Thirty. He knew the history of the last time the two cities had fought against each other for control of the valley. Fascinating to be sure, but it had little bearing on the day's issues.

Only one thing stood out for Jasfer. At one point in his speech, another prince, Bunaran, stood up to get himself some tisane or other refreshment. Far from the only prince to do so but when he did, a surprising number of princes watched him, as if he drew their influence with him.

Bunaran was a little older than Jasfer and had never struck him as being especially powerful or even influential, within the Thirty or outside. So why did so many look his way?

He would have to have Datri look into Bunaran's history and relatives for anything noteworthy.

Other princes came and went, each sharing variations of the same thing. Send the wolf jati soldiers. Gather an army of other jatis.

No, others argued, an outright assault wasn't the best idea, without a clearer idea of how things stood within the city. They needed a more subtle approach, something to reveal where the miners got their support. There was no way they had achieved this much without some sort of hidden leadership coordinating it all. Plots like this often collapsed once their details came to light. Maybe they could make it impossible for the rebel leaders to hide. Was there a festival coming up to hide an attempt to infiltrate the rebels? Nothing worthy for their purposes. Perhaps they might dedicate a building of some kind. Or establish a new rail line to go direct from Romnai to Pashun.

Jasfer liked that last, for his own purposes. How much better to get his goods directly from the mines rather than having to switch from wagon to train halfway. But the steambeds made such a route a challenge. The land in between was not well suited to roads of any kind, much less railroad tracks. There was a reason the ore traveled the way it did, but it was an idea he'd like to see pursued. Even so, the connection to putting down the insurrection seemed like a stretch.

Finally, the High Prince spoke up. "We are ranging too far, twisting ourselves into nagas. Untie the monster, as the saying goes. Keep it simple. It isn't as if we need to hide our purpose, only learn what we can and decide what actions would best serve it."

Nriteesh stood slowly, leaning on a cane, not because of age but because of some recent injury. While riding a horse? Jasfer couldn't recall exactly. He was a muscular man and wore his silks in a new pattern, looped in such a way that made his shoulders look even broader than they were. "Let us take this time to celebrate our longstanding connections with Pashun." His voice had the lilt of the Jarnur accent, the sing-song of fishermen and dock workers. Maybe Jarnur was the origin of the new way he wore his robe. "As you can guess, I have no relatives there at all. But High Prince, your wife's people are from there, are they not? Could you not coordinate matters through your relatives, find what's happening, craft us a plan for helping rescue them?"

Baram demurred with a wave of his hand. "Not I. Not openly, anyway. I am gathering what information I can through my connections there, but we need a visible liaison as well. The last thing we wish is to draw the rebels' attention to me personally. I would be too clear a target."

"Who else has connections to the city?" Nriteesh scanned the room and settled on Jasfer. "Prince Jasfer, of course. You would be perfect for this."

"I?" Jasfer shook his head. "I have no relatives there that I know of. None who are close, anyway."

"You have the mines, though. Going back to your father and even further, if I remember right. Who else would be better to deal directly with the rebellious miners?" Nriteesh's words sped up, as if he was thinking this through as he spoke. "Isn't it your responsibility, at some level?"

Jasfer's breath caught. Was that a challenge? Nriteesh's

pose was nothing but respectful. The implication was to blame him, and yet…

Yatim wasn't present, and neither was Mahendri. Either one would have been worth consulting with for one reason or another. But it was Datri he really wished he could ask for advice. "I would have some pull there." Good to hold onto his image as someone with influence. "It may take time to arrange. My contacts are uniquely caught up in the difficulties, and likely have little direct contact with the princes in Pashun. But I will begin to make the arrangements." He'd never imagined himself acting in such a role, but if he could use it to increase his power among the princes…

Datri would be the one to figure out how to best deal with it.

"I will consult some of my people and let the High Prince know my plans as soon as they are set."

***

Sulfur snow fell as Jasfer and Datri made their way to Romnai's grand temple near the river, but they chose to walk regardless, protected by a handheld umbrella-canopy. It was tradition to arrive by foot for the Festival of the Weary Fire, to wear old clothes, and the very real splashing of coal-fouled snow-melt would add to the image. More importantly, though, the snow muffled their voices, isolated them so they could talk. Even Yatim and their other servants, who walked close enough to protect them, would overhear nothing.

"I hate this nonsense," Jasfer said as they passed the manor of another prince. "Schemes and subterfuge." He shifted his grip on the umbrella so he could better protect them both from the snow. "Not the change itself. I mean, I want to see changes, too, things working better, people treated better. But why not work in the open, try to find allies to make our home a better place that way?"

"Oh my sweet prince." Datri took a draw of clove-scented smoke from her clay pipe and laughed as she released the smoke. "This is exactly what we were born for. The schemes give us life. Without that, why, we're little better than merchants."

Merchants who scheme in their own way, Jasfer thought. And what's wrong with being no better than them, anyway? Aloud he said, "Well, I'll leave that part of life to you, then, dear. Have you found anything about Nriteesh?"

"From Jarnur, but you knew that. All his family lives there, servants from there. No great scandals here, and no clear connection to any one group within the princes."

"And Bunaran? He once gave me an old hunting saber as a present. Maybe when I succeeded my father. I can't say I thought much of the gift."

"He gives lots of gifts, though. I couldn't pick up any pattern, except it's to other princes. The Thirty and beyond, including a fair number of princes in Pashun, back before these current challenges. It makes him a well-liked prince."

A lot of nothing. They passed a small group of beggars—few were out in this weather, but even in the snow the untouchables needed to do something for food. Jaritta would have had some years when she had no other choice. Why must his thoughts turn to her? He forced them back to the upcoming celebrations.

"Any other new discoveries?"

They spoke of the other princes, little things Datri had teased from her own sources and uncovered beneath the innocent gossip of her acquaintances and friends. She seemed to be avoiding some part of her information, though.

At last, Jasfer said, "Go ahead, say what else you've learned. I can see there's something."

Instead of her familiar, playful laugh, she surprised him with a darting look around them, a look that spoke of worry, perhaps even a touch of fear. Jasfer pursed his lips and looked around as well. Another *kortru* household walked the mendicants' way toward the temple a block behind them. Nothing suspicious in that, nor in the few other people in sight in front of them.

Datri put her hand in front of her mouth and spoke around it. "It's Baram."

Jasfer nearly forgot to turn his face to the side to hide his own mouth. "Baram? There's no reason for him to be— I mean, he's the one with power. Why would he support…"

Datri held up her hand to silence him. The noise of a band of musicians, marching up a nearby street, pierced the muffling effect of the snow. None of the beautiful, stringed instruments out in this weather—they weren't a part of the festival of mendicants anyway—but the crashing of various kinds of metal plates and fire tongs set the beat as they marched past. Datri waited until the music passed farther along the street.

"I don't mean he's behind the insurrection. He's not scheming against himself. It's that I'm not sure he trusts you, not sure he would protect you." She paused then added, "If it ever came to that."

Would the High Prince betray him? Jasfer felt the cobbles open up beneath him as the question played out in his mind. They had never been friends exactly, but allies, near equals. No other prince was as high in Baram's regard as Jasfer.

Which made him more vulnerable than he'd been willing to recognize in the past. And if Baram had to sacrifice Jasfer to save himself?

Jasfer willed himself to see the street as solid and kept walking. Datri would have noted his hesitation, but any outside observer likely wouldn't. "We will have to prepare for that. Protect ourselves."

She touched his hand holding the umbrella, a rare public

sign of affection—as public as the nearly empty street could be—and they continued on toward the temple together.

The temple was surrounded by false ruin, by charred items that could have been anything, salvaged and burned for the festival. The *kortru*-caste people, princes and priests and silk-weavers, walked in wearing tatters. Or false tatters, much like the fake ruins, but certainly no silks. Soot or something resembling soot was the dominant color.

Jasfer and Datri greeted the others silently, as words broke the solemnity of the festival. A priest entered. In the paradox of the festival, he wore the finest silks, an ostentatious display of silk over silk, wrapped and arranged into an elaborate costume.

"The fire is rich," he intoned. "The fire is poor. It burns us to our blood, burns away our chaff and deadness. It gives us light and warmth and the rich colors of flames."

He continued on in this vein for what felt like a long time, and at the same time a group of the women from the priestly jati acted out a solemn dance behind him. They held wooden forms that didn't represent anything Jasfer could identify. Gray shapes, the color of ashes.

Jasfer turned his attention to the others in the temple. Kortru, almost all of them. Some few brenil servants had entered along with their masters, but most remained out in the entryway. Influence lines were too ephemeral to trace, as everyone focused on the rites. Or made a show of focusing on them.

As the ceremonies came to their end, a sound rose from the entryway. Jasfer turned in time to see a man burst through the temple doors. He wore fancy clothes, fancy for a nefli laborer. No silks, nothing compared to the priests' garb, but still the kind of clothes a laborer wore to an important occasion. Servants shouted and grabbed at him, but he flung his arms open.

In a loud voice that echoed off the rafters, he cried, "The fire comes to all who beg! In the name of the gods and of their children it comes!"

For a moment, Jasfer thought it sounded like simple, fairly anodyne piety, but then he realized the colors coming from the man were not a part of his costume but flames, real flames.

Other fires were spreading nearby, as if in the act of flinging his arms open, the man had flung fire to every side as well. Cries of alarm became screams, and a smoke that wasn't incense rose to fill the sanctuary.

For a moment the lines of influence snapped into clarity, but they didn't lead to the intruder. Someone else directed the action, someone the intruder deferred to. Before Jasfer could follow that line, a blast of the spreading fire forced Jasfer backwards. He stumbled, fell against another prince or silk weaver, lost his footing.

Datri grabbed Jasfer's arm and pulled him to his feet. "We have to go." Her voice was distant. He clung to it, just as he clung to her arm to keep his balance.

When he locked around the room, all was chaos. The line of influence he'd seen was gone, and all such lines impossible to follow. The only influence was the fire.

Ducking low and keeping a tight grip on Datri, Jasfer moved away from the fires. New flames appeared in front of them. How could they avoid it? The entire temple seemed to smolder, each space merely a thin sheen of reality laid over the potential fire beneath. A beam crashed down from above. Jasfer pulled Datri back, wrapping his arms around her. When it bounced off the floor and sheered toward them, Datri was the one to yank him to the side, throwing them both to the floor.

Ash fell, the remains of some portion of the temple's roof floating delicately down toward the floor.

"We have to get out of here!" Jasfer shouted, but he

couldn't tell if his voice carried even as far as Datri. He began to crawl, dragging her along with him until she was crawling beside him on her own.

Someone running tripped over them and cursed. The fire spread, seemed to be on every side. Datri nudged him to the side where a gap opened up between the fires. They were in the midst of the flames when the fire flashed outward.

Heat seared Jasfer's side. He screamed as the flames on each side closed around him. There was an inhuman shriek like the sound of wind as the fire closed together. He pushed Datri forward and scrambled after.

She turned and pulled at his arms. Tears ran down her face. When had he ever seen his wife cry? Or were her eyes simply reacting to the smoke? Heat lapped at his back.

At the doorway, the propped doors like arms reaching toward him and the others who had made it through the fire, Jasfer collapsed, unable to push any more.

***

The pain never went away. Awake, asleep, he always felt it. To the touch, his skin around his back and legs felt cool, but that was false. It burned. Inside, the pain kept coming in wave after wave, and the salves they (who? he wasn't even sure) applied periodically only barely touched the deeper pain.

Some medicines made him sleep through the pain. He woke dull and restless, as if he'd been aware of the burns and writhing from them even as he slept.

Servants carried Datri in to visit him every day. Her legs were badly burnt, but as far as she admitted, the pain was nothing like what he felt. A large portion of her hair had burned away, leaving stubble behind. When he could piece two thoughts together around the pain, he asked her, "What are they saying about the fire?"

The first time, Datri shook her head. "Haven't been able to

find out."

Another day he asked, and again later, each time with the same answer. Her voice grew stronger, though. She moved about Jasfer's room on her own now, one step at a time.

After nearly a twelve-day, her answer became, "The man died, the one who started the fire. He was the first victim."

"First? Of how many?"

"I don't know yet. Nothing official has been announced."

Waiting to see if Jasfer or one of the other injured people would die, most likely. Some days the pain was enough to make him wish he would. Nights he screamed, trying to sleep, until whatever medications they gave him began to work. Then the numbing would spread, and he'd be back in his pain-wracked sleep that was never a complete respite from his injuries.

Had Jaritta felt pain like this after the fire burned her face? He shouldn't let himself think of her, but he couldn't force the images from his mind. The flames of the temple became the smaller flames in his family's old chapel that had burned her face. How terrible to be cast out, the pain of being thrown from her family, her whole world, at the same time that the physical pain must have been unbearable as well. How had she not thrown herself into the geysers or from some high building to end it all?

Several days later, the burns on his back were actually subsiding. Datri entered, on her own feet. "Fourteen dead. That's the official number. Fourteen, not including the assailant."

Fourteen, and most of those gathered had been of their caste, many of their jati. "People we know?"

Datri nodded, lips pursed. "Prince Vedu." Not a powerful prince, but a long ruling one and wealthy. Jasfer silently wished the gods' blessing on his family. Datri listed some other names. Acquaintances. A month ago, he would have been sad to hear of any of them dying but wouldn't have felt it deeply. Now it hit closer, caught up in the pain of his own brush with death. Each name throbbed, made his injuries pulse in sympathy. Each left behind family, and he pictured their faces as they watched the funeral rites that maybe had already taken place or soon would. Would the bodies be burned, or would they decide the flames had already taken their share? Or perhaps there would be nothing left either way, only the death jati attendants standing in useless silence for all to avoid.

Jasfer's stomach clenched. After Datri left, he was sick the rest of the day.

One of the dead had been a ruling prince, and two more were family members of the Thirty. When they gathered together next, it would be a different gathering.

The pain in his legs didn't ease up, but Jasfer forced himself to turn his mind to other things, to matters of the valley, of ruling.

His opening questions for Datri changed. "What are they saying about the High Prince?" "What are they saying about Pashun?" "What are they saying about the plans to send soldiers there?"

One day Datri entered with a worried frown. She walked easily now, and her hair was mostly grown back, though the new hair was a darker color than it had been and more stringy looking. She held a bolt of silk in her hands, as if she'd forgotten that she was holding it.

"Is all well?" Jasfer's legs still throbbed with a distant pain—they probably always would somewhat—but he scooted forward in his bed and leaned toward her.

Datri shook her head. "Memories are too long here in Romnai. We never should have let Baram drag your history back into the light."

His history? What did that mean? "Is there some scandal?"

"Is there some scandal? Of course there is. You can't have forgotten your sister." Datri worried the silk with her fists, a wealth beyond imagining, squeezed absentmindedly.

Forgotten? Of course not, much as he tried to pretend he could. When Jasfer said nothing, Datri added, "Romnai hasn't forgotten, I assure you."

"But what does she have to do..." The answer occurred to him as he asked. Of course her history touched on his own legacy. How could it not? He'd tried to convince himself that people would ignore it, forget it, but it was all self-delusion. His parents had two children. One had been rejected by the fire and cast out. Years later she'd tried to lead a coup against the ruling princes.

Jasfer had disowned her then, had expected her to be executed, but she fled. Now she came back to haunt him.

"It isn't just her, though, is it? Are they saying I'm rejected by the fire as well?"

Datri nodded. "You and me both."

"You? But you're hardly—"

"I haven't appeared in public since then. And I wouldn't either, not without you at my side. For me to appear in public alone while you recover—that would be worse than the rumors people are already spreading. And they're bad enough."

Jasfer ran a hand through his hair. Her appearing alone *would* emphasize how badly wounded he was and make the rumors grow much worse. If neither of them came, they could keep up a fiction that their injuries weren't as serious. Or that both of them were invalid.

Two children, and both rejected by fire. Rejected—that was what the priests had claimed when Jaritta was burned as a fifteen year old. A fire scar like hers was proof that she was not forgiven, proof that she deserved to be cast out, labeled untouchable. Now the fire struck him as well, and even his wife had been drawn into the fire's punishment.

At least his scars would be hidden beneath his clothing, and Datri's hair could be made to look whole.

"The princes of Pashun have already said they will attend no festivities." Datri set the silk down on the foot of Jasfer's bed. So much for the High Prince's scheming. "And that's not all. There are rumors your sister is leaving the city of outcasts."

Now, of all times to have her back, drawing attention to herself.

"I'll have to denounce her again." Jasfer forced himself to his feet. "Show that the fire hasn't touched me, and that she has nothing to do with me."

His first time standing, and the waves of pain forced him back down to his bed. He lowered his head. "Soon. As soon as I can manage."

Datri gathered up her silk again and held it to her face as she left the room.

CHAPTER 11

The streets and buildings of Pashun funneled the heat from the steam beds up through the streets of the city, even early in the morning. Valni seldom felt the need for warmer clothing, even when she was simply passing through the streets. Now, sparring with Lodnan, a young man of one of the innumerable minor soldier jatis of the city, the snow and wind of her journey here seemed like a welcome memory of relief.

She swung a practice sword low and caught Lodnan's parry near his hilt. A simple twist, and she could disarm him. Instead, she pulled back and made another pass at a different angle.

He was a decent swordsman. The little soldier jatis here, like the Madrur that secured this small stretch of the city, trained their acolytes in traditional forms. But there was an emphasis on balance that the soldiers in Romnai didn't always learn. She appreciated that. It was nothing like her falcon jati training, but at least it wasn't mindless muscle work.

When Lodnan left an obvious opening, Valni took it. His intent was plain, to trap her sword with the stiff armor of his upper arm and then easily score a winning tap. The smile on his face, as if she'd fallen for the trap, vanished when she managed to avoid his armor and tag him just above its upper edge.

"How…" Lodnan took off his practice helmet and wiped the sweat from above his eyes. "You're fast. I've never seen anyone faster with a sword."

Valni sketched an easy bow. "Speed's important when you're out fighting mumblers. Or…whatever else you find yourself fighting."

When she'd arrived, Valni had kept her story simple. She was a soldier trainer, a sort of servant to the wolf jati, not a real member. When the streets of Romnai became too dangerous, she'd taken her leave. The reputation of the wolf jati meant the soldiers would clamor to have her train them, but the mistrust of the wolf jati would mean no one would hold it against her that she'd left.

They didn't trust her, not fully. Enough that she could learn how things were in this corner of the city, though, and that was all she needed. As the days had passed, they had started trusting her more.

As she wiped her face dry, she repeated her question in another way. "You think the soldiers above you are trained as well as you are?" She pointed vaguely toward the streets above.

"The Anguch? They're a pretty small jati. Used to be, anyway. Much less important than us. But they got in with the miners right away, and then the Sons of Ryo allied with them. With the miners, I mean, but that's both of them now. Who knows what's happened to their jati since then."

The Sons of Ryo. They'd been causing problems in Romnai too. "Can you show me? Maybe I can help you set up your defenses."

Lodnan pursed his lips and considered the streets leading upward. "I suppose so. We can use whatever help we get."

They tossed the practice swords beside the plaza, which had become a practice yard for many of the soldiers. Valni grabbed her staff, and they set off up the cobbled street.

A cart stood in the middle of the street, a street not made for a cart that size. As they came closer, she realized it wasn't a cart at all. It was a train car, taken apart and assembled into a shape that only resembled a cart. It was wedged against the buildings and held a post for a couple of soldiers. They might squeeze a handful more if necessary.

"Are the cart drivers any good at fighting, if you need thm?"

"They're bodies." Lodnan shrugged.

When the miners had rebelled, the cart drivers who had been here already hadn't wanted to join them, but they hadn't trusted the princes in the upper city, either. So, since the Madrur jati was based in the same part of the city where the carters stayed when they weren't out on the trade routes, they'd joined forces. Valni got the impression that similar patterns held in other pockets of the city, though the miners themselves occupied the bulk of the city.

She peered past the wedged train car pieces at the barriers the miners had set up on the other side, barriers of mined rock and the rubble pulled from decrepit houses. The people she could see moved with the certain discipline of true soldiers, not untrained rabble. "Who are their soldiers? Anguch, you said?"

"Yes, Anguch." Lodnan spat on the cobbles. "A weak jati before this. But well-enough trained, I guess. They were supposed to be putting down some kind of fight in one of the mines and turned against their orders. Came back here and allied with the Sons of Ryo, whatever they are. And now..." he swept his hand at the barriers before them, "now this."

Valni opened her mouth to ask more about them when someone shouted a warning. "Get down! Get back!"

Valni ducked just as a whistling sound approached. A rock crashed with a bang into the building beside the barricade. She scrambled back, Valni beside her. The soldiers from the outpost crawled back as well, joining them around the corner of a building. No one was injured.

"Do they do that often?" Valni asked, catching her breath through the dust and debris.

The soldiers couldn't answer through their coughing. Lodnan checked on them and said over his shoulder, "Not like that. But smaller volleys. Don't want us to forget they're there."

Valni crawled closer to the debris so she could see better.

From behind, Lodnan added, "I bet they did it on all sides. The priests on one edge, the princes above, and all kinds of smaller ones around. But they want our carts for trade, that's—"

Valni saw movement in front of her, a figure stepping through rubble. "They're coming through this time! Get ready to fight."

Lodnan scrambled forward to her side as Valni took a fighting stance. A glance back told her the coughing soldiers were in no shape to help them yet. How many Anguch soldiers were there?

Two more figures came through the dust, slings ready with deadly bullets. Even the most graceful of sword fighters was just another target for a weapon like that. They had to find a different way to stop them. Valni had her own sling. She picked up a fragment of rock and shifted into a throwing stance. One fighter against how many?

A balcony above the street had a number of pots, etched clay and fancy ceramics. If they could get someone up there, they might at least keep the enemies from using their slings.

More soldiers came through. "We have to go," Lodnan said, pulling at her arm.

Where were the other Madrur soldiers to help? She spun and helped him with the other soldiers. "Can we sound an alarm?"

One of the soldiers said, "I had a horn." They staggered into the nearby alley as he spoke. "It's back there."

"A place to gather?" Valni slowed as they came to an intersection in case the Anguch were attacking from multiple points. It looked clear for now.

The soldier who was supposed to have the horn finally

took charge, pausing in the middle of the intersection. "I'll go down and find others, gather up what I can. There will be more signaling horns there. But I need all of you to continue along this edge and warn people. They could have other attacks coming across. Or they might sweep through from behind, so we need to be alert on all sides."

Without another word, he raced downhill. The remaining group ran up to the barricade above them to spread the warning.

They were already engaged in fighting when they got there, and the soldiers with them fell into positions to help them. "At least it doesn't look like as many," Lodnan said as they crouched a short way behind the other soldiers. "They can hold off here until more help comes up."

Valni looked back the way they'd come. "Unless the point is just to pin the soldiers here until a bigger force traps them from behind."

The barricade was a good defense, but it wouldn't do any good if they were attacked from below.

Lodnan grimaced and called out. "We need to fall back, find a better place."

The soldiers at the barricade ignored him.

"Sir!" Lodnan forced himself into the space with the other soldiers. "Sir, there are enemies—"

"Stand down. We don't need a trainee telling us how to defend the place."

Lodnan reeled back as if the words were physical. And they would prove deadly, if Valni let the soldiers stay here. The alley below them might be easily blocked with the pieces of this barricade if they hurried. Or even... She scanned the street beneath the intersection. No other carts in sight, but there was a wheeled stand—a handcart, she supposed—like some sellers used for setting up shop on a street corner. Abandoned.

"Lodnan," she said, loud enough to snap him out of his shock, "help me make a second barricade."

They ran down to the handcart. By the time they had it upright and heading the right way, there were shouts from the barricade. A wave of soldiers was pressing on them, testing their defense.

"We need to help." Lodnan let go of the cart as if to run up toward the fighting without it.

Valni grabbed his arm and propelled him back to where he could help her push. "This *is* how we help."

They kept pushing the handcart toward the mouth of the alley.

Too slow.

The shouting of a crowd of soldiers warned Valni away. She pulled Lodnan away from the cart toward the other side of the street. "Behind you!" she shouted up the street as one last chance to warn the soldiers there. She and Lodnan raced across. There was no alley directly opposite the mouth of the other, but they made it to another alley just as the soldiers came through behind them.

No, not soldiers. This was rabble, miners and insurrectionists who fancied themselves soldiers. Valni hesitated. It was an insult to run from such a crowd. She could fight them, drive them back into the alley… No, they were too many, and real soldiers came along behind the undisciplined fighters. Her task was to learn things, not to fight needlessly, not to give her life away for nothing.

She and Lodnan ran into the new alley, again paralleling the upper edge of the Madrur-controlled region. Horns were sounding now, some from behind them and some from up ahead.

The next street was already flooded with fighting. The barricade at the top of this street had broken, and the fighting was all around. No alley led onward from there.

Lodnan didn't hesitate but quickly found a unit to join. Valni lingered to the side to try to understand the full scene. It was a small group that had broken through, and what looked like two units had converged in the scene from below. Should be an easy place to defend, at least until the mob broke through from the alley.

But the Madrur soldiers were struggling.

It took a moment before Valni saw the way the light gleamed off patches of the street. The Anguch or the Sons of Ryo or whoever it was fighting had poured something down the steep slope of the street once they'd broken through the barricade. Even when the units had arrived, they couldn't mount an effective defense.

But what could she do? The falcon jati soldiers were experts at a graceful way of hand-to-hand fighting. The slippery cobbles would take away much of her advantage.

Some of the Sons of Ryo were carrying more of the slick oil down from above. If she could get to them…

Beside the alley was a balcony. She leaped and pulled herself up on its railing. Moving quickly, she got far enough to be past the slippery cobbles. She jumped down and ran close to the walls. The soldiers didn't appear to notice her circling around behind them.

When she was above the fighting and any glint of slickness on the stones, she dashed across toward the people carrying the vat of liquid.

Even before she reached them, one dropped his side of the vessel. Oil spilled dramatically onto the street. The other carrier looked at the mess and ran as well. The sound of metal on cobbles echoed over the sounds of battle. Valni rolled the vat directly up the street from the fighting. The gaslights, already lit this time of day, reflected off the oil slick as it oozed downward. Then she spun toward the other pair bringing more oil.

They had already turned around to go back, still carrying their burden. She shouted a ululating war cry. Terrified, they both let it drop and fled.

The vat was too heavy for her to carry alone, so she tipped it where it landed. The oil spread over the stones. Already the earlier drop was disrupting the fighters of both sides. Valni ran back and made her way down the side of the street. The invaders had scrambled back to one point, and the defenders were clustered together below.

Movement below showed more soldiers coming up to join in, but there were the sounds of the Sons of Ryo rabble coming from the alley, and who could say how far they'd already infiltrated down the other streets. The neighborhood might well be fallen, for all they knew—everywhere but here.

Valni joined the Madrur cluster. "You need a better defensive position fast. Defensive from all sides, until we know what's happening elsewhere."

"Who are you?"

"Listen to her, sir," Lodnan said. Valni was pleased to see that he looked uninjured. "She's—"

The mass of enemy fighters burst through at that moment, both from the alley she and Lodnan had taken earlier and from streets and alleys below them. They blew their own horns, the notes echoing up and down the city and making the stones reverberate with the noise.

Instead of attacking, they flew a parley flag. A miner stepped forward, dressed as if to work in the mines—even to carrying a pickaxe on his shoulder for a prop. His voice carried over the street. "We do not wish to continue this fight. We would have you join us instead, work with us against our true enemies, the princes."

The Madrur milled about, muttering to each other. No one gave any official kind of answer. Below them a group of carts gathered, as if preparing to join in. What they could do to help was unclear.

"You may retreat to discuss with the others. We will maintain our positions until later today, an hour before dusk. Let us know of your intent by then. Or we will advance."

***

"What will your jati do?" Valni asked Lodnan as the soldiers around broke into little clusters to talk. Most began making their way down toward the carts below. "What do you expect?"

Lodnan shook his head. "The Anguch want our carts. They want trade. That's all they're after. Control of the trade road."

"It isn't as if you've done anything with trade yet."

"No." Lodnan shrugged. "No one's dared do anything that direct against the princes. As for what we'll answer, at this point, I think we just want to protect our homes. They'll find a way to work together, I guess."

Working together with the rebellious miners might not be safe for her. Not if there was any chance of them discovering her identity. It would give her access to information she might need, but was it worth the risk? Or could she find a way to create a more defensible situation?

She trailed along down the street to where a crowd was gathering.

No one trusted the Sons of Ryo, that much was clear from what she overheard. They seemed to be the wild stone in this strange game of kiwan. The Anguch were a soldier jati, not especially friendly with the Madrur but people they understood and could form some kind of agreement with.

The miners…were miners, common laborers, beneath the soldiers except as battle fodder. Valni could hear the way the Madrur sneered at them, even if they never said it out loud. But they valued the goods those miners provided. And an alliance with them might give the cart-drivers some leverage to help trade resume.

No such agreements would be of any value if they couldn't trust the mysterious Sons of Ryo. Based on what little anyone knew of them, they were zealots, wanting violence for its own sake.

The afternoon passed quickly, and Valni was unable to plan anything to help them. Probably better to slip away while she could, see what there was to see in the rest of the city.

But she lingered.

The common sentiment was moving steadily toward making some kind of agreement with the invaders. What good were the carts doing them, anyway?

Valni decided to head down to the steambeds. She could skirt around the part controlled by the Sons of Ryo and see how things stood in the other parts of the city. The priests would welcome her, if she revealed who she really was. Or the many small neighborhoods, each with its own jati of soldiers, might welcome a new soldier to help their defense. She could learn what she needed in other parts of the city.

As she headed down the street, slipping now and then on streams of oil that had reached even this low, a commotion came from the strip of city just north of there, an area controlled by a different jati.

There were no barricades on this side, because the two jatis had an old friendship, but they had resisted uniting fully. Now through those empty streets a mass of soldiers advanced. At their front was a man who wore odd clothes like nothing Valni had seen before. Thin and wiry, he looked, but he was no soldier.

Valni hovered at the edge of the steambeds, watching.

There were hundreds of them, well-disciplined and armed. Either they were a bigger jati than the Madrur or they united several jatis already. Given their location, they were probably the ones whose camp she'd avoided on her way in. Soldiers guarding the trade lines, surely that was an important piece of the puzzle to report back to the High Prince. If they could unite with the carters, it might make them a powerful force. Whether they ended up helping secure the neighborhood or not, maybe that was the way she should go to learn more. She headed back upward to be able to hear the conversations.

"The Gwalpi have long been the allies of the Madrur," one of the soldiers said as they neared the gathering of soldiers. "We are now here to honor our friendship."

One of the leaders of the Madrur jati, Lodnan's uncle, answered, "The Anguch were once allies, as well. Why should we turn to you and not them?"

"*They* attacked you. What kind of ally is that?"

The strangely dressed man cut the soldier off and offered Lodnan's uncle a peculiar bow. "I am a stranger here. I cannot speak to your allyships or history." He spoke with a strange accent as unfamiliar as his clothing. "I come from far away, but I can tell you I have experience with these Sons of Ryo. If you once trusted the Anguch, you must know that once they allied with that sect, you can trust them no longer."

"Where are you from, then, stranger? Do they come from your land, too?"

"No." A private smile, as if only for himself, passed across his face. "I only learned of them when I arrived here from my own land, which was right as they seized power. But let me introduce myself. I am Sembaari, and I come to you from across the mountains, with the wisdom of the Forgotten South. It is with those ghosts of the past that I say we will take your side in this battle."

The gasps and cries of wonder told Valni all she needed to know. The Madrur would welcome their rescuers, and they would join neighborhoods to add to this stranger's power and control.

But how did he fit in with the princes and miners in revolt and the High Prince back in Romnai? That was what Valni needed to watch for.

The milling chaos of the crowd grew without any sense of any new information forthcoming. Valni stepped away, toward the quieter streets of the Gwalpi neighborhood.

***

Valni watched the stranger from a distance. He looked like anyone else from the neighborhood at first glance—skin color and facial features could have been anyone from Eghsal Valley. Yet there was something strange about him that she couldn't define. A way he held his body, maybe. The way his head bobbed as he looked at each person who spoke to him.

Was that evidence he'd come from the Forgotten South? What was that land truly like? She knew the stories as well as anyone. Were they lands of the mythical naga, imparting wisdom to wanderers? Did the gods come down to bless their soldiers and give them battle advice?

The questions kept coming, especially about what his presence would mean for the High Prince. He might prove a useful ally. Or an enemy. But she hadn't had a chance yet to get closer. He seemed so young to have such an appearance of power.

There was often a man near him who didn't speak to the gathered crowds but whispered to Sembaari. He was a slight man who moved with a dancer's grace that seemed almost to equal Valni's own. A soldier like her? No, he didn't look like he had the bulk for that. Strong but wiry.

When he stepped away, Valni followed.

A moss-covered waterway lined with buildings separated much of this neighborhood from the one occupied by the Sons of Ryo. It made for an easier stretch of city to defend than the Madrur place had been. An army could certainly cross that way, but they wouldn't surprise anyone. The man headed upward toward the city's upper reaches.

The man stopped by the one large street that crossed the waterway. Its barricade was well set up to defend the crossing and guarded by vigilant soldiers. Valni observed from a distance. When the man continued, she followed again, right up to the upper edge of the neighborhood.

Here a path of rubble cut the city in two. Toppled buildings and piles of debris separated the neighborhoods below from the manors above. The rubble built gradually into an impenetrable wall. Soldiers patrolled above, the Vainath jati. Valni had heard their name from the traders and princes. These were her allies, in the end, the ones who would support the High Prince when all the unrest was finally put to rest.

These other soldiers below that wall—the Madrur, the Gwalpi, the Anguch—they would be suspect, at the least. Probably her enemies, if the fighting spread to involve the Falcon jati.

She found it hard not to sneer at the way the Vainath hid as if in fear behind their wall. Real soldiers, if they wanted to be trustworthy allies, should be attacking and not hiding. They should be able put down the riots and revolutions and restore the city to peace.

And if they couldn't, then it would be up to her and the other real soldiers to do the work, in the name of the High Prince.

When Valni tore her eyes away from the wall of debris, the graceful man she'd been following had disappeared. From above the wall, she heard the sound of crowds passing by, the people visible occasionally where the gaps in the buildings let her see through. And for a moment she thought she glimpsed him, joining in with the crowds.

Chapter 12

Harkala welcomed the visiting scholars to the excavation site. Nakhil, as a mere student, stood several steps behind them, head lowered.

"Thank you for being here." She studied the scholars as she spoke. They wore rough clothes, but it was for the trek to the site rather than poverty. They'd been given time to refresh themselves when they arrived, so now they stood before her, nine scholars with slicked back hair, a mix of gray and black, with the solemn bearing shared by scholars everywhere.

No one especially prominent, but at least they'd shown up to learn what she'd uncovered. Given the unrest elsewhere in the valley, she shouldn't expect anything more. In time these few would become multitudes. "As you can see, our work on the site has progressed well over the past half a year. This ridge was untouched when we started, but now the excavations have extended beyond even my highest hopes. We are uncovering more of our history every twelve-day."

The top of the ridge was curtained off into small sections, curtains that kept out the winds and also, more importantly at this stage, allowed Harkala to present the pieces of history in her own order—and to preserve the mystery of the tour, keep her guests curious and surprised. Harkala walked to the rope around one part of the excavation and gestured for the scholars to join her.

"The ground here showed no hint of the boat beneath it. As you can see, though, we have found the stern of an ancient boat. The style matches previous reconstructions of what our ancestors must have sailed, though with some differences. You'll notice—"

One of the scholars spoke over her. "This looks like a

depth of what, at least a hand-span? How would it be fully covered after six hundred years?"

Best not to be annoyed at the interruption. At least they were listening, willing to consider her findings. Better than many scholars. Still, she had to take a calming breath. "Yes, that surprised me. Our estimates in other parts of the valley indicated a much shallower depth over that time span. Taking those calculations, these boats would have to have been left here several centuries too early. But that implies mumbler ships, and no one has ever known the mumblers to build anything beyond a simple rowboat. All I can suggest is that those estimates were made from studies within the valley, not out here so close to the sea. Perhaps the ocean winds carry more debris."

That or the timelines of their own history were far off, but she didn't feel comfortable suggesting that possibility.

She went back to what she'd been saying, as if the interruption were nothing. "These boats have a considerably wider beam than other scholars' recreations of early fishing boats. That makes sense, if it was able to cross the rough seas. Later boats would have grown narrower as they were used for fishing near to shore." She used a stripped branch to point out the space from side to side. Then she pointed at a feature that stuck up from the stern.

"This structure puzzled us. We found something like it on each of the ships we've excavated, but nothing similar exists in the fishing boats of the following centuries."

"It appears to be the stump of a mast. How many masts did these ships appear to have?"

Harkala nodded. There *was* a stumpy look to the structure, as if something had broken off or worn away. "We wondered that same thing. No ancient fishing boats we've found had a third mast back here—they have one or sometimes two, but never one so close to the stern. We tried a model to recreate it, and a mast at this location added nothing and in fact made the models less stable."

She waited to see if anyone had other suggestions. When no one else spoke, she said, "We brought a local fisherman up here to see if he had any insight. He said he'd seen some boats use a device back here to hold their nets for them. As they drag the nets through the water."

"But then, are we looking at fishing boats rather than the ships that brought our ancestors?" Always the same scholar asking the questions. Suvril. He taught some of the high caste children, the older ones who began to show some aptitude for scholarly thought. He was a frequent contributor to the Society papers as well. Skeptical but curious, she'd have to be sure to cater her explanations to him. The others, seemingly, would just follow along.

"No, but I think there may be an ancient connection. Our visitor mentioned that sometimes ships with their nets here will leave them to drag when the seas grow rough. It stabilizes the boat, but only under the right conditions, with the wind and currents working with the boat. When they have to leave their nets like that, they often end up needing to cut the nets free as the winds shift, so the fishermen don't like to do it."

Harkala stepped delicately over the rope and traced her stick upward from the mysterious stump. "What if our ancestors had some other version of that? Some device they could drag in the water but with better control than fishing nets? It may explain how they could cross seas that no one has managed to cross in the centuries since then, either coming or going."

The scholars had no answer to this question. In truth, Harkala didn't know if her guess was even close to true, but it was a good working idea as she continued to study.

After she'd let the image sink in for a few moments, Harkala led them to another part of the excavation.

"Our best-preserved ship is around this way." The area of the excavations was not large—there wasn't space on the ridge for much—so the walk was short.

They had only gone a short way when they passed around one of the curtains to view another part of the ridge. One of the scholars gasped. Harkala allowed herself a smile and continued to lead them.

"Oh, look at that," another said as they came along the edge.

"Wow."

Harkala let the expressions of surprise and appreciation flow through her. So good to receive that rather than the scorn and skepticism she'd heard so often over the years. She lingered in the moment, slowing her steps and enjoying this view of the ship.

It *was* an impressive sight. They'd uncovered the full gunwale line and excavated down the whole depth of the hull along a good stretch of it. The entire mast, though broken off, had been laid carefully beside the boat. Nakhil had devised a way to arrange the mast as it must have looked, stretching up above the deck. The same strange structure that might have held a net of some kind looked as mysterious as ever, but intriguing rather than simply incomplete.

The hull still had hints of paint above the waterline. Nakhil had wanted to repaint the entire thing as it might have looked. Harkala had resisted that, since the flecks of paint hadn't been enough to be sure how it had looked. But she'd allowed Nahkil to paint one possible pattern onto a hide and drape that over the hull, to hint at what it might have been.

It was an uncanny pattern they'd recreated—or perhaps merely created themselves, she had to admit—a dizzying up-and-down, in-and-out arranging that never completely settled into anything regular. Perhaps the ancient silk-weavers had worn cloth much the same. She should bring them out to visit sometime, if the rumors of unrest in the valley didn't prevent them from traveling. Perhaps they would be so impressed with the history that they could fund the excavation in exchange for using the pattern on clothing.

When she felt the scholars had had enough time to take in the sight, she spoke. "This gives you a good view of the depth of the ships. It would have sat in the water deeper than the early fishing vessels we've found."

One of the scholars who hadn't yet spoken leaned down toward the ship and asked, "Is this how it was found in the dirt? How much have you relied on those other fishing vessels?"

Harkala picked her way around to the boat's prow where all the scholars should be able to see her. "This one is recreated to a certain extent, more than some of the others. The wood was rotting away, so we took care to match everything exactly as it was or as we found analogous parts in the other boats. Nothing is reduced to mere guesses. We puzzled for a long time over what seemed to be missing struts. All the fishing boats we've studied had struts here and here." She pointed with her stick to several points along the gunwales. "It's the type of structure that might easily break off from one boat or even two. But to break off from all five of these we've uncovered so far and never leave beyond any hint of their existence? Highly unlikely, so much as to be essentially impossible. So I suspect there must be something about the flexibility of the boat that makes a strut detrimental on the open sea. Though what that could be, I can't imagine. The fisherman we consulted did not have any insight."

One scholar rubbed her chin and tilted her head. "Or the sturdiness might come from some other factor in the boat."

"Perhaps." Someone could argue those details in some comfortable classroom back in the city. "The key point is that these are undeniably distinct from any comparable boats we've found from the early days of our settlement of the valley. Those differences will be one of the great legacies of this site. Scholars like yourselves will come to view this excavation as the most important source of information we have for our earliest ancestors. They will debate the theories that you yourselves present to your students and develop in the years to come."

Let them envision that, the glory of having their own ideas passed down. And known as theirs. Bodies might be given to the fires—and minds with them—but ideas could be as immortal as the gods. A scholars' vanity made them all crave such a legacy, far beyond any money or even fame today.

"Come and see the other ships we have been excavating. The site is small, but full of new findings at every turn. If you see anything you want explained or anything you wish to examine more closely, let me know."

After their tour of the site, admittedly short with how small the area was, and answering a handful of questions, they were back where they'd started. Suvril requested to speak. She acknowledged him, guessing already what he would ask.

"But these look so small for an ocean journey. How many people could have fit in each ship?"

Not exactly the question she was expecting, but leading up to it.

"Our estimate is that each ship might have fit four dozen people. Perhaps as many as five dozen, including all sailors, but that would have been a very uncomfortable journey."

"That's not enough." Here, what she was waiting for. "There must have been ten times as many ships. Where are the others?"

"If not more." She nodded and let the mystery linger. "That's the biggest question, yes."

Harkala paced, looking at the signs of their digging instead of the visiting scholars. Where were the other ships? Some cannibalized into fishing boats that sank over the years? Or even into the earliest dwellings? That's what people had thought when she began her search for the remains, that she'd never find them. Now that she had found some…

"We may never find all of them. Nor should we expect to. The first colonists may well have made use of much of the timber. But it is true that I had expected to find bigger ships. Or more ships in one location, or both."

Harkala pointed down the ridge behind the scholars. "Turn around and you can see the river as it is today. If you've read my brief report, you may be able to make out where the riverbed used to be. That is what led me to this site, that intuition of the river's changing course. I have only intuition at the moment to answer the question. But what I suspect is that most of the colonists used their ships for whatever shelter or trades they undertook. And only one jati brought their ships here and left them."

Suvril broke the silence that greeting her claim. "Which jati?"

The silk jati, she wanted to say. It fit so well with the story she had begun weaving together out of the fragments they were finding. But the evidence wasn't there yet. "That is where my studies of the dig site will be turning next. I hope to search for some clue to answer that question, and I hope to enlist all of you in figuring out what clues we might be able to find and what those traces could mean."

The scholars left late in the afternoon, with assurances that they would help her investigate, each from their own expertise. Fire and the gods of excavation willing.

***

The thrill of finding a new structure and uncovering a new expanse every day with shovels and picks passed into the slower progress of brushing the dirt back bit by bit. Which didn't mean a lack of excitement in its own way. Harkala wielded the tiny tweezers and brushes with the same fierce focus as she did a shovel. The end of each day always had less to show for all the work, though.

After many days of toil, Nakhil called out to Harkala. "This looks like some fabric."

Simple words, but Harkala's heart sped up. She had to force her hand to calmly set her brush down instead of tossing it aside. Had to force herself to calmly make a mark in the dirt with one tool and a similar mark in her book in ink.

Only when the ink was dry did she allow herself to walk, as if calm, across the excavation to where Nakhil was working.

She crouched beside him. "Does it look like cotton or wool?" She couldn't let herself hope that it would be silk.

"Not much to judge by." Nakhil held a few fibers, still stuck in the dirt around them, in a pair of tweezers. "We might learn the color." He licked his lips as if he wanted to say more but stayed quiet.

She looked carefully before speaking. "The strands aren't wool." Old wool had a particular shape, visible even to the naked eye. "Let me look with my lens."

Could it be silk? No, she shouldn't even let herself think the word. The glass lens she drew out of a velvet pouch was a precious tool, worth more than any of the other excavating tools or even all of them together.

It wasn't the glass alone. The glass-worker jati was fairly small and certainly lacked the power of the silk weavers, but it was a solidly *brenil* caste. But to get the exact gradations of this glass lens required far more specialized labor. And that required money a scholar on the outside of the major institutions could only afford by much saving and scraping.

Harkala held it close to the fibers and leaned herself close so she wouldn't bump the glass as she moved. "Flecks of green dye," she said. "Would green still look green after this long?"

Nakhil couldn't shrug without jolting the fibers, but his tone might as well have been a shrug. "We would have to consult someone. That question has never come up in my studies." His eyes were bright, already moving on to the next question, the next possibility. He was a good student for her, no matter his parentage or birth jati.

"Maybe it used to be something else then. We'll have to ask around." She moved her head from side to side without moving the lens. "Might be blue. Maybe both or maybe one fades to the other."

Now to examine the shapes of the fibers themselves. "Definitely not wool. There's no twist to it." That much she'd already identified. "It…it looks smooth. Maybe a slight twist to it…" That might mean it was cotton, but even as she thought it, she knew it wasn't true. "No, it's smooth all the way."

Lifting her eyes to meet Nakhil's, she said what she hadn't dared. "It's silk, beyond any doubt." Nakhil let a grin touch the edges of his lips.

Harkala managed to keep her excitement in check long enough to carefully put the lens away. Then she shouted without words.

Nakhil set his tweezers down and then let himself join her. He walked a pace away from the dig and danced a quick step. "So it's silk weavers? Can we call this proof?"

Harkala sobered up at the question. "Not definitive yet. But a step in the right direction. If this was the silk jati, that places them here at the right time. Gives us our reason for these specific boats to be here."

"Maybe the first Silk City, of sorts, was even near here." Nakhil scanned the land around as if to find where they could excavate next, for signs of some ancient settlement.

And that was why having a student willing to dream the

next question was so important. "Good thinking, Nakhil. We'll have to consider where to dig next, once this site is complete."

The excitement carried them through the next days, days of no more hints of silk but some day to day implements that told them little.

Until Harkala found other scraps that looked at first like fabric. "Hold this," she called to Nakhil while she took out her lens.

She brushed a bit more dirt away from the scraps and then leaned in close to her lens. Even before seeing the magnified version, she guessed what she'd see, and the disappointment felt like a shovel-full of dirt being poured over her head. The scraps were part of a larger piece of something, but there was no weave to the piece, no threads to examine. It was a solid, though fragile, section of a leather strap.

Not just any leather, but clearly an early sling.

Nakhil frowned when she identified it. "Even the silk weavers would have needed weapons to protect themselves, right?"

True. She shouldn't let one find alone strip away the excitement they'd been feeling. But more ancient slings came to light over the next days, as well as a pitted blade and a stock of sling bullets.

"Bullets. Not just pebbles. That implies they were relying on the sling for fighting and hunting, not just having some nearby in case of emergencies."

Nakhil agreed. After a moment, he said, "What if the silk was a mislead, though? Maybe it was a soldier jati all along, and they happened to leave behind evidence of the few fancy clothes of one of their commanders?"

If it was even fancy, by that point. What if silk was still seen as common and the problem of preserving it in this climate not yet understood? They might have taken a bit of an old robe, cast off by the high caste leaders back in what was now Jarnur, and used it as a rag to clean off a bloody sword. Sacrilegious as the idea of silk-as-rag was.

Yet she'd so wanted this site to be tied to the silk jati. It was a neat story, easy to explain, easy to study further. They'd have come here after leaving Jarnur, established a camp for a time, and eventually moved on eastward, until they finally settled in their remote city far inland. If she could present that history, the silk jati themselves would fund her continued excavations. If she could present that story, then even the simplest person on the street would understand the narrative. If she could present it, then history would seem, for a brief moment, to make sense of the chaos and uncertainty of the past.

The gods knew the chaos and uncertainty of the present could use some solid sense rising from history.

And her name would go down as a great scholar.

But if not…

Maybe the wolf jati soldiers would be an answer. That cut out the wealthy patrons but left the rest in place. A good narrative, a sense of history fitting the stories they all knew. Fame, or at least—and more importantly—respect.

She nodded reluctantly. "We'll have to keep putting together the clues and see what develops."

The clues over the next days only added to the uncertainty. A metal pouch of some kind that appeared to have held food, but the time she spent puzzling over what food it had been and what it meant yielded nothing. More scraps of fabric, one of silk but the others of wool—or something similar to wool that she didn't recognize. Had the animals of the Forgotten South been different? It would make sense. Even within Eghsal Valley the animals varied as you went inland or to higher elevations away from the river. A fragment of old pottery held a faint promise of providing more clues, but the pattern, what little of it they could make out, meant nothing to Harkala. All they could do was sketch out the piece and send it away to one of the scholars who'd visited the site.

Who had these people been?

Were they soldiers, who left behind such a strange assortment of scraps? Silk weavers along with a few guards? Some other jati whose identity would become clear only after years of labor?

"I'm going to climb up the trail here," she called to Nakhil at the end of a day's work.

Nakhil leaned on his shovel—he'd begun digging some paces away from the rest of the excavation in hopes that Harkala didn't share that there might be more evidence, more ship remains hidden there. "Will you be safe alone?"

A double-edged question. He'd no doubt seen the growing signs of her melancholy as the dig dragged on, and the trail led to some high places with steep drops. He was asking both for herself and for the dangers posed by others. The stories of unrest in Jarnur and the inland cities added a concern for danger to any activity. And while there had been no sign of mumblers in the area recently, a number of old fire scars up the mountainside beyond it testified to a history of their presence, and relatively recently.

To both unspoken parts of the question, she answered only, "Yes, I should be fine. Keep the lanterns on down here in case it's dark by the time I return."

She took a small lantern herself for the hike back down, since she hoped to watch the sunset over the ocean, late as that would be today.

The trail had been no more than a game trail when she and her team set up the site. Now months later, they'd worn down a smooth path, though it still led over rocks and fallen trees here and there. The ocean's salty snow was thin this time of year as summer moved toward autumn, so she made quick progress.

As she rounded a promontory, though, the wind off the sea struck her. Salt and cold turned into tiny pricks of needles. She pulled her hood over her face and stumbled back around the curve in the trail.

No matter. She could see the ocean from here, sheltered by the slope above, nearly as well. She couldn't see far south, where she really wanted to direct her thoughts, but then that was fitting. It was like studying history, peering into the ground for clues about what lay forever outside her reach.

The water below and outward well to the west of her was a terror of waves, even from this distance. No wonder the ships never ventured far. The white crashing of waves churned the black sea into chaos. It was a chaos that had given birth to the people of Eghsal. Somehow, in some way.

"Who were you?" she called out into the wind. "How did you come through that impossible sea? What gods or fire guided you?"

There was no answer, of course, only the wind.

The roots of their history lay in that wind, across those waves. So the stories told. What if the stories were wrong in some key way? What if only five ships came this way? Could those ships have carried all their ancestors? No. Not even if nine out of ten ships had ended up cannibalized for buildings would it suffice for how many of their ancestors must have come. There had to be more, but where did they all end up?

"Show me!"

No gods came to answer her questions. She watched the sun drop far beyond the edge of the water without learning any new intuitions or discovering a new direction to explore. Only silence, the blustery silence of an unchanging pattern that stretched as far as she could see or imagine, in location and time.

Chapter 13

One hundred seventy-three people stood before Jaritta and the other self-proclaimed leaders, in the rock-strewn plain south of Old Eghsal City. Was it enough? She moved her hands, as if they were so many lumps of clay for her to sculpt. Twelve others, led by Pavresh and Azheeran, were already scouting the path ahead and would protect them on their way. Scattered camps around the mines or other sites began with fewer, but they had the cities to supply and support them. Had Romnai begun with so few? Perhaps. Maybe even Eghsal Valley itself, with those bedraggled refugees from the Forgotten South.

Less than two hundred, setting out. It felt like the kind of epic journey those ancestors had once made. And she to lead them.

Well then, best to begin.

She pitched her voice to carry through the crowds, and they quieted to listen.

"We are the outcasts. The untouchables. The...the mumblers." She stuttered over those words, strange and even heretical to lay claim to, but pressed on. "We are the ones they've pushed aside. Out of touch, out of sight, don't think about who we were or who we are. It makes it easier for them in Romnai and Pashun and Jarnur to pretend we don't exist.

"Well, let us *not exist* somewhere else, then. Let them ignore us in our new homes, even as we move closer to their cities."

She paused and looked behind her at the geyser field and ramshackle homes. The catch in her throat was more than just a performance. "This has been our home. Some of us for many years. It welcomed us when nowhere else would. Many of us will miss what it used to be, but it has already changed. It has become unsafe. Don't think of it as the land turning against you, though. Eghsal Valley has not made you untouchable in a new way, has not cast you out or judged you unworthy."

She had them, all leaning forward, letting themselves be shaped by her words. She had to take a deep breath and release it before she could continue.

"It was the people of this place who accepted you, not the place itself. And we are taking that same thing to a new place. So bid goodbye to the rocks and geysers. Bid goodbye to the particular view we had from the lava field—of the river, of the mountains. Those are worth remembering. But don't feel like you're saying goodbye to your homes. You take your home with you.

"We will set up a new home, welcoming to all. A new home that will surpass what Eghsal City has been to us. And let not the princes in their plush cities come and take it away from you. We will make our claim and demand that we not be turned away."

As they cheered, Jaritta took a last look across the ruins of the old city. A geyser now would be fitting, the perfect farewell. There was a faint rumble underground, but nothing more. Even that could easily be lost in the claps and shouts of the crowd.

She would have to accept that. Lifting her chin, she set out through the crowd, and they turned with her to stream out to the assortment of carts and makeshift sleighs that would carry what goods they didn't have on their backs. Beyond the heat of the lava fields, a thin snow covered the ground.

A pair of the scouts stood at the edge of Jaritta's line of sight and waved to her. All clear for the moment, then, the path they'd planned out acceptable. She set out on foot, amid the creaking and groaning of wheels and skids.

Few of them had any animals to pull the possessions, so

most either carried what they needed on their own shoulders or worked with a small group of families to pull a small cart or sleigh by hand. Jaritta had little herself and carried what she owned. A far cry from her childhood, but not so different from her years on the streets of Romnai.

Would their food and supplies last the whole journey? They were hardened by want, used to getting by on little, but that very fact made them weakened to begin with. They carried as many dried fish as they'd found room for, and Jaritta prayed to whatever gods would listen that they would find food to scavenge along the way.

No, not to any god. She amended her thought. Not to the god Ryo. And not to his sons. Let the god of rules and social mores remain ignorant of them as long as they traveled. And may his sons, whoever those vandals really were, not bother them along the way. They'd chosen a time when the number of soldiers watching them looked fewer, though she knew they'd prove a challenge along the way at some point.

Over the course of the day, several dozen more outcasts arrived to join them, people from the city who'd initially rejected Jaritta's arguments. Maybe they'd heard reports of Jaritta's speech. She liked to think it might have swayed some of them, anyway. Or a new geyser somewhere spooked them into fleeing. More likely the sight of that many people leaving together was the final argument they needed to join in.

No matter what, Jaritta welcomed their presence. The more people they had, the easier it would be to stand up to the princes in the existent cities.

That night they camped before the sun had set, near a mostly frozen stream. The lava glow of the sky to the north was still bright, as if to mock how little distance they'd actually traveled. No worries. Jaritta expected a slow pace and wouldn't let that leave her or any of the travelers disappointed.

A man who'd been a dancer before he was cast out entertained them with a performance of an old dance about the founding of the Eghsal Valley. Somewhat apart, the two dozen mumblers with the group played odd stringed instruments and sang as the sun dipped below the southern mountain peaks.

By the time the camp was waking for a new day's journey, another family had straggled in from Eghsal. Jaritta personally welcomed them. Then she moved around to the front of the camp to lead the people, her people. They were all packed up and moving within an hour of waking.

They'd only gone a short way when they found the family of outcasts wasn't the only group to find them overnight. A group of soldiers stood in their way, one of the scouts stripped and bound and held before them like a shield. A mumbler. His skin looked almost blue in the cold air.

The mass of people creaked to a stop, compressing together as those in front stopped first. Jaritta strode ahead, alone, her fire-scarred face bare.

Was this band a part of the Sons of Ryo? They looked like wolf jati soldiers, though any other faction might have chosen wolf jati style clothing as they wandered the wilderness.

Summoning the full authority she'd learned in her parents' household, she spoke to the commander of the small group. "Release that man at once. He is under my protection."

"Your protection? A mumbler under the protection of a band of beggars?"

She lifted herself even higher, though it wouldn't have seemed possible, and looked down her nose at the soldier. "I am authorized to hire whomever I choose, even a mumbler. By whose authority do you detain him?"

The commander hesitated, and she knew she had him. Whatever cutting response he'd planned to give fluttered away beneath her gaze. He looked behind Jaritta toward her people, their gathered mass leaning toward his few soldiers as if ready to fight. He broke away and spat on the frozen ground. "Authority? We'll see by whose."

Slashing the scout's ropes roughly, he shoved the man toward Jaritta.

Better if the soldiers never tried to find out and learn that she had no authority, no matter the way she spoke. Could she give a signal to her scouts and the fighters among the mass of people and make sure this band of soldiers never managed to leave this place? Slaughtering these scoundrels would save many lives of her own people. Perhaps. What kind of leader was she, and what kind of city would their destination prove to be? The answer to that question would stem from what she did here. She twitched, trying to decide.

Too long.

The soldiers headed up the hillside while Jaritta bent over the mumbler scout. Any attack now, and trained soldiers like these would be prepared. Her people might kill them, but not without many deaths of their own.

By the time she turned again to the scout, the mumbler women Chhayasheela and her mother had come forward from the horde to tend to the man. Was it her husband? She looked again at the man's pale face. She didn't think so, though he was one of the mumblers working as a scout. They wrapped the man in furs, as much as they could while still making sure they could check on what looked like a few superficial cuts on his torso. She left him to their care.

Two other scouts came down to the group, riding stocky ponies. One carried the other scout's clothes and handed them off to the people caring for him.

"How did that happen?" Her voice cut through the cold air like a leather sling snapping back to its owner. "Your job is to see danger like that and warn us."

One scout shook his head and grimaced. "We rode right

by them. They must have hidden themselves for the night. There's a stand of trees up ahead that looks too small to hide anyone, but…that's where we found his clothes, after we heard the cries from here and came back."

"Our other scouts?"

"Accounted for. Searching more carefully for hiding places."

"And watching those soldiers leave?"

The scout nodded. "We set three to monitor them, at least until it's clear they're not turning around to bother us again."

Jaritta passed a hand over her eyes and opened them again. "Good. We cannot, must not be surprised by anything like that again."

"No, tisrah."

As the scout backed away and mounted his pony, she muttered, "Let it happen again, and I'll cast you out."

She hadn't meant for him to hear the words. They were bitter sarcasm, neither a cold threat nor a joke, but only after she said them did she realize how they might sound to someone else. His eyes widened, but before he could respond, she waved him wearily on his way to guard and guide them through the land.

***

Two days later, the scouts returned to warn them that a larger group of soldiers blocked their path. Jaritta rode ahead, with the other leaders and some of the scouts including Pavresh, to try to bluff her way past again. She rode close to Pavresh, hoping he might lend her some kind of arcist courage or wisdom. The soldiers stood in ranks in a narrow saddle of the land, where there was no choice to go around.

Many soldiers. The numbers dizzied her. What chance did her paltry group of pilgrims have? She needed the authority of the jati of her birth, the certainty of power as simply her right. But the fire scar on her face itched, reminding her of her past, her loss of that power. She slowed down, desperate for something else, for some secret route around the soldiers for some…

Magic.

That was what she needed. Arcist magic to get them through.

"Pavresh. Can you get them to let us by?"

He hesitated before answering, mouth tight. "I…maybe I can try something, but I'm not sure how it'll work here."

"Shall we wait here for you to figure it out? Or pull back for now?"

He shook his head, a tight motion as if he didn't want a distraction from what he was doing. "Keep moving toward them. I'll center the magic on us."

Jaritta didn't feel anything as they neared the soldiers, and they didn't put away their swords. She slowed down, began looking for a place to hide.

"Jaritta, formerly Talai, the untouchable," the commander said. "We are her to escort you to Romnai. And all your followers with you."

As if she were the only person with any authority, controlling them all. And yet a part of her relished the implication, the sense that she was the one molding and shaping the events of the world.

"We will not go with you." Jaritta tried to summon her authority. "You do not command us here."

The commander sneered and gave a signal to his soldiers. They stepped forward, swords out, menacing. "This is not a request. Accept that we can cut down every one of your followers with little danger to ourselves." He lifted his chin and made a show of scanning the group of scouts as if contemplating how each of them would die.

People dying for her. It wouldn't be the first time. Her

resolve turned fragile. What would happen if Pavresh's magic failed? What would happen to the others if she turned herself in? Maybe they could continue on without her. Maybe it would be for the best.

As she wavered, she felt the wave of Pavresh's magic. A pulse of some strange energy that went through her and then built up in power. It didn't affect her directly, and she couldn't identify what it was doing, but she felt a sense of some kind of emotion wash over her, a feeling of having accomplished an important task, a sense of needing to go complete something new.

She spared a glance toward Pavresh. His face was tense with focus. Or pain? She didn't have time to figure out what was wrong. The soldiers in front of her were too close, too much a threat.

"Make your choice. Come peacefully or we begin to cull the weakest from your herd. I don't need to prove to you..." A look of surprise crossed the commander's face. He stared for a moment at Jaritta as if willing his body to do something, to attack, to command his soldiers, yet his body wasn't obeying. The soldiers under his command had blank expressions, their eyes seeming to go distant and unseeing. Another pulse of magic passed through Jaritta, and something snapped in the commander's bearing. He made a sharp gesture and led the soldiers up the side of the saddle, leaving the route open for the outcasts to pass through. They marched at a fast clip off toward the west. None of them looked back.

Jaritta had to force her mouth closed as she faced Pavresh. "That was amazing that you could do that. What else—"

Pavresh's groan cut her off, as he slid sideways almost off his horse. One of the other scouts leaned over to prop him up. The look of pain had only grown worse in his face. His eyes were squeezed shut.

"Are you well?" She looked around for a place to lay him

down. "Put down a blanket, someone. Do you need shade? Water?"

Pavresh let them guide him to a place to rest before saying anything. When he did, he simply said, "That was awful."

"Drink," Jaritta said. "Rest." How long until the spell lost its power, though? She itched to be on their way. If Pavresh's magic faded, it wouldn't take them long to turn around and catch up to her people on their slow journey.

Eventually Pavresh ran his hand over his face. "I feel weak. Sick. That's not how the magic is supposed to be."

"Will it hold?"

Pavresh gave her a look of loathing, as if the question itself were cruel. But after a moment, he gave a weak nod. "Should. Maybe not until they get to Romnai, but enough to give us a solid start."

Then they'd better go and take full advantage of it. "We'll find a place in a wagon for you. Thank you." She made sure her full gratitude came through to make up for any uncaring that had come through in her question. "You've saved our journey. Or else it might have ended before it was hardly started.

***

The land they passed through was a barren, rocky region, far from the trade road that led to Pashun, and far from any other place where people were likely to be. No farms, no mines, no strategic value. Even the mumblers appeared to avoid the region.

Just enough hard, icy snow covered the land between the rocks that those with runners kept pace, and those without weren't stopped cold.

They saw little game, and what trees grew there provided little shelter, so no wonder. Jaritta was pleased she'd insisted on everyone taking as much food as they had. If anyone ran out, they would have to spend a long time in that harsh landscape trying to find food, and the rest of them would begin to run out as well, while waiting.

They ate light and moved as far into the twilight as they could, taking advantage of the long days. Their pace was slow, even so. Carts got stuck. Sprained ankles and twisted knees slowed down those who walked, and the land twisted and buckled in every direction. The scouts might have missed their one encounter with the small band of soldiers, but they earned their keep as they guided the mass of outcasts on southward along bands of snowy landscapes.

A ridge well to the east kept a steady distance from them, as if pointing the way they should go. The trade road would be up there, though Jaritta wasn't sure if it was right at the edge or further, well out of sight. As far as that, the edge itself wasn't always distinct, as if the land were trying to decide whether to force itself into a true ridge or simply fold gently from high to low.

Jaritta memorized the way the colors of the rocks moved in gentle swells from gray to yellow, with lines of red breaking the patterns now and then. Once she'd dreamed of crafting clay pots. Those rock patterns would have looked good in clay.

Even away from that ridge, the stark rocks of the land had their own kind of beauty. Boulders stood above their route, too small to be hills and too wide at their bases to be towers. Ice gave way to stone only to take it back. Woody shrubs twined about themselves as if huddled in coarse furs for warmth.

Some kind of ground rodent made homes among those shrubs. Jaritta never got a good view of them. They were too shy to be studied, too quick to be hunted, though some of her people tried. Fresh meat would have been welcome. Jaritta refused to let them slow down and devise traps of any kind.

Better to press onward, even as their stores ran low. They scraped the lichen from the rocks to eat with their dried fish and kept moving.

Finally, after nearly thirty days, a group of scouts came back to meet with Jaritta and the other leaders. Only when Pavresh came forward did she recognize him beneath the heavy furs. After his spell saving them from the soldiers, he'd spent a few days riding in a wagon to recover. Since then, he'd gone off with the scouts, never coming back to share information on what they'd seen. Avoiding her. Or maybe so engrossed in whatever stories it was the other scouts could tell him. She hadn't even been sure he was still traveling with her.

"You're getting close," he said, his voice muffled beneath his furs. "Should see the lava fields within a day or two, at most."

This statement wasn't news to Jaritta, as they'd been able to smell the sulfur of the lava field for the past two days. But it was a curious way to phrase it. "*We* are? Not you?"

Pavresh shook his head. "I...I'm sorry, Jaritta, but I'm not well. Not recovered yet. I promised I'd help you get to the site, but I can't keep going." His voice sounded tired.

"Surely you can't go off on your own, either. That would be worse. Ride in a wagon again until we get there."

Pavresh grimaced. "It's not the travel that's hurting me. It's my magic. It's...there's something wrong with the magic, something sick in it. Or in me." He held his hands to his head in pain. "I can't shake it free. And I'm afraid what I might do."

Jaritta couldn't answer. Without his magic, they would have failed. *She* would have failed—again.

"Afraid of what I might do to myself," Pavresh repeated, "but what I might do to others as well. I'm not safe to be around." He shuffled away from her to dramatize his worries. "But there's a healing pool that I've been hearing of. Maybe that will help. I hope it will, anyway, but to get there I need to head off to the west now." He gestured off through the pine trees, their scraggly trunks had been straightening, growing, coming closer together as they'd journeyed. A ridge of more rugged rock marched toward them from the southwest. She could imagine it would form a more difficult barrier to cross, if he wanted to be on the opposite side of it from her destination.

But so what? What did he need to go that way for in the first place, except to chase after more of his silly stories. "You know this land, then. You've been here before. That's exactly why I need you to stick with us a little farther. Then you can go off on your own."

Pavresh shook his head. "I don't, actually. I've been learning everything I can from the other scouts. Ellechandran mostly. He's from here originally, or not so far beyond your destination. Chhayasheela, too. She probably knows how to navigate these lands even better than he does. And some of the other mumblers know the land too. They're your experts here, not me."

Let him go. Let him go where he wouldn't betray her again. There would be no attempt at a coup this time and no way for Pavresh to warn her brother, to swoop in and end her claim to lead the people of the valley. Better to simply be free of those terrible memories, of the people who had died and the people who were now dead to her. And yet... He was a connection to Chaitan and Rashul and all the rest of those who'd dreamed of exactly what she was doing now. Without them she never would have set out in this way, leading a horde of untouchables to found a city without castes.

Her relationship to Pavresh had never been romantic, but it was real nonetheless. She wanted him at the city because then it felt like Chaitan could be there in some way, too.

Not that she was going to admit as much to him.

"I wish you'd continue with us, a little farther at least."

Pavresh shook his head. "I believe in what you're doing, Jaritta. I do. But I won't be any help to your city now." He looked around at the carts, at the people on foot. "Not until I'm healed." He gazed off westward and then toward the north. "Besides, I need to know what's happening in other places. In Romnai. What happens there can't help but affect you."

Jaritta set her jaw and pretended that she didn't care. "It's our horse, I think."

"I paid for it," he said as he wheeled the mountain pony around. "Bought from a family that chose to stay in the camp by the ruins." He looked back at Jaritta and then at the route ahead. "I wish you luck, Jaritta. All of you. I'll learn what I can and send you word, maybe even be back myself and see the city you've founded. May the Fire bless your journeys." Then he trotted off to the west, alone, up the sparsely wooded slope.

***

They caught their first glimpse of the lava fields late the next day, a flat expanse of mud and rock and strangely tinted plants. The pale green that shaded toward blue contrasted with the orangish brown rocks. Pashun itself lay on the northeastern edge of the fields. The scouts had led them well to the west, to decrease the chances they might run afoul of the residents there.

Jaritta, Thamiba, and the widow Driyya made their way to the front so she could be ready to address the people when the time was right. To further mold and shape them into the city she hoped to establish.

The pines opened up, revealing the stunning blues and yellows of stagnant water, rich with the minerals that gave off such a stench. It would be a good place to pause, to speak to her people.

As Thamiba gave the signal to halt, Jaritta noticed movement down near the water. Soldiers. The same they'd already encountered? She studied them a moment and saw the colors of their jati. No, the others must have returned to Romnai, as Pavresh had promised. This was a local jati, Pashun soldiers. Still, they stood in plain view, waiting just long enough for their message to be clear. This time she had no magic to call on to drive the soldiers away.

A scout was racing along the pines toward them. A belated warning, but she didn't care. This troop was no danger to her people, not directly, and they would have planned exactly how to position themselves to avoid even the best of scouts. Being familiar with the land was a powerful weapon. They themselves were a warning, a notice that she and her people were being watched.

Even before her scouts reached her, the Pashun soldiers had wheeled away, gone from sight among the rock formations at the edge of the lava field.

Let them go. Let them watch. She would not be intimidated, would not be driven off.

But forget the speech. She could save that for when they reached the actual site where she would found her city.

"Nevermind," she told the scout before he could speak. "Westward we go. Watch for them to return, but only defend us. I want no aggression on our part, no matter how few you happen across. We will be their neighbors soon."

The stench of the lava field settled over them, invaded even their pores. They stayed at the edge of it, where the ground was at least stable, but the sulfur smells spread far from their precise sources. A geyser blew as they walked, more mud than steam, then another a short time later, as if the land itself could not stomach the water for long.

But what was a smell compared to safety, a home? She could endure. As could they all, her people.

The trees—and all vegetation—ended abruptly, giving them a convenient line of open land to traverse. The lava likely poisoned any plant that came too close, she supposed. Or maybe the ground was often too hot, though it didn't feel especially warm through her travel-thinned soles. The hard-packed soil was a deep orange next to the trees, paling to yellow as it neared the swampy land beyond. As long as they stayed within the band of orange, they should be safe.

She hoped.

Their progress remained slow but steady, and the lava fields vast. The scouts told her to expect at least three days of travel before they came to the place they'd settled on.

Pashun soldiers harassed them as they went, never attacking outright, but darting in to steal supplies—out of what little remained—and spooking the pack animals. Petty things and not terribly dangerous, but a constant reminder that they were there.

Even worse was the possibility of other soldiers keeping an eye on them. She thought she saw glimpses of shadowy figures ahead now and then, soldiers without the colors of the Pashun jati. Spying on them? Hiding from someone else entirely? She had the sick suspicion that the Romnai soldiers they'd met early in their journey had escaped Pavresh's spell and doubled back to finish their task. The Sons of Ryo or the wolf jati or whoever they had been.

The edge of the lava fields curved southward. The southern foothills marched closer, great ridges that led right up to the edge of the orange soil and then dropped abruptly. So far, the route near the fields stayed solid, though with increasing stretches of marshland for them to ford or circle around. She didn't like the idea of having to lead the entire group over any of those ridges.

After a day of skirting their edge, a scout beckoned for Jaritta to lead the group away from the fields entirely, up an incline between two ridges. The land ahead appeared to grow wetter, a swampland full of clouds of insects. A narrow river flowed into the lava field, cutting across—and no doubt helping to create—the swamp. This was the kind of land she'd pictured from Pavresh's descriptions. Houses on stilts amid the stink and the swarms of gnats and biting flies.

But clean water—that she hadn't dared hope for.

The river, narrow as it was, was a welcome relief. The rugged sides of the ridges rose up steeply on either side of the water, and the water too rose, in a snaking waterfall up toward the snow-covered mountains to the south.

Would it be warm enough year round?

"We are almost there." Jaritta tried to make her voice carry over the crash of the waterfall to her whole mass of settlers. "You have traveled far, endured the barrenness and cold, the soldiers who would mock you, the sore feet and long days. Now we are come to our destination, to our new home. You will see the river rise above us, the cliff walls closing in. There we will make our homes, of hide and caves, of wood and stone. You will be free to build where you want, how you want. But we will be a city, united, ready to help each other and defend ourselves against our enemies."

That last would be a change from the ruins of the old city, where each had been left alone and no defense was needed because the unstable land was its own defense. Or should have been and had been for many years. Such a change in their mindset needed to be hammered home, over and over.

"Together we will build this city where there are no outcasts and no untouchables. A city without castes, where even the mumblers as well as the people of Eghsal can work together to make it a city for us all."

The route up beside the water was slower than she'd imagined, because it was so steep and without any established path. They camped on one ridge that night and finally reached the slight widening between the ridges where her scouts had planned to establish the city by midday.

A thin layer of snow covered the valley. No doubt it would be much deeper some times of the year. Yet, the cold was bearable. Heat rose up from the lava fields, and the ridges trapped it within. The dark evergreens promised a place for game as well as food to be grown. Several good-sized caves could house dozens of them while they worked to build new houses.

Why had no one come to settle here before? She asked Azheeran that very question.

"I cannot speak for the peoples who lived near here. My tribe was traveling the foothills far to the east of here. We are not all the same. Chhayasheela is from somewhere closer by."

With the scouts mostly back among the people, she and her husband Ellechandran as well as her mother were nearby. Summoning the three of them, Jaritta repeated her question.

When she asked them, he lowered his eyes as if in shame. "It is too close to your people," Azheeran translated for him. "Our village did not allow our people to come in view of your people. When they did, they were…punished, even cast out."

Before Jaritta could react to what he'd said, something that was clearly personal to their family, Chhayasheela added something else, and Azheeran said, "The river has changed, too. You can see on the walls of the ridges that it used to be higher. It may not have been safe until more recently."

Were those truly high-water marks or only the coloring of the stone? Well, no matter. It was a good place, and the trees told of many decades of safety. Far better than the constant threat of deadly vents of gas and lava.

"We will make sure it is safe now, for everyone," Jaritta said as she moved on to explore the area.

She'd only seen a small portion of the village site when a call rose from the scouts. She hurried over to the lip of the waterfall. A troop of soldiers was climbing up the riverside. Some forty of them, she guessed at a glance. At least they were coming openly—for now.

She took a deep breath of the cold, sulfur-tinted air to steel herself.

Time to defend the city, her city. To discover if it would last long enough to be molded into the shape she imagined or if it would be cast back to the ground before she had any chance.

As she waited, Driyya, Thamiba, and the death jati woman Poorma came up on either side of her to support her. Along with Azheeran who was organizing the scouts for their defense, these were the new leaders of the new city. Let everyone see them, enemies and friends alike. Let them see their resolve and the inevitability of the new future being shaped before their eyes.

CHAPTER 14

Prince Jasfer winced as he swallowed a dram of medicine. The pain wouldn't go away, but at least the medicine would let him ignore it. Long enough to get through the morning.

Even before the medicine had begun to kick in, Datri was pulling him out of his couch. "You'll be at your best if we go now."

True. If he waited too long, the medicine would leave him unable to stand straight. Didn't make him want to get up yet, but he let her help him to his feet. His back and the backs of his legs screamed in agony, screams that he swallowed behind pursed lips.

Yatim helped him out of the house to the waiting carriage, Datri a proper and regal distance behind. Her hair no longer looked charred, and both burned and unburned sides were blended together smoothly. In case anyone was watching, Jasfer forced his back straight and tried to make it look like Yatim wasn't actually assisting him as much as he was. During the carriage ride, the medicine began its work. Jasfer's back relaxed, and the pain seemed to be happening to someone else.

At the High Assembly, Mahednri stood outside, offering a nod of silent support as the prince headed in. Jasfer made his way to the front. Datri stood with him, though a step behind and to the side, as she was there by special permission, not as a ruler in her own right.

The room was a solemn place, built of dark wood that even the angled windows in the ceiling could not fully lighten. The years of snow falling on the glass windows to melt had left them grimy, so that even on a summer day like this, it looked like there was snow gathering on the panes. The princes reclined on piles of pillows or sat on low chairs, but no amount of soft pillows could take the hard edges away from the room. It was a place of difficult decisions and harsh lines. Servants came and went with gourds of tisane and small foods to keep the princes refreshed. The ruling princes quieted down to hear what Jasfer would say. He still had power and influence, but it was a tainted power compared to before, one shadowed by mistrust because of his former sister.

"Fellow princes, it is good to be back among you. These months of healing have made me miss your presence, your wisdom, and your leadership. I mourn with you for those we lost in the attack on the temple on such a holy day, especially our brother Prince Vedu. He served our people well and long and should be remembered with honor. May the Fire of the gods welcome their spirits into its holy flames."

The princes muttered their assent as Jasfer paused. Before he continued, he tried to trace the flow of power in the room, but already the medicine was making it difficult to pay attention to what used to come without thought. Had he shifted the sense of suspicion from him, or was it unchanged? Baram, as High Prince, certainly held the naga's share of power. Which others exerted influence over the room and how it related to him, he couldn't pin down.

"I come before you for another reason, however. Word has come that the pretender Jaritta, who once was a part of my parents' household, is creating chaos in our valley. She has led a group of outcasts from the old ruins, where they'd scrabbled for years and never threatened usm to a new location. She seems to be setting up a village of her own, under her rule, near the city of Pashun. Their actions make peace in Pashun even more difficult to achieve

"I denounce her work.

"Let there be no question in this body nor throughout the

city. Her act is a betrayal of the Valley, and of my family. May the Fire judge her. Her act of uniting the outcasts threatens all of society. We can sympathize with her wish to help those who are untouchable, to make their lives less burdensome, but not to do so in ways that could upend the peaceful cities of Eghsal Valley. Now of all times, we need to be able to extend the peace we enjoy into the battle-torn city of Pashun. We can't be distracted by that woman's misguided venture.

"In this, let us be clear that we stand for the Fire that creates the world, not a fire that destroys and warps the lives of the Valley's residents. We must do all we can to prevent the pretender's actions from disrupting the castes and jatis of our cities."

As he spoke, he hoped to see the princes aligning his way. They certainly watched and listened. If there was any movement in the lines of influence, he couldn't read them. Soon the medicine would render him incapable of speech—or leave him babbling incoherently if he pushed himself too far.

To avoid any such risk, he ended by saying, "As we grieve and as we look to guide this land forward for the sake of the gods and all its people, let us keep the Fire of the cosmos burning pure and bright within this chamber and in our cities."

The other princes applauded. Whether it was enthusiastic or merely courtesy he could no longer distinguish. He focused on keeping his back straight and head held high as he left the room and refused any help getting into the carriage. By the time Yatim closed the door on the carriage, he was aware of nothing else besides the sound of Datri settling herself into the seat and the touch of soft leather cradling his face.

***

Jasfer sat at his desk, Datri in the chair beside him. It was a solid, wooden desk, stained dark to remind visitors of the color of the High Assembly, with matching chairs and bookshelves. A desk to intimidate. A desk that spoke of history and power. The shelves held rare books more than a century old. Ledgers on another shelf recorded the wealth of raw ore that channeled through his family, minerals from a dozen mines scattered all over the Eghsal Valley. A large ingot of pure iron, set into a wooden display stand, decorated his desk, emphasizing the same points told by the ledgers.

He did not recognize the person across the desk from him, but Datri knew her.

"Yes, tisrah," she said. "I worked for your lady wife when she came to Romnai to marry you. I served in your house for the first year, as her attendant, but would not have had cause to speak with you."

"I presume you wore finer clothes then." He frowned at the rags she wore, the look of the streets. He had made sure Jaritta never needed to go dressed like that, back when…well, before he'd broken off contact. Before her betrayal.

"Yes, tisrah."

"Yet we dismissed you at some point. Why? What was the cause?"

"I…" The woman opened her mouth without words.

Datri cut in. "No, husband. Sashyu still works for our household. Or rather for me, as my attendant. Of sorts."

An image flashed through his head of the arcist he'd once hired to be a spy for him. Pavresh, who might have become among his most trusted servants, if he'd stayed. "You'll need to explain," he said, though he suspected she didn't.

"I sent her to live in another part of the city, to be my ears where I can't listen. She is one of the reasons I am able to learn things that are useful to us."

One of. How many other spies did she employ without his knowledge? But then, he'd known that she did such things. In fact it was Pavresh who had tipped him off to this side of his then-new wife's expertise.

"Very well, I won't ask more. What have you learned? And why make yourself vulnerable by coming directly to me?"

"I work as a *walla*, tisrah. I deliver food to workers near the river."

As if it mattered to him exactly how she did her work. He gestured for her to continue.

"I've come in contact with the...the people who are agitating. The ones behind the attack on you. In the temple. The Children of Kwona."

Is that who was behind it? Jasfer leaned forward. "I didn't know there was more than the one attacker, and he died in it. What do you know of them? Are they planning something else?"

"Maybe. I think so." Sashyu moved her head nervously from him to Datri and back as if not sure whom to address. "I'll give you all the names and what I know, only..."

Datri tapped her hand on the edge of Jasfer's desk. "What is it, Sashyu? You have something else to say?"

"It's...I'm scared to go back. I may...they may already know me. May have seen me come to visit you."

So why did she then? He gestured for Datri to handle this request. Her former servant and current spy. She would know better what to do.

Before Datri could respond, Sashyu pressed. "Please, isn't there any position in the house I can take? I've served you well, here and back home."

Datri put on a big smile that Jasfer recognized as false to a degree. "Of course we'll find you a position, Sashyu. Let's take a look at the names you have and what you've learned about the Children of Kwona. Kalvandi will see you to my own office, and I will be there shortly to record what you have."

After Sashyu had left, Datri rested her forehead in her

hand. "She's probably fine to keep here, but I don't like relying on *probably*. I'll have a better sense after I talk to her more. She's been on the streets long enough that people might recognize her, even dressed in a cheetah jati's dress. I might be able to come up with an excuse to send her to the Silk City—it's what she wants, I'm sure, if she can't stay here. You heard how she still called it *home*?"

"I did notice that. You haven't called it home since moving here."

Datri shrugged. "It's not, to me. *This* is. But if you have some other task to send her on, think on it."

Jasfer nodded. Someone would have to go to Pashun, to deliver letters and help everyone make their plans. Would probably have to try to deal with Jaritta, somehow. Or at least deal with the situation there. Unfortunately, that someone would not be some minor servant but himself. He'd known *that* since even before the High Prince sent his falcon jati soldier to investigate the city. But how could he leave, in his condition? Someone would have to go in his place, and he couldn't imagine who. He ran through plans and possibilities in his head as Datri slipped from the room.

***

The first units of the army he'd put together would set out without any official from his household. Instead, he was sending Mahendri as his liaison and hoped it wouldn't be seen as an insult. They would finish the work of the wolf jati in opening the trade route most of the way toward Pashun and then secure the new bypass the southern princes had created. A high-ranking official might look good for that person, but it would do little to help the soldiers achieve their objectives. Regardless, they would go with the blessing of the princes and the pomp of heroes. Datri sent out invitations to the other princes—ruling and otherwise—as well as the silk weavers and even some prominent priestly families.

He would have to be the gracious host to his peers as well as the inspiring voice commissioning the soldiers.

Except, day after day the invitations were declined. Each came with an excuse. A family member departing for the Silk City meant the invitees would be spending the day with their loved ones. A long-planned event downriver in Jarnur. An elderly mother in failing health. One after another the people of their caste gave their reasons for staying away.

"These are barely more than outright lies," Datri told him as she read the apology from Prince Nriteesh. "His old injury is bothering him? No more than it always does. And he was the one who suggested putting this on you in the first place!"

"It makes no sense. But you're right. They're avoiding me ever since the fire in the temple. The priests declared me spared by the fire, honored even, in the way I survived. But it's as if they treat me as still suspect."

"It has nothing to do with the temple fire, husband."

Jasfer cocked his head.

"It's Jaritta and her silly city of outcasts. No one wants anything to do with you because of the shame of your association with her."

Jasfer lowered his head as if he felt the shame as well.

By the time the day approached, Jasfer wanted nothing to do with it. Let the soldiers be off to rescue the city of Pashun, but leave aside the pomp of their departure. As much power as he might have in many ways, that kind of decision was not up to him. So, he dressed in his finest silks, set his face to look solemn yet sure of the soldiers' success, and rode his carriage to the Tanan Square beside the lava fields to see the soldiers off.

The soldiers stood in ranks that filled the square, and his feelings rose at the sight. The wild ox soldiers formed a smaller jati, one trained to defend the city from mumblers attacking, which hadn't happened in Jasfer's lifetime. Even so, their numbers were impressive. Mahendri had suggested this jati, and they looked the part, standing in perfect ranks, ready to do the princes' bidding. To do Jasfer's bidding. Surely they could put down a few unruly miners and their supporters.

As part of the pomp, the commander of the troops walked Jasfer and his entourage on a tour of the soldiers. It was a blur of units, of "And this formation assisted in the riots of…" Mahendri nodded and appeared to listen more closely to the details, which surely mattered more. Jasfer examined their uniforms and gear for any sign they might prove lazy in that regard, which was the best he could do to judge them. By all indications they were taking this task seriously.

The tour ended, and Prince Jasfer took his place before the assembled people, the few princes and priests who had deigned to come taking up places behind him and around the sides—a short way around the sides. The architecture of the square made his voice carry.

"Soldiers of the wild ox jati, thank you for your service. The city of Pashun needs you, but do not think you go only for them. You go for Romnai, for your home city needs your success as much as that other city does. You go for me, in the name of Prince Jasfer and all the princes who rule this land. And you go for the gods, who serve the Sacred Fire in all things."

Propriety would have him speak more. He should seize this chance to claim the admiration of the soldiers as well as the honor of his peers. But with so few peers present, the effort wasn't worth such small reward. He moved on to the next part of the proceedings.

"Mahendri, come forward."

After he had spoken similar words of sending over Mahendri, a priest came forward and did little more than repeat the same ideas, only turning them into prayers. Jasfer's thoughts wavered between finding the fanfare impressive and finding it tedious, and as his mind swayed, he felt his body swaying as well.

Datri rushed up from behind him with a gourd of tisane. It made him look weak, so he must have already looked in bad condition for Datri to do so. He took the drink and forced himself upright through the rest of the prayers and a flourish of horns and drums to set them on their way east.

As soon as he could, he bid farewell to the few princes who lingered behind and collapsed into the seats of his carriage. His back and legs were fire. By the time they reached the manor, they had tightened up so much he couldn't even walk inside on his own. Yatim and another servant carried him between them to his room and into his bed.

***

Rashul entered Jasfer's office a broken man. He had come meekly enough at Jasfer's summons, no hint of the rebellion he had once inspired. His clothes were fine, for a typical mid-caste brenil man, and his hair neatly combed. Nothing on the surface that looked unkempt. Underneath, though, his brokenness was clear. Empty eyes, a slowness to his speech that wasn't thoughtfulness but simply a lack of caring.

"No. I know nothing of the attacker. I don't involve myself in such things."

Jasfer spun the iron ingot from his desk in his hands. "And you're sure it wasn't any of the people who used to gather with you at Chaitan's house?"

Rashul shrugged. "Who can be sure of anything? I don't think about that time much anymore."

"Is that the kind of actions you planned back then? Or that others planned?"

"No, tisrah. We wanted to overthrow the princes but not burn them."

Sarcasm or some other hint of mockery? But his voice was too lazy to take his own jabs seriously.

Jasfer leaned across his desk and placed a single finger on Rashul's chest. A controlled threat. "Are you familiar with the Children of Kwona? Are they inspired by your old speeches? Have you encouraged their rise in any way?"

"Children of Kwona?" Rashul snorted. "I met one once. He didn't like me at all. They like the castes, want them even stronger. They just don't trust the soldier jatis and maybe the princes, but only specific princes. It isn't the idea of princes that gets them riled up."

That was worth exploring more. Maybe Sashyu would have insight into that part of the faction's appeal. It was clearly the extent of Rashul's knowledge, so Jasfer moved to a different line of questions, though he hated even bringing it up. "What about my sister, the outcast Jaritta? Would she have been involved?"

"I had nothing to do with her coup." This time the words came out fast, with greater energy. "You know that. Asked me often enough back then. That had nothing to do with me. Nothing with my ideas. I wanted no castes, not just to set up a different prince."

"I remember the facts. That's not what I asked, though. Jaritta has been on the move outside the cities. Causing problems. Could she still have contacts in Romnai who are acting to support her?"

"Is she causing problems? Well, that's interesting." Rashul leaned back away from Jasfer's threatening finger. "But as far as her using fire to attack? There's some poetic justice to it, but it doesn't seem like her. Or what I knew of her before her coup."

No, it didn't. At least it didn't fit the Jaritta he used to know. But now—how could he say for sure?

"And you maintain that you've had no contact with her

since then, either? You have no knowledge of her new city, no knowledge of any people here in Romnai who might support her efforts?"

"A new city?" Rashul sat bolt upright. Almost immediately he shrunk back into his former posture. "No, I know nothing of that." His voice had resumed its earlier, lazy drawl, but there was no hiding the interest he had in the idea, no hiding the spark that lit in his eyes.

Jasfer flipped the ingot around in his hands, tracing the lines and bulges as if they held hidden information. For all his outward nonchalance, Rashul still had the revolutionary spark he'd once cultivated. Muted and wary but not gone. Jasfer might need to take advantage of that.

Making his voice dismissive, he said, "Some city of outcasts and mumblers down south, near Pashun. They'll probably all dissipate as winter sets in, with no real force to unite them. Back into the streets or out into the mountains. I'm sure it's nothing that will last."

Words to cut, but words to make Rashul burn with a wish to go help her.

The question would be if he went on his own or if he contacted others in the city to join him. And who those others might be.

When Rashul left, with Yatim arranging for him to be observed, Datri entered. She took the ingot from his hand and set it down hard on the desk.

"It's not working."

"What?"

"We're finding out about the agitators behind the attack, but there's not much there. Just a few angry people."

"Good." Better than there being some vast conspiracy to put down. But as the silence stretched, he thought about how Datri had said it. He thought of the invitations declined and the tiny crowd of spectators for the soldiers. It had been almost a month, but still too soon to hear any news on what progress they might have made in Pashun. "Ah, and that won't satisfy the other princes, will it?"

Datri shook her head. "You're not redeeming yourself in their eyes. You need something that shows your power."

Would his burns allow him to do anything? The pain had been lessening over the past twelve-day. If it continued, he might be able to travel. It was a gamble, but he wasn't sure he'd been left with any choice. "I have an idea. It will mean traveling."

Datri narrowed her eyes. "I can handle some travel if I must."

Jasfer shook his head. "This one will have to be me. Officially I'll be going to Pashun with additional soldiers to complete the battle with the insurgents. Unofficially, I'll be finding more about my sister's little venture." He took the ingot back from where Datri had slammed it and squeezed it hard enough to make the veins stand out on the back of his hand.

"And making sure it fails."

CHAPTER 15

It hadn't been easy for Pavresh to leave Jaritta's horde of outcasts. They were making good progress, at least, and the smells of the lava fields had begun to waft their way. The empty, sick feeling inside him wouldn't let him stay, no matter how much he felt obligated to help. And the stories of the people no longer put off the sickness. The words grew muddled as the travelers' weariness increased, until no one could spare the breath to tell him anything new.

Chhayasheela and Ellechandran had spoken of a strange village to the south with healing pools. It sounded like the kind of tales he gathered, a mysterious *other* place where magic happened. He could even tease out the arcist themes that wrapped themselves around the idea, even if there was no such place. The deep sense of wrongness that had invaded his sense of the magic made the effort to find it anyway worthwhile, even if all he ended up doing was chase rumors with no referents. The solitude alone may be healing. On his pony, his own though Jaritta had only reluctantly allowed him to take it, he headed westward into a part of the valley he'd never visited.

The rocky terrain grew formidable. To the west and north lay the great lava fields of Romnai, though the city itself was still far out of sight. Here, it seemed as if all the debris of those geysers and mudpots had been left to cool and harden in disarray. Perhaps like the volcanic activity around Old Eghsal City, these fields had once moved, gradually shifted west and northward.

That idea didn't bode well for Romnai someday. The future might well betray the capital city eventually.

Pavresh's pony stepped carefully among the rocks. The

land itself was tricky, channeling travelers either into the dangerously unstable lava fields or south into impassable mountains. As they'd scouted out the route for Jaritta's horde, Ellechandran had told him of a way through that land, not a path of any real kind, but a way to keep from either edge. It required him to stay alert and watch for certain ridges and low rock formations. Weaving between the landmarks, he made for the very southern edge of the lava fields.

The mountains loomed in over the route as the days passed. The air grew warm and thick with the geyser outflow—not as bad smelling as the Pashun fields, but thicker with something like ash that fell and coated Pavresh's hair and clothes. It fit the arcist theme of desolation, of ancient ruin and emptiness. A place unfit for humans.

When he was beyond any guidance from Ellechandran's recollections, he simply did his best to stay away from both fire and ice, the lava and the mountains. A narrowing band of stable ground gave him little choice except to hope that he hadn't already missed some turning point behind him.

Little food grew in that land. He carried enough to last him for a long journey, but he hated to deplete it so soon. He scrounged what he could and limited his rations as much as he dared, a balancing act that was never completely second nature no matter how much time he spent traveling.

At last he came to a place where he had no choice, where the rugged mountains came right to the edge of the lava fields. And there, just as he'd been told, a gap between higher peaks promised a route into the mountains.

Before he pressed on, Pavresh climbed to where he could see the lava fields spreading outward. Ash obscured much of the fields to the west, but the air straight across was mostly clear. Romnai's buildings were visible, dark gray against the landscape. Directly around it were the green fields where much of the city's food grew, a bright expanse of color taking full advantage of the growing season. Beyond that, the melt caused by the lava fields and the sun's rays gave way to the white of ice and snow that covered everything in sight, even at this time of year.

How long since he'd visited those streets? And who remained from his time there? The stories he heard made it seem a far more violent place than he recalled, full of the danger of powerful princes and mysterious factions. There should be an arcist image for this moment. What would fit? It wasn't exactly nostalgia, or not merely that. The thoughts of the past, woven with all the choices he'd made since walking away. It wasn't regret he felt, but seemed like a cousin to that feeling, one he had no word for.

He would remember that mixture of emotions, add it to the themes he could draw from for his magic.

A vent opened between him and the city. The steam didn't completely block the view of the city, but it grew hazy and dreamlike, shimmering in the changing heat of the air between them.

Turning his pony's head, he moved on between the ridges into the southern mountains.

***

The mumbler villages Pavresh encountered in the southern mountains were small but otherwise little different from any others he'd ever found. The pale-skinned people within blurred into his memories of countless other mumblers he'd met in his travels. Each village had at least one member who spoke the trade pidgin.

Pavresh classified the stories he heard by how they fit with all the stories he'd collected from his travels. Twice he heard a variation on the tale he called "The Danger of Dark Caves," in which a hero or heroine falls prey to an unnamed monster. In one village, the heroine managed to kill the monster and escape on her own. In the other village, the hero was trapped for four hundred years, only to find, when another hero entered, that he himself had become the new monster of the cave.

That was a noteworthy variation. He let it play in his mind many times as he traveled onward.

He also heard the Dima story once, the tale he'd once thought as coming from the Forgotten South—of a seamstress who refused to use her magic for the king. Here it was a woman who made carvings of the gods. Interesting that, as gods of any sort rarely showed up in the mumbler tales.

Three different wolf tales, each following a different pattern, a foundling who becomes a chief, a family lost in the mountains. Each was different in some ways from tales he'd heard elsewhere, but each fit with so many of the folk tales he'd heard throughout the mumbler villages.

When he wasn't learning folk tales, he learned and shared what news and stories of the area he could. One key detail caught his attention in their news. A bigger village lay to the south, a tribe that kept to itself. They would trade, but only rarely and always by visiting the smaller villages, not by letting others come to their home. And in appearance they…well, that part was unclear, but they were somehow different from the mumbler tribes around them.

Was it a real village, or no more than another folk tale? The lost village, the mysterious city with healing pools of heated water. It certainly fit an arcist theme, but that didn't mean it was *only* myth.

So he continued, further into the southern mountains even as the snow grew deeper and the passes more trying, more difficult even to find.

His stores grew scant. He chewed pine sap to distract himself from his hunger, dug open pinecones in hopes of finding the tiny nuts within, with little success. These pines had tough cones, and even when he found one he could open that hadn't already released its seeds, the nuts were small and far from filling. He climbed a ridge only to find an impassable mountain beyond it, descended and pressed on at another slope, another ridge. The summer sun let him spend long days searching, but no matter how long the light lasted, there were always roadblocks and new detours.

Eventually there was no going further. The snow too deep, the cliffs too steep, the peaks too high. Pavresh found himself turned back yet again. He descended back to where he thought he'd been, but the high valley looked different, cut off from where he'd been by a sheer ravine.

He paced the rim, hoping for a way across, and found a narrow game trail that swung away into a gap in the mountains. Mountain goat hoofprints led him, made him worry that he'd end up at some steep rock face where only a goat could go. The padded paw prints of some hunting cat did little to reassure him. Instead, the path widened and dropped down into a pocket of evergreens. Every few steps he took revealed that expanse of trees to be wider and more hidden than he'd thought.

Soon he saw bootprints beside the animal tracks. And human-built walls became visible between the tree trunks.

For days he'd spared little thought for the magic. Or rather, few thoughts for the magic glamor he could wear like the furs that kept him warm. He'd thought often of the themes and images of his magic but he hadn't needed any magic himself. Now he reached for it, pulled the trader image down around himself by second nature. The wanderer. The traveler. The welcome guest. The pang of using the magic wrongly was still there, tugging at him, but it was distant. He kept his spells subtle to stave off the feeling.

He stopped and quickly arranged his pack with the traditional trader signal, the willow branches laid atop his bag. Then he came a few dozen steps closer until he found a tree with its lower branches gone, apart from the bigger stand of pines, and sat down against the trunk.

And waited.

How would these mumblers be different? They would speak/trade, certainly. At least, the stories he'd heard implied as much. Perhaps they would style their hair differently, somehow, though he might never know that unless he was invited inside a building. Maybe their skin and hair would both be the color of snow, to better blend in. He imagined an extreme version of the mumblers' pale skin, a step farther into true white instead of the lightness of the other villages.

Odd. As soon as he pictured their pale skin—the key distinguishing feature of mumblers in every story he'd heard since childhood—he realized that in the villages he'd come through recently, their skin was not as pale. Not the deep brown of his own skin of course, but still not as light as he was used to. Perhaps that created the difference they'd spoken of. If these villagers had extra light skin to blend into the snow while the mumblers nearby had skin not quite as pale as many of their tribes, then the difference might be striking to them.

Or could there be something even more extreme, some coloring or body shape that he'd never imagined? Pavresh had seen many animals in his travels. The difference between one type of deer and another was great. Between the heavily furred hunting cats of the mountains and the sleek felines that lived in the shadows beside the Eghsal River, between maned wolves and tamed dogs. Each was far greater than the difference between mumblers and his own people.

Who could say if there might be people far more different? Shorter or taller, with longer legs, fur-like hair, a strange build. The longer he waited for a trader from the village to recognize him, the more he imagined the possibilities. People with spots or striped skin. A people whose bodies were suited for the healing pools he'd come to find, with fins or gills or the sparkle of fish scales. Something truly strange might come visit him at any moment.

He sat up straight when he noticed movement among the trees. The three people who walked out looked entirely normal, though their heavy furs made it impossible to see more.

Pavresh prepared to speak the traditional pidgin words, requesting a trade. Before he could speak, one figure pulled her hood back from her face.

From her brown face, with the fine features of a high-caste kortru. The pidgin words fell away. Instead, he blurted out in the language of Eghsal, "What are you doing here, tisrah?"

Had she been abducted as a child and raised here? It happened in stories often enough to be an arcist theme. The Lost Princess or perhaps something along the lines of The Foundling. How had she come here? What did she think of life among these hidden mumblers?

Did it fall to him to rescue her? That was an arcist theme, too.

But she cocked her head in confusion at his words, and the other two pulled back their hoods from their faces as well.

All three had brown skin the color of a soft leather cloak.

While his tongue stumbled over what to say next, in the language of Eghsal, the woman said in the trade pidgin, "Are you here to trade/speak?"

No hint of an Eghsal accent to the words.

"I…yes. I am a trader/speaker. I wish to trade/speak for your stories."

"Come, then," the woman said. "It is cold, and we do not…" some word that Pavresh didn't know, "the same as other villages. We will trade in the shelter of the woods."

Or *of the buildings*? The way she said it almost seemed to elide the two distinct words into one.

"I would be honored." He struggled to put himself into the habits of his story-trading persona. He had once spent his days collecting stories on the streets of Romnai. Drawing on that memory, he managed to reclaim his balance. "Please, lead the way."

The trees sheltered more buildings than Pavresh could count. The buildings themselves even incorporated the tree trunks into their structures so they could crowd close together without losing the protection of the branches above. Most buildings shared at least one wall with a neighboring house as well, though there was nothing uniform about their sizes. As far as he could see, there was no single main route or path through the village. The trail they came in on ended after passing a few buildings. They turned, went past a single building, and then turned again toward the center of the wooded grove.

There was no sign of any healing pool.

By then he was already struggling—again—with his persona. Every person he saw, several dozen or so, could have been a citizen of Romnai or Jarnur or Pashun. They didn't all have an identical shade of brown to each other, but the variations were no different than those he might have seen among his own people growing up.

How could they have ended up here?

He tried to speak in the language of Eghsal. "Who are you people? What brought you so far into the mountains?"

His guides frowned without answering.

"Have you been here many years? Were you cast out of the cities?"

The woman leading the way shook her head and said in trade-pidgin, "We do not speak your language." Or, "We do not trade your trade," but that statement made no sense.

Pavresh strained his ears to hear the people talking within their houses, to hear what they spoke to each other when they met on the path. Would he hear the words of Romnai, be able to pretend he was back among his own people?

The snippets were hard to interpret. Might that be... No. Or that...

It was easy to convince himself that some sound or combination of words reminded him of his own language. But being honest, he knew he was only wanting to hear familiar rhythms. What he heard was not the words of the language of his people. Instead, it closely resembled the trade pidgin. Some words even sounded identical. *Visitor. Trade*, though that might be influenced by the pidgin itself rather than a native word. *Snow. Food.* The words weren't merely similar but exactly the same, though weaving in among them were other words he couldn't identify.

It was as if they spoke the language the trade pidgin came from.

After a few more turns, Pavresh's guides brought him inside an enclosed room that looked like neither house nor shop. One of the men held out a dish of food. Pavresh scooped a small amount onto a wedge of dark bread and ate without looking too closely at the unfamiliar texture. It tasted nutty, a roasted mash of things he couldn't identify. Dried berries perhaps? Nothing he'd ever eaten among his own people or the many distinct mumbler tribes and villages.

Something other than travel rations, though. He longed to gobble more, but to do so would not have been polite.

"I, I trade in stories, in news of the villages around you and news from farther off." And I desperately want to know your story, he wanted to add, but he couldn't rush the order of things without offending them. Though if they weren't true mumblers, did they follow the patterns of shame and honor that carried through all the other tribes?

Best to proceed as if they did. He settled into his role, and they responded as mumblers in other villages did, offering him shelter and food and sharing their stories.

Even so, he pushed his questions sooner than he otherwise might have, trying to learn the history of the village.

All he could pull from them were myths that didn't fit any of the ideas he'd formed.

"The gods formed us from the ice of the mountain peaks," the trader/speaker said. "As they did for all people, so our stories say. Or at least all the tribes who live nearby. Then they sent the eagles to carry us, one mother and one father, each to our own places. An evil giant owned these trees and didn't want to let us in. The eagle who carried our mother and father was a trickster eagle who disguised their skin so they could blend in with the pine bark. They scared him when they came out from between the trees, and he fled."

Nothing of a recent arrival from the cities he knew. The disguising showed they knew their skin coloring was different, but what did that even mean for their history? No hint of a caste or even the idea that they were all one jati once, as Rashul had once suggested for the history of the people of the cities of Eghsal. And if they were from so long ago that they'd forgotten those parts, shouldn't they at least tell of fire and nagas, not ice and eagles?

He found himself slipping into his own language far more often than he usually did among mumblers. Once in a while these people recognized an Eghsal word if he happened to speak it, or at least seemed aware that it was a language of his people in Eghsal Valley. They were not so isolated that they knew nothing of his home. But it wasn't the words he would expect to be preserved, and usually they only recognized it as foreign, with no idea what it meant.

They must have separated from his people and come here long, long ago. If more settlers had arrived from the Forgotten South than he'd always assumed, a small group might have split off. Maybe they tried to find a land way through the mountains to return home and ended up here. And as the years passed, they could have taken myths from the surrounding mumblers.

Maybe.

He listened to their other stories over the following days. A Dima tale which, in a rare twist, had her attack the chieftain and become chief herself. Tales of mountain spirits. Of gods who resembled neither the pantheonic deities of the Valley nor the disembodied Fire of the splinter Enshi religion, which was Pavresh's own. These were gods of the heights, of snow and storms and avalanche.

One god seemed vaguely familiar. The name was different, and within the pantheonic religion, it was the goddess Aoso who filled the role rather than a god. But their god of the dawn was a strange figure whose stories overlapped with hers more than seemed likely if it were merely a chance filling of the same arcist niche. What that meant and why no others struck him as familiar, he couldn't answer.

The language he heard when no one spoke to him in the trade pidgin—there was never a real hint of any connection to the language of Eghsal Valley. It seemed far closer to the pidgin itself than even most mumbler languages. They might even have been the source of that language as he'd first wondered, though if so, then both it and their own had meandered apart in the years since its spread.

But how could that possibly be, if as a people they resembled his own so closely?

Applying an arcist theme, they were the Lost Cousins, but only at the surface. Nothing in their language or stories matched that theme. Instead, they were the source, the Old Ones, as much a part of the mumbler past as any tribe he'd ever encountered.

There was no resolving those two opposite images.

As if arcist magic itself was in error.

***

There was no healing pool in the village. The best his guide could suggest was that their word for the type of pines that defined their village sounded like the word for a steam-warmed pool. Or maybe the healing pools were somewhere else entirely, in some village he'd passed by, along some route he'd missed.

Even so, he did find something healing in being beneath those pines, in spending time wrapped in furs and sitting beneath their snow-weighted boughs.

After some six days among them, Pavresh noticed a low table in the shadowed corner of the room where he always met to trade/speak with the three people. Those three were not elders exactly—too young for that—but they were the voices of the village when it came to trade. These houses, all that he'd had a chance to enter, were lit by a few candles and nothing more, leaving the edges of the rooms in full darkness.

He approached the table, feeling something was familiar about it.

A sloping wall led down to lines in the middle of the table. A *kiwan* board. The game of strategy and skill that the people of Eghsal, especially the high caste kortru jatis, played religiously.

His breath caught in his throat.

Was this the connection he'd looked for? *Kiwan* was no mumbler game, after all. It came from the Forgotten South. It defined them as a people in many ways.

And here it was, the proof that this dark-skinned village of mumblers were descended from Pavresh's ancestors, that they were the Lost Cousins after all.

He struggled to keep his voice calm as he spoke over his shoulder. "You play *kiwan*." There was no word for *kiwan* in the trade pidgin, so he left it untranslated.

His guide sauntered over and picked up a bag of *kiwan* stones. "Yes, this game. We try, but we are not very good."

Not good? Had he misunderstood some phrasing and she merely meant that *she* wasn't good at it?

"Is it an old game?" he asked. "An old part of your village?"

"This, old?" She held up a handful of stones and let them spill through her fingers back into the bag as she laughed. "No, we don't usually play such games. It was a visitor, one of your people. He lived here for several years and tried to teach us, but he left last spring. Only my brother was able to really learn."

Her brother? Was that someone he'd met? But even more critical, a visitor? Pavresh groped his way to a stool and sat down heavily. He picked up the other bag of *kiwan* stones and ran his hand through them. They fell between his fingers with a familiar, smooth weight. His mind ran through the thought of someone else traveling here. Who, how, when? He'd never seen other people of Eghsal willing to meet—and live with!—the mumblers. The brother might know more.

"Where is your brother? I would enjoy a game of *kiwan*."

"Hmm, I'm sorry. He would have enjoyed meeting you, too. He learned to speak your valley language quite well from our visitor, and no doubt he would have liked to practice speaking with you."

"Is he…did something bad happen to him?"

"Bad, no. Sad for us, but not bad. He left with the visitor. Last spring, when Ekana left, he chose to join him in visiting your cities."

Ekana. Pavresh couldn't catch his breath. Could it be the same? He had fled into the mountains after his masters' plot had failed. The man who'd betrayed Chaitan, who'd worked with the princes to manipulate Jaritta's coup. A name to haunt him. The *kiwan* stones spilled out of Pavresh's hands onto the floor.

Chapter 16

The sacred sequences carried Indima from the central circle of the temple, out to one of the twelve shrines that lined the building, and then back to the middle. It made little difference whether she was back in the familiar temple of the Silk City or here, visiting the temples of Pashun as a special guest. The sequences were the same, each movement done in honor of the Fire and the gods.

She danced alone.

The shrine to Tiespetre, father of the gods, was filled with a massive fire table, which held burning coal. A priest lifted a coal out and set it into the clay censer that Indima held. The husks inside ignited, and incense rose from the flared top of the censer.

Indima swung it in a careful arc, drawing a line of smoky incense through the shrine. The smoke dissipated quickly from sight, but the smell lingered as she moved around the fire table.

Back out in the central circle, the grids on the floor guided her footsteps. She lifted her censer and let it swing down or out as the dance demanded. Bracelets jangled against her wrists with each movement.

It was not *her* dancing. Only her body, her arms, her hips, her feet. Not herself, not her fire.

Was that sacrilege?

So what if it was. She would never speak the words aloud to any priest. As for the gods divining her secret, what attention had they ever spared for her?

As she danced across from shrine to shrine, never in a direct line and never two shrines side by side, she exchanged her censer for others. Each god or goddess worshiped here had its own form of incense. Pleasant within its own shrine, but each one lingered with her as she took the next. The mixture grew cloying.

Ryo, the god of propriety and marriage laws. She cursed him inwardly as she danced. Take his rules back to the Forgotten South. They didn't need such things here. Indima let none of her thoughts influence the calm beauty of her dancing. Grace and honor carried through each movement.

Then she was on to Kwona, the rebellious goddess, ruler of wild horses, who had taken many a lover of her own over the years, without bowing to Ryo's rules. Here was a deity she could honor. Except the goddess seemed to have no power to extend her ways to her worshipers. What was a goddess for, if her worshipers couldn't follow in her footsteps?

As for that, Indima's own footsteps were light and sweeping as she switched Ryo's incense for Kwona's. Not rebellious.

Rebelliousness was a childish thing, after all, a part of her past. She set even those emotions aside and immersed herself in the sacred dance.

For all she might incline toward Kwona's stories, she wouldn't ever join with those who claimed themselves her children. She'd observed their gatherings from a distance in the Silk City and wanted nothing to do with them. They were as rigid and backward-looking as any other faction these days, no matter what their patroness might stand for. Might as well conform to Ryo's strictures as submit to such a group.

She moved to Saeldagtre's shrine, which was shaped like the chariot the goddess used to transport the sun. Alas that it could not carry Indima away as well. Then on to the twins, who were both confusingly named Tiessen. One was supposed to be a dancer, and if she were as devout as she made herself appear she might be able to identify which one. To her they looked the same, and their stories blended into one. After, she came to Paxu's shrine, where a corded jug held a vast quantity of wine. Another form of escape, but not one she chose. For now.

A cluster of priests gathered to watch her. They'd arranged for her to come after hearing reports of her dancing in the Silk City temple, arranged for her to spend some time in Pashun, despite the unrest and dangers in the lower part of the city. She would dance in the two temples that stood behind the protective wall cutting the city in two, dances that would culminate in some great festival. Which god or goddess was this one to? She couldn't keep track, couldn't care, though she'd have to at least know on the day so she could perform the correct dance.

It was originally to be a simple twelve-day span of time, and she would leave after the festival. It would give her father a reprieve from worrying about her dancing so he could focus on the new fabrics he was developing. But she'd arrived with her entourage to find the city in chaos. Representatives from the princes had intercepted them and guided them safely to the upper reaches of the city. Most of the priests were cut off in a corner of the city, leaving only this small group to keep the upper temples open. Now, with plans changing often, she didn't know how long she would end up dancing here.

But Indima didn't bother with that. It didn't matter. So little mattered these days. She could dance here as well as anywhere. Behind walls or in the wilds. Let the slings fly overhead, and she would ignore it all.

The common worshipers watched as well, coming to pray but staying to take in the sacred dance of a silk-clad, otherworldly waif. She could imagine their thoughts: to them the distance in her face was a sign of the gods; surely she moved with their sacred presence, borne by their fire, enraptured in worship of their mysterious transcendence.

If only they knew that *distance* meant *emptiness*.

***

Because the temples in the upper part of the city were cut off from their seminary below, Indima ended up instead in an inn of sorts that stood among the princely manors. Anyone needing a room in that neighborhood before the unrest would have come with their own entourage of servants and attendants, so it hardly seemed like an inn. It was fancy and riddled with extra rooms, which filled quickly with the Silk City priests and many servants attending them all. The building stood high above the mudpots and geysers, with a cold wind blowing up behind it.

She insisted on a room at the rear, where the cold crept in whatever cracks it could find. It found few, as the place was well built and staffed by cheetah jati servants who made sure every fireplace was always burning.

The priests had their own jati of soldiers to guard her as she returned from her dancing, and the silk weavers had sent along a squad of their soldiers as well, some of whom were among the servants who accompanied her. Indima let them walk around her but never acknowledged their presence. Let them think her still so focused on the gods that she had no thoughts for anything else.

She watched her surroundings. Beneath her seeming indifference, she did her best to stay alert to everything there was to see. What would Rashul have made of this city, as stuck in the rigid castes as Romnai had been, if not more so? It would have incensed him, just as Romnai did, inspired him to gather revolutionaries around himself. What would Pavresh have said and what tales might he have told, pulling from the patterns of life in that city? Even now she didn't fully grasp arcist magic, but she supposed he might make something of the steep hillside and the ways people arranged their lives to fit it. He might have woven those stories into her dancing.

Oh, the dancing.

What would Ekana have thought? She couldn't suppress the memories once she started thinking about her time in Romnai. The lover she could almost convince herself she'd forgotten, whose face blurred into forgetfulness. But not his touch, not the way he danced opposite her in Chaitan's house. She recalled the mingling of arcist magic with artful music and the perfectly matched grace of a pair of dancing masters.

Maybe it was only the thoughts of Ekana, who'd grown up a fisherman in Jarnur, but suddenly she thought she heard that seaside accent calling from the streets below the wall. She veered that way, and after a moment's stumble, her honor guard swung around and continued to pace her. They made no attempt to ask her what she was doing or why.

At the wall she looked down on a gathered crowd. Soldiers stood around the square, their attention on the wall above them. They were not the soldiers protecting the princes. She found herself wanting to dance for them instead. Better yet, for the people in the crowd who weren't soldiers of any jati. It was a mix of castes and jatis—wallas and merchants, laborers who would have looked at home in the mines. Were these the miner rebels who terrified the princes so? They surely didn't look like a terrible threat. It was almost as if life went on in that neighborhood below, just as it always had, and the removal of the kortru upper caste made no real difference.

Nothing about the young man who commanded such attention was familiar. His thin, dark face could have been at home in any of the cities of Eghsal Valley, his dark hair shaggy but no more than many men wore their own hair, especially when the disruptions of life made something as simple as a haircut into a rare event. The hints of the Jarnur accent faded as she listened more closely. Why had she thought that, anyway? Perhaps it was merely imagination.

He spoke to the crowd, but she had no doubt he pitched

his voice to carry up to the soldiers and people on the wall above.

"I am no threat to anyone. No part of any faction. Not a prince and not a miner," he said. He *did* have an accent of some kind, but nothing Indima could place. "I can lead us forward, but first I want you to know me, to understand why what I say is different. How the wisdom of my homeland can guide us to a better way."

A better way. That made her think of Rashul. Indima leaned out to be sure she caught his words.

"This time I will speak of the mountain passes. Not all the way through. Some stories I must save to another day." He smiled and winked at his audience as he spoke. A showman, nothing more.

Indima turned away in disappointment. She already knew her share of people who spoke nonsense about things they didn't believe themselves. For a moment she'd thought she heard echoes of bigger dreams, of Rashul's ideals and Chaitan's fierce rebelliousness. But this? A weaker tisane that failed to satisfy.

"The passes require a dancer's movements," the man continued, and Indima paused to hear more. Skeptical but curious. "As I shuffled around one bend in the trail, the wind blew me into the rock face. But wind is a trickster, we say in the South. The...Forgotten South, as you call it. The Remembered South let us call it now. I knew it would reverse itself, snatch me away again. That I would fall. So I moved into a dance pattern called Crows in Snow."

Indima caught her breath. It was a real dance, though only a tame variation of it existed within the sacred canon. And he was actually performing a portion of it down below on his stage as he spoke. Only a trained dancer should know even that much.

"Stepping just so, I tricked the wind itself. It whistled

against me but did not throw me off the mountain. Then I performed the Fire Dance of Paxu and made it off the height, away from wind and danger."

The Fire Dance she knew as well, a wild dance of abandonment. In fact, it formed a brief part of the dance she had made that morning, as she moved from Paxu's wine-laden shrine toward the shrine of Brilith, goddess of the sea. Most curious, that a stranger, some wanderer from…was he really from the Forgotten South? How could that be? But if so, for him to know those dances…

Only as she neared her inn did it occur to her that Crows in Snow was always a two-person dance. He'd performed a tiny portion that worked alone, but it wouldn't have served him any good on a mountain pass, not without a partner. Whom had he danced with, as he traveled among those mountains? It wasn't a romantic dance really, but the steps required two people, ducking around each other, leaning together and balancing each other as they leaned apart.

And as she thought it through, she could see how those combinations might help a pair of travelers to stay safe on a narrow mountain path, buffeted by the wind. Two dancers could adapt the steps and holds and make it through.

Two, though. From his stories he made it sound as if he'd come to Pashun alone. There was more to this stranger, more than he was telling his adoring audiences.

***

When her attendants had left and she had feigned sleep long enough, Indima left her room and made her way back to the wall. There was a way through the wall, something most people wouldn't notice, but her dancers' feet found the route. Over a culvert, along a narrow pipe, and down into a dark dead-end. It was not a soldier-friendly path, nothing that would be an easy weak spot for either side, but for her it was a simple way to cross through.

Once below the princes' wall, she made her way to a house she'd seen from above. Nothing specific marked the house as different, not in a way that stood out to others. She found it as she'd found Chaitan's so many years earlier: a whisper here, a hint, a rumor. People like this were cautious about allowing high caste strangers inside. She gave the correct responses and waited quietly until she was ushered through the front room and into a room that might have been called a ballroom in a fancier house. The tensions that turned the city into a war zone simply dissipated, like fog when the summer sun rises.

The memories of Chaitan's bustling house made for a poor comparison. This was a minor imitation of what had been so perfect and authentic. But then such was life, always a poor comparison to memories.

Music was playing. Indima had to twist her head to find the two musicians in the corner of the room. One played a short-stringed gourd instrument with a curiously shaped neck; the other also had a stringed instrument, but it lay across her lap. Their melody was usually lost in the noise of the others in the room, drinking and smoking a variety of substances.

None of that mattered to Indima. She ignored them all and went to the center of the ballroom. People moved aside without her needing to acknowledge them.

The dance moves had all the beauty and grace of the temple-sanctioned dances, but Indima turned them on their head. She added hand movements that would have been scandalous and joined up passes that would be sacrilegious in the temple. Here they were neither for nor against the gods in the pantheon. The dance was unconnected to anything but herself, an expression of herself, of the things she was thinking and the things inside her that she didn't even know she was thinking. An outpouring of the fire, and whether that was deeply religious or completely antithetical to the priests and their rules, she didn't really care.

The dancing lacked an arcist to give it depth and edge, so she made do by adjusting her movements, some wider and some clipped, so they might carry a touch of that magic. Her bracelets gave the dance a counter beat that never completely matched the musicians' playing.

She danced of Jarnur, of fishing boats and the river's mouth, though she'd never seen either herself.

She danced a version of the Crows in Snow, adapting it for a single person. The solo version would have done nothing to protect her from wind and snow and fatal drop-offs, but it was beautiful in its solitary grace.

She danced of Silk City, of being sealed within, cut off, denied a part of herself. Danced of suitors rejected, and of finding a way to dance in the temple that didn't completely kill the part of her that wanted this other form of dancing as well. Danced of loneliness, cramped in and crowded.

As one song ended and another began, some of those there tried to applaud. She shrugged them off and kept dancing. At another break, a man approached her. "You're amazing. I love to watch you dance."

She said nothing.

"I mean it. I could just watch you all night. Do you always dance alone?"

It might have been a salacious comment from someone else. Indima didn't think this man meant anything but what he said. Either way, she saw no need to answer.

"You see, I'm a dancer, too. Would you show me some of your ways of dancing? I realize you want to just dance now, but sometime. Would you take a partner ever?"

She spun around twice then met his eyes only briefly. "No, I don't. Not anymore."

Then away again and lost in the movement of her body.

Maybe the priests were wrong. It wasn't fire that gave birth to the world, but dancing. If you cut the world down into its smallest parts, you'd find those parts dancing, always moving in their patterns that encompassed every step and pass of the sacred dances and every other dance move as well. Fire was a key part of the wonder of the cosmos, but even it only took its power and energy from the dance of the smallest of flames.

When the short night was nearly gone, the sun already rising before any honest folk dreamed of waking, she left with only a nod of her head to those people she passed.

Some knew who she was, no doubt, that she was the very dancer the priests had invited as a special guest, sneaking down into their neighborhood. But how would they tell that she'd been dancing at the secret ballroom without implicating themselves in the room's other activities? At the least it would make their reports suspect and easy for Indima to dismiss.

In her room she slept, and encouraging the image of herself as a temperamental artist who must be catered to, she refused any intrusion on her sleep until the morning was gone away and the sun already past its noon height.

***

The festival arrived. It celebrated the cattle goddess Gouwind. Whereas her sister Kwona, goddess of horses, was infamous for her affairs and all around wildness, Gouwind was revered as the faithful wife, the one who kept the house whole.

Indima preferred Kwona.

She was here to dance, though, not to care about her own preferences. There were new soldiers in the city, new talk about taking control of the rest of the city. They would want the blessing of the gods, which meant the blessing of Indima's dancing. The festival would end at one of the temples, at Gouwind's shrine. Indima began her dance several streets away, at the city's main government building, a towering structure hung with ivy.

She began in a circle, arms tight to her side as if it wasn't her at all that mattered but the circle her feet made in the cobbles of the square. The circle was usually the symbol of Little Fire, an odd goddess who had no real name like the rest of the pantheon. Little Fire was goddess of the hearth, and on days like this she seemed to become subsumed into the identity of Gouwind. The dance, then, began with her, evoking the well-tended home and the comforts of a cooking fireplace that were also a part of Gouwind's remit.

As she opened up the circle, winding outward, she brought in other parts of Gouwind's mythology, dancing the patterns that had been passed down for centuries.

There was no real creativity in sacred dancing, none of the open discovery that she relished in her clandestine dancing. Yet she was a celebrated dancer, not for how she interpreted each deity but for how entirely she submitted to the movements, when she chose to; for how smoothly she moved from form into form, without creativity, without inserting herself into the dance in any way.

She moved outward along the streets between the city building and the temple—not the temple she'd danced at before, but the dance knew no difference. The shrines might vary, but the movements would be the same. The steps took her to one side of the street, nearly brushing the brick wall. Then she swept across, avoiding a wind-blown bit of trash without changing her stride. Soldiers or priests or someone cleared the way for her so no passerby might interfere. The street constrained her movements, but even then the dance itself adapted to the close buildings and brief disruptions.

It was her ability to separate from herself that let her dance so well, she decided. Sacred dance meant leaving all thought behind, becoming something that wasn't herself. Call it gods or the fire or simply the cosmos that rose from them, it was not her who danced along through the street.

In front of the temple her dancing opened wide again. She circled, though it was no longer Little Fire's plain circle that had begun the dance. She spun and twirled and moved her arms. The bracelets on her wrists sparkled as if aflame.

One flame seemed to burn her eyes, and she stumbled. She, who never missed a step, tripped, was it possible? It wasn't as if she fell flat on her face. Likely no one watching her had any idea that she'd lost her balance for a moment.

Or almost no one.

"Indima!" Her name came as a gasp from someone's lips. Someone standing right where she'd distantly moved her gaze before she stumbled. Someone was moving there, pulling an edge of a cloak up over the side of his face, turning away from the temple. Heading, it seemed, for the same dancer's path she had taken in the night.

No way to identify him.

She kept moving, graceful and flawless, but her movement lacked the elegant distance it had earlier. Who could that have been? The stranger who claimed to come from the South? That didn't fit, not with her own reaction, not with the involuntary crying out of her name. Whoever it was had gone away, and no peering into the crowd told her more.

She danced on, taking her easy grace into the temple, through the center and to the shrine of Gouwind. But now it was her, entirely her, trying to fake the easy distance and absence of her usual sacred dancing.

Her name. Whoever it was, he'd known her name.

CHAPTER 17

Prince Jasfer's burns healed enough for him to walk around normally, enough for him to ignore the pain as the new skin stretched and pulled across the scars. He still took large doses of medicine to dull the pain and could only hope it wasn't dulling his thoughts too much as well.

He could travel, at least, at last. All the news from watching Rashul showed him likely to be leaving soon…soon, but not yet.

When another day came with no indication that he was close to departing, Jasfer spoke with Datri over the breakfast table.

"How wise is it to stay in Romnai? We court suspicions and rumors every day I stay here and do nothing."

Datri, chewing a piece of sweet melon, nodded. When she could speak, she said, "No, you're right. We need to get you away from here for a while. You still think you can manage to go to Pashun? I'll send Sashyu with you."

The spy who'd shown up the other day? Not the most trustworthy person, despite Datri's couched reassurances. "I thought she would be going to the Silk City. Unless you've come up with some other reason to have her in Pashun. Either way, I'll want Yatim with me. For protection and for appearances. He can choose a few other servants to help keep me safe." Yatim had been his primary personal attendant for years, and anyone who had looked into Jasfer's rule would know that fact.

"No, you're right again. I should send her to visit my parents, not with you. Just a few household servants then, or are you thinking of something bigger?"

No, he needed something more dramatic, something to

proclaim his importance, no matter what his sister did to undermine him. "I'll lead an army, the rest of the soldiers of the wild ox jati." He scanned the table but had no appetite for what was there. The meat, too spicy, the fruits likely to upset his stomach. He swallowed a spoonful of a cool soup made of mashed up gourds and bland herbs. Then he added, "No invitations or awkward speeches, but we'll still keep the pomp as we head out, in Baram's name, to save Pashun.

"Eat," Datri said. "We'll find our way through this, but not if you starve first."

Starve. What would it take to starve Jaritta's little city thing into failure? Certainly more likely to work than the outright attack some of the other jatis and even princes would be pushing for. Jasfer ate—without thought for what exactly he was eating—and began to lay out the plans.

***

As a prince, he traveled to Pashun in comfort, such as traveling with an army made that possible. Which meant not very comfortable at all. Every jolt of the train made his burns flare as if they hadn't even begun to heal. So he spent the journey, both by train and carriage, largely unaware because of the large doses of medicine. Yatim and a pair of lesser household servants tended to him in the midst of the army on the move.

The earlier soldiers, accompanied by Mahendri, had cleared the route to the princes' new road, driving the miners and other rebels back to their own corners of the city. They kept a large presence, riding the trains and patrolling the trade road to keep it safe.

The wild ox jati sent an additional three hundred soldiers with him. That was the rest of their fighters in Romnai, so most of the members of the jati who did not fight traveled with them as well. Jasfer knew they were a crowd, but he paid no attention to the effect their passing had on the train workers, the inns, the animals that claimed those empty lands. He gave himself up to his medicine and left such concerns to others.

As they approached the city, he had them ease off the drugs so he could be alert when they arrived. The new trade road was even rougher than the other had been. He gritted his teeth and watched the icy countryside pass by. The sounds of their soldiers filled the rocky shadows and echoed off the snow fields.

The rest of their jati met them outside the city, gathered in a growing camp of sturdy tents and large outdoor fires in the empty, rugged land above the steep city streets.

Mahendri welcomed them to the army camp.

"Are you ready to take this city for me, Mahendri?"

Mahendri offered Jasfer a deep bow. "We have begun to set out plans, tisrah. It will be good to add more soldiers to those plans. I have been sure of our success, ever since hearing word that you were on your way."

Standing made Jasfer dizzy. He put a hand down on the side of the carriage to prop himself straight. A subtle motion, or so he tried to make it. But before Yatim could step in to support Jasfer, Mahendri said, "Before anything else, let me see you to your rooms. Get yourself settled, and we can address plans after that."

Jasfer nodded his thanks, and they rode in the carriage into the city proper and up to one of the finest of the buildings.

The manors of Pashun had great walls of windows facing the lava fields. The glass was thick enough to distort the view, as if the thickness of the windows would protect the residents from the foul air. And perhaps it did. Smaller windows, open to the cold air from the east, kept the insides fresh, but never fully warm.

Mahendri led Jasfer to one of the finest mansions, the mansion of the mayor himself, a Prince Hrisha. He welcomed Jasfer with due respect, and guided him personally up to the rooms prepared for him. Jasfer slept until late in the day.

When he finally felt refreshed enough to leave his rooms, Jasfer wore a rich—and heavy—coat to keep himself warm as he descended from his east-facing bedroom to meet with his hosts. A crowd of non-ruling princes had gathered in the south-facing solarium. The sun shone in weakly as it bounded along above the southern peaks.

"What is Romnai doing about the untouchables?" someone asked.

Before Jasfer could say anything, another blurted, "We need soldiers. Is your army big enough to put down the rebels?"

Other princes then tried to add their voices to the din. Jasfer held up his hands until they were quiet. "I do not think we should be discussing specifics here. I came with soldiers, but they are not a full army to themselves. We will need to work through the details with the leaders of your own soldier jati. But Romnai is aware of the situation outside your city as well. I am here, in part, to decide what to do about the untouchables."

Of all times for his sister to cause such problems. He kept the grimace off his face and went through the motions with these princes as long as his energy allowed. Soon—probably sooner than he should have—he begged his leave and headed back to his rooms for a light meal and bed.

***

At Jasfer's insistence, Hrisha took him on a tour of the wall the following day. Mahendri joined them.

In the center of the city, the wall towered over the streets. Jasfer looked down on rubble where buildings had once been.

No miners and their rebellious supporters would be able to advance on the princes from that direction. There was a lot of city below them, though, much more than Jasfer had expected to see.

"The miners control all that much of the city? How did you let it get so out of control, Lord Mayor?"

The words were deliberately blunt to gauge Hrisha's character.

The mayor took the question in stride. "The miners were only one piece of it. They rose up, and while we were trying to respond to them, various groups of malcontents in the city each managed to subvert a jati of soldiers and set up their own fiefdoms around the city."

Smaller fiefdoms. That should make it easier to reconquer the city. "Then let's start with the smallest of those, pick them off one by one."

"We lose the protection of our wall once we move below it," Hrisha said. "We'll need to be strategic about where we advance and how quickly we can build on that progress."

Did the mayor think he could claim the influence for himself with a little complaint like that? Jasfer kept his voice even in responding. "Naturally. But what good is a wall if you just hide behind it? Eventually it traps us inside."

On the surface, both of them spoke mildly, but there was definitely a competitive undercurrent, one Mahendri must have picked up on, because he swept in with a reassuring voice, saying, "I believe I have the perfect jati to attack first, tisrae. I've studied the layout of the forces, and on the southern flank there is a small neighborhood, tucked in close to the wall. They have set their forces to defend from the other neighborhoods rather than from us. A quick, decisive battle there may be just what our soldiers need. And once we control those streets, they should be easily defensible with our soldiers."

A good warmup. Jasfer nodded. "I like the idea. Show me the place."

The wall wasn't as impressive along its entire length as it had been in the center of the city. In places it was no more than the original wall of a building, its windows and doors sealed shut. "This looks harder to defend," Jasfer said at one place where the alley between two buildings had been filled with debris to create a sort of wall. "There must be a danger of people crossing. Smuggling? Enemy soldiers getting through?"

"We haven't seen anything here," Hrisha said. "But we know it's a danger and keep a closer watch on this section. We have found some smuggling on the north side of the city. The wall runs into some older features there, waterways and sewers and angled streets that are difficult to block entirely. It makes it more porous. We should look into conquering that area soon, if we want to be sure our protection will hold."

"Yes, show me a map when we return, so we can plan out the rest of our strategy."

The neighborhood to the south that Mahendri had chosen sat in the shadow of a larger segment of the wall. Jasfer didn't like the idea of giving up such a formidable protection. It increased their vulnerabilities, but apart from that, this section of the city looked like a good opening. The neighborhood was small and had its own natural defenses with the edge of the city to one side and a wider boulevard providing a clear boundary to defend.

Jasfer leaned out to see the line of that boulevard snaking around beneath them. "Who are they?"

Hrisha answered, "Servants. Not cheetah jati, so they felt disrespected. But I think it was more that they feared the other jatis would try to make them their servants. Instead, they allied with some soldiers and held this little area."

Servants. Maybe he could offer them something to

willingly ally with the princes. He would have to consider that. "Very good. Mahendri, I'll leave it to you to plan with the army leaders when to stage the attack and how. But I want a show of forces, something impressive up here on the wall. And I want to address the people below personally."

It took some days to get everything into place, but when it was, it matched exactly what Jasfer had planned. All morning, soldiers filed into positions along the wall, rank after rank arranged to look like even more soldiers than it was. Jasfer watched from a comfortable seat behind the wall.

At midday, Jasfer—strengthened by his medicine—made his way up to a position in the center of the soldiers where he could see down into the neighborhood. A speaking horn awaited him, fixed to the edge. No one waited below—not visibly—but he was certain many people were watching with fear. Within the neighborhood and probably as far as they were visible into the one beside it, in fact. They would hang on every word he spoke.

"I am Prince Jasfer Talai, of the Ruling Thirty." His voice thundered through the horn to fill the streets below. "We are here to restore peace to this city. You have rebelled, but we are benevolent. You reacted out of fear, but we come with an offer of forgiveness. An improvement in your positions, for your assistance."

Hrisha stiffened beside him but knew enough not to interrupt.

"Think on that. You will rise in status as a jati, you and your children given greater honor than you had. But it is an offer that only lasts until we open the gates to come through. There is no forgiveness for those who resist our army."

The door beneath him began to creak open. He let the noise echo through the city for a moment and then said, "There will be no time to debate your answer. Welcome us or fall."

The soldiers' boots were made to echo loudly as they marched into the neighborhood. The servants and soldiers of the neighborhood threw down their weapons before a single bullet was slung or arrow released.

"They'll be disappointed not to have a chance to fight," Hrisha said as the neighborhood fell so easily. "Maybe we should have allowed them at least a skirmish before letting those rebels off."

"They will have plenty of fighting soon enough, I wager," Jasfer said. To Mahendri he added, "Put half of the conquered soldier jati along the new border, and twice as many of our soldiers. Let them know they are free to use their slings and bows to attack anyone across the line but not to cross it themselves without orders."

Mahendri left to speak with the army leaders, which now included the wild ox jati they'd brought from Romnai, the Vainath jati that served the princes here, and the new, smaller jati of conquered soldiers. He'd been a liaison to the soldier jatis even before he'd gone to Romnai, so Jasfer trusted he could figure out how to balance the different groups. It seemed to be a particular skill of the man.

"Lord Mayor." Jasfer held out his hand, inviting him to lead the way. "Now that we know how well this has worked, I would like to see that map of the city you have. Let's plan our next steps together."

****

There were three choices on how to proceed.

They could use the opening they'd created on the southern side to cut down and meet up with the priests in their seminary. Hrisha pressed for that option, and there was some sense in it. That side of the city gave access to the mines, so it was an important place to control. The priests were trapped in their sprawling complex, without even any soldiers to protect them, only their ranks of cheetah jati servants. Yet no one dared attack, and clearly they would side with the princes once set free. What they lacked in fighting forces, they could make up for with their voices, encouraging people to give up their rebellion and submit to the princes.

Jasfer hated the thought of having to rely on the priests.

The second choice was to move right into the biggest section of the city. The bulk of the miners had taken over a large swath of buildings in the middle, and they were supported by one of the bigger local soldier jatis, the Anguch. It was the biggest gamble, but Jasfer had brought the soldiers to do what they needed. If they could take down the insurrectionists quickly, any remaining opposition along the edges would crumble. No one would expect to stand against an army that had taken down the strongest faction.

Or they could take the neighborhood on the northern edge of the city. It was where the wall was already weakest, and once taken, it would be easy to defend from the miners because of a water spillway that made one east-west boundary. It might also open the city back up to the normal trade road, though the intelligence of what was happening farther downslope beside the carters' road was scant. They were the neighborhood with pieces of train cars and other goods stolen by raiders. Whether that was because they'd been the raiders or had simply been the logical destination for the parts, no one could say.

There was something strange about that neighborhood's leader.

"He truly claims to be from the Forgotten South?"

"So he says," Hrisha said. "We hadn't heard of him before the miners' revolt. But he showed up in the middle of it, speaking with a strange accent and telling wild tales. His own people seem to believe him, anyway."

It was the safest route to reconquering the city, but Jasfer kept studying the map. "On the southern side, we would have to cut through the miners and the Anguch, right?"

Hrisha nodded and pointed at a small section of the city. "They control a bit right here, mainly where the routes from the mines come in. I suspect they would fall back quickly, once we're above them. They wouldn't have the best defenses there."

"How did that group get so powerful, though? I guess since they control so much of the city, and they control so much because they're powerful. It feeds into itself, in some ways.'

"The miners had the emotions, and they allied with the strongest of the soldier jatis, apart from our Vainath." Hrisha dipped his head toward the corner of the table where the Vainath commander sat. "But they also got that cult on their side."

"Cult?"

"The Sons of Ryo. We still don't know the full connection there. Some of our people wonder if they prodded the miners to rebel in the first place. Some think that the miners would have risen up anyway, and the Sons of Ryo rushed to join in. But they took advantage, anyway, and took over…"

Hrisha's answer droned on, but Jasfer felt his mind float away, into memory, into the pain of the fire scars on his legs. The Sons of Ryo. He hated them, hated the destruction they left in their wake. They had to be the first to fall. To be crushed utterly.

When Hrisha paused, Jasfer said, "We have the numbers. I want to get some forces in the mountains near the mines. Not to attack anyone yet, but to get a sense of the area."

"We do have some small units out that way, and others we've sent to keep any eye on the untouchables across the steam fields," Mahendri said. "We can reach out, call some of them closer if we need to, and get the information from them."

Jaritta's city. Jasfer hid a wince. Addressing that folly would have to come later. "I want more than information," Jasfer said. "I want a presence. I want the miners to know we're there, to think we might try to cut them off there or take the mines back without them."

"Which wouldn't be a bad route to reconquer that southern edge." Hrisha traced his hand toward the neighborhoods near the seminary.

Jasfer held up a single finger to stop him. "Not exactly what I had in mind yet. We'll give them a few days to get in place and be seen. Actually, make it a twelve-day at least. Our line below the wall seems secure, as long as we have the numbers to watch it. Meanwhile, mass the rest of our soldiers beside the wall. Place a good number of them at the northern edge, enough to make it look like that's where we'll go next."

How would the person from the Forgotten South react to that? Someone who grew up so far away might be more difficult to predict. His plan relied on that neighborhood not becoming an aggressor.

"But keep the bulk of the army ready to send through the center and crush the Sons of Ryo. In the meantime, Mahendri, send a message to the Prince of the Forgotten South that I would like to meet him. A public message, such that even the rest of the city will know it's happening."

If Hrisha or Mahendri or any of the others wished to argue, they kept silent. The power in the room, the authority and influence, it all went to Jasfer. He claimed it, made it clear in the pitch of his voice and the way he held his body. His years as a ruling prince were worth something, at least.

"Then while everyone is waiting for the outcome of my meeting with that man, our soldiers will catch the Sons of Ryo by surprise and end this before anyone can even blink."

Jasfer rose. "I'll leave it to you to figure out how to make that part of the plan work." Then he left and sought out his rooms, his next dose of medication, and the darkness of a quiet room so he could sleep.

CHAPTER 18

The attack came just after dark. By this time of the summer, that meant late, but not so long after people had gone to sleep. The nightly air currents reversed direction, carrying a stink from the lava beds but also warm air to make sleeping pleasant. If only they were allowed to sleep. The timing was much as Jaritta had expected, but that didn't make it any less heart-stopping to see them coming in toward the new camp, to hear the cries of her soldiers fighting and calling for help.

Soldiers, had she named them such? They belonged to no soldier jati. Her *defenders*, anyway. Not born to fight, but choosing to, while the born soldiers battered their way closer so they could destroy Jaritta and the dream city she was building. She ran toward the cries, little as she might do to help.

Her people had done their job creating the camp's defenses. She watched from behind a rock wall with Poorma beside her.

The attackers came in an organized mass, a hammer stroke to smash through their little camp at a single blow. They came from the most obvious direction, probably certain they could brush these interlopers away without difficulty.

Her soldiers needed to pull back, let the attackers get higher so their defenses could work. She clenched her fists and breathed, "Now, drop back."

Poorma put her hand on Jaritta's back. It didn't make her relax. Thamiba should be calling them back. Why were they still fighting so low on the slope?

Even as she thought it, she heard a brief horn blast, and the fighters tried to disengage. The soldiers pressed them, not letting them get any space to breathe, much less withdraw.

The whole mass—retreating and attacking—scrambled up the steep slope. Jaritta loosened the knife at her side. If it came to fighting, she wouldn't be much help. But she'd rather die fighting than be captured and carted off to Romnai.

As soon as the front line crossed a certain point, Jaritta hissed, "Now!" Another horn blast sounded, as if created by her voice. The defenders who weren't fighting hauled on some ropes, bringing up a wall of sharpened stakes. Rather than rising high into a wall, the stakes came to rest pointing outward at chest height.

The leading soldiers continued on as if their comrades were still behind them. The line of stakes didn't quite stretch the full width of the attacking column, so some soldiers managed to pour around the sides, especially those who'd been farther back. But it disrupted their charge thoroughly.

She leaned her cheek against the cool rock and watched for movement from the side. There, a flash of something among the shadows that became an advancing mob.

The counterattack, led by Ellechandran, came as a mixture of mumbler tactics and mob violence. For all Jaritta knew, maybe that was how the mumblers fought regardless. She wished she could be with them. His wife Chhayasheela was among them, as well as some other mumbler women. They swarmed the isolated soldiers and struck the sides of the column as soldiers stumbled around the wall of stakes.

The sounds of the fighting echoed off the rocks, the harsh grating noise of blades on leather, the cries and groans of the wounded. They lasted only a short time before a trumpet blast cut through all other sound.

Retreat.

Jaritta's heart raced as the soldiers stumbled back past the dead and the wall of stakes. Was it over already? Merely the first wave of an attack that would last all night? She couldn't guess, but she knew for certain that in the bigger picture this was only the first of many attempts to come.

Climbing down from her position, she called out, "Well done." Her voice caught. She took a deep breath to steady herself. "Let's get some people who know about healing in here." Groans and calls for help. It twisted her stomach, but she let them subside. "And put the stakes back down. Probably won't be effective a second time, but worth keeping it there in case." She had to draw on all her childhood training in the princely jati to keep her voice from cracking.

The defenders had taken three soldiers captive. That could prove very useful in bringing about peace. She had to hope, at least. If the cities of her people ever gave her the chance to make her argument, to stake her claim.

The jati soldiers didn't attack again that night. Eight of her own people died.

Eight who'd made the journey. Only eight, and yet... Eight who'd survived all the struggle of the cold desert, who'd come so far and begun to believe in the city she was founding. Dead.

She wanted to lash out and burn down the city, whichever city these soldiers had come from. Or else stamp out the entire jati they belonged to, let them be only a memory of what happened to those who fought against her vision.

But she couldn't do that. If the cities ever reached a point where they might sit down and come to an agreement, she'd have to forget about those deaths, pretend they were just a part of what founding a new city meant.

Her fingers clenched and squeezed into fists. Until that time came, she could let herself imagine snuffing her enemies out. Let the images of vengeance push her to shape her people into the city they would have to become.

***

Jaritta wrote a letter to be copied and sent to the princes and soldier jatis of Pashun and Romnai. In it, she made her claim for the unoccupied land west of Pashun. Driyya helped her establish the exact location in the detailed language of a scribe, but she put in the flourishes of a prince-born high-caste.

Then the letter shifted into accusation. Still couched in a patina of politeness, but she attacked the decision to send soldiers against her. Betrayed, outraged, she let the anger bleed through in the words. Even then she had to bite back a portion of the pain she felt at the eight who were killed. Likely there would be many more before they were truly safe.

From there she circled back again to their claim on the site of their new city.

"This land belongs to us now. We are not a threat to the other cities. We lay no claim to the productive citizens of Pashun or any other place. If we are permitted to establish ourselves in peace, then we will not raid your mines for workers. We will not lure soldiers away to form our own jati, our own army.

"But we will exist. We will be permitted to govern ourselves in—"

Jaritta tapped the nib of her pen against the field table. "We need a name for our city. How have we not set that up already? Thamiba, you're better at those kinds of decisions."

"A name." Thamiba walked across the tent floor and peered over her shoulder as if she hadn't already been reading the entire note aloud as she wrote. "A name is good. I say we name it for Chaitan."

"Are you crazy?" Jaritta spun on her stool to face Thamiba directly. "Name it for Chaitan?"

"Sounds like a good idea to me," Tanjali added. "Chaitanshehar has a good sound."

Jaritta didn't respond to her, only held Thamiba firmly with her gaze. "We're trying to tamp down their worries. I can't think of a single name we could choose that wouldn't aggravate them more."

"I could."

"What? Whose name?"

Oh, to wipe off that knowing, mocking smile from Thamiba's face.

Rather than answering directly, he said, "You're going to be signing the letter, aren't you?"

"Of course. And you will, and Driyya. All us leaders of…of the city." She had to get used to calling it a city if she wanted others to see it that way. "We'll all sign it."

"A letter signed by someone famous for an attempted coup. You don't think they'll have forgotten your name, do you?"

No, of course not. She waved the argument away. "I'm not naming it after myself. Is that what you were saying?"

Thamiba laughed as if she'd guessed his suggestion. "Not really. But I'm just saying that having your name on the letter is provocation enough. Naming the city after Chaitan doesn't add to that at all. We could try to hide your presence here, not have you sign it, but I have no doubt they'll already know. So we bank on the name, stake our claim boldly."

Jaritta looked down at the letter she'd been writing, the beautiful, high-caste script, the bold words. Yes, she wanted it to be audacious, inspiring. And if she could honor Chaitan with it as well…

"Chaitanshehar it is. You're right. It will send the right message to the right people, even if it makes others afraid."

***

Before sending out the letter, they decided they needed to make the miner threat real. While Azheeran and Thamiba oversaw strengthening their perimeter, Jaritta went with a band of her people to a nearby mine, eight of them including herself. She passed on the message that she was accompanying the group by messenger as she was leaving, so they wouldn't have a chance to argue she would be needed in the city. Driyya could handle whatever came up, even defend the city again if it came to that, though so far the soldiers had held off on a second attack. This shouldn't be a dangerous task, any more than scouting out rivers and swampland had been. At least that was how she defended her decision.

The mines were around the lava fields from the newly named Chaitanshehar. Pavresh had told her enough about how his father's mine was run that she had an idea of what to expect. Empty land until they came close. Roads and noise, but few people.

The noise part was accurate. The heavy sounds of newfangled steam engines sounded through the pines more than a day before she expected to come close. She had heard those sounds in Romnai from the steamships, and sometimes a ship would pass by the ruins. But what were they using them for out here, she wasn't sure. Pumping the mines free of water or pulling ore up out of the depths, she supposed.

The lack of people he'd suggested…that didn't prove true at all.

Chhayasheela, familiar with the slopes and foothills to the south of here, led the band. She spoke the mumbler languages and let others do the translating, leaving Jaritta to only guess at the events had driven her away from her own village. Jaritta imagined a history of terror, of a band of Pashun soldiers who destroyed her village, or a monster from childhood tales rising up from a cave beneath their camp. But that didn't really fit how Chhayasheela acted. There was no deep fear, only a resigned sense of returning to something sad or shameful. Chhayasheela slowed them down when they began to hear the noises. With several other mumblers as guides, they crept through the wooded slopes of the southern mountains.

They'd only gone a short way when Chhayasheela gestured for everyone to freeze. They dropped to the ground, as their guides had trained them. Paramyan, a mumbler who could speak Jaritta's language, slithered over, pulling himself with his elbows to Jaritta.

"Lots of people in the woods here."

"Miners? We shouldn't be that close yet. Or do you think they're some kind of soldiers, out here guarding the mines?"

"Soldiers, yes." He shrugged. "Guarding the mines or watching them, it looks like. Maybe doing something else, I don't know."

Something else. Like preparing to attack Chaitanshehar? Maybe they should look for weaponry to sabotage while they were here.

"I guess we should try to find a way around. Let Chhayasheela know. They can't have a full perimeter, not this far out."

Words to haunt her. Chhayasheela found them no route that was both far enough from soldiers and still offered cover for them to move ahead.

"It isn't just a single camp of soldiers," Paramyan explained after returning exhausted from yet another scouting mission. "A clump here, a clump there. They don't always even seem aware of each other. They complain about the woods, the camps, the cold. But someone's sent them to be here."

She had to send them back then, before they could attack her city. But how?

"Can we trick one group of soldiers to fight another?"

Paramyan consulted with Chhayaseheela before answering. "Can try. Probably put us at a lot of risk too, though."

Worth it if it could protect the city. As he described the layouts of some of the camps, though, the doubts grew. She was responsible for the city as a whole, but she was responsible for this band of scouts too. They hadn't agreed to come just to be sacrificed for something that only *might* help the city.

"Hold off on that, then." She studied the sticks and pine needles he and Chhayasheela had used to describe the soldier camps. "I don't think we should. Unless you see a way we could do it without too much risk to ourselves."

He was silent.

"There do seem to be some gaps between camps where we might sneak through, don't you think?" She pointed at a few places where the soldiers looked to be farther apart.

"At night, I might make it through. Chhayasheela and I probably could." He paused to say something to her in their shared language, and she gave a very small nod. "But the whole band? No, I don't think we'd escape notice."

"Then take the letters with you. Get as close as you safely can, and leave them where some miners might find them."

Jaritta stayed with the other five from their party while the two mumbler scouts set out that night. They had a good hollow among the pines where they could keep their camp and be pretty sure they wouldn't be found. The rest of the band spent most of the time on lookout to be sure, rotating around the camp and the several hidden posts they established between them and the groups of soldiers.

Jaritta spent most of her time doing her best to map out the soldiers' camps—as the mumblers had described them to her—onto paper. Then she wrote some letters, so that each camp would know where the others were located.

"Did you know there are other soldier jatis stationed near you? Why are they there? Are they preparing to attack you?" After those lines, she set about trying to lay out where each group was, relative to the others. Likely it wouldn't be a surprise to some of them. Their scouts couldn't be so unaware of their surroundings. But it might set some soldiers on edge, make it harder for them to trust each other.

Just in case some authority in Pashun recruited several jatis to work together against Jaritta's city.

Even better if the different soldiers represented rival factions within Pashun. If they could focus on whatever arguments they had with each other, it might keep them away from Chaitanshehar long enough for them to truly establish themselves.

Paramyan came back during the second night since he left. He had someone with him, but it wasn't Chhayasheela.

"This is Bripin. He will join our city."

He looked strong and healthy, though he shied from the shaded light of their little campfire.

"Welcome." Jaritta wished she looked more like a prince than a common hunter. "Our city welcomes everyone willing to be a real part of the city's future. Thank you for joining us."

As he mumbled his thanks, she asked Paramyan, "And Chhayasheela? She isn't…" There would be many deaths and injuries, but she didn't want another one now. She held her breath.

"Took a different way back. We decided she could drop off letters outside some of the other mines and then make her way back higher up in the mountains."

Just going off on her own, without an order to do so. A part of Jaritta wanted to explode at the man for letting her do so without any effort to consult with the others. Was Jaritta in charge of this band, like a prince, or a part of it, like she had been in the ruins of Eghsal City? It came to her that how she reacted to this change in plans had implications for much more, back in the new city. About the level of power she and the others wielded, about the expectations for their people. Strict obedience? Or would they allow their people to make other choices, if they thought it would be right for the city? What would the other leaders say?

The report would come back, not just an official report, but the stories told by the others.

After swallowing the lump in her throat, Jaritta said, "Well done. She's a capable scout and knows these lands. I hope she made the right choice to help us all. Now rest a few hours, both of you. We should be on our way back home before sunrise." Home. The word had almost tripped her tongue as she said it. But maybe it could become home, in time.

***

Daylight came. Jaritta and the band of scouts made their way back to Chaitanshehar. It should be a calm time of day, a safe moment to move quickly to their destination. She pressed them to hurry, anxious to see how the city, her city, was doing. A movement out of the corner of her eye made her stop.

"What's wrong?" Paramyan asked.

"There was something over that way. Someone, I think. Movement, anyway. You notice anything strange?"

Paramyan stood very still and listened. "No…" He drew out the word as if he was still considering. "It *is* very quiet. Not many birds, but I wouldn't necessarily expect to hear a lot from them. Some squirrels moving around. They always sound loud for such a little animal."

He made no move to continue, though, so Jaritta waited.

Before he could say anything else, a shout sounded across the rocky terrain from the direction of the city. A battle cry. The sound of swords.

Paramyan's eyes grew wide. Hers probably as well, but she recovered and gestured upslope. "The ridge," she mouthed more than actually saying. She led the way.

Climbing up, they came to a ridge that blocked them. The natural route would be to go around, away from the city and come down from higher up the mountainside. The base of the ridge led into an impassable clutter of boulders then back to the main climb where the fighting seemed to be. Either route would bring them to the city's guards, who might not recognize them until too late.

But Jaritta had grown up exploring the hallways of the old manors in Romnai and later, cast out, she became adept at finding routes over the roofs and through the alleys of the city. There was another way up the face of the ridge that would lead them inside the city, such as it was, without running into the fighting. "Stay close," she said over her shoulder, and Paramyan passed it along to those behind him.

She had to jump into a shadowy recess to get onto the narrow path. Then they edged along, hidden at times by trees but often only by shadows and the shape of the ridge. A slow journey and tense. At last, they came out behind the fighting, just as the attackers appeared to be pulling back. A retreat? Had they been defeated? Or was it merely to find a new angle to attack?

Jaritta wanted to throw herself into the fight, though she was no fighter. Instead, she sent her band, including the miner who'd joined them, to refresh themselves, and she sought out Thamiba.

Poorma was bandaging a wound on his side. The sight of her, once a death jati worker, tending to him gave Jaritta a start, but he spoke, his voice tinged with laughter, before she could even say anything. "You're back, good. The fighting here's been so trivial even our death jati is stuck tending scratches." He winced as she tightened the bandage.

When she looked at Poorma, a question in her eyes, Poorma shrugged. "Nothing bad. Him or anyone. They're sacrificing their soldiers for nothing."

Likely not for nothing. No soldier commander would be that callous. "So what's the story, then?"

Thamiba stood up. "Thanks, Poorma. That'll be fine."

When he started walking, Jaritta fell in step with him toward the defense line. "It's Romnai soldiers, the ones the arcist sent running away, I think. They've been attacking now and then. Nothing serious. Poorma's right, they have sacrificed some soldiers, but probably not as many as it seems to us. And they have more to lose, I suppose, than our little city."

At least they had one new person, the miner Bripin. He looked like a man who might fight hard if put to it.

"They're just testing, though. Sending up a few at a time to learn the routes, to see where our defenses are. They'll probably keep doing it for a while before they decide to send a full-scale attack."

And by then, they'd know exactly where to send that bigger force. Meanwhile her own defenders would have been kept too busy to establish the city in the meantime. She looked across the haphazard scattering of shelters thrown up in the space they were calling a city. Walls of stone, half finished. Tents made of furs and branches, the brown pine needles still attached. Cave mouths leading into the darkness. "We have to stop them somehow, or we'll never get the city built."

Jaritta sent out a message that same day to meet with the commander of the soldiers. He accepted her request surprisingly fast, riding out at sunset before the city's defenses with only a single attendant. So much for the summons itself being a good delaying tactic, as she'd half dared to hope. Jaritta and Thamiba rode out to meet with him. Poorma and Tanjali rode behind as if their attendants. At the meeting site, the two death jati women dismounted, but Jaritta and Thamiba stayed on their horses.

"This is the city of Chaitanshehar," Jaritta announced as soon as they stopped. "We claim this land as our own. By what right and under whose orders do you attack us?"

It would have been better to have Pavresh with them, to

use his magic to convince them to leave. Instead, it fell to her to try to mold the world to fit her hopes.

"I do not treat with traitors and outcasts." He turned deliberately away from her and addressed Thamiba. "By order of the princes of Romnai, you are to leave this site."

Before Jaritta could give the coldly high-caste response his words deserved, Thamiba laughed.

"You don't treat with outcasts? Then why are you talking to me? Or any of us. We are all outcasts of one kind or another. Yet we still claim this place as our own. So cast yourself away from here."

The commander looked from one to the other as if they made him sick. Then addressing the air above them, he said, "Then I command you all to vacate the region. This place is under the jurisdiction of Pashun, under the protection of the Thirty Ruling princes and the soldiers they send to secure it. You are outcasts and untouchables and not worth the effort to resolve this peacefully. Anyone still here by the end of a twelve-day will be presumed a criminal and punished, up to death."

At these words, Poorma threw off her warm cloak to reveal the death worker clothes beneath. "Did you summon us?"

Tanjali stood beside her in matching black rags. She stretched out a finger, and the commander shrank back. The death workers were an anomaly in the valley, a jati, but untouchable. Everywhere, no matter the caste, they were feared, and soldiers were often more superstitious than most.

"Then in the sight of all your soldiers, I summon you." Poorma walked forward, her finger stretched out, Tanjali a silent, menacing shadow beside her.

Caught between not wanting to look the coward and not wanting to be touched, the commander stood his ground and only leaned farther away. The women continued forward, right up to him.

Touching him plainly in the middle of the forehead, Poorma said in a voice to carry across the rocky land before them, "You fear the untouchables? You are untouched by death. I claim you as mine, and all whom you command."

The distant soldiers murmured at the words, and Jaritta thought she heard a shield being thrown to the ground in fear.

The commander scrambled onto his horse, and he and his attendant rode quickly away.

Chapter 19

Pavresh left the mumbler village, his mind still awhirl. Was it really even a mumbler village? They didn't look like the mumblers he'd known before, even if their village *felt* like a mumbler one. Were they his own distant cousins, some group who'd left the others behind shortly after arriving from the Forgotten South? Yet not a single one of their stories referred to an ancient southern homeland.

The only stories they had in common with Pavresh's people were those they shared with other mumblers as well.

And then there was the presence of Ekana in the village. He'd spent more than two years there, had learned to speak their language, become friends with some of their younger members. And only left a few months before Pavresh arrived. He struggled to wrap his mind around that. What would have happened if they'd met in Pavresh's travels, if he'd come this way sooner?

They'd been friends once.

Then Ekana had fled, returning only to betray them all. How many had died for his actions? If Pavresh had met him, he might well have attacked. There was something of that story arc inside him—the one who finds revenge in the wilderness. It might have risen up at that moment. An ambush among the snowy peaks. Or a duel, fought face to face, with sword or sling or even bare hands. He could easily imagine that story, as he conformed to the archetype of a definitive judgment, vigilante justice.

But he could also see another story that might take over, the one of two enemies setting aside their differences in the wilderness. It could have played out that way as well, with him rescuing Ekana somehow or the two helping each other through difficult terrain. They might have struggled to accept each other, eventually coming to a grudging sort of acceptance. Perhaps even something like respect.

Which possibility would have happened? Only the sacred Fire of the cosmos could answer that question.

The terrain certainly was difficult. Pavresh had a vague thought of following in Ekana's footprints, trying to discover where he had gone. As he left the trees of that strange village behind, he felt their healing touch fade as well. The ache of misusing his magic still pulsed within. He still pondered the nature of arcist magic but determined to use it only sparingly when he met the people who lived in this remote land.

The first village he found, cold and weary from traveling, had no recollection of Ekana passing through. What they did have were more people who looked just like Pavresh himself, their dark skin such a contrast with the mumblers that Pavresh had to constantly remind himself to speak the trade pidgin.

When he left their village, they showed him a narrow path heading westward, told him they had never seen the sea but that the trail was called the Sea Path. If Ekana had wanted to return to his home in Jarnur, then he might have attempted such a trail.

The path kept low in the deepest parts of the valleys, sometimes even descending into deep canyons. He had to lead his pony through the snow along frozen streams for long stretches to get through from one valley to the next. There were no side trails leading south. The mountains crowded in close to each other, the passes between them so high he doubted anyone could climb to them. From here the Forgotten South was utterly inaccessible, as he'd always been told. The hints of paths to the north looked unreliable as well, leaving this an isolated land.

When he eventuality came to another village, they were

again a darker skinned group and unused to visitors. Their trader/speaker struggled to make himself understood in the trade pidgin. Pavresh did his best to piece together the stories of their people. It all fit in with the recent villages, mumblers tales coming from Eghsal faces.

No one had seen any sign of Ekana, as far as he could learn.

The same interactions repeated themselves in a half dozen other villages and tribes he met as he made his way toward the sea. Despite the remoteness, he made good progress, slowed only by the brief time he spent in those few villages The series of high valleys were remote and cold, with more wild animals than people. The tribes—he could never decide whether to think of them as mumblers or not—lived off hunting deer, woodland wisents, and bear. Their stories were full of hunters and shapeshifting animals and the cold night sky.

No Forgotten South. No sacred fires. No journey by sea.

***

At the last, he needed a guide to bring him down through a terrifying trail that led to the sea. The closer he'd come to the end of that Sea Path, the more comfortable the villagers' traders/speakers seemed with the trade pidgin. Familiar sounds crept into the accents he heard. Finding a willing guide who could speak with him proved easier than he would have guessed.

In a village that clung to the edge of a sea-facing mountain like a strange bird nest, the pidgin trader was a woman named Kuliya. She seemed only a little older than he was but was in charge of trading not only for that village but for a few other tiny villages that clung to those cliffs as well. When Pavresh told her where he was trying to go, she said that she'd had plans to do some trading down near the coast. She agreed to accompany him through the narrow defile that was the only safe route and then down beside a fast-moving stream. He would have to leave his pony behind in the village as a gift to them. They gave him a gift of stories and as many traveling supplies as he wished to carry.

Not only did Kuliya speak the pidgin, but she had even picked up some of the Eghsal language, overhearing words here and there, even trading with some of the valley people. They must not have realized she was a mumbler, he decided, when the shock of hearing this wore off. They probably thought her a simple woman who spoke little, but made no connection to the dreaded mumblers they heard of in tales.

She helped Pavresh down a final drop, where they had to brace themselves against the sides of a narrow slot canyon, their feet brushing the white tips of the rushing stream's rapids. At the bottom, the stream ran out onto a rocky beach and into the saltwater.

Pavresh leaned his hands on his knees and breathed deeply. The smell of fish and salt filled each breath.

Kuliya smiled. "Good thing you had a mumbler to help you through that, huh?"

He nodded, unable to react at first to the Eghsal word *mumbler*. When he caught his breath, he blurted out, "But are you a mumbler, really?"

Kuliya cocked her head. "Of course. You saw our village. We are speaking/trading. What else could I be?"

"But your skin." He touched his own cheek. "It looks like mine. The other tribes farther inland, they look pale, like the snow has leached away their color. But not your village."

"Come, let's talk as we keep going."

Kuliya was silent as they made their way away from the stream. The shore was a ragged and wild land, no place to land a ship, no place to build a house. Finally, she said, "Being a mumbler has nothing to do with my skin color. It's about being a part of a tribe of people."

"Is that so different from being a part of a city, though? Or even a family? I came from a small family out away from the cities."

"But you *speak*." She used the Eghsal Valley word for speaking. "That marks you. Makes you a part of the power of the cities. Of the valley."

Pavresh had to focus on walking for a moment so he didn't twist an ankle. Once past the rough ground, he said, "So as you learn to *speak*, are you no longer a mumbler?"

"Only if I get accepted in your cities. If they extend me that power that comes from being a part of them, then sure. Then I'm a city-dweller, for as long as I choose to claim it for myself."

As if someone could switch back and forth? In all the stories he'd collected and catalogued over the years, the idea had never even occurred to him. What would it mean to be whichever one he wanted? Or to move back and forth without ever being an outsider in either setting?

But as he tried to imagine a mumbler becoming a part of the patterns in Romnai or any of the other cities, he ran into the question of skin color again.

"*You* might pass as a city dweller, but not all mumblers could, because they'd stand out with their pale skin."

Kuliya nodded. "True. Your cities set up the divisions they want to keep. *Speaking* won't overcome that. But don't blame the mumblers for that. It's a quirk of your people."

And one that might change? He added that question to the mix of stories he'd collected and arranged over the years. He imagined the cities becoming places where mumbler-shaded faces were as common as any other. It would be an idea that twisted and rearranged so much of what he'd thought he'd learned.

One that would take time to understand. For now, he asked, "And I? I'm speaking/trading with you, wandering alone through the mountains. Perhaps I've become more of a mumbler than you give me credit for."

Kuliya looked him over, a quirk of a smile on her lips. "You? No, you belong to no tribe of mumblers. But I think you belong to no tribe of your own people either. You're not a part of the people of the cities or the mountains or anywhere. A part of the land, alone."

No doubt true. He was the lone wanderer, a powerful arcist image, and one he often leaned into heavily when he approached a new village, when the magic didn't pain him. But he'd never considered that this one image was so overpowering that it cancelled out his own place among the people of Eghsal Valley. Did he truly belong nowhere?

He let the question play out among the stories and images of his magic the rest of their journey. Kuliya left him a few hours before reaching Jarnur so she could trade with an isolated group of pale-skinned mumblers in a cove south of the city. Pavresh entered Jarnur alone.

***

No one had seen Ekana in Jarnur. Pavresh looked for those who had known him as a child but learned nothing. A woman he was told was Ekana's mother simply cursed him until he left. At the fishing boats, people were kind...until he mentioned Ekana's name. No, no one knew him, no one who would admit to it. *Now leave.* It was never worded quite so bluntly, but that was the message up and down the wharf.

The Enshi religion, at best tolerated in the rest of the valley, was prominent here, so Pavresh sought out a holy site, a plaza on a cliff above the port where a flame was always kept burning. He touched the kusti around his waist, tracing the sacred knots. He'd tried to keep faithfully performing the kusti ritual, but he hadn't always done it as often as he knew he should.

Others of his faith were beside the flame, performing with their belts. He felt like an outsider, a lesser member of the religion. Someone who didn't belong, just like Kuliya had said. He'd never tried to become one with the fire with others right there beside him, not since he was a child. What if the passes he knew were wrong?

Worry and self-consciousness. They were the opposite of the religious practice of joining the fire. He'd have thought he was beyond such matters, but as soon as he identified it, he saw how those ideas played out within the arcist themes. He resisted the urge to make himself belong by using his magic, and unwound his belt. The fire didn't care if he was an outsider. Neither would he.

The flames were holy.

All flames were holy, but he felt it more here as he knotted and unknotted his kusti and moved through the ritual poses. Like the trees, the forms provided a sort of healing. Something in his connection to his arcist powers became freer, unclenched. The sun had set by the time he became aware of himself again. A few worshipers remained, themselves looking the same way he felt—dazed and still somewhat groggy with the fire's presence.

None of them looked at him as if he didn't belong.

He greeted them in the name of the fire, and one older couple invited him to stay at their home.

Pavresh had intended to ask these people if they knew anything of Ekana, but the reaction of the others made him pause. When the time seemed right, he asked more generally. "Have many travelers come through recently that you've seen? I'd been following rumors of a man who was visiting mumbler tribes."

"Troubled times," the man said. "Few people dare travel far these days."

His wife nodded. "Have you heard of the man who's come from the Forgotten South, though? They say he came to Pashun through the mountains."

More about those rumors. "I can't imagine there's any route there. Not in the mountains I visited."

"You visited them?" They looked at him with a touch of awe, and the woman continued, "So far from any fire. What do those lands tell you of the world?"

They were looking for a spiritual answer, not any of the truths he'd learned. The religious yearning was clear in their eyes. So he answered, "Many things, too many to retell. But this is one truth. Even where the flame is forgotten and the ashes have cooled to snow and stone, a traveler is part of the fire." That sounded vaguely insightful, but true as well to what he'd felt on his travels. Then he added, "And whether in the southern mountains or staying at home beside the river, we're all travelers in our own ways."

They nodded at the made-up wisdom. "Thank you," the man whispered, deeply moved.

Pavresh stayed with them that night, welcomed without the need of his magic, refreshed to reconnect with the ideas of his youth. But by morning he was ready to move on.

After that, he took to wandering through the city, learning stories, listening, never mentioning Ekana's name. He avoided the soldiers, who were widespread in certain parts of Jarnur, but spoke with anyone else who would talk to him. The people of Jarnur told tales of the sea. They told of sea creatures that swamped the fishing boats or haunted those who traveled too far out to sea.

Going too far was a big part of their stories, an underlying sense that danger lay beyond the unknown. A key arcist theme, but inland it was more tied with dangerous knowledge or sometimes with journeys too far into the mountains.

Here every arcist image was translated into the sea.

But the tales of the Forgotten South were unchanged. A distant land, a terrible voyage. He listened to the way people told the stories for any differences, but they told the same things he'd heard growing up, of the gods rescuing the hero Gauran and helping him lead the people northward to safety.

If it was so constant, did that mean there was truth to the stories? The mumblers who looked so much like the people from the Forgotten South might be a simple quirk of history. Or maybe they had come too, long ago and forgotten, while the valley people preserved the real memories.

Or did the constancy mean something else? Did it mean the stories were more recent, with little time to change? Rashul had always claimed that the ruling princes manipulated the history everyone accepted as true, making up the parts that helped them hold onto power. A made-up story, enforced by those in charge, might change less than a folk tale, which spread from teller to teller.

Who benefited from the common threads of those stories? The ones helped by the stories of the Forgotten South were those in the cities—not just the ruling princes, but all of them—against the supposedly primitive mumbler tribes all around. It gave them roots, a sense of history that was denied to the mumblers.

No, that wasn't quite right. The mumblers had their own history. The roots denied them were entirely in the minds of the city dwellers, a willful ignorance.

These musings he also added to the mixture of stories, not finding an answer but letting them all mix and blend with each other within the magic, within his mind.

After he'd been in Jarnur for a twelve-day, Pavresh happened by a tisane bar near the city's university. Students filled the chairs even out into the street, where umbrellas kept off most of the seaside mist.

Pavresh found a chair deep inside. He had to share the very

small table with a young man who didn't appear to fit with the students. Still young—younger than Pavresh—but older than the other students. Perhaps set apart in some other way as well, a different jati, a different focus in his studies. He called himself a scholar after Pavresh had introduced himself.

While he waited for his tisane to cool, Pavresh asked, "You say you're a scholar. What can you tell me about the people who came from the Forgotten South? I mean, not the stories, but what do we actually know?"

The young man, Tekhel, laughed. "Oh, no, not you too."

"What do you mean?"

The man took a deep drink from his tisane. "It's just what we've been trying to figure out for the last year. Looking for ships, looking for clues. It seems the more we discover, the less we know."

Pavresh leaned over the table. "Do you have ships? Anything you've found?"

"Some." Tekhel waved his hand as if it was nothing, but then his tone changed. "I mean, we did find some. And it was a very exciting find. No one thought we could or would. But who were they? It's only a few ships. Nowhere near enough to have carried everyone here from the Forgotten South. So now we're wandering around, looking for other clues to the rest of the ships and where they all ended up." He swung his empty gourd of tisane through the air to add some drama. "Under the river, maybe, and we'll never find them. So, I guess we're stuck with the site we found."

What stories could ancient ships tell him? What arcist themes might they reveal? "Could I see it, the site? I would love to find out whatever you've learned."

"Are you a scholar, then? I thought you said you were here from Romnai, looking for an old friend."

"A scholar, you could call me that. A scholar of stories, wherever I find them."

Tekhel shrugged. "We have stories, I suppose, but more questions than stories. Harkala's still there at the site, and I'm heading back in a few days. You may come with, if you can supply your own needs on the way."

Pavresh agreed and made the necessary plans. When Tekhel left the bar, he thought through what he'd said. Ships, but too few. A Forgotten South, maybe, but no real evidence for it. And meanwhile Pavresh knew of a people in the mountains who looked just like the people of Eghsal.

What if it was all lies? What if history itself had betrayed them all along, and there were no ancestors who sailed here, no difference between the valley people of Eghsal and the mumblers except for Kuliya's explanation of power and belonging? What if there was never a Forgotten South anywhere?

CHAPTER 20

The soldiers went through their drills outside the city where the wild ox jati had been camped since their arrival. Jasfer was no soldier, but he could read body language. The divisions between jatis were clear, the wild ox, the Vainath, and the other smaller ones they'd begun to bring in. They didn't work as one army but as hesitant allies. One unit nearly collided with another as they each marched and took their turns. Soon they would have to work together to fight the Anguch. What would happen then?

When he said as much to the others observing with him, Mahendri agreed. "It is always the nature of the jatis. Or any groups. We used to have fewer soldier jatis in Pashun, and they'd end up forming their own smaller groups within the jatis.

"Surely it will only get worse as we bring in other groups. What will we do with them as we conquer the city?" They couldn't blithely take those other soldiers back in as if they had nothing to do with the rebellions. But they couldn't very well throw them all in jail or set up a mass execution, not without creating the ground for future rebellions.

"Jail the leaders," Mahendri said without hesitation. "And give the other soldiers specific tasks to demonstrate their loyalty. It might start with patrolling the mines as they return to full operation, to make sure the miners aren't agitating again."

Maybe even work in the mines. They would have to execute many of the ringleaders of the miners and jail others, so there might be a need for workers.

Unless…

"We should send them out to the outcast city. Do we have soldiers out there already?"

"We haven't had the numbers to spare from here," Hrisha said. "It's possible Romnai sent a company of the wolf jati."

The soldiers drilling came together into a single formation and turned as one, giving a loud shout to mark the change. They looked united for a moment, as if in defiance of Jasfer's analysis. But after they'd moved through a few more exercises as one, they broke again into smaller groups to train.

When the noise and movement decreased enough to let them speak comfortably again, Mahendri said, "I don't know that we want to put the task of conquering the outcasts on soldiers we don't know we can trust."

"Not to conquer them," Jasfer said. "To monitor, disrupt them maybe." He thought about the barren land they'd passed through on the way, the flickering memories of what he'd seen through the haze of medications. "To keep them trapped while they starve themselves into failure." Let his sister's foolishness collapse on itself, and they might not need soldiers driving them away at all.

Many of the soldiers below switched from movement drills to sword practice, and the cacophony of their blows drowned out further discussion.

***

Jasfer gestured for his visitor to take a seat. Kamlash had lost weight since Jasfer had seen him at his cousin Samatrit's reinstatement celebration. He still had the same shrewd way of narrowing his eyes as before, a shifting look as he studied the room, the walls, briefly meeting Jasfer's gaze, and then away.

"Thank you, tisrah."

"How is my cousin? Are you here for something related to him?"

"Samatrit fares…well enough. The city is dangerous, and I think he is relieved not to be involved. At least after the attack on the princes when you were burned, tisrah." Kamlash leaned forward. "But that is not what I came to speak of. I came on matters of my own business."

He was a silk trader, if Jasfer recalled correctly. "Speak, then. What business do you wish to discuss?"

"We had spoken once of your interest in the silk trade. I have considered the matter and wonder if you would like to sell any portion of your mine holdings."

They had discussed such a thing, though on Jasfer's part it had been more curiosity to learn what he could about Samatrit's future than actual interest in selling his mines. Something about Kamlash's demeanor made him suspect his current interest was feigned as well.

"I've brought a map of some of the mines near here. I wonder if we might discuss them?"

Kamlash unrolled a paper with a number of mines marked. The Gaentsi mine was circled once. Another, the Kaladnagar, had a marking beside it. The Badayar and the Wampi were each circled twice.

There were other marks on the paper as well, and they didn't correspond to the mines or anything on the map itself. They were a coded message from Datri.

Jasfer licked his lips and looked carefully at Kamlash. He only shrugged and mouthed the word, "Samatrit."

A way of thanking Jasfer for sponsoring his cousin's return to society. Or more likely, Datri had some hold on the family that kept them loyal to Jasfer even now. "Thank you," he mouthed back. "I will remember." Then in a normal voice he said, "Let's see about these mines."

"*Watch out,*" Datri had written. Long practice let him read the code without extra thought, almost as if it were normal writing. "*I've heard disturbing rumors of the factions in Pashun.*

Some of the soldier jatis there are compromised by old allegiances. There is something in their past, in the events that led to them being split into so many smaller jatis, that is shrouded in mystery. I can't tell if the princes are involved in those matters, but I can tell that there is deep unrest and shifting loyalties among the princes of the city. Almost as if they might split into several different jatis, much as the soldiers did. If you can make contact with our liaison, you would do well to learn what she has uncovered."

No room for more on the map. He wished he could talk to Datri directly. "How recent is this…map? All relevant information included?"

"Very recent," Kamlash said. "At least, it was up to date when I left Romnai fifteen days ago."

Fifteen days. That was when Datri wrote it, then. By then they were already engaged in conquering the first neighborhood beneath the wall and making plans for the rest of the city. Too bad he couldn't have communicated directly. Would her warnings have changed the plans he'd given the armies?

Jasfer made a show of considering the business that was Kamlash's cover, discussing the mines and their value compared to the silk trade. Kamlash seemed genuinely interested in such a trade, even now, but for Jasfer it was a matter of going through the motions. It was a way to thank Kamlash and through him Samatrit for providing Datri with their own sort of support. Begrudging as it might be.

He left off with a promise to consider Kamlash's proposals.

***

A procession of soldiers led the way into the square where Prince Jasfer would meet the supposed traveler from the Forgotten South. They took up their positions along one side, wearing ceremonial uniforms but practical and seemingly well used swords at their sides.

What did it mean to have someone from the Forgotten South as leader? Did he come here with the magic of the naga? The blessing of some forgotten gods of the South? Or maybe he came from a city, caste, and jati not so different from their own.

A second line of soldiers entered, dressed in completely different uniforms. They headed along the other edge of the square, as if forming two completely distinct wings of the neighborhood's army.

As they took their positions around the lower edge of the square, Jasfer leaned over to the Lord Mayor Hrisha. "I don't understand why you have so many little jatis. We have a few, but nothing like this. Where do they all come from?"

"Ah." Hrisha gave a sheepish shrug. "That's simply a part of Pashun's history. We do seem to have a lot of splintered soldier jatis. And others, too. The merchants are split into so many we can never keep track. Even they can't entirely—they only know which jati is their nemesis and which is their ally. There must be some history there, competition or something. But I don't know what its origin is."

What would that mean once this was done? He'd made his plan with Mahendri for sending them to Chaitanshehar, but would that even work? "Are they so splintered that you can't get them to cooperate if you have to rely on them, though?"

"Oh no." Hrisha gave a knowing, superior chuckle. "We learn to handle them. That's what being a prince in Pashun is all about. Learning to manipulate this jati and that to get what we want."

So an all-out assault on Jaritta's city—if he granted their term for it—was still a possibility. But the different jatis might be useful in taking a more tactical approach. Set one to patrol the mountains above them for their penance, cut off both trade and hunting grounds. Set another jati to prove themselves by harassing the untouchables' guards, keep them from devoting their full populace to gathering food. And others as needed, searching out ways to prevent them from establishing their ideas for the city.

Give them a year, he'd have them dislodged from their location. As long as the princes here truly knew how to handle the various factions.

The traveler from the Forgotten South entered, walking faster than his strange clothing—a robe wrapped so tight it looked uncomfortable—really permitted. He tripped on an uneven paving stone, caught himself with surprising grace, and continued over to meet with Jasfer at a more stately pace.

He was younger than Jasfer had expected. In his twenties, maybe, but surely no older than that. Unless the people of the Forgotten South aged differently? His skin was a deep brown that caught the thin sunlight. Apart from his strange clothes, he might have blended in with any mid-caste group in the cities of Eghsal and would not seem completely out of place among the princes. It was more than his appearance, though. His mannerisms seemed young, awkward.

He stopped a few steps away, gave an awkward half bow, and then stood there as if waiting.

Jasfer waited as well. The longer the silence stretched out, and the more awkwardly, the more the power of the situation rested in Jasfer's hands.

Finally, a slight man who'd come in behind the traveler cleared his throat and announced, "Sembaari, a lord of Pashun, liege of the Madrur and the Gwalpi, and prince of the Forgotten South, greets you and thanks you for this chance to meet."

Sembaari dipped his head more naturally this time.

Jasfer responded, letting arrogance fill his words. "Prince Jasfer, ruler of this valley." It was a true confidence he felt but with casual superiority feigned over top of that. "With Lord

Hrisha, mayor. And other peers of this city. I think this will be a brief meeting. I hope you have come prepared to not waste our time."

Sembaari swallowed hard. "Of course not. I mean, of course I have prepared. Of course, I won't waste your time." His voice was halting, uncertain. He passed a hand over his eyes, and when he opened them again there was a focus there that hadn't been visible before, an intensity that made Jasfer lean forward.

"Sirs," he said. "Tisrae, I think is the word you use. I do not know your ways well yet. In the Forgotten South we are blunt and speak what we mean."

He spoke with an accent Jasfer had never heard before, a hint of Jarnur and stronger notes of other languages. Even so, it was an impressive command of a language he must have begun to learn within the last year or two.

"So, know this," Sembaari continued. "I am not your enemy. My enemies are and always have been the Sons of Ryo."

That was promising for his hopes to reconquer the city. It almost made him reconsider the plans he'd laid. A route through this man's fiefdom could give them another front to push into the neighborhood and root out the cultists and their allies.

The big question was where it left the man standing awkwardly before him. Imprisoned for treason or celebrated as a visitor from far off? Executed or allowed to go back to his own lands?

"All I insist on," Sembaari continued, "is fair treatment of these soldiers who have come to join me. They did not plan rebellion, only sought to protect their own from the rebels. They will be loyal to your rule, if you simply grant them your pardon."

Which was all good, except not for what Jasfer was

planning. Accept Sembaari's terms, and the Sons of Ryo would know they were next and prepare. The street-by-street fighting would be brutal. The numbers of soldiers at his disposal meant they would win in time. But he didn't like the casualties that would come with that.

Keeping his arrogant facade, he answered, "You insist? That is not how these things work." He had to make this a demand Sembaari couldn't accept. "You are not in position to insist on anything. We will accept your common soldiers, if they swear to serve us. Some will be mixed into new jatis, and the current jati leaders will be imprisoned until all can prove their loyalty."

"There will be no need to imprison—"

"We may need to execute some to discourage other rebels. And you as well. We will try you and determine your fate."

Sembaari shifted his stance, as if he might have to run to flee the square. "That is not... I am willing to return to my people, if it is necessary, but—"

"And perhaps we will determine that you may. Exile may serve the cause of justice. But until your trial, I promise nothing."

"No." Sembaari shook his head. "I can't agree to this, to your terms. We will return to our neighborhood and hope that you reconsider, with the hope of peace."

Jasfer made his face hard and answered, "It may be your survivors reconsidering their options." He dismissed the so-called prince from the Forgotten South with a casual swipe of his hand and made a show of ignoring the man's handful of soldiers as he left.

Word would reach the Sons of Ryo. He didn't know how, but he was sure that they would hear enough to believe he was preparing to attack that way.

***

Everything was in place for the attack to begin early in the morning, before the sun had risen above the mountains. Jasfer went to bed early to be able to watch the battle progress.

An urgent summons woke Jasfer from a deep sleep. He stumbled from his room, unsure of the time. One of Yatim's subordinates put a dressing robe around his shoulders and followed him down the stairs. A cold wind howled outside the open vent windows, and no light shown through from the east. No stars, even. Low clouds turned the sky a grayish brown at the very edge of black.

Hrisha waited for him downstairs, looking also recently awakened but much more alert than Jasfer felt. Others of the Pashun princes were there as well, some from the neighboring mansions and manors. Whatever was so urgent, it involved many people. Had something gone wrong with the soldiers? A change in the plans for reconquering the city?

Cheetah jati servants brought out newly brewed tisane to wake them up.

He began to drink it before he realized Yatim wasn't there.

"What is happening?" Jasfer tried to read the room for influence, but he was too tired to follow, even with so few people there. Someone was knocking at the door. "Is my manservant out there?"

Hrisha ignored the second question and said only, "News from Romnai. Grim news, I'm afraid. Please take a seat, everyone."

Yatim entered the room and dipped his head at the princes.

"This is not the place for servants." Before Jasfer could protest that Yatim had his full confidence, he added, "Even the highest ranking of servants."

"I understand, tisrae." To Jasfer he said, "I have an urgent letter from your wife, when you are able to receive it." Then he bowed his way out of the room.

Jasfer frowned. Why was Datri sending him a letter so urgent that it arrived in the middle of the night? He lifted his head to call Yatim back inside, but Hrisha cut him off with a chopping motion.

"We need to address this first." In his other hand, the one he hadn't chopped through the air a moment before, he held a paper. "There may be a new High Prince."

Jasfer burst from his low couch. "A coup? Who is making the attempt?"

His heart racing, he pictured the room in the High Assembly where a claimant could try to force himself to power. Jaritta had made the attempt six years ago and failed, bringing him a shame that still hung over him and the rest of the household. But surely she wouldn't have made the attempt a second time. "Has Baram been able to dislodge them yet?"

"No, not a coup. Not yet. The High Prince Baram was attacked yesterday."

Attacked. Jasfer's mouth went dry.

"An assassin. I know little more. He has survived so far and is being treated. But the news is not promising."

Jasfer sank back into the chair. "May the gods protect him," he mumbled as his thoughts raced. Baram dead? Perhaps not, but it sounded likely. What did that mean for him, for the ruling princes, for Eghsal Valley?

And who would be High Prince next?

With Datri's help he'd made himself in many ways the second highest ruler in the land. He could try to push himself into Baram's position, as the legitimate successor. History gave him power here. It also made him dangerously vulnerable. Anyone wanting to take on the role of High Prince would fear Jasfer, either as a rival for the High Prince title or simply as a too-powerful subordinate. He should have brought more servants for his own protection.

He should have arranged for better protection for Datri

while he was gone as well.

"I need to see my wife's letter."

"You need to stay sitting now."

The force of Hrisha's words shocked Jasfer. He leaned back against the couch.

"There are concerns about what will happen next. Concerns about what you will do now."

As if he knew yet what he should do on such short notice. "What concerns?"

Hrisha leaned forward on his couch to say, "You may be tempted to rush back to Romnai. You may be tempted to be with your wife and household. But you must know that there is danger in going back too quickly, especially this time of year. We simply want to protect you."

Jasfer studied Hrisha's body language. What was he trying to say? Bringing up his wife, was *she* in danger? Was it truly for Jasfer's danger, or to keep him away while someone else took over? Nothing in the prince's posture answered any of his questions.

"Thank you for your concern. I would like to read my wife's letter now, as I try to decide what to do." He paused then added, "We will continue with our plans to retake the city."

As he left the room and received the letter from the waiting Yatim, Jasfer noticed a contingent of Pashun soldiers outside the mansion. No wild ox soldiers, only the Vainath. They should be down at the wall, preparing for the attack. Why were they here instead?

To protect him. No doubt that's what Hrisha and the other princes in Pashun would tell him if he asked. But if Jasfer tried to return to Romnai over their objections… The soldiers might well turn into jailors. With soft gloves, no doubt—at least at first—but unmoving bars and solid chains.

CHAPTER 21

Valni made good use of her falcon soldier training as she navigated the routes into the lava fields and back. At the moment, early in the morning as the sun was behind the city's heights, she and Lodnan balanced on the rocks above the mud pots, following the route laid out for them by the soldiers in training. Pashun disappeared into the sulfur haze behind and above them.

They wanted to see through that haze, though, to find out what the princes' soldiers were doing. To learn when the attack would begin so they could relay that information.

There were many such routes through the edges of the lava fields, paths of rock and solid ground that flirted with the edges of danger. The soldiers used them often to develop their reflexes, and even those who would never become full soldiers tested themselves on the paths.

Never alone, though. That was an iron-clad rule of the jatis, never to tempt the lava fields, for once tempted, the lava would be sure to claim a solitary soldier.

While they had a vital task out here, they still took advantage of the route's challenges to test themselves.

Their path was marked with a symbol, etched into stone or carved into wood, of a naga wrapped around some kind of rock. An ingot of gold, perhaps, or maybe simply a piece of coal. Even the most carefully carved symbols were little more than hints at whatever the symbol had originally meant. Lodnan hopped onto a fallen tree trunk, bleached by years of exposure. The wood under one foot crumbled, and his foot gave way.

Before he could even cry out, Valni leapt up beside him and pulled him to the safety of a solid portion of the tree.

While he caught his breath, Valni tried to make light of his close brush with failure. And possibly death. "Someone will have to plan a new route through here, won't they? That tree shouldn't be a part of the course anymore." She slapped the symbol carved into the wood.

"You…" Lodnan gasped quick breaths and held his head in his hands. "Thanks, that was quick thinking." He looked at the weak part of the tree then down where they sat. "Is this safe?"

"At the moment. You were just unlucky where your foot landed."

"Thanks. Again." He shook his head and shuddered. "You've got quick reflexes. Maybe you should be a soldier, not just a trainer. We have women soldiers in our jati, you know. Maybe not back where you came from, but we do."

Valni forced a smile and shook her head. "I'll train your soldiers, if I have the chance. But the fighting, that's not for me." Tempting to show just what she could do, but of course that was exactly why she had to avoid it. Put her in a real fight, and everyone would know she was from the falcon jati. Pointing ahead at the next naga symbol, she said, "When you're ready we should keep moving. Or do you want to head back?" Probably just as easy one way as the other.

Lodnan looked where she pointed and took a deep breath. "Give me a moment yet. Then we should keep on forward."

In the days following the cooperation between the Madrur and their neighbors, the Gwalpi, a sort of peace had taken over their portion of the city. The Sons of Ryo and their miners had pulled back to regroup, and the princes ignored them.

Now all that had changed, and the man behind the change was the one who had sent her here, though of course on the High Prince's behalf. Now Prince Jasfer was preparing the soldiers to attack her allies. Her friends? It felt like it some days, but since she could never tell her own story, the friendships never deepened.

There was little movement up above, no sign that an attack was imminent. Some hints of people directly above their own lines, but those had been visible from up close as well. She shielded her eyes. Actually, there were a number of people moving rapidly between the manors at the top, well above the wall itself. Were they cheetah jati servants carrying urgent messages? Though given what she'd seen of the Pashun princes, it was probably little more than, *Quick, Prince Arrogant needs new bath oil! Hurry, the Lady Delicate needs her smelling salts!*

Or was this yet another soldier jati, getting things arranged in the background while the real fighters waited below, ready at a word to attack?

There were so many soldier jatis in this foolish city. So inefficient. Romnai had its wolf jati base, though their soldiers spent most of their time far from any city. And Romnai had Valni's own falcon jati, which exclusively guarded the High Prince. Beyond that, the wild ox jati and the wisent jati handled almost everything else soldier-related, which mostly meant patrolling the streets and guarding the princes when needed. Maybe there were a few smaller groups that straddled the line between workers and soldiers, guarding warehouses at the docks and the like, but such work was beneath a real soldier.

Here, every sector of the city seemed to have a different faction. It made them powerful in a way. Or at least very present in the city, visible and accepted almost anywhere. But that power got spread thin and divided into tiny slices for each little group.

As critical as she was of the idea, at least it had made it easy for her to join in, with their soldiers anxious for her training knowledge.

When he seemed to have recovered enough, she held out

her hand and helped him to his feet. "I don't see anything up there yet, but we can go a little farther out, it looks like. Want me to lead this stretch?"

Before he could answer, bells sounded in the city. Great, heavy bells she'd never heard since coming to Pashun. "What's—"

"Something's wrong." Lodnan peered back through the haze toward the city. He hesitated, cocking his head to listen. "I don't know what. We need to get back there."

The bells that rang first were high in the city, among the princely manors. It might have been some signal to begin the attack, but there was no new movement along the wall. And a moment later, other, lower bells began to ring as well, the sound coming first from the seminary but then spreading out even into the neighborhoods allied with the various rebellious factions. A mournful terrible sound that settled in over the city.

"Ahead or back? One's still as fast as the other, I'd guess."

"Back now. We know what to expect this way." Without waiting, Lodnan began jumping along the route they'd taken.

Valni followed, scrambling over the rocks of their outward route. The naga symbols were placed to be visible from the other direction, but Lodnan proceeded as if he'd memorized exactly where they'd come. Maybe he had, but Valni found herself often glancing backward to make sure they were still on the right path.

The seminary's bells were the closest to them, ringing, solemn and slow. with the others. A pair of funnel horns added their droning notes from somewhere within the city, as if to bring out the sadness of the peeling bells.

After a surprisingly short time, the haze opened up, and the city was before them. The slope of buildings climbed up toward the sky. The bells still rang, heavy and solemn.

Valni ran to keep up with Lodnan as he made his way up

the streets to the section of the city where his jati's leadership gathered, along with the Gwalpi. She wanted to stop and ask someone what was going on, but she didn't have the breath to ask without slowing down and losing sight of him.

The gathering place was only a short way up the slope and then around the hill for several blocks. Lodnan stopped abruptly a little ways before he reached it. Valni had to rely on her own reflexes to keep from running into him. Another of their jati was also hurrying through the streets.

Lodnan called out to him. "Puneev, do you know what's happening? Is it an attack? Why—"

"Death. Someone in Romnai."

The answer struck Valni like a sword to her chest. Or a knife to her back. A death? She blurted out a half choked, "Who?" But she already feared the answer. Who would be important enough for all the bells of Pashun? A priest, maybe, if he was at the pinnacle of the temple's hierarchy. Much more likely a ruling prince, though even one of them wouldn't likely be prominent enough to provoke this reaction in a different city. There were thirty, after all. One of them probably died often, only to be replaced by a son or cousin. Each one alone meant little outside the confines of their assembly. Which only left one possibility.

"The High Prince. Baram."

Whether it was Puneev who answered or some other passerby who overheard them, Valni had no idea. Her body went distant. Her mind floated, dizzy, apart from everything.

Baram, dead. The High Prince, the one her jati was charged to protect. Dead.

"What? How?"

The other soldier didn't know her and only gave her a strange look, as if she shouldn't care how it had happened. But, of course she did. Was it some fluke that no one could have prevented? An illness that no one could heal?

Or had her jati failed him?

Had she, stuck in this distant city, failed him?

If anyone answered, she didn't hear the words. In a daze she wandered to her room within the jati's warren and lay down.

***

As she often did when her mind couldn't settle down, Valni wandered. The streets of their neighborhood—squeezed among the cramped buildings between the wall above, the waterway to the south, the rugged hillside to the north—gave her few choices. She had no destination in mind.

The bells had stopped their incessant tolling, though every once in a while, perhaps on the hour, they rang out again to mourn the High Prince. Valni still had no answers to her questions about his death.

Some cheer rose from the street ahead, counterpoint to the bells. The celebrant followed the cheer with a cry of, "The Sons of Ryo have struck!" She tensed for an attack to come over the waterway, but there was no sound of fighting. Was that who had attacked the High Prince, the group who claimed the center of the city? Valni ran forward, itching to fight anyone cheering on her prince's death, but the street was empty of any celebration.

Let them fall. If those cultists had anything to do with the attack, then they deserved no mercy.

She slowed down and resumed her aimless wandering. Her feet took her to a bar-room. Sitting at the bar with a few others was the man from the Forgotten South, deep in discussions with his soldiers.

She took a step toward him, curious, then pulled back. What would he think of some girl from this rustic valley talking to him? She'd never considered herself especially shy, but she felt awkward suddenly, wanting to turn around and leave. Instead, she took a seat away from the traveler.

He was the leader of their neighborhood and had been threatened by the princes already. Their allied groups were a small enough combination of people that being a leader didn't separate him entirely from everyone else. But the attack made everyone around him, soldiers of the Gwalpi jati, alert and suspicious as they watched the patrons and the doorway.

The talk in the bar was about the High Prince, of course. She wanted to hear every tidbit, every hint of what had happened. She wanted to block out all the news and pretend it had never happened. The two impulses warred inside her. She sipped her tisane and sat in the corner, her whole body tense.

At last, she stood up. The tension made her clumsy, and she bumped the chair beside her, which fell with a bang. Fighting the urge to cover her face and leave, Valni marched straight to the traveler.

"Are there princes in the Forgotten South? Is there a High Prince?"

One of the soldiers half stood to put himself between her and the traveler. Inside Valni laughed. If she wanted to, she could throw the man to the floor of the bar before he had a chance to draw his ostentatious sword.

The traveler put his hand on the soldier's arm, and he sat back down.

"There are many tribes in the Forgotten South."

Tribes? What, were they no better than the mumblers back in that land of history? She cocked an eyebrow at him, waiting for a better answer.

"Some have princes, and some high princes. And other titles that don't exist in your language."

Tribes and other languages. "You make them sound like mumblers in hide houses and caves."

He bit his lip as if to stop himself from saying something he didn't want to say.

Rather than waiting to see if he'd say anything, she pressed on. "Who guards the princes there? Is there one jati that protects them?"

He waved a hand at her and turned away, saying only, "Your jatis are nothing from the Forgotten South. Where there are princes, they choose their protection. Or decide they don't need it."

No jatis. Her mind caught at that for a moment, but then the idea of not needing protection grabbed her. The conversation was clearly over, and she no longer felt welcome in the bar with how the soldiers watched her. Maybe she'd judged their jati wrong. Maybe it didn't matter.

She left to wander some more, and in her mind she turned over the idea of a place where the High Princes had no need of protection. How could that ever be? A place of such peace that their version of the falcon jati could be freed to any kind of soldierly work. A land where the burdensome weight of protecting a single person would never fall on their shoulders. No matter how agile and battle-ready those shoulders might be, they weren't made for so heavy a weight.

***

The city held its breath, waiting for the princes to send their soldiers to attack, waiting for more news of the High Prince. Some said he was not dead after all, only sick. Some said that the Sons of Ryo were to blame, others that the Children of Kwona had orchestrated it all and would be coming for the soldiers next. Some that the news had been mistaken all along. Valni did her best to continue her attempts to be a part of the Madrur jati. She trained the younger soldiers, took part in keeping the shared rooms neat, joined the others for communal meals whenever they happened, and watched for the soldiers above to begin their attack.

But what exactly was her purpose anymore? She'd been sent by the High Prince Baram to spy. Not a very specific task, just to learn what she could about the factions of the city in its unrest and rebellion. Secrets among the princes, secrets among the soldiers.

So, what did she have to show Baram for her work? What did she have to show his successor, whoever that might be?

She needed to *do* something, work her muscles so sore that the pain woke up her mind. She wished the promised battle would finally begin. Or that she could cross into the streets of the Sons of Ryo and fight against them. Maybe then she could plan how to move forward.

Both waits broke at once. The battle started with the same bells they'd been hearing for days. As she raced up toward the wall to watch and join in, she discovered that the soldiers weren't attacking them after all. A huge wave of the princes' army streamed down into the center of the city, brushing aside the defenses set up by the Sons of Ryo and their allies.

She should join in, jump the waterway and fight or come up from beneath where the Sons of Ryo would be neglectful. As she vacillated, Lodnan rushed up beside her. "They've found the assassin."

"Assassin?" Valni's voice squeaked over the word. The air seemed to tighten around her chest.

"Yes." Lodnan let out a deep breath through his nose. "That news was confirmed. The High Prince was assassinated. A knife to his neck as he was watching some chariots or something like that."

The ice chariots. A vision of that slick ice flashed before her eyes, of all the ways she and her sisters used to make sure that place was safe. Valni let her sword drop to the ground. Her jati had failed, then. An assassination right beneath their noses. They were disgraced, all of them. Whether they were present or not, as falcon jati they were no longer…anything.

A cry rose up in her throat, and she knew it would come out as a keening wail if she let it. She swallowed, forced her voice to be as flat and lifeless as she could. "But how did he get there unseen?"

"She. I haven't heard exactly. Sounds like she may have joined months ago as a house servant and waited until now to strike."

No, Baram didn't have house servants. All work in his house was done by the falon jati. People knew the falcon jati for their fierce women soldiers, but they were more than that. The men and women of her jati protected the High Prince by being his servants, his cleaning staff, his cooks. Had one of their own betrayed him?

No, that would be to betray themselves, who they were as a jati.

A brief cry escaped her lips, and she clamped them shut.

Lodnan pressed on as if he hadn't noticed. "But that's not the biggest news. They caught her trying to flee the city."

What did that matter? Valni let her leaden feet carry her to the wall, where she leaned her forehead. Details, when the only thing that mattered was her jati's complete failure.

"Reports are that the assassin was from here, from Pashun somewhere, probably even from one of the miner families."

Valni lifted her head. If so, then she had to cross over the water and join in the battle, find the miner families, take her revenge. But even if it was true, it only revealed her own failure as well as her jati's. She let her shoulders drop and avoided looking at Lodnan.

"Others say no way. Someone in Romnai is trying to blame us to sow discord, but it's not true. The assassin was from Romnai. A malcontent of some kind trying to overthrow the city. Or maybe some untouchable—"

Valni slammed a hand against the wall. She couldn't listen

to him any longer, couldn't handle the speculation, the theories. It didn't matter! None of it. Turning on a heel, she stalked away, down toward the steambeds that led away from this cesspool of a city.

What was a jati without honor? What was a soldier without a jati? A *falcon* jati soldier without purpose, without a High Prince? It didn't do any good to fight the miners or the Sons of Ryo or anyone else when no one knew the truth. When no one would probably ever know the truth. Should she return to Romnai, offer herself to the new High Prince? Or maybe offer herself to whatever shame and judgment fell on the jati as a whole. It would be fitting for the priests to judge them all as shamed by the gods.

Beside the lava fields, she followed the naga route she'd attempted before the bells rang. Alone, breaking the soldier taboo. She hesitated for a moment as she stepped out toward the naga symbols, but she was already shamed. Let the taboo slide off her as if she were from a Forgotten South land where the High Princes had no need of soldiers. Honor was pointless, a lie, and truth itself a betrayal.

Where she and Lodnan turned around the other day, she stopped and let the wail finally escape her lungs. The cries came in waves and echoed across the lava fields and mudpots. A geyser coming from inside her to match the geysers all around. Or rather more like the mudpots, a bubbling and ugly outward sign of the chaos trembling underneath.

Night fell with her still out there, and no one had come to find her. So it was when you belonged to no jati. She should expect nothing more.

She made her way forward, guessing at the route since she couldn't see any symbols, scarcely caring if she lost her way and fell into lava. Rocks rose up, solid ground appeared between scalding pools of water, and she stumbled onward all night long.

When the sun rose, she'd left the route far behind, even left the city behind. Pashun was visible as a wall of houses, but no ringing of its bells carried to where she stood, far out in the lava field, no sound of a battle that surely still raged on. Or had the city fallen so fast?

Rather than heading back, she made her way onward, into the sulfurous air, twisting and moving in the way she'd been trained but not to fight an enemy and not to protect anyone. Only to protect herself for as long as the fire permitted her to live.

Chapter 22

The archaeological site was smaller than Pavresh had pictured, but that made it no less impressive. The shapes of the ancient ships were clear, majestic and ancient. Too bad they might have nothing to do with the arrival of the earliest ancestors of their people.

The scholar in charge of the site, Harkala, welcomed him. "Tekhel says you are interested in our history. That you might even have something to add?"

Maybe, though he was more interested in hearing her story than in telling the loose outlines of the idea that was forming in his mind. Before his arrival he'd wrestled with using his magic or not—the memory of what he'd done still ached, but magic was a part of him as well, a part of how he interacted with people. It helped people understand him in ways that he couldn't seem to convey through ordinary words or body language. In the end he'd given himself a touch of the scholar's demeanor and an elder's wisdom, but most of all the eager curiosity of a young acolyte, something he sensed in Tekhel as a fading part of who he'd been until this past year or so. "Tell me what you've learned from this site."

Harkala waved her hands over the view of the ships. "It was a small group of ships that ended up here. Small, but a complex grouping of people already. This would have been a good site to set up a more permanent camp at the time. We have begun to find some evidence of buildings down the slope a little ways." She pointed back upriver where Pavresh could see new excavations.

"When the river changed course, it appears that they abandoned the site. Maybe that was when they moved inland, discovered the warm air around the lava fields, and founded

Eghsal City."

"What evidence do you have that these were people from the Forgotten South? Have you found graves? Any hint of their rituals or habits?"

Harkala shook her head. "No bodies. Surely, they would have been burned. Perhaps we will find charred bones as we dig through the buildings."

Unless they didn't revere the Fire yet. Perhaps that was the real difference between the people of Eghsal and the mumblers, a sense of worshiping the Fire, whether that meant as part of the pantheonic religion or as a part of the Enshi religion, as Pavresh had been brought up. Even the mystery religion of the wolf jati soldiers was centered on the Fire, though for them it was their rival rather than something above them. A devout person might even say that the Fire had chosen one group of mumblers and made them different for that very reason, except for where that left the stories of gods and Gauran.

When he didn't answer, Harkala continued. "The ships themselves match the style of the fishing boats of the river mouth from the centuries after their arrival. They are not identical, but the connection is clear."

Time to express what he was wondering. "So, is there any chance that, let's say, a group of mumblers began building fishing boats and for whatever reason dragged a few of them up this way and tried to establish a new village?"

"Mumblers? No. Well…" Harkala cocked her head to think it through, which immediately made him trust her scholarly ideas more. So many of their people would have dismissed the idea out of hand without even giving it a second thought.

"I do think there are mumblers who have contributed more to our society than we tend to think. Some of my colleagues have found clues that imply the mumblers founded a city where Romnai is, centuries before our arrival here."

Well, that was very interesting and bolstered his thought that the mumblers may be their ancestors after all.

"The main reason to doubt it, though, is the wood of these ships. It is not a native tree. The pattern of the grain and the way the wood ages do not match anything we are familiar with here."

"Could it simply come from somewhere up in the mountains near here, a tree you wouldn't really have a reason to know about?" There were the trees in that high valley where he'd found the first village of Eghsal skin tones, though they'd looked like any other pines that grew in the area. And elsewhere in the mountains, if you went high enough to find anything unfamiliar, only scraggly trees grew. Nothing that would produce enough timber. "Or even an extinct tree that used to grow here, until some of our ancestors used it all for ships?"

"Not likely, unless it used to be warmer here. At least, if you compare the wood from trees that grow near the warm lava fields to trees from higher elevations, and extrapolate, the grain of this wood seems to come from even warmer lands. I would not say it's impossible. We scholars don't like that word. But unlikely."

There was something about being within the dig that calmed Pavresh. It had a feel of antiquity, much like the pines had, a sense of the past reaching into the present to soothe his aches. He wandered between the recreated ship and the visible portions of others. Were they a memory of the stories he'd always known, a proof that the past still touched the present? Or were they simply a salve, false but comforting? He lingered over the fragments of an unknown past. If his magic could be as fragmented as that, instead of an overwhelming force, then it didn't have to be an evil thing. The magic might leave space for people to wonder and question and find their own response. Arcist magic could be the overlapping flames that sparked curiosity, but not a wildfire to destroy everything it touched.

"What do you think it was like when they arrived?" he asked Harkala after he'd wandered the site for some time. "Did the mumblers try to keep them out?"

"We've never seen any evidence of fighting from that time period."

"Not even, I don't know, sling bullets or a bunch of death memorials from a single time? Remnants of a wall to keep them out?"

Harkala shook her head. "There are old records of the dead in Pashun, but they don't go all the way to the beginning, and there's no indication that many died at once that I've heard of. As far as a wall, well, it would leave behind its foundations, I imagine. Nothing like that I've seen."

If he could only piece it all together. It felt like a cornerstone that could shore up his use of the magic. The past, with its continued influence on the present, was one part of the magic he still felt like he didn't understand.

Though he would have liked to linger, it was time to head back into the interior, drop in at Romnai, then on toward Jaritta's city. He needed to know how they fared, if she could possibly be successful with her dream. Early the next morning Pavresh thanked Harkala and Tekhel and left.

His thoughts worked through the implications of Harkala's findings as he went. Too few ships. No signs of a distinct jati. But also, there was the nature of the unknown, ancient wood. And, could the rumors really be true of a traveler from the Forgotten South who'd come through the mountains to Pashun? Rumors and the grain patterns of some ancient wood were not much of a foundation to build on. Still, maybe there was truth to the old stories. Some slim version of the truth.

A tiny band of refugees from...someplace warmer,

crashing on this northern valley and either killed by the local mumbler tribes or absorbed into them. And their journey remembered and elaborated in legends as the real ancestors of Eghsal Valley rose to prominence.

A sliver of truth that was still entirely false, history itself betraying the stories and lies that had built their people, their identity.

At the Eghsal River, a train was making its way up into the interior. Once upon a time he'd looked at those engines as instruments of terror, an abomination he would never use himself. He couldn't summon that earlier fear anymore. The upheaval of clashing stories made it difficult to recall much that he had felt in the past. And the years of weary legs as he walked the valley and mountains made the prospect of riding a train far more attractive.

He walked adjacent to the track, watching for a place to sneak aboard. Nothing appeared before the train was far away. Late in the day he came across a small trainpost, where a cluster of buildings stood beside the river: a hunting camp and slaughterhouse. Carcasses would be frozen solid and then loaded on the trains.

Instead of sneaking on a stopped train, he decided to rely on his magic, cautiously testing each layer he added, like a traveler testing the ice over a probably-frozen pond. In his off-kilter mood, the magic came with difficulty, but the unclean feel of the magic felt distant as well, less distasteful. An official. That was an easy image to reach for. A minor official with an important task. Boring, but not someone to be hindered.

He brushed the dirt from his clothes and made himself look as presentable as he could, then marched into the station.

"I must reach Romnai. When is the next upriver train?" Believe in his own claims. Act certain. He'd always had a gift, even apart from the arcist magic, of seeming to fit in, of seeming to be whoever he claimed to be.

The stationmaster had blood on his butcher's apron. Such a small affair that he handled both roles? No, not likely with how many frozen animal carcasses stood ready to be loaded. Probably rather that the butchers needed extra help, and he earned a little side income by pitching in.

He glanced at Pavresh's clothes and seemed to decide he could leave the bloody clothes on. "Should have been one an hour ago. Must be delayed. So maybe any time now. Or not till morning. You a soldier or a hunter?"

Were those the only ones who boarded near here? Pavresh shook his head. "Neither. A servant." He drew on the artist image of the high-ranking servant to someone influential. It started to strain his control, so he eased back. "On my way back to report to my master." Someone much too important to be questioned. He left that part unsaid, except through his magic. "What's the delay from?"

"Who knows. Deer on the tracks? Too many soldiers heading upriver? Might be anything. Probably not a snowstorm this time, not for an upriver train. At least I haven't seen storm clouds that way."

Soldiers heading upriver. He repressed the chill that made him shudder. "Where can I stay until it comes?"

The stationmaster swept his hand at the sawdust filled room with a few empty benches. "Take your pick." Without waiting for Pavresh, he turned away, tightening his apron strings, heading back to more butchering work.

Pavresh touched the knots on his own rope belt, his kusti. Too public a place to perform the sacred patterns, but he ran his hand over the knots, allowing himself to rest and his mind to enter that space where it was only the sacred fire and himself.

How much time had passed when the train arrived he didn't know. He simply returned to himself and climbed aboard without a word to anyone. There were soldiers on board, more than he liked to see in a single place. They carried themselves with a sort of excited solemnity that reminded Pavresh of priests and rituals. Whatever brought them on that train, they considered it a serious duty, a chance to prove themselves in service to something far bigger than they were.

A sense of foreboding threatened the inner calm he'd been able to achieve. Rather than speak with the soldiers or listen to any stories they might tell, he retreated to a quiet car on the train, sat in the corner, and blocked out all thoughts of soldiers or delays.

The train pulled away. A herd of elk moved off away from the tracks as they picked up speed. Pavresh watched the light of the train's swaying lantern pick out the ripples on the river.

Rashul used to talk about the stories from the past being false. About hidden histories and how the truth might have been deliberately forgotten to set up the highest jatis as those rightfully in power. He would be the one to talk to about what he'd learned.

The train clicked onward, a rhythm that reminded Pavresh of poetry. Bad poetry, no doubt. Iksheen wouldn't have touched such a rhythm. Marankiya might have, though. He would have taken the beats Iksheen despised and turned them into something masterful, just like he'd taken Rashul's ideas of the past and mixed them with the traditional form of epic poetry and created art for the ages.

That's who would know what to say about Pavresh's discoveries and ideas. If only he hadn't been killed by the priests and princes.

He imagined Marankiya taking a swallow of his nasty fire liquor and then sitting down to write out a new version of his epic. It would still have the human hero Gauran, forced to flee the battles of the south, lost in a storm at sea with his people.

But when he came to shore, he wouldn't find an empty

land—empty apart from the pale-faced mumblers, which was as good as empty in the way they usually told the story—but instead a civilized land that took him in, that made him and his rough and weary people a welcome part of the civilization they were already beginning to create.

Was that what had really happened?

No, that wasn't the real question. Within the arcist magic what mattered wasn't always what was real, but how a story fit. The real question was, would anyone believe it, and how would they respond if they did?

****

Romnai was in turmoil. Soldiers paced the train platform, watching the workers and anyone arriving, greeting their fellow soldiers as they disembarked. Pavresh relied on his magic to make himself fit in. The ache opened up again inside him, but he didn't dare release the magic entirely. A common worker with a touch of authority not his own, as if given a task by someone important. A person who belonged there. Without the magic, no doubt he would have been stopped and questioned. He saw others pulled aside, herded along into nearby houses where there were other officials waiting. Pavresh caught a glimpse of massive ledgers and lines of scribes taking down detailed information, but he managed to leave the station without extra notice, hoping to find his way to Rashul's house. Even in the streets the soldiers were out in force.

When he'd returned from the Silk City five years earlier, the city had felt much the same. The people on edge, worried, trying to get through the day without lifting their eyes to see what was going on. And how soon after that return had Jaritta made her attempt at a coup? Perhaps history was repeating itself or simply betraying someone new.

A short way from the station, Pavresh came across a

beggar sitting beside the street. Pavresh never traveled with money, but he had a little food that he'd requested as his right on the train. Tossing a piece of cheese in the man's open hands, Pavresh crouched down beside him.

While the beggar ate, Pavresh said, "Rough times here, it looks like. It wasn't this way last time I came through, but I just returned from Jarnur. Why are so many soldiers out?"

"Princes. Who knows?"

Princes? "Something going on with the Thirty?"

"Don't know. Don't involve myself."

A shout came from down the street. Even before the soldier called out, "Clear out, beggars!" the beggar was on his feet and shuffling away. Pavresh turned his back on the soldier and walked away, as if he had no reason to worry.

Even so, he released his breath when he turned a corner and left the soldiers behind. This street had only a few people hurrying along, heads down and covered against the falling wet snowflakes. Pavresh cast about himself the aspect of a walla, without taking anything to deliver to complete the impression. He made his way into the brenil streets north of the city center.

Had this been a part of the city that was, before it was Romnai? Had mumblers built these streets? He looked for any hints of ancient architecture, but everything was far too new. These streets wouldn't have been the original city. He should look nearer the river or beside the steam beds for real evidence.

An image came back to him of hiding in a strange tunnel of sorts, right before the coup. Jaritta and Bhadrik and Ekana had been there. The walls had seemed ancient, covered with artwork he hadn't recognized from anywhere, except now they reminded him of the walls of the mumbler cave where he'd met Chhayasheela and Ellechandran. Surely those must have been a part of the older city, a physical reminder of the mumblers who'd begun to create the civilization Pavresh and his people now claimed as their own.

Rashul's house no longer had soldiers guarding it, as it had five years earlier. He knocked on the door.

No one answered.

The door was locked, so Pavresh peered through the windows. No sign of anyone inside. He walked around its sides. Unlike many in the city, it wasn't connected to the houses at either side—one reason the princes chose it for his house arrest. The windows along the side and back showed him nothing else. A brick-covered yard in the rear was well cared for, though the snow showed no recent footprints. How long ago would the oldest snow here be? This time of year, with fall heading toward winter, that might only mean no one had come out here in the past day or so. In the shaded corners the snow lay somewhat deeper. Anyone walking there would have left footprints even longer ago, perhaps as long as a twelve-day, and there was nothing to be seen.

"Who's wandering around back there?" A woman's voice, coming from the house next door. Probably innocent of Rashul's past, but almost certainly she was paid by the soldiers to inform them of anything strange going on at his house.

Pavresh made himself a friendly shopkeeper, quiet and not the least challenging to anyone or anything. A simple, superficial spell that put no strain on him.

"An old friend of Rashul's. Does he still live here?" He walked over to the stone fence as he spoke. "I haven't seen him in years, but he used to live here."

The woman was elderly and smiled at him when he looked over the fence. "Used to, yes. Even last twelve-day. You see him, tell him I'm worried about his ivy. Needs trimming."

Until so recently. In that case... "What happened to him? Is something wrong?"

The backyard of the woman's house was a garden of

stones, beautifully arranged into gravel pathways that wound around rock piles and one single stone placed upright as if in a position of reverence. It had the look of an altar. It would be hidden from sight, but he guessed there would be some sort of alcove near the bottom or at the side facing the house where a small flame could be lit. No follower of the official temple would place an altar at her own house, but a follower of the splinter religion might. He touched the Enshi sacred knots that tied his belt around his waist.

The woman shook her head. "Don't know. Disappeared about the same time everything else went crazy in this town. Haven't seen him, but I hope he's not hurt."

Images of the coup again filled his mind, flashes of their planning, of the hiding places they'd gone to. But Rashul hadn't been a part of that. Last Pavresh spoke with him, he was resigned to a brenil life away from any kind of intrigue.

"What went crazy? What does that mean? I just arrived, and everyone walks around as if they're scared."

"Scared is right. The High Prince was assassinated." The old woman peered more closely at him. "How, you mean you haven't even heard that?"

Assassinated. Pavresh closed his eyes. He'd observed the man, when he worked for Prince Jasfer. A decent prince, as far as those things went. Not corrupt, even if not willing to allow society to change as much as it should. He'd struck a noble figure when he'd presided over the High Assembly of Princes, not so much of distant pride as of deserved respect.

He'd also sentenced Jaritta, Marankiya, and others to death.

"I hadn't heard," he said at last and opened his eyes. "I was traveling outside the city." His eyes ran along the gravel path in the woman's yard and then back to the bricks of Rashul's and up to his house. "But surely Rashul had nothing to do with that. Why would he disappear?"

The woman shook her head. "He had more to do with things beyond this house than you might know. Soldiers were here looking for him a few days ago. Some prince's servants a twelve-day before that. You're not the first."

Not the first. He looked again at the woman's innocent face, at the Enshi altar in the yard. And now some of those others would learn that he was here. He wouldn't deceive himself. Even if he shared a religion with her, even if she seemed the kindly neighbor, she was here because she kept someone informed about Rashul's activities. And she would tell that someone about Pavresh's interest as well.

Or perhaps already had.

Yet another path to betrayal.

Pavresh thanked her and said, "Well, I would have liked to have seen him again, after all these years. I'll see what other friends I can still find in the area."

Then without making his hurrying obvious, he left, quickly turning down one street and then another and hoping he was sufficiently away before anyone came to investigate.

Maybe now he could find that place they'd hidden in before, look for other clues about the ancient mumblers.

As he walked toward the lava fields, he tried to imagine how Rashul might have become entangled again in such a thing as assassination. He'd sworn off his rage and revolution, had become a quiet part of the city. Someone like that might be drawn back into politics, if the right trigger came along, but the farther he walked the more sure he grew that it wasn't the case here. Rashul was not a suspect. Pavresh would have never come so close to the house if they'd had any thought he might be connected.

Despite all that, for some reason, Rashul had disappeared, right at the same time that the city had become so chaotic, so fraught with danger. What news could have triggered him to leave?

The last time Pavresh had walked here along the steam beds, there had been many more beggars. Many untouchables who weren't allowed to work and could only eat what they begged from the passersby. The princes always wanted fewer out in the streets, but they could only do so much. Even in times of upheaval the untouchables needed to eat. The risk of a soldier's boot was worth the chance to survive another day.

A group of wolf jati soldiers marched along the boulevard. Even with his magic cloaking him and his head down, he didn't avoid their notice. They veered directly behind him and matched his pace for more than a block. When he turned aside, at a street that led away from the edge of the city, they paused as if to taunt him, make him afraid they might pursue him. Then they continued on their way.

It rattled him, just as it rattled the beggars, no doubt. But it didn't make him flee. Ah, he realized the answer to both the beggars' absence and what triggered Rashul's disappearance. News of Jaritta. They'd heard of the city she was founding and left to join her. There was an arcist certainty to the answer. Even without being sure it had happened exactly as he pictured it, he was certain it explained at least part of what he was seeing in Romnai.

Eyes peeled, he eventually found a crack in a foundation that looked familiar. He crawled inside, into a tunnel of ancient walls strangely painted, just as he remembered from so long ago. He used a small lamp from the last mumbler village he'd visited to give himself some light. By its light, he peered at the odd colors and patterns that covered the ancient wall.

Like mumbler artwork. Or was that only a connection his mind was forcing on him, a new piece to fit a bigger narrative he'd already decided on? He traced the figures that moved along the wall. The figures moved as if in some sort of primitive dance. Or was that merely a narrative as well?

A civilized dance might look little different when painted in this style. Here they might be building the city, raising walls, founding armies. Creating today's civilization, both its good aspects and crooked, out of a wandering, mumbler past.

A noise made him stop, drew his eyes away from the walls. A cluster of untouchables had already claimed a part of the place as their own. Taking on the aura of a storyteller, he approached their huddle against one wall to ask them their stories and find out what they knew of Jaritta and her new city where no one was untouchable.

Under that guise, the magic gave him no discomfort at all.

CHAPTER 23

The first wave of soldiers broke the defenders and sent them scrambling backwards down through the city. Of *Jasfer's* soldiers, he reminded himself, no matter what Hrisha had done to change Jasfer's orders. The delay had grated on him, but there was some wisdom in the pause they'd allowed so they could all absorb the news of the attack on the High Prince and figure out what it meant for the city.

The Sons of Ryo took advantage of the time. Instead of a surprise attack at dawn, as Jasfer had commanded, the attack played out several days later, the surprise largely undone by the movement of troops above the wall over the intervening days.

The noise of celebrations hardened Jasfer's resolve. The bells rang in mourning, and each time the people below them lifted their voices to cheer, as if they could drown out the bells. Their defiance of the princes and pleasure at the attack on Baram was a disgusting thing. All the more reason to stomp them, grind them underfoot.

Maybe they should have put their efforts toward their defenses instead of celebrating. The extra days of preparation didn't appear to have helped them much.

"Well, this might be quick," he said aloud.

Beside him in a box, as if they were enjoying some gruesome theater from up in the balcony, Mahendri leaned forward. "May not do to rush to conclusions. But they've fallen back, that's certain."

"Lord Mayor," Jasfer said to the man on his other side, "I wish to descend to view the streets of the battle."

"It will not be safe yet."

"I did not mean now." He glanced around for a messenger,

but he wasn't sure which servants to trust and didn't want Yatim to leave him alone among these princes. "Mahendri, would you take a message for me? Tell that prince of the Forgotten South that if he's willing to bend his knee, I'm interested in some proof. Tell him to gather his soldiers and attack the Sons of Ryo from below. When his soldiers meet ours in the middle, we will accept his surrender."

"Yes, tirsrah." Mahendri hurried off, and Jasfer made his way out of the box toward the wall. There were no arrows flying this far, no stones slung to these heights. But the sound of battle was loud, an animal noise, or something lower than the animals, as if in fighting the soldiers became less than human. Certainly those they fought against became less than human—had to be less to keep the soldiers killing.

"When this fighting is done," he said, "I want the leaders of this cult brought before me. The others—the miners, the leaders of the Anguch jati—I'll leave them to your punishments or clemency, as befits the situation. But the Sons of Ryo, I need to see them face to face and punish them myself."

As he looked down, the view grew hazy as if with fog. Or smoke? The soldiers, his soldiers, advanced steadily, making sure to check each building before passing it by. The different jatis worked together with none of the awkwardness Jasfer had observed in their training.

Suddenly, a line of fire cut across the middle of the neighborhood, behind the leading edge of the soldiers. Jasfer felt the searing pain of his scars as he flinched away. The princes cried out.

There was no way to see how many died in the flames, but they appeared to be in a narrow line, not spreading into the buildings either above or below. The fire stayed there, a wall of flames that forced the army in two. The Sons of Ryo rushed out from hiding places in great number and advanced toward the trapped soldiers at the front while the commanders called for those in the rear to try to give them cover with bows and slings.

Burning arrows fell among the soldiers of each side. Jasfer couldn't watch any more. The pain along the backs of his legs made his muscles spasm. He hobbled along, with Yatim's assistance, as the princes' guards ushered them back, away from any chance of the battle shifting up toward them.

***

"Dearest husband," the letter began. It was not the loving opening it seemed. Years ago they'd decided on a code for addressing correspondence to each other. This one meant they were both in danger. His fingers clenched on the edges of the letter. He read on, hoping to erase the image of the fires of battle from his mind.

"I write to you with a sense of foreboding," did nothing to alleviate his fears. There was nothing coded in the line, but the fact that she was willing to say as much openly made her fears perfectly clear.

She went on to describe a nonsense story about seers and stars, all of which was included to throw off anyone snooping on the letter. The key point within it all was a reference to a knife the supposed seer had used to cut open a fruit and read its seeds. The details were meaningless except for the knife itself.

A knife attack on the High Prince. She'd known that much before sending the letter with all haste. Dead or not, she didn't specify, so likely it was sent before she knew.

The foreboding, though, wasn't for the High Prince but for him. She turned the letter to discussing his journey to Pashun. Pleasantries, people she wanted him to greet.

"Be cautious at the lava field. I know, you will as always. My worries are no more than a wife's simple fears."

Meaning there were complex motivations at play here and he should beware of the princes in Pashun.

The letter went on. She had no suspicions yet about who could be behind the attack. If it was the so-called Sons of Ryo, they'd become no more visible than they were before the attack. From her various sources, she'd still learned nothing of that group. She did, however, suspect that Jasfer's enemies among the Thirty would use the attack against him. Whether that meant a move to cut his power among them, to maneuver him from his position entirely, with a new High Prince and new Thirty, she couldn't say. Or they might even take advantage of the chaos to simply get rid of him. What was one more assassination amid such chaos?

Well, that was always a possibility for a ruling prince. He would have Yatim look into increasing his protection, for as long as he was here in Pashun.

More worrying, was that Datri feared for herself. If their enemies felt confident enough to attack a prince's family, then it was far more dangerous than anything he could remember. He needed to get back to her, so at least they could be together and have their full house and staff to protect them.

Even as he continued reading, he began thinking through what it would take to travel back to Romnai, even against the wishes of his hosts. The city would be theirs soon, his task here complete. He should go back to Romnai and take charge of the Assembly of Princes, at least until they could agree on a new High Prince.

One paragraph confused Jasfer. "I was practicing kiwan to pass the time." That was a reference to spying or some clandestine work along those lines, but the rest he couldn't figure out. "You will recall the piece you were going to take with you to Pashun. It went missing. I spent some time searching for it among the other pieces, on the floor under the table. It was gone. I finally found it again, fallen back behind a chair. I am watching it carefully now. If it goes into play, then I will attempt to make the move you had planned."

What did that mean? Was it Sashyu, the girl who'd been her spy? They'd thought about sending her to Pashun but ended up sending her to Datri's parents in Silk City instead. Had she gone missing on the way?

The falcon jati soldier Valni? No, she'd been sent to Pashun much earlier. Yatim had finally tracked down some rumor of her activity. She'd ended up with a soldier jati, the Madrur who supported the prince from the Forgotten South. But she'd disappeared suddenly, and Yatim hadn't been able to learn what she'd uncovered.

But either way, it didn't explain what was in the letter.

Datri clearly thought he would be able to put it together, but nothing he thought of quite fit.

Given its position within the letter, he had the feeling it was a key part of what she wanted to tell him. Until he figured it out, he couldn't be sure exactly what steps she thought he should take next. He hesitated over the plans and strategies.

Certainly, he would have to set aside any plans for dealing with Jaritta until everything else was settled.

***

The sorry lot huddled in the plaza before the wall. A half dozen bedraggled men, most with more white in their beards than black. Their hands were bound behind their backs, and the Vainath soldiers loomed above them. These were the cult leaders that had spread such violence and disorder in the valley?

"Who *are* they?" Jasfer asked Mahendri. "What kind of fanatic gets involved in something like this? Are they untouchables?"

"There are brenil caste mostly, actually."

Jasfer stared at Mahendri. "Merchants? I figured it would

be neflis and outcasts. Not…" He gestured, as if his hands could encompass the jatis of the mid-caste brenils.

Mahendri shrugged. "Shopkeepers who struggled to earn as much money as they thought they should. Traders who saw others earning more and grew jealous."

Jasfer strode toward them. The nearest to him kept his eyes down, but the man beside him glared up at the prince in defiance. The scars on Jasfer's legs twinged with a memory of pain.

"Do we have any evidence of contact with similar groups in the capital?"

"Nothing certain," Mahendri said, apologetically. "But we are looking into it. They had associates hiding outside the city. We've brought them in also, to be questioned, tried."

Bringing in the people outside the city. It reminded him of Mahendri wanting to bring in the outcasts of Eghsal City. Of course, that had fallen apart when Jaritta led her followers away. And a good thing. Many more people would have flooded the capital, the streets would have ended up even more dangerous, and the attack on the temple probably would have come even sooner.

Did this man look like a person who would send someone to start a fire in a temple? A man who would plan an assassination? He looked like a person resigned to his fate, a person who'd followed orders and knew the risks. Who might have given those orders? There was surely someone else above this sorry lot coordinating them. "We don't need certainty. If we find any ties at all, take them to the executioner."

The man didn't flinch, but did his eyes look more worried now, or was that only Jasfer's imagination?

Mahendri bowed and answered, "Yes, tisrah. A scaffold is set up, and an executioner is ready to come at a moment's notice."

Good. Let the cultists fear. And if the scaffolding ended up as punishment for Jaritta as well? He forced his lips to harden. Anything that happened to her was only what she brought on herself. He would continue to do what was right for the valley as a whole, no matter who got in the way.

***

When two days passed with no news from Romnai, Jasfer confronted Hrisha in his sitting room.

"I can't sit here waiting for events in the capital to transpire. I have done what I came for, freed you from your enemies. Now I must get back and help the other princes rule as we are charged by the gods and the Fire of the cosmos."

Hrisha stood behind his desk and offered Jasfer a shallow bow. "I understand your wishes, tisrah. You have an important and holy task, and your concern for the entire valley is clear. I will do all I can to assist you. You must understand, though, that bandits are out along the travel routes. The soldiers you brought to patrol came back here to assist our fight against the miners, so there's no knowing what outcasts or other criminals might have taken advantage of their absence. And the weather will continue to be terrible for the next while."

"I have my soldiers. Some will stay with you, and I intend to have Mahendri stay here and help you establish peace." Jasfer leaned across the desk far enough that Hrisha pulled back from him.

"That...yes, that may work. I had begun wondering about your sister's city. The more soldiers we know are loyal, the better that attack may go."

"You will have the soldiers you need for that. Mahendri has my instructions for how to proceed."

"Very well." Hrisha rearranged the papers on his desk. "We will begin to make the arrangements. Before anything else, there is a new message that has just arrived. Let's take a look at that and not rush off while everything remains unsettled."

Was he merely trying to put off Jasfer's demands, delay, deny? Jasfer exhaled through his nose and kept his chin high. "I will take a look at that letter."

Hrisha handed over the paper. The seal was already broken.

Jasfer made a point of looking at the cracked wax in silence before giving Hrisha a hard stare. "In the future anything not addressed personally to you should be opened in my presence."

Hrisha sat heavily down. "Yes, tisrah."

The first thing he saw in the letter was that Baram had died. Hrisha nodded to a cheetah jati servant, who brought a chair over for Jasfer. He sat down and leaned his head back against the cushioned back. Then he read the rest carefully.

An assassin had infiltrated in the High Prince's guards and stabbed him while he was watching the ice chariots race. That confirmed what Datri had uncovered. The authorities were tracking down the assassin's background but had nothing to share at this time, only a fierce promise to uncover every secret and learn the truth. The Thirty Princes had declared a period of mourning of three months. In theory that gave him plenty of time to delay his traveling.

What would Datri want him to do? She had the mind for this kind of intrigue, not him. He set the letter down on the arm of his chair. Smooth cloth covered the arm, as if to soothe away his thoughts of the harsh conditions that traveling would entail.

"Make what plans you need," he finally said to Hrisha, "for my departure with a contingent of my soldiers, if that is what I choose to do. For the moment I will hold off and give the princes in Romnai time to make their arrangements."

Hrisha nodded. "As you wish, tisrah."

Back in his own rooms, Jasfer took out paper and pen to write his own official letter.

It is with sorrow that I hear of the death of my friend and colleague, the High Prince Baram. He was a powerful leader of our valley, loyal to our people above all other considerations, and a voice of reason whose presence will be missed.

He was a prince among princes, raised with honor in Romnai and married into a prominent family of Pashun. He united the different voices and garnered respect at every juncture of his life. It was for this reason he was urged to become High Prince, and he achieved that distinction without bloodshed. There have been attempted coups during his tenure, as there are for every High Prince. Even these he handled adroitly. He cut off rebellion before it could reach the inner chamber. Or he rallied everyone to oppose the destabilizing forces when revolution became a real threat.

We will be hard pressed to find a prince to replace him. Nevertheless, I urge us all to seek that same legacy among our number, to find a new High Prince worthy of Baram's calm power.

I am not writing to make this claim for myself. I know how some have viewed me, in support or in opposition, as among the most influential princes beneath Baram. But I do not set myself up as his successor. I state clearly that I have no aims to make the attempt myself and withdraw my name from any consideration. I wish to continue to serve this land, as my father did and as I have these past years. Not as High Prince, but as one among the great leaders of our Assembly.

It is difficult to be away from Romnai when such events are taking place. I was sent here by Baram's command, and I will return without ever presenting my findings to him. With a heavy heart. Until that time, I am mourning here and continuing the work of a ruling prince, to guide and lead Eghsal Valley forward to continued greatness.

—Prince Jasfer Talai.

Would Datri approve of him removing himself from the High Prince-ship? It would have meant more power and prestige to take Baram's place, two things his wife placed high value on. Five years ago, she might have disagreed with his actions, but not today, he thought. She could clearly see by now that the power of a high-ranking prince was itself great, and the power of the High Prince came at a steep price.

And if they decided together that he *should* still make an attempt, he could claim the situation had changed since he'd written this letter. Three months was a long time for plans to change and develop. At the least, this might provide some protection for both herself and him in the days ahead.

***

When the next letter from Romnai came two more days later, Hrisha opened it with Jasfer and some other Pashun princes in attendance.

"There has been a coup," Hrisha said as he handed it to Jasfer.

So much for three months. Jasfer's hand shook as he took the paper. A minor, non-ruling prince from Romnai had attempted to proclaim himself the new High Prince. He'd been heard proclaiming that princes from Jarnur were to blame for the assassination, and that the only answer was a strong Romnai to force the other cities to bow to its power.

The falcon jati soldiers, loyal to the late High Prince and to the three months imposed by the High Assembly, counterattacked to drive him from the inner room. They slaughtered the pretender and his retinue with much greater violence than necessary.

Afterwards they claimed they were merely following the call for three months mourning. There could be no doubt that their response also stemmed from shame over allowing the assassination. A soldier commander, from a different jati and chosen by the priests, was placed within the falcon jati to help coordinate any future actions they might take.

The period of mourning was upheld again by the Thirty.

After reading the letter aloud, Jasfer looked around the room. "They will hate that, having someone from another jati controlling them."

"I am sure they will," Hrisha said. "Perhaps they shouldn't though. It is a common action we have learned to take here with our many jatis, a good way to keep any one group from becoming too powerful. Already we have begun pursuing the same with the jatis here, as they show whether they are worthy of our trust or not. Once they remember their place, beneath the princes and priests, then the stranger can be recalled to their own jati."

A Pashun strategy, used by the priests in Romnai. Yet another sign that there was more going on behind the scenes than he could guess. He only wished he could see the connections that must be hiding in plain sight, if he could only find the right way to look at them.

***

A new letter arrived from Datri, after most of a twelve-day had passed with no communication coming through whatsoever. Hrisha blamed the roads on keeping them cut off from the rest of the valley. The new peace that settled over Pashun wore on, the trials, executions, and offers of pardon. Jasfer found it difficult to focus on those matters when he was constantly wondering about the events back home.

He shattered the wax seal as he tore the letter open.

Dearest husband,

The kiwan piece I mentioned in my last letter has been put into play. The game board has been completely remade since we set our plans, and I suspect this piece may serve us in quite a different way than we had thought. Our opponent's pieces now occupy a large section of the board where we had sought to establish our pieces. It is no longer a safe strategy. So, where we had meant to tear down the opposite corner to strengthen our base, I propose moving our base entirely to this new corner.

I am setting out with the piece in question, along with a small retinue in disguise.

Datri.

The closing was surprisingly uncloaked in game terms. She was setting out from Romnai, in disguise. To where? And if the roads weren't safe for him and a group of well-trained soldiers, surely they wouldn't be safe for her. The rest was still frustratingly opaque. What or who was this kiwan piece?

He went back and reread the earlier letter and tried to think back to what they'd planned before he departed Romnai. So much had happened since then that it was a blur. He'd planned to come here to free the city from the rebels, and at the same time to find some way to undermine Jaritta. That was...

He sat back and touched the words of the new letter. *Tearing down the opposite corner.* That was Jaritta's supposed city. She meant to...

No, not possible. Except, the other part of their original plan jumped into his mind. Rashul. He had meant to journey here with Rashul, but the man had dithered and then seemingly disappeared.

Like a lost kiwan stone.

That's what her comments on kiwan had meant. She'd found the hiding Rashul and was watching his movements at first. The ruling Thirty had changed the playing table so much that it was no longer safe to keep doing what they'd planned, carving out their position in Romnai among the Thirty. She proposed leaving it entirely behind and joining in with his sister. His outcast sister whom he'd forcefully and publicly denounced.

And had she already left?

He flew from his room into Hrisha's study. "I must travel to Romnai right away. I trust that your plans for dealing with the city are set, with the soldiers I will leave behind?"

Hrisha steepled his hands and did not rise from his chair. "There is a new letter from Romnai, which has just arrived. From Prince Bunaran, one of your ruling colleagues. You may wish to hear it."

Jasfer took a deep breath. Not bad news, he prayed to the gods and goddesses. "Yes, I can open it and read it."

"No need." Hrisha tapped his desk where an open letter lay. "I have already read it." Before Jasfer could reprimand him for not waiting until he was present, Hrisha continued. "There has been another coup attempt. This one successful."

Jasfer staggered backward, but there was no chair for him to fall into this time. "Who was it?" His voice quavered.

"Akhash. Of Pashun, actually, though he has lived in Romnai for many years."

Jasfer shook his head. He didn't even know the name. How could an unknown prince take power? "I don't know him."

"He would not have drawn attention to himself. Our emissary to Romnai reported to him, but otherwise you would have had no reason to interact with him." Hrisha let out a dramatic, false-seeming sigh and said, "I'm sorry to inform you, Jasfer, that you are no longer among the Thirty."

His limbs felt like they belonged to someone else. He

looked around, pressed a stranger's hand against his forehead, finally found his balance by leaning against the wall. "Who are they? It must have been the plan all along. Murdering Baram, creating this chaos, just so this unknown Prince Akhash could take over. A puppet for some upstart Pashun princes." His voice rose almost to a shout, but he didn't care to control it. "Who is behind it, Hrisha? Is it Bunaran? Is it some princes here? The priests? We can't let them get away with murder."

Hrisha waited until he was done and looking his way. Then in a calm, emotionless voice he said, "We can't have such rumors tearing apart our valley, Jasfer. Especially now when we must all be united to rebuild this city. The new High Prince has taken over, but that does not mean he was behind the terrible attack on his predecessor. I'm sure he is only seeking a peaceful future for us all."

But how likely was that? Surely this prince had laid his plans long ago.

Without giving Jasfer time to reply, Hrisha said, "Remember that you are still a prince for now, but you can be stripped of your jati, cast out just as your sister was." He turned in his chair and stood. "And from now on, you will address me as *tisrah*. As a ruling prince it is, after all, my due."

Chapter 24

Jaritta climbed down the slope to greet the latest group of miners to flee the fighting in Pashun. One was bent double, coughing. Another leaned on his neighbor as if too weak to stand. None of them looked likely to last through the winter. More might still come. They heard stories from the people they welcomed, about Pashun and the rebellious miners and others, people who might have hoped to carve out a place in that fractured city who now fled.

Could they trust such people to help them? If they were able to fight and willing to do so on their behalf, then she couldn't think that they had much of a choice.

She painted a friendly smile on her face. "Welcome to Chaitanshehar. Anyone is welcome here who is willing to work toward building the city and protecting it. No other demand is placed on you, and you will demand nothing of your neighbors apart from that. We have no castes and no jatis, and even mumblers are a part of our city. If any of that bothers you, then you still have a chance to leave."

She gestured at the bundles lined up beside her feet. "This is food, one bundle for each of you. It should last a few days. Longer if you can find food to supplement it with. Your new neighbors may be able to help you with that.

"Even if you choose to leave the city, you may take one bundle of food to get you on your way. At this time of year, I would suggest staying close to the steam beds. Return to Pashun and try to hide there until warmer weather arrives, if you think you can avoid the soldiers.

"If you leave, do not return. Your welcome today is your one chance to be a part of our new city. It will not be extended a second time."

As soon as she stepped away, two miners rushed the food, with the others running or hobbling behind. Ilshu had to make sure each of them received exactly one. Jaritta trusted that they would and made her way further down the slope to where their defenses were growing apace.

Thamiba stood on the wall, leaning slightly to favor his wounded side.

"Looking good here," she said to him.

He scanned the wall and nodded. "Any attack up this route would be foolish at this point. We should finish what we have, but even as is I can't imagine any army would be so stupid as to try."

A path led up from the steam beds, cutting back and forth as it climbed. Plenty of exposure coming up that way. An army might ignore the trail and try to forge straight up—it wasn't so steep that the switchbacks were completely necessary—but they'd find plenty of loose scree, hidden pits, and weakened rock formations that way, slowing them down. And above all that, a solid wall with Jaritta's soldiers stationed along it, ready to spread the word to others in the city.

"Good. But you think we need to focus on the other defenses at this point?"

Thamiba nodded.

That was more difficult. They talked about the walls to the right and left, along the northern and southern edges of the city. They had raised some defenses there immediately, blocking the most open access, but the walls were disjointed, and the geography of the place made connecting the existing parts a challenge. Upslope, the city was completely open, and the needs for hunting and foraging meant the people resisted any defense that would end up cutting them off completely from those lands.

Thamiba rubbed his jaw. "How long do you think Poorma's death jati threat will hold?"

Jaritta glanced around for either Poorma or Tanjali, but they were elsewhere in the city, taking care of some of the constant demands on the leaders' time. The superstition about the death jati was powerful among most people, and soldiers especially. Their task was to touch the bodies of the dead, to prepare them for burning. To be touched by one while alive was seen as a curse, a promise that death itself would come soon. "It's held this far. That's more than I expected."

The hold hadn't been perfect. One small band of soldiers had decided to take a chance on avoiding the death witch, as they called her. Jaritta had had a large group of women dress like death jati workers and simply stare down the attackers. Their spirits broke before a single arrow was shot. Nearly everyone in the city, men and women, now kept a death jati disguise in case it would prove useful.

Chaitanshehar, the city of the death jati. It was not what she'd had in mind when she set out.

"Maybe they'll wait for better weather," Jaritta added. "These long nights probably make it more difficult to distract their soldiers from superstition. Longer days, and we can expect a much bigger force coming against us."

And she could scarcely afford to lose the fighters they would be forced to rely on, while Pashun had more than enough soldiers to throw their way. So far, they'd never even made a real attempt to root them out of their growing city. And when they did, a coordinated attack with seasoned soldiers...

A dozen miners here and a dozen there, along with a trickle of untouchables and others from the cities had swelled their numbers. Even a good number of stragglers from the Old Eghsal ruins had come in before the weather had turned too bad.

It wouldn't be enough, she was sure. They needed

something more than numbers to distract the cities from bothering them while they established themselves.

"Someone's coming up the trail," Thamiba said.

More miners. Hopefully this group would be healthier and able to contribute to the city's protection. She leaned out to watch them come around one switchback and cross below them. Didn't actually look like miners. The miners arrived with nothing, often not even enough clothes to keep them warm on the journey between the mines and the city. By design the mine owners gave them as little as possible, warmed the living areas rather than giving them extra clothes they might steal. Those who'd managed to revolt earlier, which hadn't been successful in all the mines, were fleeing the fresh attack by the owners' soldiers. Either way gave them little chance to prepare fully for a winter journey.

This group of around a dozen travelers were wrapped in thick robes. They carried bags and packs. No pack animals, but the furs spoke of access to a mid-caste kind of money.

"Any idea who they are?" she finally asked Thamiba.

He shook his head. "I didn't see them until just a moment ago. They were already on their way up."

The miners sometimes hit the switchbacks from the side, coming around the ridge to the south of the lava fields. This group appeared to have come the whole way up the path, or near enough. Were they here to join the city? Or might they be some other, clandestine way for Pashun to attack, a delegation meant to drive them away?

"Guards, be alert," she called out. "Thamiba, let's meet them below the wall to be safe."

"Not safe for us," he muttered, but two guards joined them going through the door in the wall, and they began the descent to meet the travelers.

It was the first time Jaritta had descended since their arrival. The trail felt more protected than it had looked from above—intentionally so. Shrubs and rocks afforded an illusion of cover. The smell of sulfur met them before they'd gone down the second switchback.

The travelers were still below them, with one switchback corner in between, when one of them called up, "Hello. Are we to the new city, then?"

Thamiba waved down and said, "Almost. Come meet us up ahead where the trail turns."

The switchback was sharp, with no room to gather, so Jaritta continued a short way past the actual turning and waited for the travelers in the lee of a small rock formation.

She had been close when she guessed there were a dozen travelers. They were eleven, six women and four men, plus one child of about ten. They'd traveled far. The dust on their clothes told as much, the color tones recording the story of where they'd been, if anyone could read it. But they looked strong. Nothing like the sickly miners who trickled in. Their leader was tall and wrapped in so many furs she could make out little more about him. Young or old? Perhaps he'd do as a fighter for their city, though she doubted he had the build of a true soldier.

Her own guards stood to either side of Jaritta as she greeted them. Hardly seemed necessary. This was not a group arriving to attack her.

"You are approaching the city of Chaitanshehar. Please tell us your purpose and reasons for coming."

The leader choked on whatever he'd been about to say. When his coughing fit had passed, he said in a weak voice, "What do you call it? Tell me again the name, please."

"Chaitanshehar."

"You named it for him?" His voice grew stronger, and it suddenly snapped into familiarity. "Oh, Jaritta. You can't imagine how it thrills me to hear his name again. To dream his dreams."

"Rashul?" She couldn't keep the incredulity from her voice. "Rashul, it is you." Rashul who had inspired her and her co-conspirators in their coup. Rashul who had never reached out to her after its failure, but sat in his house, rumor was, and let himself be a pawn for the princes. Rashul who was standing right here, amid the stink and the wild of that new land.

"Have you come…" She couldn't bring herself to put the hope into words. Maybe his adopted masters had sent him for some ulterior purpose.

"I heard of your city, Jaritta. That's what they call it in Romnai, Jaritta's city. I had to go into hiding if I hoped to sneak out here without the princes knowing. It took longer than I had hoped, but now I am here."

And here to stay? "Your voice…" She had to swallow a lump in her throat. All the memories came tumbling through her mind, of sitting around Chaitan's house while Rashul dreamed for them all and inspired them. "We need your voice here, Rashul. I am thrilled to welcome you to the city."

She turned and gestured up the slope to the wall above them. "My city? No, a city *we* are building, a city for everyone. As Chaitan would have wanted. Come inside so we can talk more. About the past and about the future."

Rashul walked beside her. "I have little to offer these days. What I can, I will. But you… You have built this. A place to make the society we always dreamed of."

Only if the princes and priests didn't send their soldiers marching in and turn it all to nightmare. With Rashul's presence, that suddenly seemed less likely than it had earlier. The soldiers might come, but with Rashul's charisma to inspire them all, the defenders were surely turn any attack away.

They talked as they climbed, skating across the time directly around her attempted coup, but skipping back and forth between the more distant past and these last months spent founding the city and fighting to keep it alive.

When they passed through the heavy doors at the base of the wall, Chaitanshehar seemed much more real, much more the place she'd always had in mind that it could be. The tough stone walls and makeshift shelters were only the beginning, hints of the city to come.

***

Rashul's companions had faded into the background. One of the men, Tarnmai, had spent some time at Chaitan's, but he was only scarcely familiar. A face, aged by the years, that she vaguely remembered. He had been no part of her coup. The others were more recent friends of Rashul, people he had gathered around him quietly over the past few years. An older woman who had lived nearby. A couple and their child who'd come to know him at the market.

The most recent of these friends was a woman in her mid-twenties who carried herself as if she were much older. She'd met Rashul when he was already in hiding but proved herself a resourceful part of their final preparations, even securing them extra food for the journey.

Jaritta didn't like her. Something about her was false.

No, not only something. Everything. Her name was not Matral, though she answered to that. She hadn't met Rashul by chance, though Jaritta couldn't quite figure out how she knew that. But most of all, she was higher caste than she let on. Jaritta had always been good at identifying a person's caste—a combination of how her mind worked and the training she'd had as a young girl in a family of the princely jati. But Matral, as she called herself, was kortru through and through. Prince or priest, she couldn't tell through observing, but there was no doubting her high-born caste.

After a few days observing her, Jaritta confronted her. They were walking along what was becoming a street with buildings rising on either side. Without offering any warning, Jaritta put her hand on Matral's shoulder.

"Who are you?"

She lowered her head in a way that was probably supposed to look meek. It didn't. The way her shoulder flinched from Jaritta's touch told as much. "Matral, tisrah. I came with Rashul, remember?"

"I am not *tisrah*. Not back home and not here. And you, I think, are not Matral." With a slight signal from her, three soldiers converged toward them but kept just enough distance to keep their conversation private. "Don't think I didn't notice how you flinched to be touched by someone untouchable."

"I am sorry, Jaritta. A lifetime of reactions are not easy to overcome."

Absolutely true, yet not the full story. "I can have you thrown out. An easy explanation to Rashul, and no one else would even miss you. So, try again. Who are you?"

Matral hesitated, eyeing the street and the soldiers and the people going about their business. Her shoulders dropped, and she said quietly, "Can we go somewhere to talk instead? I'll tell you."

Jaritta studied the woman's face, still travel-worn, but its high-born beauty visible under the strain of more recent days. Nothing there to make her trust the woman more. But it wasn't as if she feared Matral would attack her, not that kind of distrust. If she pulled a knife, she'd find Jaritta's years of living on the street made her more than a match for a high-caste woman like this. It was instead the woman's words, her reasons for being in Chaitanshehar to begin with, whatever devious and unspoken plans passed behind her kortru eyes.

"Follow me."

The soldiers fell in with them as she led the way to the humble house she'd claimed for herself. It was made of mud bricks, baked to a color that matched her skin. The roof was stretched hide from some mountain beast that had been hunted for her. Inside was a sitting room of sorts, the most she would concede to her status as a leader of the city. They each took a seat on opposite sides of a wooden plank that could serve as a desk or table. The guards stayed on their feet beside the door.

Matral looked around the room in silence before saying, "It reminds me of your brother's study. You resemble him, I think more than either of you would admit."

"My...brother?"

"Please, let me introduce myself. My name is Datri. My husband is Prince Jasfer Talai, your brother." She opened her arms as if to offer Jaritta a hug. "Sister?"

It was a half mocking offer, and Jaritta didn't deign to answer. She sat frozen on her side of the plank. Of course, she'd heard that Jasfer had married and knew something of Datri by reputation.

Which is what made her stand up abruptly. "Get out." She pointed at the door, but to be clear she added, "I don't want you in my city."

Datri didn't move. "I thought all people were welcomed. As long as they have something to offer. I have much to offer you."

"I suppose my brother heard about this city and rushed to support me in any way he could." Jaritta crossed her arms over her chest.

"Quite the opposite. He came here to try to stop you, only something else happened along the way, and our plans have changed. And those changes affect you far more than you must realize."

It was playing into the woman's games to even listen, but she couldn't ignore her either, if what she knew was really so important.

"You don't trust me, I see that. And I understand why, but first let me tell you a brief story from six, almost seven years ago."

Seven years. Her coup. Jasfer's marriage ceremony shortly afterward. Jaritta sat down on the edge of her chair and gestured for Datri to speak.

"I was newly arrived in your brother's household. Not yet married. In his household was a young arcist who wanted to leave. I wanted him gone as well, to be honest. His influence on my husband-to-be threatened to be a counterweight to whatever arguments I might make. What gave the arcist pause was that you were imprisoned, and he wanted to do what he could to free you. Jasfer would not listen to his pleas. *Couldn't* listen, to be fair to him. The risk to his own tenuous position was too great.

"So I stepped in. Even now I won't say exactly how I did it, but I arranged a distraction for your guards. I showed the arcist how to rescue you and made sure he was successful. I won't claim I did these things for you or for him. They were done for Jasfer's sake, to take away the one thing that might weigh on him over the years ahead. Your execution. And I would do it again. For him, not you."

She met Jaritta's eyes as if daring her to respond.

Jaritta couldn't. She had her own memories of that time, some of them thoughts she hadn't allowed herself ever since. The anger at her brother, the betrayal at Pavresh's hands…but then also his rescuing her. And it all came together in this devious woman?

Finally, she managed to say, "Fine, I will listen. What else can you say before I send you off alone? And it had better not be more rumors of a traveler from the Forgotten South. We've all heard that one plenty of times now. What big event has transpired in Romnai now?"

"The High Prince has been assassinated."

Jaritta gasped. Baram's face flashed before her eyes. She'd sought to unseat him, of course, but it had never been about him personally. It had been the system, one he was too much a part of. But who would take his place instead? Probably someone far worse.

"That's what changed our plans. That and a new Thirty that does not include your brother. He is in Pashun, but I haven't heard from him since the new Thirty were named."

Jaritta's thoughts spun. A coup. A new Thirty. What would they make of Jaritta's city? Would they step away and let them succeed or fail on their own? Or would they prove more aggressive still in crushing Chaitanshehar before it had a chance?

"I still don't trust you."

"You shouldn't. If you're to be the leader of this new city, then you need to not trust me. Nor most people you meet, even those you know."

Jaritta accepted the advice with a single nod of her head. "I won't send you off alone, not yet. And I have no jail cell to keep you in. But I will put Rashul in charge of watching over you, once I make sure he realizes exactly who you are."

Datri grimaced, exactly the way any high-born person would at being put beneath a brenil-caste lesser. But she didn't argue.

As they made their way back through the city toward where Rashul and his other friends had established themselves, something seemed wrong. The quiet. Muffled noises that she couldn't identify.

"An attack!" One of her guards pointed, not at the walls but down the street toward what was as much the center of town as anything.

"No soldiers could have made it that far…"

"The miners could," Datri said. "If they weren't all real miners." She held out her wrists to Jaritta as if to be handcuffed. "Take me to Rashul, if that's what you want. But be fast or you might have a whole city collapsing into chaos if you can't stop those miners now."

Jaritta took one look at Datri's wrists then shoved her away. "Get the guards from the walls," she told her guards. "We need everyone we can spare. Now!"

CHAPTER 25

The steam beds continued to open before Valni. A path would seem to end, the deadly pools closing in, but as she pressed ahead, each time a passage materialized, a route to lead her onward, deeper, farther from anything human.

A river frothed upward from the middle of the lava field. It stank of sulfur, even more than the worst mudpots clustered at the base of Pashun. It scalded the rock as it flowed outward, through a series of rapids. Valni followed, leaping from rock to rock of the river bank, well away from the water itself.

The river led down into a depression in the lava fields, a low point of scattered rocks and uneven ground. The water poured in and then seeped down through the rocks to disappear. And would a person disappear into that as well? Valni paused at the edge of the hollow to catch her breath. The air was thick and pungent.

From this point Pashun was hidden. Even the upper buildings lay behind the slope of the land. All she could see was the lava fields themselves and far above them, as if they belonged to another world, the hazy peaks of the southern mountains.

Another world. Perhaps she should go there, into the mountains where shame and a jati's failure were unknown or unimportant. Or beyond them, to the traveler's Forgotten South, where there were many kingdoms, some of them surely in need of soldiers to protect their rulers.

Edging around the hollow, she pictured herself leaving Eghsal behind. To never see her home or anyone she knew again. But also, to never have to endure the shame of her sisters' failure.

When she put it that way, she knew her answer. Tempting

to leave, no doubt. And she could if forced to, could find her own way among the mountains and live—or die—as events transpired. But if her purpose was simply to avoid shame, then it was a cowardly retreat, selfish and unworthy of a falcon jati warrior.

That didn't mean going back immediately, though. She came up the far side of the hollow and saw a new route leading onward across the lava fields. A possible route, though it might well end or turn her around toward some new place. But she climbed onto a rock and jumped to the next.

The route was full of false paths and dead ends, wide stretches of foul mud and sudden gaps of deadly pools of something that merely resembled water. Valni nearly fell into one pool of mud and slipped down the bank beside another. She slept in a break in a rock formation and continued the next day, faint with hunger. The day was nearly over when she came out the other side. Pashun was far away in the yellow haze behind her.

Who ruled it today? Who would rule it tomorrow?

This edge of the swamp was soft and still treacherous. But the shrubs held small patches of solid ground with their roots, so she went from shrub to shrub with no destination in mind.

As she came around a large stand of shrubs, a trio of soldiers popped up on the other side. She dropped into a crouch.

"Who do we have here?"

"No one," she said. "Just passing through." A silly claim, she knew as soon as it left her mouth. No one would be passing through such a swamp for no reason. She waited in silence for their answer, her staff poised to strike them if they came close.

A fight, with her outnumbered and weak with hunger. Against three trained soldiers? Her falcon jati training meant it would still favor her—as long as she could strike first.

Or was that the overconfidence that had led her jati to shame?

"Well, pass on through then," one soldier said with a smirk. "Don't let us delay you."

Valni didn't move. She should try to learn something from these soldiers. She tried to look more relaxed without actually lowering her guard. "Maybe you can help me. I got lost in there. I didn't expect to come out over here, on this side of the geysers. Where exactly am I?"

"Geysers is the polite word for it," one mocked.

"Not the word we use around here, though, is it?"

They began to spread out. She couldn't afford to wait much longer.

"Some untouchable then, on your way to the untouchable city over here? We've been seeing your kind going west here all these past twelve-days. Well, we're not afraid of some little untouchable, are we?" Violence made his words ragged.

Before his companions could answer, Valni leaped forward and swung her staff at his head. He dropped into the mud as she shifted direction toward the second soldier. His eyes widened as it must have dawned on him that she was more than a simple beggar girl. He managed to deflect her staff with his sword, but that only made it swing down and strike his leg with a crack. His counter was mere reflex, likely coming before the pain even registered. His blade cut her below her arm just before it fell from his hand.

While he screamed at the broken bone, she swung the other end around into his ribs, knocking the breath from him. He fell, and she didn't think he'd be rising.

That left one. She winced as she moved to face him. The cut across the side of her ribs wasn't deep, but she shouldn't have let him even wound her that much. It was the hunger, the poor sleep. But that brief weakness wouldn't save the last soldier.

The smart move for him would be to flee, but he stood his ground and shouted for help. How many other soldiers were nearby? Probably a score or so if it was a unit of one of the local jatis. He wore no insignia for her to identify, but he must be expecting others to be within earshot. She needed to deal with this one and be gone before they came to his rescue.

He'd seen her skill with the staff, though, and kept his distance while he put a stone in his sling.

What he must not have realized was how quickly she'd moved even before her first swing of her staff. As he began to bring the leather sling around, she vaulted to the side to throw off his aim then charged.

The slung stone went far wide of the mark, striking the mud with a squelch, and she ripped the sling from his hands with one end of her staff then knocked him into the swamp with the other.

She grabbed the sling and ran off before any other soldiers could pop up from the surrounding land.

West. When she had a chance to slow down and think about where to go, she remembered what the late soldier had said about the untouchable city. They'd seen many untouchables heading west. She cleaned out the wound on her side as well as she could and looked across the swamp.

There was something untouchable about the shame she knew her jati deserved. Perhaps such a city of untouchables would be a place for her as well. She directed her path westward, toward drier ground and what looked like a shift from mud to stone.

***

The swampland at the edge of the lava fields was much wider than she'd pictured. And even here, pits of sulfur-smelling mud dotted the swamp. She climbed a tree to spend the night, and even by the time the following night was falling she hadn't reached the edge of the wetland.

Other soldier groups were about throughout the area.

Why? Were they all watching for people heading toward the city of untouchables? That seemed hard to credit, but she didn't dare approach anyone to ask. Maybe they were fleeing the fighting in Pashun. Even if so, she didn't trust whether she'd be able to identify enemy from friend. Or if she could count any of them as friend. She kept her own travels to the shadows and thickets, watching always and hiding rather than take a chance at being seen. She scavenged little blue berries from the thickets, hoping they were safe to eat. They gave her a thin, wavering sort of energy that came and went.

Again she slept high in a tree, tying herself into the crook of a branch. It became the pattern of her life, the pattern of shame and self-exile. For days she made her way westward as much as she could without revealing her presence to the small bands of soldiers. In truth, it was often a journey northward or southward, ending up scarcely any nearer the edge than she'd begun, not because she was lost but simply out of extreme caution of remaining unseen.

Her wound healed without becoming inflamed, a true blessing out in this unclean land. She poached food and safe water from the camps when she could manage without being seen and ate what berries she could find, but mostly lived off nothing, off the chemicals that weighed down the air and the thoughts of her jati's failure.

One night she'd dozed off when the light of a campfire woke her back up. A group of soldiers had set up camp only a short way from the base of her own tree. She lay there watching them, wondering if they knew the dances she would have danced with her jati sisters, wondering what food they ate and what stories they told to pass the time. Wondering what shame they *didn't* have to feel.

She finally slept, but when morning came it was far from sufficient. Her movements as she crept down the tree were leaden and her thoughts slow like the mud.

Maybe that was why she was seen as soon as she left the tree to slink away. At least she could blame it on weariness.

"Valni?"

She had to squint to make out the figure who spoke to her. The sunlight was behind the man, but she managed to make out enough of his face to recognize him. It was Lodnan, from the Madrur jati she'd sort of joined while in Pashun.

"Lodnan. What are you doing away from Pashun?"

"Why are *you* out here? We have orders, as many of us as we could get out here fast. The princes will forgive everything if we move quick enough. But it's not going to be safe. You should still be back there." He looked around at the harsh landscape, as if puzzled to find her here. "You just disappeared though."

Not, *why didn't you help us fight?* Not, *we thought you might have been injured in battle.* Just, that she shouldn't be here.

Because she wasn't a soldier in his eyes.

She looked away. Best to keep as close to the truth as possible. "I was following a training route and got lost. Thought I'd find my way back eventually but ended up out here instead. What are your orders way out this way?"

"Followed a route all the way across? For this long? That's some training. Though you know not to enter the lava fields alone."

Valni shrugged. She was so far beyond feeling embarrassed at breaking that taboo, she couldn't even think how to explain it to him.

He let the taboo go as well, likely too focused on finally having his own chance to join the fighters. "You must be starving." Lodnan tossed her a chunk of bread.

"Thank you. Thirsty too, if you have anything."

While she drank from the small cup he offered her, he gazed out to the west where a series of broken foothills huddled beneath the higher peaks. After a moment, he seemed to recall her question about their orders. "Some sort of uprising out here. Can't imagine who it'd be, but we're coming in to enforce the peace, I guess. Round up some bandits who've built walls and a little camp of some kind."

"Planning to actually fight, then? Or is this just a chance to march into the woods and scare them?"

Lodnan laughed. "Oh, I think there'll be fighting. I hope so. No one wants to come this far just to march back home, and the princes are calling this our penance. But I don't imagine it'll take much of a fight to send them fleeing. A little fighting, and then we go back with the Madrur reputation fully restored."

As easy as that, to absolve them? She could join them. The thought made her dizzy. She'd always fought for her own jati and the honor of the High Prince, not deigning to enter into the squabbles that demanded soldiers of other jatis. But if her own people had become shamed, could she regain honor by fighting for another jati? For other princes? If she fought honorably for someone else, did it say anything about her jati's shame and her own honor? "I'll head that way with you, then."

"What? No, we don't need a lot of extra support members. It's only the soldiers for this mission. Real members of the jati." He looked around at the swamp and pursed his lips. "But I suppose someone should escort you back…"

Valni swept away the idea with her hand. "See, that's why I'll just join you for a little while. I don't need to be part of the fighting, but traveling together would be better for you soldiers and for me."

Lodnan pursed his lips and looked back at the camp as the other soldiers quickly packed up and prepared to move. "No," he said at last, shaking his head. "You made it out here on your own. We can't slow down to have you join us, and we're not going to spare anyone to guide you back. I don't mean to sound cruel, but you'll have to make your own route again."

Valni blinked at the man's tone, the clear dismissal of any responsibility toward her, the barest hint of an apology—and even that gone by the end.

Over his shoulder he added, "And stay out of the way. We aren't the only soldier group out here this morning. I wouldn't want you to make it so we can't do our job against these upstarts."

So, that was the way of it. She hadn't expected it to feel so much like a slap across the cheek to be dismissed that way. Would it have been different if she'd truly been a part of their jati instead of someone who'd simply shown up and associated with them for a time? More than likely. If she'd grown up among these soldiers, they'd think of her as one of their own.

Instead, she was still simply a stranger.

Well, then. So much for fighting for another jati to establish her honor. She could just as well go be a stranger among the untouchables and see what they would do when she came.

As soon as the soldiers had decamped and set out, she rushed ahead, paralleling them on the other sides of trees, no longer so concerned with not being seen by other groups of soldiers as long as she could avoid the attention of the Madrur group. Finally, for the first time in days, she made real progress that wasn't undone by backtracking to avoid any other people. Soon she'd far outpaced Lodnan's troop.

By midday the swamp was ending, and she approached a sloping path up toward the foothills. The noise of hammers echoed off the rocks. Not making any effort to hide where they were then, or what they were doing. She made her way up the gentle incline of a trail that looked to cut back and forth half a dozen times to reach the wall above.

A surprisingly sturdy looking wall, given how dismissive

Lodnan had been of these upstarts. Maybe it was more of a city than he'd implied.

She made her way around the first two corners of the trail and paused. The noise of the hammer didn't sound so much like hammers anymore. Swords?

A game path cut off from the main trail at the next switchback. Valni dashed that way, in among a group of large boulders. When the path faded into nothing, she climbed up onto one to see the route ahead. There were soldiers climbing up the face of the rock, hidden from the trail.

Rather than going back, she leaped to the next boulder and on from there, rock to rock over dizzying drops. Even her path across the lava fields had been nothing to this. She didn't let the danger slow her down. No squad of soldiers could have climbed that way, but a falcon jati soldier had training beyond that of any normal soldier. She leaped and clung and inched her way around to the next jump.

On one side were the soldiers, as yet unaware of her. On the other side, the switchbacks came and went and came again. She was even with the top of the trail and a solid wall that certainly undercut Lodnan's claims of how easy this would be. And yet, only a few guards stood on the wall. So maybe it would be as quick as he thought.

One guard, fully exposed to the trail below, had his head cocked backward, as if watching whatever was happening with the sound of swords and hammers.

Valni climbed around another rock and dropped onto the wall.

She was about to warn the guards when a woman came up onto the wall along with a large group of other guards. The woman halted and stared at Valni.

Valni took the moment to study these untouchables. The woman's face was scarred across her forehead and one cheek but otherwise had the fine features of a high-born lady. The guards with her looked like they'd just come from fighting. All four of them were wearing death jati robes, and one had the skin tone of a mumbler. His appearance gave Valni pause. The mumblers were the enemy and always had been, the threat in the wilds that could take down a High Prince no matter what her jati did to defend him.

But if shame brought her down to the level of an untouchable, no reason why honor couldn't raise a mumbler up to the same state.

Sketching a bow, Valni asked, "Is this the city of the untouchables I've heard of? I wish to join it."

"And attack from within once you've joined?" the woman asked with a dismissive wave of her hand. "We can't accept any newcomers now. Lock her up until we've had a chance to question her."

As several guards came forward, Valni held up a hand. "Wait. I saw soldiers climbing up the rocks here, below where I was. You'll need to fight them off. I can help."

The woman released a weary breath and turned to her guards. "Our fighting isn't done, then. Once you have her locked up, come so we can set up our defense."

The guards again moved toward her.

Valni shouted, "No! *I am* your defense. Let me help. I was told this is the city of untouchables. That those without a jati will be welcomed here. You need my help to fight them off."

"I wish I could. We've welcomed others, but they betrayed us. Until we can question you—"

"Those soldiers won't give you time to question me. I've seen them converging from all over the swamp down there. Seen other soldiers already climbing. If you wait to question me, your city won't last long enough." She drew herself up with all the strength and power of a soldier-jati-trained warrior. "You need a soldier to direct your defenses or you won't have a chance. My sisters may have failed to protect the

High Prince. I will not fail to protect your city, if you give me the chance *now*. There is no time to delay."

The scarred woman hesitated a moment, studying her face. She might have whispered something like, "Falcon jati," but the words were lost in the noise of the mountains. Then with a decisive nod she said, "This woman is a true soldier. Whether we can trust her or not, I don't know. Put her to work though. We need any help we can get."

Valni didn't wait for anything more but began directing the tired guards to new positions along the wall and in the rocks where no wall had yet been built.

Let them try to invade this city now. She would not allow it to fall, this she swore.

On the last vestiges of her falcon jati honor.

Chapter 26

Pavresh found the old mumbler trail through the lava field south of Romnai just as he'd been told he would. It cut between a relatively predictable geyser and a toxic pond, the way marked by low piles of carefully arranged stones.

"Come." He gestured behind him at the mass of untouchables who'd decided to follow him. "This is the trail I'd heard of. Mumblers used it long before our ancestors even founded the city." Or rather back when the mumblers were the ones founding cities, including what would become Romnai. So, it might have been their ancestors after all, and the stories they'd all known all their lives merely lies. He wasn't about to confuse his followers by explaining all of that.

The followers were a surprise wrinkle to his plans. After hearing the stories from the one group of untouchables in the subterranean remains of the ancient mumbler city, he'd shared what he'd known of Jaritta's city. They'd heard rumors and were desperate to hear any direct knowledge.

By morning the entire group of untouchables wanted to go with him.

By the time the next night fell, they'd reached out to other friends, relatives, untouchables throughout the city. Three dozen people, none with any resources for such a journey, clamored to join them.

Pavresh chose one woman, Juishika, to be in charge of arranging their plans. "I'll be going there, and they can come along with me. But I'm not gathering food and supplies for dozens of people. Tell them they each need to put together enough for a twelve-day journey."

"We're beggars and worse. How do we manage that?"

Pavresh didn't answer directly. They would figure it out,

or they wouldn't go. "And it might take longer than that. The more people in a group, often the slower it moves. So, food that's filling, that lasts, that isn't heavy or bulky. And shoes, good shoes for walking many miles."

He left her to it and made his own plans for the best route, talking to travelers who spoke of an old trail through the steam beds. The trail had lain in disuse for many years but perhaps would still be of use to him. The last time it was used was during the Mumbler War, which ended over forty-five years earlier. The mumblers had tried to sneak into the city from beyond the lava fields early in the war, which pushed the time back another decade or more. They were turned back. Later during the conflict, when they were a bigger threat to Romnai, they hadn't returned to the route, as if they'd found it lacking. No one ever learned the reasoning for that or any of the mumbler decisions during those battles. The story of the war was told entirely by Pavresh's people.

Now not only had he found the remnants of that old trail, but he had a swelling mass of untouchables coming along after him. The three dozen had added even more. A dozen or so handcarts, shared among them, helped carry some of the food and blankets they would need. Mostly they carried their goods in their arms or in bags strapped around waists and over shoulders. Quite a few used a curious satchel with a long strap that rested on their foreheads. Pavresh thought his head would be pounding after a few hours, but no one complained.

"Can they make this journey?" he'd asked Juishika.

Juishika lifted her chin and said, "I hear there's a man from the Forgotten South came through the mountains last fall. If he can make that journey, then we can make this one."

So that rumor had come here as well. Curious. Whether true or not, it was an arcist image with its own power, one that caused it to spread. The intrepid traveler. If it could inspire these beggars to keep pace, then all the better. He wove a glimmer of that same image around himself as he led the way. Casting the spell in that way, to help the travelers with what they wanted to do anyway, didn't feel wrong in the way some of his other spells had. In fact, in a surprising way, it healed him. There was still something valuable in arcist magic, a story it could tell that added value to the world.

The mumbler path wound southward. The Romnai lava fields were a land of geysers and bare rock forming pillars and dry gullies. Scattered lines of pine trees offered the appearance of safety, but they often grew where the geyser ash enriched the soil, so an eruption could take place at any time. The path would sometimes come close to those trees but always veered away before reaching them.

Juishika sang as they marched, leading the others in silly children's songs that many seemed to already know. Maybe something about growing up in Romnai meant they'd all absorbed them in childhood. Pavresh, having grown up on his father's mine to the north, knew none of the songs. They were about animals and the naga of myth, about armies getting lost and fishermen finding nonsense things beneath the sea—cattle and castles and carriages.

Singing passed the time, so Pavresh didn't complain. He missed the silence of traveling alone, the sounds of the land itself all around. Rather than dwell on that change, he chose to think of the songs as their own source of arcist images, a parallel to the folk tales he always sought to learn. The trail meandered across the geyser field, from stone pile to stone pile while they sang.

On the third day the complaining commenced. As they came down past a pool of bright green water surrounded by rings of brilliantly colored soil, without any warning Pavresh could identify, a large portion of the group slowed down together. They dawdled behind, separating from the others, calling out for the rest to slow down and wait.

Pavresh slowed his own pace, but the stragglers fell even further behind.

"You know them," he said to Juishika. "Find out what's slowing them down."

She gave him a look that said she thought it should be his job. But she took a break until the rest caught up while Pavresh slowed the leading group even more.

When she came back up by him, she shrugged. "Nothing specific. They're just tired. Want to leave the geysers, want to rest some, want more food. And wish the food they're carrying weren't so heavy."

But they couldn't leave the lava field faster *and* rest. Couldn't eat more *and* carry less. Or at least, any solution to that would be decidedly short-lasting. When he opened his mouth to say as much, she shook her head.

"They know they can't have all of that. Just remember, these aren't great travelers like you, used to the road. They're beggars, some because they're too often sick to work, some too old or young. You are their leader. You need to come down to their level some."

Pavresh picked up a stone from the mumbler path and moved it out of the way so no one would trip on it. "I didn't ask to be their leader. They just chose to tag along. Can't you get them singing again, or something?"

It sounded petulant, even to his own ears. He pretended to find something interesting on the path ahead so he wouldn't have to meet Juishika's eyes. As she made her way back along the line, she called over her shoulder, "Of course you didn't ask. Maybe the best kind of leaders don't. But you're stuck with them, either way. So better decide what kind of leader you'll be."

What kind of leader was he? Not a leader at all, if he could choose. Let him sit in the shadows and watch, learn, turn the stories he observed into magic. But his own story kept shifting away from that idea. Now he was the leader in the wilderness. He'd better fulfill the role as best he could, at least until he could give the responsibility to someone else.

Then he could shape his life around some other story, some other role.

The mumbler path appeared to be reaching its end, along the southeastern side of the lava fields. Maybe once they made it out, then the complaining would stop. They'd just press onward without incident until they reached Jaritta's city at last.

He could hope.

First, they had to get through this last stretch of the lava field. He cleared the irritation from his mind and drew on the arcist magic of the situation. Leader in the Wilderness, that was an easy place to start. He built up his own authority, drawing the threads of power in toward himself. The magic strained against that invisible line between the magic working well and the magic feeling wrong. He threaded it carefully to keep on the good side of that line, made sure he didn't push for more power than he could control, for more control than was humane.

A good start, but he needed the untouchables to move. Fear. He could draw on the fear of the unknown to get them back on their feet. Nothing too extreme or they'd simply give up. But he made them fear the geysers and pools nearby, added in a fear of wild beasts—though there was precious little wildlife out here. Fear that they would fall too far behind.

The beggars at the front, around him, suddenly sped up.

"Wait." He held up his arms and leaned more heavily on the wilderness leader image to get them to slow down.

Arcist magic wasn't something he could simply direct toward one direction or one group of people, but he did his best to focus the fear on something behind them, on the idea of being too far from him, their leader. The discomfort returned, the feeling of the magic as unclean. He held back from adding anything more to the mix, gritted his teeth against the feeling, and held the magic in place.

The beggars in the rear sped up.

They reached the edge of the geyser field, a region of bare rock and scattered trees that differed only in that it felt colder, with at least an hour to go before sundown. But Pavresh was weary and nauseated. He called for them to make camp, and as soon as it was clear the work was getting done, he let go of his magic, lay down, and slept, deep and dreamless and free from any hint of fear.

***

At first as they made their way through the barrens that edged the eastern side of the lava fields, Pavresh thought they might truly be past the struggles of the journey. All downhill from there, figuratively at least. The path did climb up as it left the warmth of the geysers. Not enough to slow them down.

They crossed the route Pavresh had taken on his way westward. He paused there. To the right, a narrow path led along the lava fields and into the southern mountains. At the end of that path was a mumbler village hidden in a stand of pines where the people had the dark skin and features of his own people.

And to the left the trail, such as it was, led into the wastes where he'd left Jaritta's pilgrimage. Now he came back to this crossroads and to her impossible venture, hoping to find she'd succeeded. At the time he left, he'd been told the route from her destination westward was too difficult, cut off by a ridge of high land. The ridge lay ahead, but looked passable from this direction. The ancient mumbler path, which he'd not even noticed on his way through, led upward from the lava fields.

His own pilgrimage of untouchables wouldn't survive a journey into those wastes to the east. They didn't have the food or the supplies. But if he pushed them, they might follow the old route up over the ridge. And some might survive.

He shook the morbid thought from his head as they continued upward. They settled into the rhythm of the journey for another day and then two, but by then the pace had tired out almost all of the untouchables. He could not get them to speed up anymore. The constant climbing wore them down. Even using his magic to inspire them with fear couldn't make them shake off their lethargy, and it left him feeling sick.

Juishika puffed along beside him, struggling just as the others were. Pavresh pursed his lips and forced himself to slow down even more.

"They're tired, tisrah. You have to understand that our feet aren't used to this."

"I'm not sure people call each other *tisrah* in Jaritta's city." Pavresh swerved to avoid a small rock in the trail as Juishika swerved around the other side of it. "I do understand, though. I only wish it weren't so. That we could keep our pace up."

"As well wish the sun wouldn't set." After a few paces in silence, Juishika added, "We used to call those mumbler wishes. But you said even mumblers are living in this new city? I wonder if we can still call them that."

Pavresh didn't know what to answer, so he said nothing. What would it be like to have a city with both mumblers and the people of Eghsal? Maybe it was simply a return to their real origins, a mixed people who created their identity out of a false past. Or at least a past so twisted by vague memories that it could be made into something new. Now they might do it again. Living together, would their descendants look back on Jaritta's city as their own ancestral land, and the other cities as foreign rivals?

Chaitan would have loved to tease out the storylines of such a new venture. Although, come to think of it, he'd never been fond of the mumblers. It was in fighting against them during the Mumbler Wars that he'd stumbled across arcist magic and begun to understand how it could be used.

Chaitan had been the wilderness leader back then. He'd been the one to inspire his followers into doing the impossible by playing on the arcist themes of justice, of heroes defending their homes.

Pavresh stopped in the middle of the path. Not fear. Chaitan *could* have tried to push his soldiers to fight stronger by using any number of variations on the idea of fear. But he hadn't. Maybe fear was too weak to inspire greatness, too easily accepted as normal. Fear might spur a quick action, but too much and the people became numb to it or gave in to despair.

That was what Pavresh was doing wrong now. He'd forgotten the first lessons of Chaitan's example, the very origin of the magic.

The weariness of Juishika and the rest was clear in the fact that no one asked him if he was well or why he'd stopped. They only took his pause as permission to rest.

Pavresh looked over them, seated or leaning on each other over a large stretch of the trail behind him. Barely a trail, a hint of a history of many travelers but never enough to make their individual paths clear. He might be veering away from and onto a thousand different slight variations of the trail used by mumblers who had come this way over the years. Small in number—this crowd of untouchables probably dwarfed the largest of those groups of hunting parties and small family tribes.

This was the new history, then. People could tell stories centuries from now of this journey.

He hadn't used his magic on a grand scale often. He'd

used it to affect how people saw him—or ignored him. He used it to understand and influence single people and small groups. He'd used it to force his captors to release him and the soldiers to let Jaritta's pilgrimage pass, but that had twisted the magic into something that damaged him inside.

The ambitious way he'd used fear to spur this crowd to hurry from the lava fields had really been his first attempt at the kind of thing Chaitan had done in the Mumbler Wars. And that had been a spur of the moment use, without planning or strategy, one that veered closer to the unhealthy ways he'd allowed his magic to go.

Now he began weaving a bigger effect through the magic, one that could hold them together for this entire journey, no matter how sore their feet or empty their bellies. He started on himself, not on how others would perceive him—as he had done to spy and so much else—but rather on how he pictured the venture. The patient leader. The visionary. He had to be the leader they needed if they were going to make it through.

Only when he could feel himself believing in this journey—for all of them, not only himself—did he turn his attention to weaving the magic for the rest of them. A promised land, a hard journey. They'd survived the streets of Romnai, after all. How could this be so much worse? The pride of overcoming past difficulties gave a surprising boost to the magic. Sore, even bleeding feet couldn't stop their journey.

It took much more energy to cast the magic over so many people, an intense focus that he didn't think he could maintain for long periods of time. Some of the strands unraveled. They whipped about as if to destroy the other parts of the magic, but he reached out to them and pulled them back into the magic.

A journey. All on its own that was a powerful arcist theme. He drew from the stories of the journey from the Forgotten

South. Even if it was false, in part or in whole, it played a role in the stories they all knew and accepted. But that wasn't the only journey in their past. Their ancestors had come to Romnai from Jarnur, at the least. Some must have lived in the old Eghsal City. The journey there would have been harsh. The journey away might well have been a flight from terror, filled with the same mixture of sadness and longing as their current journey.

And the mumblers had their own histories of journeying. Pavresh knew the many stories from the tribes he'd visited. Made into myth and magical folk tales, but still a record of groups traveling to new lands. Did it matter whether those mumblers shared an ancestry with his crowd or not? The untouchables didn't need to know that part of the past. The truth still mattered to Pavresh, but it was the image of those journeys that mattered within the magic.

As he let the complex mixture of magics settle over the crowd, their eyes brightened. Juishika raised her head from where it had been drooping down toward her chest. Others looked ahead as if seeing their path for the first time.

Pavresh was the only one weary now. Weary but not sickened by the magic. Maybe it wasn't how strong the magic was that mattered but what he used it for. He drew back what energy he could from the inspiration of the spell he'd woven. He was their leader. He would accept the tiredness and keep going as if it didn't slow him down.

They set off, not as fast as Pavresh might have liked but still at a pace they could maintain for many days. If the magic would last that long. As much as he could feel the effects of the magic filling him with resolve, it didn't restore the energy it had taken to weave the magic in the first place. If he had to recreate it every day, he didn't think he'd be able to continue, but he hoped he might have to do nothing more than strengthen any fraying edges as the days went by.

The next morning, he was surprised that even that kind of maintenance wasn't necessary. The magic was as strong as it had been when he set it to work, as if their own belief in the spell—in themselves—sustained it. They veered upward into the edge of the mountains, coming over the crest of the ridge. They followed a smooth trail that hugged the ridgeline for most of the day. Still buoyed by magic, they traveled far that day.

Over the following days, the cold settled in, and they didn't always make it as far. Their slowing had nothing to do with the arcist spell waning. It was merely a normal aspect of this road Pavresh had chosen. They traveled through snow and into rugged foothills that kept them from ever speeding up.

The struggle, even apart from the magic, united them into a single people. Pavresh caught his breath at the strength of their unity as he began noticing how it affected them. The ways they leaned on and helped each other, achieving more than he ever could have expected. Carefully he added that strength to the magic, forging them into something that didn't even have a word. A jati, a tribe, a family, none were completely right. But outside of language, it kept shaping them.

They hunted as they went. Pavresh was the only experienced hunter, and he was only passable at that, but they managed to bring down a few deer and share the meat among them to keep them going. The dry shrubs that grew from the snow had tiny berries, hardly enough to eat, but chewing kept them from noticing their hunger.

After many days, they woke up to a surprisingly warm current of air rising to meet them from up ahead. Pavresh gathered them at the edge of a foothill, the view below obscured by a swirl of snow and wind and volcanic dust.

"The city lies below us," he told them. "I do not know what

we will find when we arrive. I do not know how they will welcome us or what their situation is. Perhaps they will not be pleased at first by our sudden arrival. But you have endured too much to be turned away. We will become a part of this city. And we will shape this city into a place for all people, untouchables or not, who make this journey to find a new home."

It was a short speech, but a fitting one for the cold air. Without another word he led them down out of the swirling snow into the upper reaches of the caste-less city of untouchables.

CHAPTER 27

The attacks on Chaitanshehar never seemed to cease as the twelve-days passed and Jaritta's people did what they could to establish her city, their city. Death jati costumes no longer had any effect, but at least they'd given the residents time to set up and reinforce some of their defenses. Jaritta and Azheeran climbed to the top of the wall to catalog the night's destruction. There had been no direct attacks, but that didn't mean the city's enemies had been quiet.

"Over there." Azheeran pointed toward the edge of the switchback trail. The slope between two levels of the trail had been laid bare. The traps and obstructions they'd placed to force attackers to leave themselves vulnerable on the trail had been cleared away, and a steep shortcut led straight up the side.

"Well protected from above, too," Jaritta said. The new path cut below an overhanging rock, which would shelter enemy soldiers from the wall. "Can we open that up somehow, so it's not protected?"

Azheeran frowned and studied the rock overhang. "Might. We have some heavy hammers and picks, as well as miners with the expertise to figure it out. And it looks like a section of it at least could be vulnerable. Make that fall, it might even wipe out their path. But it might take too long, be too late."

Jaritta had to fight the sigh that tried to escape her lungs. Everything they did had that same possibility, the same sense that no matter what they accomplished it would be too late to do any good. How long did they have before it all came down? How long would they have to hold out before it felt established enough to not worry? It felt like never.

They'd managed to stop the false miners who'd attacked

from within. An attack on the walls had followed. Then others from other directions, never a full-scale assault, but always one group of soldiers or another testing their defenses trying to figure out where and when to concentrate their next attack.

"Let's set some people working on it, at least see if it's worth it."

Jaritta went back into the city while Azheeran arranged for some workers to see to the overhang. She met up with widow Driyya at the house they'd made their headquarters, their less-than-grand assembly. The lower half of the walls were made of irregular shaped rocks, joined ingeniously so they were both sturdy and snug. Above about head height, the wall shifted to clay, of which there was an abundance nearby. The unfired clay bricks retained the strange colors of the mud they'd harvested down near the lava beds, back when it had been safer to travel up and down. Those bricks tapered into an impressively pointed roof above the height of the actual space inside.

It was bigger than she really felt comfortable with, as if they were trying to set themselves above the rest of the city, but they needed it as a unifying symbol for the others as well, a sign that they were more than the random conglomeration they'd been in Eghsal City.

A short time after her arrival, Azheeran joined them as well, entering along with Thamiba. The sound of someone hammering on rock came in through the open door. The people working to topple the overhang, no doubt. *Oh, may it work.* Though she wouldn't mind being there to see it fall, to be honest. It would surely be an impressive sight.

"Hunters just came back from the heights," Thamiba said as he sat down at the rough council table. "They saw what looked like people moving toward us through the mountains."

Jaritta caught Azheeran's eye. "Any chance they'd be a

mumbler tribe moving through there?"

Azheeran shook his head. "Possible, I guess, but I doubt they'd be seen. I talked to one of the hunters, one of our tribes. This sounds like a much bigger group. Not likely to be from any one tribe or village."

The last thing they needed was an attack from above. But they'd survived, if barely, all the attacks from the other directions. No surprise if their enemies chose to find some way around. "I think we need to work on those defenses, then." But there was no clear line that way, no easy way to hold off an attack short of a massive wall.

For which they had no time.

"Thamiba, see what you can come up with. I'll check on the rest of our defenses and see what we can spare to send up that way."

Azheeran left with Thamiba, leaving Driyya to go with Jaritta. They made their way through the streets to the northern edge of the city. Here there was a short stretch of wall where the surrounding land might prove vulnerable, but most of the protection came from the natural features of the foothills. The falcon jati soldier, Valni, had claimed for herself the lookout post high on a boulder that stood above the wall.

Jaritta gestured for her to come down.

Since the soldier's arrival, she'd proven an invaluable part of their defense. Her own fighting ability was unrivaled, and she had a soldier's eye for all the things the rest of them missed, of where an enemy might attack, of what they'd left vulnerable.

She landed beside them and dipped her head, as if Jaritta were the High Prince she was sworn to protect.

Jaritta flinched, reminded of the role of the cheetah jati in her coup attempt. If she'd succeeded, this kind of honor would surround her every move. The women of the cheetah jati would surround her with their confident service, a steady wall of support against her own uncertainties.

Instead, they'd been the ones who killed Bhadrik and others who'd supported her, destroying any hope of success, arresting her and throwing her into a jail cell.

Not Valni, though. She was too young to have been a part of that.

"We want to shore up our defenses from above." Jaritta kept that swirl of emotions and memories out of her voice, focusing only on the immediate needs of the city, her city. "What can we spare over here to help on that?"

"Nothing going on over here. I requested a horn, a signal of some kind. Give me that, and I'll stay here by myself and protect you better than ten soldiers."

"I brought it. Or them," Driyya said, holding out a tin whistle and a hand drum. "The best we could turn out. It seems no one knows how to fashion a decent signal horn."

Valni took the whistle and blew a piercing, off-key note. The sound seemed to carry and echo off the rocks. Jaritta waited until the last echoes died. Would people notice it if they were on the other side of the city when Valni blew it? She could only hope so.

The drum was less impressive. Valni beat a quick rhythm, but the mountainside swallowed the sound.

"It might carry better than it seems," Jaritta said. "If you can get someone to help you, blow the whistle and beat the drum. Together they'll surely get someone's attention."

Valni nodded. "I'll find someone wandering nearby. Take the other soldiers up to the top with you."

Then as if she were as much a dancer as a soldier, Valni vaulted back up the rock to her lookout perch, the whistle and drum both in her hands without seeming to slow her down at all.

The soldiers ran on ahead. Jaritta matched her pace to Driyya's, which was surprisingly fast despite her age. Driyya had a way of making each movement of her upper body a part of the step, as if she harnessed her entire body into her pace, purposeful and certain.

They made their way toward the upslope edge of the city quickly—with the city's low numbers, they didn't require a great deal of room. And those numbers dwindling as the death toll rose. If not for the new arrivals that still trickled in, the entire city would be empty but for the guards on the walls.

She couldn't keep doing this.

Jaritta didn't believe in giving up. Chaitanshehar was worth fighting for. But the feeling of doom that hung over the city made it a struggle to keep going. What good was shaping clay if the clay just turned to sand in her hands?

She wasn't the only one to feel the doom. When people peered out at her from their rough houses, they quickly looked away. Jaritta and Driyya climbed past another block, and a man in the street darted into his building, an unlovely combination of rocks, mud bricks, and branches. Vyovek. He'd once inquired after her health when an earthquake back in Eghsal City had made her fall, had gone and found her a branch to serve as a crutch. He probably thought she didn't recognize him, that she didn't know he was stockpiling food and making preparations to leave. If she couldn't protect them here, then maybe the dangers of the steam vents in Eghsal City were worth facing.

No doubt he wasn't the only one considering whether it was time to sneak away.

They passed the house where Rashul kept a watch on her sister-in-law. What of them? Would Rashul abandon the city? His voice had been quieter than she'd hoped after his arrival. He spoke at times to various groups in the city, dreamed of the city they would create, but it felt muted. As if he already feared this would collapse just like his earlier efforts to rebel against the princes. Maybe it was only her mood, affecting how she interpreted him. She hoped so.

As for his ward, Datri, she hadn't shown her face since Jaritta confronted her. Since she brought the news of the High Prince's assassination. Jaritta didn't for an instant believe that meant Datri was sitting quietly in her house and doing nothing. She was sending messages, even receiving visitors, though Jaritta had yet to intercept any. Her spies were too skilled for Jaritta's untouchables.

Rashul watched her, at least. That should keep her from any overt treachery. And as long as the mystery of what the coup leaders had done to Prince Jasfer remained—and what they intended with him, perhaps—then she wouldn't suddenly betray her new city.

That was as far as she trusted her sister-in-law, though. If it became to Datri's advantage to turn against Jaritta, she wouldn't hesitate.

They moved on past the house with no sign of either of the two and continued on to the upper edge of the city. As they approached Thamiba and Azheeran, Driyya held up her hand.

"Is that the drum I left with the soldier girl?"

Jaritta halted and strained her ears. "I don't think..." Wait, there *was* some kind of rhythmic sound, but it seemed to come from below. Probably the people hammering on the overhang to make it collapse. She turned slowly in a circle. Then a clash of swords.

"Not Valni," she said. "It's the wall. Thamiba, Azheeran." Her shouts carried in the cold air. "Something's happening down below. Get some soldiers to the wall now!"

Gathering up her dress, Jaritta ran down through the city. A squad of guards passed her by, followed a moment later by Thamiba and other soldiers. The sounds of swords continued, and the shouts of those fighting.

At the wall, the guards were already pouring over on their secret exit routes. Jaritta came right to the edge. The workers

Azheeran had set to topple the rock overhead were under assault. The lay of the land protected them from a direct attack, so three held off the attackers while the fourth and final one scrambled to continue weakening the rock.

The Pashun soldiers had them outnumbered at least ten to one. Maybe even double that. Thamiba and his few didn't come close to evening the scales, but at least they held the higher ground.

The sounds of fighting always made Jaritta wince. She clenched her teeth and made herself watch as Thamiba's squad met the Pashun soldiers. At the moment the two sides clashed, there was sudden confusion among the Pashun soldiers who weren't at the front line. Two lost their footing and then slid down the steep slope—one shouting in alarm, the other noticeably silent.

Jaritta had to lean forward to make out Azheeran and a group of mumbler guards who'd positioned themselves in the rocks above the soldiers. They would be of no direct help if it fell to hand combat nor in direct danger, but they were already picking off the soldiers in the rear. Scrambling to press closer to Thamiba's guards, those soldiers in the rear then disrupted the other attackers.

Maybe they'd even turn this attack away without casualties. She gripped the edge of the wall so she didn't fall, trying to see everything.

The view below stole away her naive optimism.

Other Pashun soldiers were swarming in the swamp below the city. It looked like it might finally be the big, coordinated fight they'd been expecting all along. The quarreling pettiness of the jatis might at last be cast aside, their rebel groups united against one enemy, herself. The time had come for them to attack as one. Jaritta wanted to cover her eyes.

The soldiers didn't all rush up the slope toward them yet,

though one group of them must have begun climbing earlier. They were already closing in on the battle from below.

Other Chaitanshehar guards were climbing down from the wall to help Thamiba's, but surely it was too late. The new troops from Pashun had almost reached the fighting. Thamiba fell from sight. Jaritta's breath caught in her throat as she looked for any sign of what happened to him.

A strange sound grew from the middle of the fight, at first a slight sound she only scarcely noticed but it grew to a roar. The rock overhang moved. It didn't fall immediately. Some loose rocks showered down, but the main mass hesitated just long enough for Jaritta to focus her attention on it. But not long enough for her to shout out a warning.

The entire side of the cliff collapsed.

Rock and air became inverted, dust so dense she couldn't see a thing. When she opened her mouth to cry out, the dust filled her lungs. She fell, gasping for breath. This was not what she'd planned for, not what the miners were supposed to do on the overhang, not what her city was supposed to be. Even as she recovered, she crawled to the edge of the wall and looked for any survivors.

Shapes moved in the dust, looking like bodies made of the same material only denser. "Thamiba!" She coughed and sputtered over his name. "Get them up here, someone."

"What if they're enemy—"

"Up here. Get them." She couldn't spare the breath to say anything more.

Thamiba was not among those who were helped up the wall. She couldn't let herself dwell on his absence. She scrambled among the survivors, tending their wounds, helping them try to breathe as the cloud of dust settled down. The downhill slope was a rocky ruin. She pushed away thoughts of survivors—an impossibility surely—and studied it as a part of their defense.

No one would be coming up the route the soldiers had cleared, in the protection of the overhang. Nor did much of an overhang remain, either. The rock fall would be loose and dangerous for many days to come, and even as it settled, the path it had cleared would not make for an easy climb. But the switchbacks themselves would be useless as well, until they could find a way to shorten the straight stretches and avoid the rock fall.

Good. No one could approach the city. The armies below wouldn't attack immediately, and probably not for a long time. That was what they needed now. If she could have carved a lava-filled moat around the city, she would. Let the land itself cut them off and protect them, at least until they could establish themselves.

But for this they lost Thamiba? For such an incremental bit of added protection he sacrificed... No, she forced her mind away from such thoughts. He wasn't dead, couldn't be dead. She glanced down at the dust-covered slope of the mountain. But he also couldn't be alive in that... If he sacrificed himself, if he was truly gone, it was for much more than one battle, much more than a rock slide and a more protected approach to the city. It was for the city itself, for its founding and its future.

Such a future as the city still had.

Azheeran scrambled over from his position above the rock fall. "Listen," he said. "You hear that noise?"

Jaritta tried to strain to hear anything beyond her own thudding heart. She shook her head.

"This wasn't the end of the attack. Someone else is coming."

Jaritta still heard nothing, but she collapsed at the idea of having to fight any more.

"I can't, Azheeran. I can't go on. Let the earth swallow them, if the gods want us here. Let them fall from the mountainside. Let the gods wash them away with a flood or send that fire the priests always talk about, I don't care. I can't do any more."

Only when she stopped talking did she hear the noise of hundreds of footfalls coming down from above. Azheeran held out a hand to her. She wanted to refuse it, to stay and mourn—her friend, her city. After a moment she took it listlessly.

As she did so, a feeling washed over her. Arcist magic. She knew it from Chaitan's house, though she hadn't realized that it would feel so familiar, knew it even before she could identify what she felt. She climbed to her feet, filled with the sense that she was about to meet people who would change the city of Chaitanshehar forever.

CHAPTER 28

The night before Indima was supposed to leave Pashun and go back to the Silk City, she returned to the secret ballroom. The two neighborhoods were united, at an uncertain peace. She still balanced her way across the pipe to get there, keeping to the shadows. It was busier than it had been other nights. A buzz of energy filled one part of the room, beyond the buzz of chemical highs. Indima veered away from that crowd and began her own, solitary dance.

Movement and form. Never to be still, except as a deliberate pause before the next movement. She removed everything from her thoughts. The situation in Pashun, with its ever-present soldiers, retaliation against the miners and the traditionalist sect that honored the god Ryo, and the often overwhelming sense of fear. The reports of the coup in Romnai, where people she'd once known had been killed or thrust out of power. The coming journey back to the Silk City now that the weather had broken and the new peace permitted her entourage to travel. What awaited her there, a city with its own tensions and the unending expectations of family and priests. One by one she subtracted them from her mind. She even removed the people all around her from her awareness. All those things were the ghosts of imagination, far from the reality of an intricate rhythm, a perfect pass, a spin that glided from character to character in sequence.

Ghosts, but they tried to intrude.

A soldier by the door caught her attention for a moment, and her hands missed one part of a difficult sequence. But it wasn't one of her guards, wasn't anyone who would care that she was there. With an effort, she made him into a phantom again without disrupting her dance.

After a few more moves, one of the ghosts stepped into her path, resolving itself into a woman who seemingly didn't notice Indima dancing there. The ghosts she was chatting with threatened to turn into real people as well, but Indima shifted her steps away. The woman's words of apology turned into butterfly shadows as she again became ephemeral nothingness.

The dance was the only real thing alive, the only thing that mattered.

Another imaginary intruder, this one taking substance first as a voice, a fisherman's voice with a strange accent. No, that wasn't quite right. The person took shape next, sitting at the bar and sipping tisane through a metal straw. It was the man from the Forgotten South. As far as the princes above knew, he'd gone into hiding. But here he must not have been concerned with being seen.

He'd claimed to come through the dangerous passes by dancing the Crows in Snow dance. Another time dancing here, she'd danced a solo variation on that dance. Now she did the original version, as closely as she could without a partner. The dance forced her motions wider, drawing in the attention of more ghosts. She had to lean forward, lean back. A lesser dancer would have toppled or needed a partner for those, but she held herself from falling as if it required no effort.

Her muscles strained to keep her going, sweeping low and continuing the movements that stretched her to either side. The stranger, like everything else in the clandestine ballroom, became again a phantom, a nothing.

The dance told a story. The original story was long lost, but hints of the story remained, of a couple fleeing through the snow, of the challenges they faced, of the forces that pulled them away from each other as they struggled to come back together. There were birds in the song, as the name implied, but Indima never thought of them as crows. These were the songbirds, small and mocking, that pestered the lovers each time they drew apart.

Perhaps there was something of the song that came all the way from the Forgotten South, though the stories made that land sound too warm for snow. Perhaps the traveler had danced it there, had known it as Sparrows on the Beach. Or else it told of some other bird, something that didn't exist up here in the north. The lovers would have been much the same, their story one that played itself out over and over, no matter the location.

As she moved into another deep, muscle-aching bow, Indima suddenly had a partner. A ghost had joined her. She refused to allow its presence to introduce the least stutter in her movements. It was still a ghost, even as it supported her in her dips, as a partner must for the dance to proceed correctly. Even as it knew the dance as perfectly as she did.

She leaned into him but refused to feel his hands, refused to admit it was more than a shadow.

Had she summoned him, by wondering about the dance as it was performed in the Forgotten South? Because surely this was the traveler, repeating the dance he'd performed on his way north. Had he simply recognized the dance by sight and become real to join in? Perhaps he knew a different version. Perhaps his ghost steps would throw off her real dancing.

If so, he would simply become a spirit again, a nothing.

She danced on, forcing her mind to focus only on the dance, not this shadow partner from far away.

Except, some part of her kept drawing her toward her partner more than the dance required. Even as she tried to keep him a faceless ghost, he resolved into real flesh and blood. Movement that she knew.

Still.

After eight years.

It was Ekana's way of dancing. The way he stepped with

her, the way he moved his arms to tell the story. Only after she'd recognized her former lover's dancing did she let herself look at him directly.

Not Ekana. He couldn't possibly look so old and ragged. And yet…those were his eyes. The shape of his cheeks, still visible under the changes caused by the years, the curve of his familiar lips. She touched her own face, wondering how much it had changed.

Such a movement broke the pattern of the dance. She couldn't. Couldn't believe it. Couldn't think about what it meant, how she should respond, how it could be. So instead, she forced herself back into the dance. Dancing required no thought, separated her from thought of any kind.

And Ekana slid perfectly into the dance as well. He said nothing, made no move to embrace her or speak. The only change from what the dance demanded was that he didn't take his eyes off her face for even a moment.

In response she avoided his eyes, looking up to the sky as if the songbirds who mocked their human loves and losses perched and flittered among the rafters.

It couldn't be possible. Ekana had left, had betrayed Rashul and all of them, had disappeared. And worst of all, had never made any attempt to follow or find her. To show up now, after such betrayal, how did he dare?

He must be a ghost indeed, not only in the way her mind ignored the people around her. He was a stranger who resembled Ekana. Or simply a portion of her imagination.

Most likely that. She'd danced the Crows in Snow with Ekana years ago. Now her mind created him, summoned him to join her. The strange drugs in the air made her brain open to weird impossibilities. The mysteries she'd encountered in this unfamiliar city—which were likely caused by little more than it being unfamiliar—led her to imagine him appearing and dancing beside her.

Nothing more than that, surely.

As the dance moved on toward its climax, she leaned farther than necessary. Maybe some part of her wanted it to happen, wanted to see if her ghost partner would really catch her. Wanted to fall into his arms.

It was too far. She felt when she passed the point where she would never manage to right herself on her own. It was be caught or crash to the floor, something she'd never done since she was a child learning her dances.

He caught her. Not Forgotten South hands. Fisherman hands, familiar hands. It was Ekana. She collapsed, not even trying to recover her dancing steps. Still cradled in his arms, she lay on the floor, half a ghost herself, half unsure if anything was real.

Except for Ekana.

He was as real as he'd ever been, crouched at her side while he held her. Speaking, but the words never reached her mind.

***

Indima refused the offered hands as she sat up on the couch. She squeezed her eyes shut to steady herself and then opened them. The couch was in a small room off to the side of the ballroom, the door still open. Music and voices came through, but distant. Was that some effect of the room, or simply her own muddled head?

"Indima, how are you feeling? Say something."

Ekana. What was there to say to him? Only everything. She couldn't answer a tiny question like that without eight years of words rushing out of her mouth as well.

"Can you hear me? Can you talk?"

She lifted her face to meet his eyes for the first time since their dance but quickly shifted away. They weren't alone in the room. The traveler from the Forgotten South was there as well. She looked at him to keep from looking at Ekana.

"Why are *you* here?" Curiosity forced the words out before she could stop them.

He glanced toward Ekana and offered her a quick bow. "I was only making sure you were well. I saw you collapse out there, and I helped this dancer carry you to this couch."

This dancer. Spoken as if he knew exactly who Ekana was but didn't want her to realize it.

"If you don't need any assistance, I can…" He backed away from the couch as if to leave the room.

"No, wait." She didn't want to be alone with Ekana just now. Didn't think she could handle that. She looked from him to Ekana, finally meeting his eyes. "You know each other."

Another glance before either answered, but she read the story as if it were a dance. The Crows in Snow, that was how the traveler had made it through the difficult mountain passes. A partner dance, one Ekana would have known. And the traveler's voice had reminded her of Ekana's all along, not because he came from Jarnur but because he'd learned the language from Ekana.

What language did they speak in the Forgotten South, then? She'd assumed it would be their own language, accented no doubt, but the same.

They were both shaking their heads after that brief hesitation, but Indima ignored it. "You guided him. Did you travel all the way to the Forgotten South?"

To think that her former lover could have traveled all that way, could have returned with this traveler to such acclaim and… No, that couldn't be true. Ekana would have returned to fame himself, not deflected it all to the traveler from the south while he kept himself hidden. They would have shared the story of both of them, of his exploits to reach the Forgotten South as well as the visitor's journey here. Would have if it were true.

She shifted on the couch to watch the traveler's full body

language. "You didn't, I know. You're not really from the Forgotten South, are you? You're another fisherman from Jarnur, just trying to trick us with false tales."

"No." The traveler shook his head furiously. "I'm not from Jarnur. I'm not a fisherman."

After a brief silence, Ekana burst out, "His name is Sembaari. He's a mumbler." The anger in his words made Indima scoot back on the couch. "There is no Forgotten South, Indima. It's time to forget those kinds of stories. The Forgotten South, the hero Gauran, the gods, the Fire, those are stories for the simple."

"And the simple are there to be fooled?" Had it been no more than a scheme to earn them some money? They'd used it to gain power, for a time. And now... She couldn't figure out what they might be after, now that he'd surrendered to the princes.

He didn't answer her question, and her mind was still reeling at the thought of this stranger—a celebrated visitor who spoke real language, not mere mumbles—as nothing more than a mumbler. Had they stained his skin somehow? How did he look like their people if he was a mumbler? She'd seen the mumblers from the Silk City walls now and then, always distant and never a direct threat. But she'd always heard of them as a danger that threatened her people, and women especially.

This traveler...he didn't seem a threat in the least.

When Ekana spoke again his voice was soft, still rough from use but no longer filled with harsh anger. It could almost have been the Ekana of years ago. "What are you doing, Indima? I don't mean now, in this room. What are you doing dancing in the temples, bowing to the priests? You're still letting your family tell you where to go. Still doing the things we fought against, at Chaitan's house."

As if he was the one to talk about turning a back on those

ideals. "I wasn't the one who betrayed them, Ekana." A whisper that might as well have been a shout for how it cut her to say it.

"But did you betray me, first?" Ekana's whisper was so quiet it might have been meant only for himself.

She wanted to shout back, *Never!* She held her tongue.

The traveler scuffed his shoe on the floor. "I should head back—"

"It is time for me to go as well. I leave early in the morning on a long journey."

Ekana put his hand on her arm. "You don't have to—"

"Yes, I do." She looked Ekana in the eyes and for the first time didn't flinch away. Here he was, so far removed from that dancer in Chaitan's house. No longer a part of that group of idealists and dreams. Instead, he was out here spreading lies. It wasn't even the lies that bothered her so much, though. The old Ekana might have made up stories and played a role if it helped to undermine the princes and lift up the people beneath them. But this? This mocked the people who were already beat down, the people grasping for some story that was new and exciting. And it did nothing at all to tear down the hierarchical system of their cities. That was what bothered her more than she could put into words. He'd betrayed truth for a cheap showmanship that bowed meekly to those who held the real power.

"What we had is in the past. If you want to honor it, though, speak the truth. If he's really a mumbler, then people need to know that. They need to hear that mumblers aren't scary creatures we need to shut out. People incapable even of speech. That's what we've been told. That's how our stories have shaped them."

She looked at this traveler, this mumbler who'd come so far, even if it wasn't from the Forgotten South. A person. Rashul would have welcomed him into their group, insisted that in a city without jatis he could belong as well as anyone from any other caste. The little city she'd heard rumors of across the lava beds, they would welcome him no doubt. Was it true that Jaritta was there, and Pavresh too? Some said that even Chaitan himself had joined the city. Surely he was too sick to travel, if he was even still alive. But could such a city be real? Probably it was as much an illusion as the people out on her dance floor.

"Don't claim he's from the Forgotten South. Tell everyone he's a mumbler." And if he wouldn't, she would send out letters, exposing the truth. No, she decided at that moment, regardless of what Ekana chose to do she would write, because she wouldn't know what he chose until some much later time. She would send letters to the new city, to Jarnur and Romnai if there were any people in those cities she could still write to. "Tell them, or I will have to inform everyone by letters."

Ekana sat at the other end of the couch, his head hanging as he listened to her words. "You could tell it with me?"

She only shook her head. The past was real, more real than ghosts or tales of the Forgotten South. But even so, it was *past*, it was no more.

"One dance, then, before you leave?"

Indima stood up and made the gesture of a leading man toward his partner. "We will dance the true story of your traveler. I'll leave it to you to explain it after I'm gone."

Then she led the way out onto the dance floor where people would see their dance. Some might even understand the story it told and spread it in their own ways across the city.

And she? Indima would return to the Silk City and the sacred, sanctioned dances, even if danced in ways that made the worshipers question and wonder.

One last story to dance that had nothing to do with gods.

Chapter 29

The city was at peace. The valley was at war.

Jasfer could see the peace below him in the city; the celebrations were stunted by uncertainty, but they still took place, dancers spilling into the pools of light, music from unseen musicians rising up among the princely manors. Laughter escaped from pent up lungs, released cautiously and then erupting into full, manic howls, under the ones who laughed ran out of breath. The streetlights revealed streamers of many colors between the revelers, banners and decorations that had been held in hiding while the city waited to see who would end up on top.

And now all was restored to its rightful way.

Maybe it was simply Jasfer's jati that was at war.

He couldn't see any hint of that war. Its battles took place in hidden rooms. Here in Pashun, far away in Romnai. And then everyone else had to accept the results of those battles. Princes and priests, soldiers and servants and everyone else below them.

Or did they?

A lightness draped over him, a sense that his arms weren't entirely attached, that his body floated. Did all those groups accept the change in princes as easily as that? Or were they given no choice?

The princes, the former ruling Thirty, had declared that the seat of the High Prince would remain vacant for three months. The priests had seemed to give their blessing to the idea. The falcon jati soldiers whose job was to protect the High Prince certainly had. What if the only thing stopping them from holding to that idea was that no one had spoken against the upstarts? Did silence alone give them power? Then it was up to him to speak up for the rightful ruling princes.

Jasfer spun on his heel and went into his room.

Despite his feeling of urgency, he kept his voice low, telling Yatim, "I need a private place to meet with Mahendri. Someplace outside the mayor's knowledge. See what you can set up and then send a word to him."

Yatim bowed and set out.

He needed some way to contact people without Hrisha noticing. Baram's falcon jati soldier would have been ideal, but she'd disappeared. The priests had their own networks and messengers, and his own antipathy toward the priests was no doubt known. No one would expect him to trust them.

But then he *didn't* trust them, didn't know how to find the individual priests whom he could dare to trust.

Hopefully Mahendri had a better suggestion.

Yatim returned before he'd had time to think much more. "Mahendri would like to meet right away, if you're able, tisrah. He suggested a place just below the wall where they have private booths."

"Now?"

Yatim helped him into his coat as he answered. "He appeared to be readying himself to leave. I wondered if he might fear the new princes himself, but he wouldn't answer me."

A relative by marriage of the assassinated High Prince, it made sense that he might be afraid, Jasfer supposed. He summoned another of his servants and followed the two out the door in a rush. Hrisha might wish that Jasfer had informed him he was leaving, but he could complain later.

The place they were meeting was a tisane shop with a large open room in the middle and many small booths and side rooms around the perimeter. Jasfer slipped into one, leaving his servants just outside.

"Thank you for meeting so swiftly, Mahendri. Are you

preparing to go somewhere?"

"Happy to meet." Mahendri gestured for Jasfer to choose a gourd of tisane. "As for where I'm going, let's just say I'm keeping my options open. A change in rulers is always a time of uncertainty, and I'd rather not be caught off guard."

"Wise words." Jasfer took a sip from his tisane, letting the sweetened heat of the drink warm his face. "Keeping the same rulers would be a welcome stability right now." He looked at Mahendri's face for any reaction.

Mahendri cocked an eyebrow and leaned forward. "Too late, don't you think?"

"Your cousin's husband was a great prince. Maybe the best our valley has ever seen. It isn't right to rush on to a new group of rulers when we are still mourning."

"What do you propose to do about that? You have soldiers, but surely they aren't enough to capture the city."

Fractured as the city was, it might not be such a far-fetched idea. But no, he didn't want to conquer anything, only to restore the order they'd had before. "I want to send some letters. To the princes in Romnai, to the leaders of the falcon jati. Maybe to the priests, so they can sanction the time of mourning that had been agreed upon. But I'm not sure how to best send the message."

Mahendri sat back and stroked his beard. "Trade is resuming along the ordinary trade road. We could get something on a messenger cart, but the princes will be watching anything you send."

Jasfer pursed his lips and nodded.

"But there's a caravan leaving shortly for the Silk City. A group of priests and silk weavers. Get your letters written as fast as you can, and I will get the papers to them. They were supposed to leave already today. I can try to delay them until tomorrow morning, but I wouldn't want to promise that. So, waste no time."

Jasfer took one more sip and stood. "Thank you. I will make sure they don't have to wait until tomorrow."

***

In the rush, Prince Jasfer only managed to get three letters written, one to the leader of the falcon jati, and one each to two of his fellow princes. He had to hope they would still be in touch with others of the Thirty, the legitimate Thirty. They would need to present a single face against the upstarts, overcome their constant bickering and rivalries—and do so without the unifying figure of Baram to keep them in line.

He almost crumpled the papers and gave up when he thought of it that way. But no, these were trying times. People rose up to face difficulties all the time. The true Thirty would do no less. Those who remained would stand united and pull the other jatis of the valley with them, to stand against these upstarts.

He dashed off as soon as the ink was sufficiently dry to deliver them to Mahendri.

This time having an excuse was probably wise, so after handing off the letters he made his way to the temple a short ways above the tisane shop. Pashun had several temples, in addition to its many smaller chapels, shrines and the seminary that dominated the lower corner of the city. This one was smaller than the big temple in Romnai but still majestic.

While Jasfer didn't trust in priests or their pronouncements, he did find comfort in the trappings of the temples, the forms and traditions. He bought a small candle and placed it at the shrine to Perkwom, where he offered the effigy of the god a low bow. Perkwom was the god of protection and of the just war, the one waged to restore peace. What could be a better image? He and the other Thirty needed all the protection they could get while they waged their fight for justice.

As he stood, he looked around the temple. Where was that dancer he'd seen in the streets? She'd been a good dancer, one who could make him forget other worries and only focus on the poetry of her dancing.

He asked an attendant sitting beside the shrine if she would perform that day.

"Ah, she has left, tisrah," the woman said. "A marvelous dancer, truly blessed by the gods. But she is journeying back to the Silk City."

"Oh, is she a part of that entourage? I hope they have good travels. Perhaps I will try to catch them as they leave and offer them a prayer of safety."

"You're too late for that, tisrah." The attendant gestured with one hand, as if toward the wastes outside the city. "They left, oh…two, three days ago, early in the morning."

Then who…

Could there have been two caravans heading to the Silk City?

He raced back to the tisane shop, but Mahendri was gone.

Surely a miscommunication, and even now he was out trying to find the promised messengers. Mahendri was Baram's family. Distant family, by marriage, but still, he wouldn't… No, he was eager to help Jasfer, had always taken his side, ever since the High Prince suggested they work together.

As much as he told himself that there was no need to panic, his steps slowed as he made his way toward his rooms in Hrisha's manor. What might Mahendri do with those letters, if he never intended to send them to Romnai?

Blackmail was the most likely. He'd return to his rooms to find Mahendri waiting there, demanding one of the reopened mines as payment. Or more likely, he'd wait a few days, give Jasfer plenty of time to worry. Then when his panic was a fever, the little man would show up and offer the letters in exchange for control of Jasfer's riches.

And he'd give it, if he had to.

In fact, he might still turn it to his advantage. Those riches would prove far more valuable if Mahendri helped Jasfer regain his position. He just had to keep calm for a few days, find his way through these new complications without running off in a panic.

When he got back, he would have Yatim search for Mahendri—assuming there was no message already. But no sense having him scour the city just yet. Mahendri would reveal his demands soon enough.

At the manor, the first thing he saw was Hrisha, sitting at his desk. The front door to his study, which he rarely used as it opened directly toward the manor entrance, was flung wide. Seated before him was Mahendri. Familiar letters sat on the desk, their seals opened. And all around the entry and the study were dozens of the Vainath jati soldiers.

Jasfer blinked at the frozen scene and knew he had time for only one response, one chance to take action that would save or doom him. "Yatim," he said from the side of his mouth, "don't let them capture you. You need to let people know."

He had a moment of imagining himself leaping out of their grasp, running into the streets with Yatim, finding some hidden resistance cell to smuggle him to safety. Instead, Jasfer held his ground while Yatim slipped away. When the soldiers rushed toward him, he held out his hands meekly to be bound.

"Well done, as always," Prince Hrisha said, and Jasfer wasn't sure whom he addressed. Jasfer for surrendering? The soldiers for their swift arrest? It rather seemed that it was Mahendri that he was congratulating, as if he had orchestrated this exact turn of events.

***

On the journey to Romnai, chained up but in a comfortable carriage, Jasfer tried to figure out a way to contact Datri and let her know what was going on in Pashun. First *he* had to figure out what had happened, and what might possibly help her in whatever was happening with Jaritta's so-called city.

She knew of the assassination, of course, and must know by now of the coup that led to a different group of ruling princes. Did she know of the infighting and all the rival groups in Pashun? Probably not in any detail yet. But he had no idea what good that would do anyone.

As the carriage left behind the stink of the mud pots, Jasfer puzzled through what Hrisha had said to Mahendri: "As always." Hadn't he always been a simple emissary to Romnai? What had Datri uncovered about him? He'd been a minor bureaucrat, for many years in Romnai and before that in Pashun. Nothing to do with the miners. Had it been as a liason to the priests? No, something with the soldier jatis.

Nothing that had raised the alarm, even within Datri's extensive range of contacts. There had been an old familiarity to the way Hrisha said it, though. Had he betrayed Baram already long ago, only pretending to help Jasfer? Nausea and numbness battled inside Jasfer as they rode away from the city.

The carriage suddenly slowed to a crawl. Jasfer peeked through the windows. A family of mumblers sat beside the road around a small fire. They watched the carriage but didn't move.

"Not a threat to us," someone called from outside the carriage. "Keep moving." They picked up speed. Jasfer watched them until they were out of sight. Ahead, the wide road continued on toward the train tracks and the river.

And then to Romnai. There would be ways to contact Datri from there, he had to hope, people he could sneak a letter to if given any sort of freedom. He would worry about that in good time. His thoughts turned again to the situation in Pashun, but now he thought of something Hrisha had said earlier, before the coup, before the assassination. They'd been talking about the many soldier jatis in the city.

And what had he said? The princes of Pashun—not yet ruling in their own right but still important parts of the city's order and governance—found the many jatis better for manipulating.

Is that what Mahendri's role among the soldiers had been, to divide and manipulate them? And then he was rewarded with a task in Romnai, at a time of growing tensions among the jatis of the city. Suddenly his suggestion of bringing so many untouchables back from the ruins to Romnai made sense as well, in the picture he was building. Jaritta had frustrated that part of his plan, and likely slowed down some of the schemes of Mahendri and the others, but unfortunately that hadn't been enough to stop him from what he was sent to do.

It was a task that ultimately led to the High Prince's assassination. Prince against prince—another potential for manipulating. Eventually it led to someone they supported becoming High Prince. But Hrisha had let something else slip earlier. Prince Akhash, the new High Prince pretender, had been living in Romnai, but someone had reported to him. Mahendri, of course, he should have known. His job done, he'd been pleased to be sent back to Pashun by Jasfer himself.

Or was his job done?

In Pashun, Mahendri might pit soldier jatis against each other to achieve the city's aims. And he might renew the push to capture Jaritta's people and force them back to the streets of the city, where they could make things more dangerous. Increase the need for a strong and violent princely jati in charge. But who could say his ambitions weren't bigger than that? Why not pit princely family against princely family, priestly faction against faction? Or even the other jatis in the city that had been such enemies during the miners' revolt? If those factions had united, the princes might never have had time to put their wall in place.

That didn't mean Mahendri was behind keeping those factions in tension. It simply indicated the style of these Pashun princes, with Mahendri playing a key part.

And if they had ways to use the lesser jatis, no doubt they had contacts with the Sons of Ryo and the Children of Kwona and probably other disruptive groups as well. Maybe he was the key spark behind the man who'd attacked the temple. The Sons of Ryo were more powerful here, but someone must have played a role in starting local cells in Romnai, and who better than someone playing the part of an unimportant bureaucrat? Mahendri hadn't attended the ceremonies, after all. And his long years working behind the scenes in Romnai might well have started the events that led to Baram's assasination.

A master at manipulations, he might be the biggest threat to Jaritta's city of any of them.

The Pashun princes all seemed complicit in these divisions. She couldn't hope to find allies there, at least until they knew more. But she had to be ready for them to attempt the same thing within Jaritta's city.

Only when they switched to the train and began the last step of the journey did he realize what to do. If there was anyone who could out-manipulate Mahendri, it was his wife. He began composing the letter he would write—in code—once he had a chance. It would start, "Declare, in formal letters to all the cities, that you are on the side of the Pashun Thirty and the Jarnur Thirty, that you support each city having its own say."

Oh, Hrisha would rage to be dismissed as the Pashun

Thirty, and as far as he knew, there was no Jarnur Thirty—yet. But might as well get a jump on Mahendri and lay the groundwork for their own manipulations. Implicate Prince Nriteesh in it while she was at it. He'd been the one to suggest having Jasfer go to Pashun, which now appeared to be a part of their attempts to destabilize the ruling Thirty. He had certainly been working his own counter goals, one way or another. If he was a co-conspirator, then it put their own leverage within the rebels' circle. And if not, well, it put a target on someone who was already compromised.

The familiar buildings of Romnai at last came into view across the river, backlit by the fires of the lava field.

***

Jasfer's captors kept him isolated and locked up in a room off the High Assembly building where only the servants usually went. It was a comfortable room, but he found no way to communicate with anyone outside. The guards were stoic and professional and spent little time with him. The princes, the members of the new Thirty, seldom visited. Some tried to assure him that he was only being held as the princes established their authority. A precaution that would soon be unnecessary. Others implied that even this imprisonment was too kind. He responded to either suggestion with the same silence.

No one else ever came to see him, which probably meant that no one even knew he was there. No messages from the deposed princes who remained in the city, no word from Kalvandi or the other servants who were surely running his household in the absence of their masters. Had Yatim escaped and gotten them word? Had any other official notice gone out? He could only sit in solitude, wondering.

Days passed, twelve-days, one month and part of another. The searing pain of his burns returned periodically, though he did nothing to aggravate them. Perhaps it was no more than the stress of being a captive.

He knew nothing of what was happening beyond his room.

A cleaning woman showed up one morning, surprising Jasfer as he mentally composed yet another code to get the information Datri needed to her. His guards had always insisted he clean his own room as well as he could, sometimes bringing him what items he needed as he requested them. He'd grown unkempt, as much as he'd tried to maintain some level of cleanliness. His first thought was to welcome the cleaner and then dismiss her from his mind.

As a prince does with servants.

But the days in isolation broke through that habit. Nothing about the woman stood out at first. She showed no emotion as she went briskly about the room cleaning. Jasfer thought of his former spy who'd used his magic to blend in. There was something about the woman that reminded him of Pavresh, though he couldn't decide if it was anything to do with magic.

He moved across the room to get a different view of her face. There was something familiar about her.

Sashyu.

Hadn't she gone to the Silk City? "I thought…" His throat was scratchy with lack of use.

Sashyu gave a quick shake of her head to keep him from speaking again. After a little while, she paused cleaning and went to the door. It was locked, as it always was when one of the servants or guards had a need to enter, but she seemed to listen for something. Then she came over close to Jasfer.

"I can't stay long." Her voice was a fierce whisper. "Yatim came back to Romnai and sent for me. We need to get a message to your wife, but we don't know what to say."

"You'll be searched when you leave, won't you?" How'd

she come in the first place? Was there any chance she could smuggle him out somehow? His mind began imagining possibilities. It was good to have something akin to hope again. Or at least some goal to shape his imaginary plans.

She nodded. "My memory is very good. That's why your wife employed me. Tell me, and I'll get the message to Yazim right away."

He nodded. He could put the message in code, even spoken. "You must remember it exactly as I tell you. Not a word changed."

She motioned for him to just speak.

"Last I knew she was in my sister's city of untouchables down near Pashun. You'll have to find some way to get it to her there." Then he carefully told her the message he needed Datri to hear. *Oh, may it help, somehow.*

When he was done, he began to ask what else she might do for him, anything she might smuggle in or messages she could bring him. She cut him off and glanced at the door.

"This wasn't easy to get in here. Their guards are...carefully chosen. I need leverage to get past them, and most don't have anything I know of."

She'd learned well from Datri, then, if she'd used that tool. He pursed his lips and nodded. Back to the days alone. Months, perhaps.

Seeing his expression she added, "I don't know if I'll be able to, but I'll try."

"More important to get that message to Datri. Do that, but then be safe."

***

His next visitor showed up only two days later.

It was a man he didn't know, but the falcon jati guards who flanked him identified him as the new High Prince himself, Prince Akhash. Behind his guards, her hands bound, came

Sashyu. Jasfer closed his eyes.

Had she betrayed him to get Datri's location out of him? No, if that were the case she wouldn't be tied up. She'd been caught. So, no message sent, and once again no way to communicate with anyone. And what punishment would they give her?

"I'm disappointed in you, Talai."

No honorific and not even his first name. A clear message that Akhash didn't consider him a part of the princely jati anymore. Akhash had the kind of voice that weak people think makes them sound tough, falsely deep and angry sounding.

"We've treated you well. Too well, I say. Yet you try to sneak information out of the city. You endanger others. You spurn our leniency."

Jasfer said nothing.

Sashyu spoke, though to do so broke any sense of propriety. "I am sorry, Prince Jasfer. I tried to find the rebels you mentioned, but they've fled the city. I only told some stranger your words."

Rebels? Fled? When had he told her to seek out any such people? And a stranger? As he thought through the mystery, a priest came inside followed by more soldiers.

He'd said nothing about any of those things. It was clearly meant as a message to him, some sort of code. She couldn't find…Datri? No, she wouldn't have had time to anyway. But she did tell a stranger. No, that was simply to hide the truth from the prince. She'd shared his words as planned. The talk of rebels had been the signal to take her words as their opposites. He had to trust that she'd told his words to Yatim before she was arrested.

Maybe.

Not easy to place his hope on such slim guessing. Akhash cut short Jasfer's wondering when he drew himself up into what was clearly meant to emphasize his status as High Prince.

"Execute the spy. Talai can keep his life for the moment, but declare him outcast. He has been judged by the gods..." Prince Akhash glanced at the priest, who nodded his approval. "And found to have offended the holy Fire, strayed from the ways of Tiespetre, and betrayed the laws of Ryo. Place him in a real jail, but a secure one."

Before Jasfer could dispute such a sentence or defend Sashyu, the priest's guards were carrying Sashyu back out the door, and the falcon jati guards were stripping Jasfer of his ragged but once fancy clothing. His burn scars flared as if once again on fire.

Naked and cast out, just as Jaritta had been twenty some years earlier. He was too stunned to say anything as they dragged him away.

Chapter 30

The clusters of Pashun soldiers milled about in confusion. For months the various jatis had been gathering, threatening, skirmishing, probing without ever quite undertaking a head-on, coordinated assault. At times the groups quarreled with each other, though as far as the people of Chaitanshehar had seen from above, their disputes had never led to actual fighting.

Alas. A full-scale fight among the factions below could have helped Jaritta's people tremendously.

The rockslide that had ended the last major attack had only meant more months to gather, to argue, to form new alliances and plans of attack. Months for the people inside the city to grow weary with anxiety. Something had changed in Pashun during that time. Datri had heard hints of it, but no one knew the full story—only that strange things had been happening since the High Prince's death, leading to chaos and unpredictability and a consolidation of power that threatened Chaitanshehar's existence.

Through a spyglass, Jaritta observed their reaction to the announcements she'd sent out to the clusters of soldiers. Her gaze moved over the rock slide where Thamiba had been killed, but she swept it immediately away. A month, or even a few months were much too few for her to accept that he'd died. The river tumbled along beside the rockslide and around and over the debris that had fallen into its rushing path.

The various leaders of the Pashun jatis puzzled over the proclamations as Jaritta looked from one camp to the next.

"I don't exactly see how this works," she said to Datri. "What do you expect to happen from this?"

Datri shook her head. "I don't quite know. Jasfer wasn't able to explain everything, I suppose, not in such a roundabout way. But there are fresh divisions in Pashun, maybe some new rivalries in the other cities too. We're trying to exploit that."

Exploit division to protect themselves. It wasn't a long-term solution. Someday their enemies would decide Chaitanshehar was too much of a threat for them to stay divided. And then they'd attack in full strength and overwhelm her city. Better for the other cities to accept them in the first place. That only mattered if the city existed at that point. If she had to manipulate things first, then she would.

But no amount of manipulating would be enough on its own.

"The prince was in little shape to share more." Kalvandi, who'd been a servant in her parents' household even before Jaritta was cast out, had carried the coded message from Jasfer and arrived two days earlier. "I think he was expecting to be better treated when he reached the capital, but he ran afoul of some more hardline faction. We eventually got this message from him, and then both he and our spy disappeared."

Yet more factions. The whole world seemed to be dividing, time and time again.

Datri took this report hard, even hearing it now for a second time since Kalvandi had arrived. As far as Jaritta was concerned, she'd said her goodbyes to her brother years ago when he stood by for her to be sentenced to death. Trying to be a sister-in-law as well as leader of the city, Jaritta placed a hand on Datri's arm. "We'll find a way to get him safe if this plan of yours works. What else did he want you to do?"

Datri gave her a knowing look. She wasn't fooled by her concern, but she answered in full seriousness. "The goal for now is to keep them off their feet, wondering. I'll send out some more letters, try to get some through to the capital.

Jasfer wanted us to try to get some messages out to Jarnur, even. I don't think we'll get anything past this blockade just now. But if the confusion delays the next attack, sends some jatis back to the city or off toward Romnai, well, it does some good."

The Pashun soldiers might be a chaos of competing groups, but they were working well together to keep Chaitanshehar cut off from the rest of the valley. Jaritta suggested, "Maybe just making these soldiers think we're reaching out to Jarnur is enough. Write the letters as if they're the continuation of discussions that are already underway."

Datri nodded. "That might do for now. I'll get some letters written and try to send something else out to be intercepted before the day is done."

She left to work on writing the letters. Something to keep her mind occupied. No doubt she needed that so she wouldn't waste her time worrying for her husband.

Jaritta left her to it and made her way up the slope of the city. The buildings nearer the wall had settled into more of a pattern than at first, with recognizable streets leading upward and paths to the sides. Most of the people had ended up using the abundant clay to make their houses, but baking the clay into bricks became more difficult as the soldiers below cut off access to the flatter land. Many buildings were a mixture of rocks and bricks and whatever else the people could find, covered with a thick layer of mud.

The caves that had been their first shelters were now used as storage, filled with as much food as they'd been able to hunt and forage.

Pavresh's caravan of untouchables had mostly settled along the upper reaches of the city. Good to have that part of the city alive, even if only here at the end. Their houses were more like the earliest buildings had been, more like the lean-tos and tents in the ruins of Old Eghsal.

"Lady Untouchable!" one called to her. "Thank you."

Another bowed in her direction and shouted, "Queen of the Untouchables!"

A few of those who'd come with Pavresh were people she'd known, years ago as an untouchable on the streets of Romnai herself. Somehow that history had turned into her being beloved, even by the others who hadn't known her. They honored Pavresh for leading them through the wilderness, loved him in a way, though he wasn't the type of person to inspire a close kind of love. Respect, and something more than respect. But they revered her in a way that was much beyond that respect, turning her into a sort of talisman for the city's—and their own—good fortune.

She could only hope she lived up to it.

She found Pavresh stalking through a wider space between houses, a space that was becoming a sort of open courtyard. Maybe someday a marketplace would pop up here. Or maybe the dust of razed buildings and soldiers' boot prints would be all there was to see. Clay turned to crumbles, idealistic dreams turned to charred logs and ashes.

She called to him, and he paused until she could catch up.

"Can't you do something?"

"Something?" He looked around with his arms open as if he was doing many things already. "What do you think I'm doing, relaxing? I'm still trying to get everyone settled, intervening in fights, and—"

"That's not what I mean." She put her hand out in front of his chest to stop him from butting back in. "Your magic. Isn't there something you can do to help?"

"No, absolutely not."

"But you cast that spell with the other soldiers on our way here, remember? Do something like that again." She grabbed his shoulders when he tried to step away from her. "Or else we will fall to them. We will die."

"You don't understand." Pavresh shivered, but not from cold. "I did that before, yes. But it, it took something from me. Made me sick. Something bigger, against all these people..." He left the imagined results of that unspoken.

Jaritta spoke with the voice the princes of her childhood would have used for chastising their servants. "Maybe that's the sacrifice you need to make, Pavresh." When he still shook his head, she added, "Would you put yourself, your brief feelings of...nausea or whatever it is—would you give up on this city named for Chaitan just to avoid that feeling?" It was a cheap blow, and she knew it, but he left her no choice.

"I..." His face crumpled as he gave in. "Maybe there is. Well...it depends. It might take time to prepare anything. But what do we need most?"

"Time. We need time to establish this city. Make it, I don't know, real. Permanent."

He shook his head. "I can't create time. It's feelings, impulses, ideas."

"Feelings don't build us a wall, either, I suppose." That had been her next suggestion, a magical shield around the city to keep them safe for a few years. She tipped her head back to watch the flakes of geyser snow drifting toward them. "I don't know. I wish I did."

"Wait, a wall. I might be able to do that."

"How? You can't build a wall out of feelings." When he didn't answer her, she added, "Can you?"

"Not a real wall, no. But something like a wall." Pavresh mumbled something to himself that seemed to be his way of steeling himself for the task. Then more clearly he said, "Give me a few hours to think it through. I'll let you know what I come up with."

***

Pavresh met Jaritta on the real wall less than an hour later.

"I think I may have your magic wall." The way he shrugged his shoulders and winced took much of the assurance out of the statement. "I don't know if this will work, but it's not that different from something I did on the way here with the untouchables."

Anything was better than nothing, whatever exactly it was he had in mind. Jaritta watched the soldiers milling about on the flat land below. Ants, but more like fire ants that were preparing to swarm. "What do you need from me?"

Pavresh shook his head. "Nothing, really. It's actually simpler than I imagined, if it works. A simple idea, at least. Just be ready. I'll be creating a sense of fear. A wall of forbidding, you might say. Once it's in place, it should keep people away from the city, but if our people in the city go too far down the slope, they might find it much easier to keep going than to come back."

A wall of forbidding. She liked that. The forbidden city of the untouchables. She hadn't known what to ask of him, but it was exactly what she'd hoped for.

"Give yourself time to prepare, then. I'll make sure none of Datri's messengers are down that way right now." She rushed off to find her sister-in-law.

Datri was in the middle of sending another batch of letters out, to add to the soldiers' confusion. "They need to come back," Jaritta said. "How long until they're all back?"

"An hour. Probably less."

"I suppose we could delay. Is there any sign that your letters are doing any good?"

Datri held her hands up toward the sky. "The gods might know. I can't tell from here. Tomorrow maybe I can try to sneak out there among the camps, see what I can learn."

"You may not be able to do that, if Pavresh's magic works. But then you may not need to worry about it either, at that point." She explained what little she knew of Pavresh's plan. Then after they both sat in silence for a time, Jaritta asked, "What do you fear? What is it that would make the wall work for you?"

Jaritta thought about her brother, Datri's husband, imprisoned in the capital. Would that be what made Datri afraid, losing him to torture or execution?

Instead, Datri answered, "Losing power. Being forced to give that up to someone else."

Kortru caste all her life, silk jati herself and princely jati by marriage, what did this woman know about losing power? Try being cast out, living on the street, fleeing the city to live in makeshift houses propped up between dangerous steam vents. Then talk to her about how terrifying it would be to lose power.

Not that they were at all close enough for Datri to share her true deepest fears, still it said something about her sister-in-law.

All she said was, "Then let's make sure we keep what power we have. Can you see your messengers now? Are they coming back?"

Once all the messengers had returned, Jaritta sought out Pavresh. He was seated, chin in his hands and eyes closed.

"You can begin."

Pavresh leaned his head back and let out his breath. "What if the mumblers had put up a magic wall before our ancestors came? Do you think it would have worked?"

What did this have to do with her wall? Pavresh had long confounded her with the direction his thoughts took him. Esoteric questions when what she needed was immediate, concrete action. She tried to steer him back to task. "Wouldn't have worked well for our ancestors, I suppose. Though there's the person in Pashun who's been claiming to have found a way through the mountains. I don't suppose any wall could be big enough to surround the whole valley. Now, let's see what we can do about making the wall work for us here."

Pavresh stood and walked with her to the edge of the wall of stone. Jaritta pictured him waving his arms in some dramatic fashion. Maybe the air would shimmer for a moment or the earth shake. Best not to be too close to the edge, just in case. The image of rock falling struck her, the memory of Thamiba's death. She put a hand to her forehead as if to draw the memory away from herself.

"But what if those are only stories? What if we never sailed here from some forgotten land? Did you know scholars have only found the remains of enough ships to carry a tiny fraction of refugees from the Forgotten South? Did you know that mumblers had already begun to build Romnai long before our ancestors supposedly landed here?"

What did this have to do with the magic? Jaritta clenched her fist and relaxed it so she didn't slap him. "The wall, Pavresh. The magic."

He didn't seem to hear. "And that traveler from the Forgotten South? Turns out he wasn't from there after all, just a mumbler with a darker complexion. And you know who was with him? Ekana."

Jaritta's heart skipped and she couldn't stop the gasp that escaped her lips. "Is he here? Where did you hear this?" Could he make a special part of his magic wall to keep that traitor even farther from the city?

"There," Pavresh said, pointing at Jaritta's throat. "That's the fear we're playing with. A fear that the past has betrayed us, that those who hurt us will come back. I don't know what really happened hundreds of years ago. I don't know who we are or what part of the oldest stories are true, but I know the people I've met. And fear is a powerful force in every one of them." He turned to meet her eyes, and his were red-rimmed with stress or worry.

Fear. It certainly might be powerful, but all the more reason to make use of it, to turn it into something good. "I understand. We are counting on you to do all you can."

He opened his hands as if he were going to do the exact thing she'd pictured, a dramatic performance to fit the drama of the moment. Instead, he stood completely still, his eyes closed, holding his breath.

After what felt like several minutes but couldn't have been more than one, Pavresh gasped in a breath and opened his eyes. He gave a single nod, and though there was no shimmer to see, Jaritta felt the wave of arcist magic strike her like a blow. She fell to a knee.

After fumbling a moment with the spyglass, she brought it up to watch the soldiers below. There were startled looks, quick consultations among the commanders. Some soldiers were already fleeing. The key moment came after only a few minutes. One commander, gesturing broadly, directed his squad of soldiers to gather their gear and march. Experienced soldiers, they still fumbled with their tents, and after a moment, the commander swept his arms downward and pointed down toward the valley. The soldiers abandoned their gear and marched at double speed. Their commander still appeared to have one of Datri's letters tucked into his belt.

Similar scenes played out across the entire slope below and no doubt into the hidden camps out to either side.

Jaritta whooped. It was not a kortru, princely jati reaction, but very much an untouchable one. She ran to embrace Pavresh.

He was lying on the wall, leaning against a block of stone as if he'd just been fighting himself. Or running from a wall of fear. He clutched at his belly with his hands, looking like he was desperately trying to hold himself together. She tried pulling him to his feet.

"You did it! They're running away. We're safe finally, safe to build and make this a real city!" She'd probably have to give a speech to the people of the city. She'd have to find a better balance between the excitement of the moment and a clear-eyed vision for the future at that point. For now, she could indulge the euphoria.

Pavresh didn't share the excitement. He groaned and slipped back from her hands into a sitting position on the wall.

Jaritta looked around at the guards on the wall. "Someone, bring water. Better yet, wine. Bring food, the best we have. This man is a hero, and he needs refreshment."

As the guards scrambled down from the wall into the newly protected city, Jaritta crouched beside Pavresh. "How long will it last? Do you…you don't need to stay awake to maintain it, or anything like that. Do you?"

Pavresh shook his head weakly. "It'll stay. Maybe longer than you want." He leaned against the rocks and closed his eyes.

Where was his refreshment? She looked around for the guards she'd sent for food and water. They weren't back yet. She walked along the wall, looking upslope at Chaitainshehar, her city, imagining what it would soon look like filled with the bustle of a living and healthy populace. She saw bustle already now. Two people, their arms loaded with what looked like hastily grabbed supplies, were running up the street. Other people too were scrambling away, up toward the far side of the city.

Something caught inside her. "What did you do, Pavresh?"

By the time she turned to look at him, he appeared to be passed out on the wall, and the feeling of fear washed over her as well. She wanted nothing to do with this city. It was a place of terror, a betrayal of those who dared to stake out their lives within. The rocks would surely crush her as they'd crushed

Thamiba. Let them crush the whole place, once she was away. The geysers below could spurt upward and tear them all to shreds. The Fire of the gods would sweep through and burn her again. The nagas of the South would smash down the mountains to come here and tear their city down.

The scars on her face itched with warning.

No dreams of a caste-free future were worth this terror. She needed to flee, to get out of here before…something. She couldn't articulate what precisely she feared, though the images kept coming and changing rapidly, only that she had to run before it was too late.

Jaritta rushed over to Pavresh's side and grabbed him beneath the arms. Dragging him away with her, she stumbled and cried on the way down from the horrible, terrifying wall and then up the slope through the rough and cursed buildings, hoping to never see the wall or the city she'd founded again.

Chapter 31

The cave overhead dripped because of the heat of so many people huddled together, melting ice that might well have existed for hundreds of years. Pavresh wiped a splash of water from his face. That water may have first frozen at the same time a small band of people sailed through the impassable waters to land here. If that had ever happened. If only there were something long frozen from that time to actually help them today instead of merely making them cold and wet. He couldn't recognize anyone in the darkness, lit only by a small fire at one end of the cave.

"How far have you carried me?" he asked whoever would answer. "Where are we now?"

"Not far." It sounded like Jaritta's voice, but he wasn't entirely sure.

"I need…I want to see it. Can we get anywhere so it's in view?"

"Not this time of night."

It *was* Jaritta. He could hear her inflections, even in the strange acoustics of the cave.

"I don't need light to see what I need to see. Help me outside the cave."

She hesitated as if to argue with him, but then she nudged a few others to help her, and they maneuvered Pavresh over to the mouth of the cave. It was low, as he'd expected given the warmth inside the cave. They crouched down, and Pavresh exerted himself more than he really had the strength for. Cold night air swirled at the cave mouth. He doubled up, coughing.

When he could stand, Jaritta supported him on one side, and one of the others on another. They'd lit a single lantern to give them some light as they climbed.

"We'll have to climb a little ways to see anything." Under her breath, Jaritta added, "Not that we'll see much even then."

He felt the fear as they made their way between some rocks toward the top of the ridge behind the cave. Tendrils of his own magic wended their way up from below, on the far side of that ridge, and echoed off the ache he felt in his own connection to arcist magic. It was wrong, what he felt down below and what he felt inside both. It didn't force him to turn back—the impact was fairly weak from this distance—but his own body's weakness nearly did. The clouded sky showed where their climb would end, thankfully not much farther. No real path climbed to the top. Pavresh relied on the others to get him the rest of the way.

The lava fields glowed below, not as brightly as the more active fields near Romnai or Eghsal City, but still enough to give a soft light to the land. Enough to see the edges of the volcanic activity—and silhouetted in front of it, the rough outline of Chaitanshehar, abandoned. A single unextinguished lamp within the city gave its melancholy light to a small section of the city, as if it wasn't quite empty yet.

It was, beyond a doubt. From here the wall of fear was much stronger, and the sick feeling of magic misused flared within him. Pavresh had to lie down so the ridge could protect him from its force. Jaritta lay beside him while the others stayed low enough so they were entirely below the rim.

Pavresh didn't need to see the wall of fear to sense its outlines. It pulsed and shimmered without light, above the city and outward well out into the lava field.

"It has to come down." As if he had the energy to do so now, yet he couldn't really wait either, could he? Every moment it was up meant the dream of Chaitanshehar faded farther into impossibility. He took a deep breath to gauge how much he had left inside to be able to manipulate magic.

"Must it?"

"Of course." He gestured at the city below with a broad sweep of his hand. "What good is that to anyone? You can't live there. No one can." Not to mention the worry he had that the longer it stayed in place, the more the magic would bind with the very rocks and become impossible for him to undo. "I need to get rid of it while I have the chance."

"I just…" Jaritta tossed a pebble down toward the city. It disappeared in the darkness long before it landed. "I was hoping maybe that the most extreme part of it would…fade, I guess. Like the smoke when you burn some food. It lingers but the worst is gone pretty soon. Then maybe we could move back in and still be protected."

Pavresh shook his head. When he realized she couldn't see the movement, he said, "I didn't make the magic to work that way. I made it something to last, bound to the city itself. I just didn't realize it would be that strong. Or affect us inside the city as well as outside." An image came to mind, a memory as he'd been losing consciousness on the wall and realized that the emotions and images he'd tried to bind together were simply too strong. He'd felt the arcist magic tearing from his control and taking root much deeper than he could have anticipated.

"You could dampen it though, right? Like a musician choosing to play more softly. I know you and Chaitan used to talk about arcist magic that way, back in his house. As if it's its own kind of music."

Could he do that? He peered down into the city, through the swirl of invisible magic. He might be able to tamp it down some, make it less powerful. It would require less of him than undoing it, certainly. At least in the short term. It might not be enough to let them back inside, even so.

Unless… He thought of his journey along the mumbler path from Romnai to Chaitanshehar.

"How many of your people are still here? In the cave or

nearby?"

Jaritta sighed. "A few dozen. Probably some more, if we seek them out. No one could have gone too much farther than this."

They'd scatter quickly, though, in the next day or two. So whatever he did, it would have to begin right away.

If he could ease the magic back just enough, then in the morning perhaps he could weave another spell around the fleeing people, a spell of solidarity, a spell of braving a difficult passage. Doing so might even heal the ache he felt. It was for the future of this people, a use for good, not for control, so maybe it fit on the correct side of the magic, the side that would bring him back from this pulsing, inner despair. If he could find the energy to perform it.

Steeling himself, he reached out through the magic to the monstrosity he'd created. It bucked and writhed against his control. He let out a whimper. He didn't have it in him to control such a thing, but he tried anyway. Pulling, easing off the fear, tying the strands into calmer knots. He introduced the idea of letting in a group that belonged, of a sense of welcome that was only for some people.

The chaotic swirl became something more manageable, something more like what he'd imagined when he began his work. Protection, not terror. Even so, the fear that seethed within the wall was more palpable than he'd expected. He couldn't be sure it wouldn't flare up and bar their entry into the city yet again.

It was all he could do for now. Leaning toward Jaritta, he said, "Sleep. I need sleep."

She nodded in the lantern light and gestured to the others to help him off the rock. As they carried him down, he told her, "In the morning don't wake me. But find everyone. Everyone you can. Bring them together in the cave or nearby, for when I wake up."

"I will do that."

Even the jostling of being awkwardly carried down into the cave couldn't keep Pavresh awake.

***

Pavresh estimated their number at more than fifty, probably closer to a hundred. Once you got that many together it was difficult to be sure, like a number you could never quite count to. Others appeared to be joining them from over the next ridge. He still had to lean on Jaritta to stand before them, but at least they looked ready to make the attempt. He had to be as well, or he'd lose them.

"You talk," he said to Jaritta. "I'll make the spell."

Jaritta nodded and straightened into a speaker's pose. "Our dream is not ended. The city of Chaitanshehar will still welcome us back. We will still create a city where no one is untouchable, no one is cast out."

Except for those cast out by the magic, Pavresh thought. He shook that thought from his head and began his work, even as Jaritta kept speaking.

"That city is still there, in our words and our plans and intentions. It will not be easy to create, but we will unite and put its flourishing above all else."

Pavresh let the rest of her words pass through him without listening. The magic still felt wrong, as if he was putting it to a lesser use that defiled it. Scanning the crowd, he sought out some of those he'd led from Romnai and began with them, finding again the unity they'd forged on their earlier journey. Jaritta's words about flourishing were good. He added the image of flowers, of cultivating a field together where the crop might take a long time to flourish. He even added an image of miners—as he'd seen them in his father's mine, as he'd learned from those who'd fled to mines to join Jaritta's city—not as slaves forced to labor but as workers enduring against the seeming permanence of stone. They would need that endurance to make their way past the sense of fear and into the city.

And where would the focus of their unity lie? He could gather it to himself, if he chose to. Be their leader once they arrived in the city and began the work. Make himself their prince, not by title or any official designation, but by default. Instead, he gave a portion of it to Jaritta's already lofty stature, wrapping it in her charisma and the skills she'd learned growing up a part of the princely jati.

But mostly he placed the authority in the idea of the city itself, in Rashul's ideals of a people without jati or caste, of a city that welcomed each of them.

As long as they were within it at the start, but that piece he couldn't weave into the magic. It would have to be enforced by the wall of fear that would soon surround them all.

He gave Jaritta a nod, and she wrapped up her speech. "So now to all people of good will and honest intent to build the city we have dreamed, you are welcome to come. The journey into that city will challenge us, but together we will reach our new homes once again."

Pavresh leaned on a makeshift crutch someone had fashioned for him, and together with Jaritta at his side he led the way around to the downslope side of the ridge and down toward the city.

When the sense of fear struck their caravan on foot, Pavresh clamped down on the magic that bound them. He also tried to ease the fear away, temporarily. The wall fought and struggled against his efforts, and doing two things at once quickly taxed him. He stopped trying to dampen the wall's magic and focused all his efforts on keeping the people united and pressing ahead.

The going was slow. Jaritta had to stay beside him in the lead, so she sent others around the edges to keep them moving. Azheeran and Driyya especially worked hard at herding people when the fears grew overwhelming. Pavresh was impressed with their work. The stiff arrogance he'd sensed in Azheeran back in Eghsal City was gone, or at least no longer directed toward Pavresh. The falcon jati soldier Valni stalked the edges of their procession like a herding dog, alert to danger within and outside their procession. He wove a little extra magic around each of them to give their encouragement extra force.

The sun was low by the time they reached the first buildings. Ellechandran and Chhayasheela helped carry Pavresh, as he struggled to keep the magic going, for a little farther. "We need… In a building," he managed to say.

Jaritta got them all going to the biggest building they'd constructed, the town hall with its upper story of unbaked bricks. It stood down the slope about halfway to the lower wall. His head was lolling in pain by the time they were inside. Despite the agony he fell quickly into a restless sleep.

He dreamed of the ancient mumblers. He dreamed that they created a wall around the valley, not a magical wall but a wall of stone. It rose into the clouds and protected them from any seaborne invaders and snow-crossing wanderers. Even the animals from outside that wall couldn't cross, so the animals within changed into strange beings, a mix of claws and teeth and antlers, of wisent horns and antelope hooves. Birds with fur-draped shoulders flew above the river. Fish with taloned feet scrambled in the mud for prey.

And in that closed off valley, the mumblers of Romnai created princes and outcasts. They fought the other tribes and made up stories about how they came from different places, the city mumblers from the sky, the nomadic mumblers from the river.

He floated over that other Eghsal, a moth with human form.

Then the dream shifted. He was himself, seated at a desk in Chaitanshehar, though the Chaitanshehar of the dream was much finer than the real one, with painted walls and cobbled streets. Horses neighed outside his room. In his hands was the letter he had received from Indima just before he'd cast his magic spell of fear. In reality, the letter had been addressed to Jaritta, and he'd merely recognized Indima's handwriting, still unchanged from years ago.

In the dream, though, it had been addressed to him, with little marks of affection around his name. When he opened it, the paper unfolded and became a figure, a doll in the shape of Indima herself. The letter began to dance. It was a traditional sort of dance, in style at least, though whether it was the temple sort of dancing or not, Pavresh couldn't say, as he'd never attended a pantheonic temple service.

Dream Pavresh could understand the dance perfectly, interpreting every step and every movement of the letter-doll's arms.

It began by dancing the same message from the original letter, of Ekana's lies and the elaborate tale he and his traveler friend created to trick the people of Pashun. Why? In the dream dance, the reason was to make themselves princes, to replace the Thirty with two rulers. They started with one jati and hoped to expand to the whole city and then the whole valley. When they failed, they fled into a wilderness Pavresh didn't recognize. A land of deep forests, but nothing like the pine forests of Eghsal Valley, a softer green lit by a warmer sun. After battling snakes and bloodthirsty birds, they reached a city.

This city he did recognize. A slope away from the forest led to a wall of stone. Beyond it lay the city of Chaitanshehar, that finer, more civilized Chaitanshehar where his dream self was watching the dance.

He woke up wondering what they would have done if Ekana and his mumbler friend had shown up in the city, before the wall of fear had gone up. The traveler he could have welcomed, even despite his lies. Ekana?

As soon as Pavresh sat up, the former beggar Juishika said, "Jaritta wants to speak with you right away." Her voice sounded tense, pained.

Pavresh didn't feel that well himself, though he'd chalked that up to his exertions in working the magic. As he gritted his teeth and made his way heavily across the main room of the city center, he noticed that the look of pain was echoed in many faces. No one appeared to be at peace. He tried to force his grimace into a smile as he met their eyes, but most looked away and said nothing.

Jaritta sighed and shook her head when she saw him. "You need to do your spell thing again. Unite us, steel us for this terrible place."

Terrible? Pavresh ran the back of his hand over his eyes. "I can try." He began reaching again for that sense of unity in the face of a difficult task. "What makes you call it..." Even as he asked, he realized why he felt so awful, why everyone seemed so lethargic. The fear reached through the walls of the building, pressing down on them all. "How bad is it outside?"

Jaritta shook her head. "I haven't checked."

Still wobbly even with his makeshift crutch, he headed for the door, Jaritta behind him almost at once. The feeling of the magic made the street outside shimmer, as if with heat. There was no way they could make a life there. He lifted his head and looked all around for any reason to hope it would improve with time.

No hope of that.

"I can't," he finally said to Jaritta. "No matter what I do to forge our little band of people into a hardened group capable of founding a city, it won't be enough."

Jaritta slumped against the doorpost. "There must...I mean, can't it get better? Can't you make it get better?"

Pavresh reached out to the wall with his magic, tried again to massage it downward to something tolerable for those within its shelter. The idea of sheltering within strong walls should exist in the magic. He could find it, try to amplify it. When he worked to pit that against the fear of the wall itself, the idea dissipated.

Perhaps not quite. He noticed a shifting of the magic, a change in how it washed over the city. Not enough to make life there comfortable.

He changed his focus to the magic he'd used to encircle the group of settlers. Their unity and sense of facing the challenges together, of working toward something better was still strong. He shored it up, added some complementary themes of arcist magic.

Would it be enough?

Pavresh tried to guess what would happen if they stayed. Arcist magic was not prophecy. He couldn't use it to divine the future. But it was about patterns, it was about knowing the stories of many people and how they usually played out over a period of time.

And this story would end up with them scratching and clawing an existence within the city, a fierce band of survivors sticking around for many years but always feeling sick, always afraid of what lurked beyond the wall. And dwindling with time until nothing remained.

The magic of the wall would infect his own use of the magic, make it bitter. No one would be able to learn it from him to keep the group going after he was gone, and that fear would always overpower any pleasures they made room for, every success they achieved.

When he turned his attention back to the group magic, he saw only one way to avoid that future. The pattern lay within what he'd already begun, but it would require something very different. A belonging like the mumbler trader Kuliya had described, one not based in fear or power or appearance. Most importantly it would mean tearing down the wall he'd constructed.

"I might be able to save the city," he finally told Jaritta. "Not if the wall is still there, though."

"Then what's the point? The soldiers will simply come back in and destroy us."

"Not…" How could he put it into words? "They'll come, yes. But if I set it right, they won't come to attack. Not by the time they get here, at least."

"How will you do that?"

Pavresh moved out into the street, leaning on his crutch to move beneath the weight of the magic. "You want a city that welcomes anyone, right?"

"Not anyone who's going to turn around and sabotage it."

Pavresh nodded. "I can prevent that. Not perfectly, I'm sure. But what if I turn this inside out? I'll take down the wall of fear and make Chaitanshehar a place that beckons people closer. That welcomes them when they arrive."

"That still doesn't keep out the traitors." Jaritta picked up a scrap of wood from the street and tossed it from hand to hand.

"That's the other part." Would this skirt too close to using the magic to control people? He wasn't sure what it would do to him, or if it would even work. But it seemed like the only choice left within arcist magic. Or at least within what he understood of it. "As they come closer, they become more and more a part of this same unity I've made among the group here. Make them anxious for the city's future, willing to work together to build that city we all want."

"Make them?" She held up the wood in front of her and eyed it, as if it were the head of one of those people coming in toward the city. "Will your magic turn them into mindless citizens of my city?"

Pavresh shook his head despite his own doubts. "Not if I can weave it right, shape it the way I expect." Of course, the wall of fear hadn't shaped up how he'd expected it to, so maybe he shouldn't be too sure of his abilities and understanding. He was playing with the powers of arcist magic in ways he'd never even suspected were possible. "Those who want no part in the city will feel themselves nudged away. They'll realize they don't want to be here and turn around and leave peacefully, on their own. They'll decide they don't want anything to do with what you're doing." Was it only her dream now, or had he united himself with it in all his work of forging the kernel of settlers into a united group? "With what we're doing."

Jaritta squeezed the wood in her hands as if to shape it into something new. "We'll have to check with the others. It'll be the decision of the group."

***

Pavresh took down the wall of fear first. It did not fall easily. The magic resisted him, as nothing he'd ever created had. He had to split his attention into what felt like infinite points, each one trying to uproot the magic he'd connected to the rocks and stones around the city.

It felt like he was uprooting a part of himself, pulling the hairs from his arms one by one and yet all at the same time. He had to fight through the pain without losing, even for a moment, the focus on each individual portion of the magic.

As it came free, he couldn't let himself rest. Chhayasheela and Ellechandran helped him stand upright, one on either side of him, as he shifted a part of his magic into the new spell he would weave. *Welcome*, the city declared. It became an invitation to all to come within, and weaving that part of the magic healed him better than the pine trees or Harkala's dig site ever had.

But it didn't end at that. The closer someone came to the city, the more it asked of them. The more they gave, the more they became a part of the city's future and the path to reach it.

He hoped, anyway. This part of the spell didn't give him the same healing as the other had, but there was no sense of it defiling the magic, either.

As he drove the magic down through stone and cliffside, anchored as deep as he could to the parts of the valley that would never change, the earth shook. He stumbled forward. Ellechandran also lost his balance, letting go of one of Pavresh's arms. On the other side, Chhayasheela toppled backward but refused to release her hold on him. Pavresh's crutch flew from his hands. It was the earth's reaction to him placing the magic, he sensed, as if to shake the magic off.

It didn't succeed. The shaking made the magic somewhat less stable than he might have liked. Not a permanent feature of the valley, but it might well last for so many hundreds of years that it wouldn't be needed anymore when at last it failed. Or maybe only a few decades, but Jaritta would do what she could in that time to make the city last.

He would do well to train many new arcists in the meantime, so that they might keep the city strong when he couldn't any longer. Fitting that in a city named for Chaitan, Chaitan's mantle would fall to him.

Pavresh fell to the dusty street as he finished the spell. From the ground he saw a bird, which had been flying past, veer suddenly and head straight for the center of the city, the city of Chaitanshehar, the city of welcoming.

CHAPTER 32

Ekana hopped across a sulfur-smelling rivulet of water and reached back to offer his hand to Sembaari. The dark-skinned mumbler, no longer pretending to be a traveler from the Forgotten South, took the hand without seeming to need it and danced across gracefully.

The ground on the other side was much the same as the land they'd crossed since leaving Pashun several days earlier. Scattered black rocks peppered the discolored dirt, rusty and streaked with pale blues and yellows. Lichen added a sheen of light green where it could manage to grow, but few other plants grew there. Ahead were finally some clusters of trees and hardy bushes.

And beyond those, the city they'd heard of. Chaitanshehar. The name took Ekana back to the house in Romnai, the people sitting around and dreaming, the dances and music and magic that mixed to inspire their dreams. That misled them all.

Sembaari took the lead but spoke over his shoulder. "Your old lover sent those letters, right? No way we can outrun them?"

Ekana clenched his fist. Indima. She was a prisoner still, whether she recognized it or not. Why hadn't she fled with him? They could have danced their way across the valley and forgotten everything else. Instead, she'd returned to the Silk City and vanished from his life. Again. He wouldn't need to invent a traveler from the Forgotten South if he had her at his side.

"She's long since sent them. Or maybe she forgot, who knows." Maybe she'd disappeared into the Silk City and forgotten all about him again. "But she might not have sent them to this city of outcasts. Doesn't matter either way. I was done pretending."

Except, was he really? Jaritta was in Chaitanshehar. Pavresh, the arcist he'd betrayed to the princes. No doubt others too, people who'd known him back in Romnai. They wouldn't let him in, knowing his past. The seven years apart might possibly be enough to disguise him, if he could find the right story to pretend. But they might not. Indima had recognized him eventually, and it had been even longer since he'd seen her.

"We'll admit you're a mumbler. That we're both mumblers, actually. We'll both be from your village."

Sembaari skirted a rock in the path, taking the opposite way Ekana had. When he came back, he grinned. "You learned to speak well," he said in the language of his own tribe. "I suppose we could pull that off, for a time at least."

Ever since Sembaari had insisted on following Ekana back to the Eghsal Valley, he'd expressed two interests, curiosity and trickery. He wanted to learn all he could about the valley people who looked like his own yet didn't speak even the mumbler pidgin language. And he'd wanted to prove himself better than them by fooling them, one way or another. He didn't say either goal outright, but they played into everything they'd done since returning to the valley.

Becoming the leader of an entire neighborhood had simply happened by a fluke of timing, and Ekana had envied the way it seemed to come so easily to him. Life had never come easy to Ekana. Cursed by the Cosmic Fire or the nagas who haunted the tales of the Forgotten South or simply a quirk of life, everything always went against him. He'd enjoyed the part he played in Sembaari's trickery, as long as it had lasted.

Now, though, the same luck had turned against Sembaari. Together on the wrong side of the Fire's blessing, it was their time to wander, and he didn't regret this change.

So now let Sembaari trick the people of Chaitanshehar, but let him do so by sheering even closer to the truth than before.

And for himself? What did it matter anymore? He wanted to be at the front of something, something new and exciting. Maybe this new city would meet his wishes, fill the void that Indima and dancing had left behind.

Or else it wouldn't. And he'd let the city crash into ruins behind him as he walked away, if that was what it would take.

As they came closer to the rising path up out of the lava fields, the pulse of powerful arcist magic struck him, almost forced him to his knees. He'd never known he could sense it so clearly, but there was no mistaking its effect here. A narrow river tumbled down the slope to soak into the swampland. Beside the river was a jumble of rocks, cut by a climbing series of switchbacks, the pathway damaged in places. Sembaari ran ahead as if unable to stop, but at the bottom edge of the scree beside the path he paused and looked back.

"This has to be the place. I can feel it, can't you?"

Oh, he did. It called to him, urged him to climb, to join in, to build the city with his own hands.

To hide nothing.

A pit in his stomach resisted that call.

Ekana climbed up from his knees and walked toward Sembaari. There were abandoned weapons on the ground. Signs of a vast army that had fled some twelve-days earlier. Some stragglers had returned to Pashun, but not enough to account for the things they'd left behind. Had they disappeared into the swamp, or turned around and climbed up to join the city? The call grew stronger. How could anyone help but rush up and into the city? Yet, his legs didn't respond when he tried to hurry. Plodding slower and slower, he eventuality reached Sembaari.

"Why so slow? You feel it, don't you?"

Ekana nodded. "I do. That's the place, and it…it wants us there, somehow." He sat down at the bottom of the scree.

"So, why stop here? Do you need to eat before we climb?"

They hadn't eaten much, but that had always been their way when they traveled together. The city above seemed to promise food. Fish, fresh like he used to eat back home. As if that were possible way out here, yet his mouth could taste it on the air. What kind of magic had Pavresh crafted?

Deception. That's all arcist magic was.

"It's a trap," he said to Sembaari. "We can't go up there."

"What do you mean, a trap? That's the best place we could be, I say."

Ekana shook his head to emphasize his answer. "No, that's the magic. It manipulates you, but it's false." He pushed himself to stand, but his body ached in reaction to the magic. "It'll welcome us in, sure. But then it'll take from us, make us do whatever Jaritta wants. Or maybe some other person, their new highest caste. Now help me up, would you?"

Once Ekana was standing, Sembaari let go of his elbow and took two steps up the scree. "Is it really so bad?"

The city called to Ekana. He didn't doubt that Sembaari found it hard to resist. It pulled at him powerfully as well, a promise of a place, a welcome, a rest. But hidden within the folds of that summons lay a request. No, a demand. Ekana couldn't put into words what it demanded of him, but he knew he couldn't accept it, couldn't submit to that summons as much as he wanted to.

"Yes, it is. If you must go, then go. But I'm not going any closer to that place."

Sembaari hesitated on the loose rocks of the path. Would he actually abandon Ekana after so much time together? They'd become like brothers. But then everyone abandoned Ekana eventually.

After a moment, Sembaari slid down the scree to stand beside Ekana. "Where will we go instead? We have to stay ahead of your old lover's letters, I suppose."

Surely it was too late for that by now. Either she'd sent the letters, and they'd arrived or she'd forgotten. "Let's go home," Ekana said, speaking the language of Sembaari's people. "Your home. We need to think, to decide what to do next."

Sembaari nodded. "We'll have to skirt this city, then, and head into the mountains. But this is the time of year for that, with the snow melting. I can find us a way." After a moment he added, "It will be good to see my sister."

****

They spent the summer among Sembaari's people. Fall came and winter threatened to seal them there in that village, and Ekana realized he didn't want to be trapped in one place any longer than necessary. He packed together his gear and was surprised that Sembaari gathered his own traveling things as well.

"There's more to see," Sembaari said with a shrug. "People I haven't met."

People he hadn't tried to trick, one way or another. Or maybe it really was curiosity that pushed him. Ekana didn't press either way. He wanted to get back to his old home in Jarnur by the sea, and that destination occupied his thoughts as they set out along a high route toward the west. The way led across snowfields and shadowed valleys, a difficult journey but one that faded into memory almost before it was over, and they reached the sea before the winter could sink its claws into their backs.

In Jarnur they heard stories of fighting, and everyone talked about the Jarnur Thirty and what Romnai would do about these rebel princes. But an uneasy peace lay over the city for the moment.

He met his family, but avoided the fishing boats. Whenever he thought of them, he remembered his old ambition to discover the Forgotten South himself, to earn fame. His attempt a half dozen years earlier to find a route through the mountains had led him to Sembaari's village. And that in turn had led to their con game of him being a traveler from beyond the mountains. If he stepped into a boat, he couldn't be sure he wouldn't make an attempt by sea.

And such an attempt would kill him, he was certain.

Still, he asked around about ships, unable to contain his curiosity entirely. *Are there any ships that* could *sail farther? Any fishing captains especially brave?*

When he asked two men at the shipyard about different designs, one said, "Ah, you should speak to that scholar. What was her name? Came around asking us about dragging nets."

"Oh yeah, her," the other man said. He didn't look up from the can of pitch he was stirring. "Don't know her name. But she came back a month ago. Started getting people to build her a ship like whatever old ones she found."

A replica of an ancient ship? Ekana leaned in close.

"No, that was a while ago. Didn't Phanin go off for a couple of months to build something for her upriver somewhere?"

"That was another one maybe. This was just recent, right here in the harbor."

The man knocked over an eel-catching hoop net as he pointed along the river mouth, but Ekana dipped down with his dancer's grace and scooped it back up before it even landed on the wooden dock. Without missing a beat, he asked, "Where can I find her?"

"Thanks. It was out away from the usual shipyards. South of the river. Just ask around for the scholar. Harkala, was it? Something like that"

Ekana was already walking away as he said, "Thank you."

Someone trying to make a ship that could escape Eghsal Valley, that was someone he wanted to meet. A project he wanted to join in on. It was ripe for new discoveries and new paths to fame or infamy. But first he'd have to talk to Sembaari, and they could decide whether to help her honestly or use her project for a new form of trickery.

The man from the Forgotten South might have to make his return, quick before any rumors of their past arrived here beside the sea.

CHAPTER 33

The spring winds, coming down from the mountains above Chaitenshehar, tossed Pavresh's hair as he performed his kusti beside the fire. Sparks flew up and into his hands as he knotted and unknotted the rope belt. He didn't flinch. He was a part of the Fire, and the Fire was here in this new city, a city on the verge of prospering.

He crouched and sprang upwards, landing with the belt held out taut above the flames, arms fully extended. A powerful position, but not at all stable.

A stronger gust burst between buildings and knocked him off his stance. He stumbled forward and caught himself before falling into the fire.

He scrambled back away from the flames. Wanting to be one with the Fire spiritually didn't mean physically joining it.

It was time to be done anyway. The demands of the new city called to him. He tied the kusti around his waist and headed through the city to find Jaritta.

She was welcoming more people into the city. He arrived just as she wrapped up. "And so, welcome to the city of Chaitanshehar. Not only the city as it is, but welcome to the city that you will help us build in the days and years to come."

Hundreds had joined the city since the arcist wall of fear had fallen. The flood of people had slowed recently, as spring progressed. They heard reports of the chaos in the other cities, but so far that hadn't led to too many refugees coming their way.

It easily might, in time, so they had to prepare.

Jaritta greeted him. "Another good-sized group ready to help. Some with experience growing food."

"Excellent. It's what you were hoping for."

Jaritta nodded. "We'll need that. The more people who come, the more we'll need that to get through next winter."

Food was definitely going to be a struggle for some time, but they were learning what to grow and where. The mumbler Ellechandran was especially interested in helping to organize that, bringing in his own knowledge and eager to learn from everyone else who came. His wife Chhayasheela had her own knowledge of hunting in these mountains. She helped the hunting parties test how far they should go, adjusting their hunting styles to match the prey. And there were the beginnings of herds and flocks of domesticated animals. Small, still, and no one with as much knowledge as they would have liked, but it was a start.

Pavresh fell in step with her as she started walking along the edge of the remainder of the stone wall. An unnecessary bit of architecture now, but a useful reminder of the recent past.

"How is your magic holding up?"

Pavresh reached out to test the edges of his handiwork. Its anchor in the earth below still held with no sign of weakening, no hint of anything beginning to unravel. And more importantly it felt…right. Maybe not quite as pure as he'd like, but most of the ache of using arcist magic wrong had faded away as the magical wall had fallen.

"It's holding well for now. I make no promises—"

"I know. No guarantees that it will hold. You've explained as much."

They walked on in silence, coming down off the wall, heading for the town hall gathering space that had sheltered them from the fear and now served as Jaritta's offices.

When they entered, he said, "I believe in this, Jaritta. I believe in what you're doing here. What we're doing here." The magic surrounding the city was the distillation of arcist magic, a way to use it that Chaitan never guessed at but would have loved. Pavresh felt no urge to wander, no need to seek out the stories of distant people.

No, that wasn't quite true. He longed to keep hearing the stories, but he was content to remain here and let the people come to him to share their folk tales and ancient stories.

For now.

"I'll be staying here to help you. You know that, right?"

Jaritta gave a noncommittal shrug. "But no guarantees that your promise will hold. I know that, too." A light smile took the sting from the words as she lengthened her stride to bend over the papers on the table.

Datri was already there, studying a variety of maps and correspondences.

Pavresh felt his arms grow awkward with memory. He bowed and excused himself from the room. Juishika waited for him outside.

"We're ready to learn, tisrah."

Four others stood with her—his students. And in desperate need of instruction if they were ever to learn arcist magic. Pavresh gestured for them to walk with him up to the roof of another building.

They sat in a circle with him. Pavresh gazed out at the land below, the switchbacks down to the swamp, the haze of volcanic steam. There were terraces of new plants leading down to the swamp and fields of food at the edge of the swamp where the lava field didn't poison the soil. A herd of sheep wandered the hillside between terraces, the herders keeping them away from the crops.

It was a land of beginnings. The arcist magic he would teach them would have to be one of beginnings, too. Of once-upon-a-time and a Forgotten South that might have never been—but that mattered for the future they were creating, whether it was real or simply a story that had grown through the years.

EPILOGUE

A letter, once decoded, from the servant Yatim to Datri of the city of Chaitanshehar, three months after that city's strange transformation.

My lady,

I continue to search out information on your husband. A part of me fears I should call him your late husband, I will not lie, but so far I cannot be sure of anything. The city is in chaos, not least the ruling princes themselves. We do not know if the Ruling Thirty are truly ruling or if they are false princes, masquerading. No doubt it will depend if they end up in power or not. The winners will decide who was true and who false.

Your courier reached me the other day. He wishes me to tell you that the journey from Chaitanshehar was difficult, not because of the weather or bandits or the roads, but because at every turn in the path he wanted to go back. Your magic is strong. I once knew the arcist who cast that spell, and I have no doubt that he has crafted it with cunning and power. I hope that the talk of him training other arcists is true and that it leads to greater stability for you and your city.

People here are beginning to speak of the magic city. At first it was in mockery. Who would choose to live among mumblers and outcasts? But as Romnai has degraded more and more, the way they say it changes. Your leaders should prepare for more pilgrims, if the situation in Romnai doesn't improve.

The Ruling Thirty of Pashun are threatening to cut the city off from Romnai again. Jarnur's Thirty are publicly considering supporting them. They are your creation, you know? The Jarnur Thirty did not exist until you sent out the declaration of Chaitanshehar's support. Though it hasn't led to them supporting you.

Jasfer never explained to us exactly what he had in mind within the instructions he sent to you. All we ever had was that one message. I suspect it was done to distract the enemies of Jaritta's city, and if so, it was well done. They have been too busy to worry about you.

But I did catch his warning that someone else was hoping to manipulate the various factions to his own benefit. Can it really be Mahendri, that minor princeling, cousin to the late High Prince, who'd helped Jasfer? I like to imagine what I would do to him if we happened to meet in a dark street here in Romnai. I wish Prince Jasfer had been able to discuss his suspicions with me at the time, but we feared being overheard. And likely he only learned the truth at the end, after he urged me to flee.

Don't become complacent, and neither shall I. We might be able to make use of the divisions in these other cities, but Mahendri will try to make use of them as well, and I have no doubt his end goals are not yours.

I will continue searching for information on Prince Jasfer and keep my ears open for anything from this Pashun mastermind. And someday, perhaps, I too will feel the pull of your new city, drawn in by its magic and conscripted to make it powerful.

Yatim

THE END

About the Author

Daniel Ausema is a stay-at-home dad and a former educator. His short fiction and poetry have appeared in many publications, including *Strange Horizons*, *Daily Science Fiction*, and *Diabolical Plots*. In addition to the Arcist Chronicles, he is the creator of the steampunk-fantasy *Spire City* series. He lives with his family in Colorado, at the foot of the Rockies.

More Fantasy novels from Guardbridge Books.

The Silk Betrayal
by Daniel Ausema

Volume 1 of The Arcist Chronicles.
A young man travels to the city to study magic,
but instead he finds intrigue and revolution.

Drakemaster
by EC Ambrose

A desperate race across medieval China during
the Mongol conquest to locate a clockwork
doomsday device that could destroy the world
with the power of the stars.

The Elephant & Macaw Banner
by Christopher Kastensmidt

Muskets, Magic, and Monsters!
A pair of brave adventurers face dangers in the
wilderness of colonial Brazil. Based on the
mythology and history of Brazil.

All are available at our website and online retailers.

http://guardbridgebooks.co.uk